PRAISE FOR

WATER HORSE

Sumptuous storytelling, well-defined characters, and superb attention to detail animate this outstanding epic fantasy from Lambda Literary Award winner Scott (*Trouble and Her Friends*). // Scott crafts an elaborate, rousing narrative of shifting alliances and supernatural intrusions into the natural world while taking the time to establish deep, handsomely delineated relationships and nuanced LGBTQ characters. This is epic fantasy done right.

— *Publishers Weekly*

Scott's complicated world fills up space, spills off the edges of the page into uncharted territory. It feels real, satisfyingly deep—and at the same time, those tantalising hints of other stories, other histories, made me intensely curious for more. I read *Water Horse* in a single afternoon's sitting, in a year in which I've frequently struggled to finish novels, or even start them at all. Deft and atmospheric, with Scott's trademark elegant prose, *Water Horse* is an engaging delight.

— Liz Bourke, *Tor.com*

An epic fantasy novel that reads like science fiction... // *Water Horse* takes place in a well-drawn, meticulously-presented world where a finely-codified technology of magic is based on music and oaths. The world has a long, eventful history and a baroque social-political structure... // Melissa Scott stirs all of this worldbuilding into her tale very artfully, in ways very familiar to science fiction readers. // ...a delicious struggle between fate and free will.

— Don Sakers, *Analog SF*

Water Horse is a magnificent and haunting book, a fantasy epic that will sweep you away. Melissa Scott is a writer at the height of her powers, and this is a virtuoso performance from a modern master. // If you are a lover of epic fantasy, queer heroes, or meticulously created worlds so real you could fall into them, you must not miss *Water Horse.*

— Jo Graham, author of the Locus-nominated *Black Ships* and the Spectrum-nominated *Stealing Fire*

A powerful tapestry of sword-forging and sorcery. // ...bad-ass harpers, a compelling bisexual king as our protagonist, // intense politics and a clever magic system, all packed into a single epic volume. This one crept up on me, and I'm still thinking about it days after I finished the final chapter.

— Tansy Rayner Roberts, author of the Creature Court trilogy, winner of multiple Ditmar, WSFA, and Atheling awards

Melissa's Scott's *Water Horse* is a rich and deep epic fantasy full of the deep worldbuilding, immersive writing, intriguing magic, and strong characters that I come to expect and crave in her writing. Just as importantly, the novel provides a framework and exemplar of a story where heroism, valor, strength of character and rising to the occasion are not trampled and mocked and denigrated... // ...a book stunningly well suited to our times.

— Paul Weimer, SFF book reviewer and Hugo finalist

I've been hearing about *Water Horse* for a couple of years now and I'm delighted to say that the wait was totally worth it. The world building is gorgeous, the plot is compelling and the characters are unforgettable. I'm already hoping for a sequel! This will definitely be one of my favorite reads of the year and beyond.

— Catherine Lundoff, award-winning fantasy author and publisher, Queen of Swords Press

WATER HORSE

MELISSA SCOTT

Candlemark & Gleam

For information, address
Candlemark & Gleam LLC,
38 Rice Street #2, Cambridge, MA 02140
eloi@candlemarkandgleam.com

Library of Congress Cataloging-in-Publication Data
In Progress

ISBN: 978-1-952456-01-5 (print), 952456-02-2 (digital)

Cover art by Eleni Tsami
Book design and composition by Athena Andreadis

Editor: Athena Andreadis
Proofreader: Patti Exster

www.candlemarkandgleam.com

To Jo, with thanks.

One omen is the best: defending one's country.

—Hector in *The Iliad*

Nothing's as soft as water,
yet who can withstand the raging flood?

—Lao Ma in *Xena, Warrior Princess*

MAP OF ALLANOTH

LIST OF MAJOR CHARACTERS

Note: in Allanoth, people are known by their given name plus the name of the parent from whom they claim their status with the "child of" suffix, -os for the father, -as for the mother.

Nen Elin
Esclin Aubrinos, Esclin Arros, ruler of the Hundred Hills
Talan Esclinos, Talan Thegen, Esclin's and Alcis's daughter and Esclin's heir
       Cat Meirin, a companion and Talan's foster-sister
       Estor, a companion
       Sian, a companion
       Ceilin, a companion
       Oriol, a companion
Kelleiden Smith, master smith, priest of the Mistress of the Fires
Rota Speaker, priestess of the White Mistress, Ruler of Death and Life
Maeslin Steward, steward of the household
       Waloner, deputy steward
Ilgae Marshal, commander of the royal levies
       Reinall Parinas, Ilgae's second-in-command
Avlen Saros, the royal healer

Nen Salter
Huwar Ellemas, lord of Nen Salter
Naïs Merinas, Huwar's second wife
Perrin Huwaros, Huwar's son and heir
Thedar Daranos, Huwar's nephew
Brelin Donderos, a wheelman, priest of the Blazing One

Nen Brethil
Wellan Prosseros, lord of Nen Brethil
Reilan Nardenos, Wellan's cousin and heir
Aillard Yrdanas, Wellan's cousin, regent in Wellan's absence
Gryffet Sinaros, holder of Nen Geyl

Esclin's Senior Commanders
Kellecost Sarrasos, commander of Nen Ddaur's levies
Torrel Engelos, lord of Nen Atha
Algrym of Nen Saal
Denior Horsemaster, commander of Esclin's cavalry
Aredan Gammelos, commander of Esclin's archers

Leicinna's troop
Leicinna Elloras, Exile-born captain of mercenary cavalry
      Fisk Ellamas, her page, daughter of her cousin Ellam
Gimmell, her second-in-command
Aylflet, an officer
Nea, an officer
Finn, the company weather-wyrd

The Westwood
Alcis Mirielos, kyra of the Westwood
Heldyn Dorthinos, Lord Winter, Alcis's consort and formerly
Esclin's companion
Rihaleth Ninnandas, Lord Summer, Alcis's consort
      Traher Alcisas, Alcis's and Esclin's son
      Helevys Alcisas, Alcis's and Heldyn's daughter
      Rocelyn Alcisas, Alcis's and Rihaleth's son
Dala Pelattas, steading holder
Ibota, Alcis's secretary
Esten Vargos, commander of Alcis's scouts
Toldra Meilanos, captain of Alcis's infantry
Roue Steward, steward of the Westwood
Savadie Observer, chief observer of the Westwood
Halcin Lanelos, commander of the Carallad's guard

Isabar Maras, captain of the Carallad's scouts
Alisand Ferentas, the Carallad's storekeeper

Riverholme
Liulf Nestaros, the Rivermaster of Riverholme
Melcana Liulfos Shield-Hand, Liulf's daughter and heir
Gelern Liulfos Sword-Hand, Liulf's son, commander of Riverholme's levies
Diran, Gelern's second-in-command

The Riders
Reys en Nevenel, lord paramount under the Blazing One
     Sunnlef en Angeiles, Nevenel's left hand
Suetrich, axial of the wheelmen, chief priest of the Blazing One
Reigar, senior wheelman, second to the axial
Lieven en Baumal, previous lord paramount, now deceased
Radoc en Martan, company commander
     Linaren en Gratoc, his steward and lover
     Graland, a guard in Radoc's service

Others
Viven Harper, a harper
Gemme Vivenas, her daughter
Pedder Annos, a harper
Amiel Harper, a harper
Verwin Grassandos, lord of Mag Talloc
     Aelin Anstellinos, his wife
Jiala, holder of Nen Soul, acknowledged as regent for her grandson by the lord paramount
     Imenor, her grandson
Faela Custanas, co-holder of Mag Ausse
Teiram Custanas, co-holder of Mag Ausse

GLOSSARY

- arros, title of the ruler of the Hundred Hills. Also, an archaic term for the shape-shifting water horse that lives among those hills
- axial, the chief priest of the wheelmen
- the Blazing One, the singular unnameable deity worshipped in Manan
- Callamben, second-largest of the Westwood's settlements, on the eastern edge of the Westwood
- the Carallad, the central holding of the Westwood, home of the kyra or kyros
- Dancing Ground, fully the Dancing Ground of War, the plains to either side of the River Lammard, now largely depopulated by the constant invasions
- Deirand Exiles, refugees from Manan who fled the rise of the Blazing One and who have been settled in Allanoth for multiple generations
- Fengal Exiles, second wave of refugees who fled Manan after the establishment of the lord paramount and the lords protector as the secular arm of the wheelmen
- Hidden River, the river that flows under the central spine of the Hundred Hills and connects the nenns carved into those mountains
- kore (masc. koros), acknowledged heir of the kyra or kyros
- kyra (masc. kyros), title of the ruler of the Westwood
- lithomancer, or stone dancer, a type of magic-worker who shapes stone through music and dance; they were instrumental in creating the nenns

- lord paramount, first servant of the Blazing One, head of Manan's army and its secular leader, chosen by the Blazing One
- lords protector, secular leaders of Manan, elected by localities under the direction of the local wheelmen
- Nen Brethil, one of the five "great nenns" along the Hidden River, between Nen Salter and Nen Ddaur
- Nen Ddaur, southernmost of the five "great nenns" along the Hidden River
- Nen Elin, the arros's fortress at the rising of the River Aurinand, backing onto the Hidden River. Greatest of the five "great nenns" along the Hidden River, between Nen Gorthen and Nen Salter
- Nen Gorthen, northernmost of the five "great nenns" along the Hidden River
- Nen Poul, a southern nenn on the edge of the Dancing Ground
- Nen Salter, one of the five "great nenns" along the Hidden River, between Nen Elin and Nen Brethil
- nenn, a fortress of the Hundred Hills, hollowed out of the mountainside, home to most of its people
- rivermaster, title of the ruler of the city-state of Riverholme
- shield-hand, title of the rivermaster's heir
- sword-hand, title of the commander of Riverholme's levies
- thegen, title of the heir to the arros or by courtesy to the heir of a major holding
- wheelman, a priest of the Blazing One, the singular deity of Manan

CHAPTER ONE

S he crouched in the stern of the barge, listening to the thud of the oxen's feet as they made their slow way up the haulage path, and the chant of the men at the wheel that opened the sluice behind the barge. Water lapped against the hull, rising slowly in the coffin that held it: this was not a great rise as the steps of the water-stair went, but even a small lift took time. The water could only flow so fast, diverted from the downstream channel. But it was enough to lift the barge, heavy with casks of the new year's wine, and she could see lights in the distance, the great smokeless flares of witchlight that illuminated the docks at Nen Elin. There was sunlight, too, narrow fingers reaching down from the cavern's roof to strike sparks from the water: even here the Blazing One was present, and she hugged that knowledge to her heart.

At the bow gate someone shouted an order and the men bent their backs to the wheel again, closing the sluice. The rush of the water slowed to a trickle, no louder than the slap of the little waves against the hull, and the captain called for poles. She was slow to respond, her eyes still drawn by the strands of light, and the bargemaster clouted her shoulder.

"Meleas! Blood and bones, your wits have been wandering since we left Nen Ddaur. Get to work, or the captain will leave you here."

She scrambled to her place, hoisting the heavy pole so as

not to foul the others or the sides of the coffin, and the gates opened in front of them releasing the barge into the docking pool. The ground was shallow here, the water of the main channel slowed and tamed, and she dug her pole into the stony bed, falling easily into the familiar rhythm. The dock drew closer, wooden pilings built out from a shelf carved from the living rock. The witchlights flared high as a man, colder than sunlight and throwing paler shadows.

She had been promised Esclin Arros, promised the ruler of the Hundred Hills, and for an instant she faltered, her pole missing its ground so that she jerked and nearly fell, but she recovered herself, her breath white in the cold air. They had promised, the Blazing One had spoken—the arros should be here. She couldn't see from the barge's deck, her view blocked by the great casks, and in desperation she leaped to the dock to take the stern line. The sternman swore at her—that was properly his job—but she ignored him, walking backward along the dock with all her weight on the heavy line. The others dug in their poles, easing the barge to its place, and she looped the line around the bollard, snugging the stern tight against the pier. The dock workers crowded close, and she put the hoist between herself and the barge. The Blazing One would not abandon her. The arros would be here; it was only her task to have faith and do as she had pledged.

She edged away from the pier, scanning the gathering crowd. The arrival of a barge was always an event, children and dogs and anyone not tied to their work glad to seize a moment's holiday. She dodged a trio in dirty smocks, obviously escaped from the kitchens, and flinched back behind a tree-carved pillar as one of the household archers hurried past. There were apprentices from the forge, come all the way from the roof— full-fledged smiths, too, their wool gowns hastily shrugged on over shirt and hose. They must have started down as soon as the barge reached the last step of the water-stair, ready now to gawp and gossip. She could feel the knife hot against her thigh beneath her worn gown. Surely the arros was not immune to such desires—surely he would come to see.

And then she saw him, coming down the shallow steps that led up into the nenn itself: a man gold as ripe wheat, his bone-white hair loose on his shoulders and the blind eye covered by a patch as red as blood. The Blazing One had put her on his blind side, the better to speed her work; she would need to strike hard and fast to get through his cloak, black lambskin with the fleece left long, but the blade was honed and blessed and ready. She glanced up at the spear of light plunging down from the vaulted ceiling, a pinpoint bright as the Blazing One, and stepped into the crowd as though into a stream, hauling at her skirts as she went.

She ducked past the first two women, dodged an archer who was shedding his gown to join the line of men helping unload the barrels. He shouted after her, more annoyed than alarmed, but then as she ignored him, boring on through the crowd, his voice rose and sharpened.

"Hey! You there!"

Meleas ignored him, the dagger in her hand now, held low against her hip. The rays of sunlight stabbed down into the dock, filling her with the Blazing One's fire; she would meet the arros in one of those shafts of light, and she exulted in the realization.

"Careful!" A woman caught at her sleeve, but she jerked free, pushing forward past a stocky man and another woman in a worn surcoat. The sunlight beckoned, the white-haired arros just outside its reach.

"Stop, you!"

She flung off the blocking arm, but other hands reached for her, and she spun free, displaying her dagger so that they fell back for the moment she needed.

"The arros!" someone shouted. "Look to the arros!"

He turned at that, the good eye widening pale as ice as he brought the lambskin cloak up like a shield. She ripped at it anyway, the blade tangling for a moment in the trailing fur, and then she'd freed it and lunged again with a cry of fear and rage. The arros turned away like a dancer, the whirl of black leather obscuring his movements, and then his men were on her, driving her to her knees and then flat on her face on the grit and stone of the dock. She had failed, failed, and the sunlight failed with her, fading as though the Blazing One turned from her in disgust, and she began to scream.

CHAPTER TWO

They gathered in the room that should have been the consort's had there been a consort at Nen Elin, Esclin Arros pacing the narrow space while his people stayed out of his path and one page built up the fire while another poured wine. Esclin reached for the first cup, but Kelleiden Smith caught his hand.

"Wait."

"A knife and poison in the same day?" Esclin paused nonetheless, and Maeslin Steward fetched a misshapen lump of nacre on a silver chain. He dipped the nacre in the wine, lips moving as he whispered the incantation. He drew out the shape unchanged, and the page from the hearth hastily produced a bit of linen to wrap it in.

"It's as well to be sure," Maeslin said, and handed the cup across.

Esclin took it, looking into the red depths for a moment before he took a swallow, barely tasting the familiar spice of this autumn's vintage. "Have you found out who she is?"

Ilgae Marshal shook her head, the red-gold curls that betrayed her Exile blood caught back hastily with a thin strip of leather. "Not yet. The barge master says she's called Meleas, he doesn't know a second name for her. He thinks she's from Ramnos, but she's been working the Hidden River since the spring."

"What does she have to say for herself?" Kelleiden asked.

"She doesn't," Ilgae said.

Esclin lifted an eyebrow at that, and Ilgae spread her

hands. "You heard her at the dock. It was all we could do to get her to stop screaming, and since then she just sits and rocks, won't say a word. She's in the cells, I've left Rota with her."

"Then you think she's mad," Kelleiden said.

"She's not acting like a sane woman," Ilgae answered.

"Mad or not," Maeslin said, "we need to know who's behind her. Who put her up to this."

"Must there be someone?" Esclin took another swallow of his wine, glancing from face to face to judge their answers.

"Does she have some quarrel with you?" Kelleiden asked in turn, and Esclin allowed himself a thin smile. Of all of them, Kelleiden had the right to that question, both as the master smith and as the man who'd shared Esclin's bed most often for the last two decades.

"I've never seen her before. Not that I remember, anyway. And I've no quarrel with Ramnos or its people." Esclin sighed. "So, yes, I take your point." He rested his hip on the long table, automatically turning so that his blind eye was toward the windowless wall.

"There are the omens to consider," Ilgae said, after a moment. She would not meet the arros's gaze, staring intently at the carved stone wall.

"I don't see that it's relevant," Esclin said. The summer's fighting had ended in stalemate, just as it had for the last four years, and at harvest-tide the public augury had been at best ambivalent. As the nenn's speaker, the White Mistress's voice, Rota had put her best interpretation on it: the day a wheelman entered Nen Elin was the day the nenn would fall. A week later, a wandering seer, a servant of the Huntress, one of the lesser gods of the hills north of Nen Gorthen, had arrived with a warning that Esclin courted his father's fate. Esclin dismissed that as one last thrust in the long quarrel between his mother's people and his father's, but he knew that he had not had the effect he'd hoped.

He saw Ilgae and Kelleiden exchange glances, and then Kelleiden said, "Is it not?"

"No."

"Our folk will think so," Ilgae said. "Whatever the truth of it."

"Let it go," Esclin said, and gestured impatiently for the page to serve the others.

Kelleiden accepted a cup from the hovering page. "Does anyone in the household know her?"

"Not that I've found," Maeslin said. "My people are still asking questions, but the dock men say she's a stranger to them. And to the kitcheners."

"They'd say that regardless," Esclin said.

"Yes, but I believe them." Maeslin gave a crooked smile. "They're not all of them that good liars."

"Why, then?" Kelleiden shook his head. "We've no quarrel with Ramnos."

"It's an Exile town," Ilgae said.

"The Exiles should have no quarrel with us." Esclin took another swallow of his wine. His free hand was trembling, pure physical reaction, and he flattened his fingers against the sanded surface.

"Manan does. From whence the Exiles come, and Ramnos is a traders' town before all. And Manan elected a new lord paramount at the equinox." Kelleiden met the arros's eyes squarely.

That was true, of course, and they were back to the truth that Esclin had been avoiding. He fixed the smith with a minatory stare. There was enough to worry about as winter settled over the Hundred Hills without raising that particular specter.

"People will talk," Maeslin said.

"I'm still alive," Esclin said, with a smile he didn't feel. "I'd call that a good portent." He won a few smiles at that, but Ilgae shook her head.

"It's not a joking matter, Sire."

"And I will consult with the speaker," Esclin said, "but that's not the matter at hand. I want to know who sent this girl—"

The door swung open, Ilgae turning automatically to place herself between it and the arros, Maeslin and Kelleiden reaching for their knives. Esclin had his own knife half drawn at the sound, and then realized that it was his daughter Talan in the doorway.

"I'm sorry, Father, but the matter's urgent. The girl—Meleas—is dying."

"Dying how?" Esclin sheathed his dagger without apology.

"Burning up with fever," Talan said. "Rota said you should come."

Esclin nodded. "Has she spoken?"

"Not a word."

Esclin closed his lips over his first response. "Maeslin, keep questioning our people, see if anyone knows anything. Ilgae, I'll want you to tighten the watch for a day or three. Kelleiden…" He looked at his daughter. "Yes, we'll come."

The cells lay toward the heart of the mountain, below the halls and storerooms and as far from the main gates and the docks as was practical. Talan knew all the shortcuts, leading them unerringly through the narrow hall between the kitchen and the armory, then down the twisting stair that led to the lowest levels. Esclin plucked witchlight from the air to supplement the hanging lamps and Talan did the same, the shadows wavering uneasily in the corners.

The corridor ended in a broad, low-ceilinged hall, the air thick with silence. More lanterns hung at stingy intervals, perpetual twilight, and at the door of the largest cell, two archers straightened to attention.

"Arros," one said, and a shadow moved within the cell, resolved into a stout woman drying her hands on her apron as she came to the door. Her hair was braided with beads and tiny bleached-white bones, the badge of her office, and at Esclin's side Kelleiden touched his heart in acknowledgment. She caught the gesture and dipped her head, but her attention was on the arros.

"You're too late."

"What?" Esclin froze. No natural illness worked so quickly. "How can that be?"

"Her god forsook her."

The speaker stepped back, beckoning them into the cell. Talan hesitated—she had not seen very much of death, after all, would only be sixteen at the spring lambing—and Esclin stepped past her. Kelleiden came with him, positioning himself in the arros's blind spot out of long habit. Talan hovered unhappily behind him. The air was cold and smelled of death, in spite of the bucket of water and the newly mopped stones. The girl's body lay on the stripped cot, the straw emptied from the mattress and swept aside to be burned, a piece of linen covering her from breast to thigh. She looked small and pinched, her skin already waxen, like a votive figure ready for the offering.

"What happened?" Esclin took a step forward, waving his ball of witchlight closer. There were no signs of injury, not even bruises from the struggle at the docks, and he looked again at Rota.

"She stopped screaming when the guards brought her down into the dark," Rota said. "They had searched her, but the only weapon on her was the knife she tried to use on you. They had sent for me straightaway, I was here within a quarter-hour, and probably less. I found her balled up in a corner, rocking back and forth. She wouldn't speak to me, and I admit I was sharp with your men, thinking they'd mishandled her."

"But they had not?" If they had, they would pay: everyone knew that rule.

"I don't believe they had." Rota dipped her head in apology.

"Well for them," Talan muttered.

Esclin put out his hand to silence her, and Rota went on as though she hadn't spoken. "I'd not been here very long— my girl had brought the water and I'd sent her for a calming tea when I saw the prisoner start to shiver. I checked her, and her skin was hot to the touch, burning hot. I got her onto the bed, though I don't think she knew herself then, and her eyes rolled back in her head. She was beyond swallowing by the time I brought a dipper to her lips." She nodded at Talan.

"The thegen was here, so I sent her to fetch you. But she didn't last."

"She never spoke," Esclin said.

"Not to me, and not to the soldiers."

"And this fever…" Esclin studied the body again, unwilling to come closer, and Rota gave a thin smile.

"Not natural. And not, I think, contagious." The White Mistress would know, ruler of both death and healing. Esclin nodded.

"There is this you should see." Rota stooped over the body, folding back the lower edge of the linen. She flexed the girl's leg, bending it and turning her knee outward to expose the inside of her thigh, revealing a round red mark. A birthmark, Esclin thought, and in the same moment realized it was too perfect a circle. It was a ring of flame burned into her flesh, the mark of Manan's newly dominant god, a red shiny scar.

"That's what you meant. 'Her god deserted her.'"

Rota nodded and eased the girl's leg straight again, adjusting the linen to cover her more completely. "She is—she was sealed to the Blazing One. She sought your death, and when she failed, she died. That's how I read the signs."

"Sent by whom?" Esclin asked. "Besides the god."

"That," Rota said, "I cannot tell you."

Kelleiden said, "The lord paramount wouldn't grieve for your death."

"He's better things to do than cultivate assassins," Esclin said. "Can we give her proper rites?"

"Not I," Rota said. "That's the master smith's domain."

"Not mine." Kelleiden straightened.

"She tried to kill you," Talan protested.

"She failed. She's dead. I won't harm her further." There was no need to court further misfortune. Esclin looked over his shoulder. "Well, Kelleiden?"

"I will not touch those rites. That fire is not mine." Kelleiden controlled himself with a visible effort. "There are Exiles in the home-guard, one of them will know what's proper."

"My people will lay her out," Rota said. "We'll shroud her, too. That can do no harm."

"Good," Esclin said, and Kelleiden caught his sleeve before he could turn away.

"Esclin. You need to take precautions. I doubt this will end here."

Esclin gave him a reproving glance, but Rota said, "The master smith is wise."

"Another augury?" Esclin asked.

"Only what I saw before. Add to that common sense and a lifetime at court." Rota gave a thin smile. "You need the royal sword."

Esclin grimaced and looked at Kelleiden, who kept his face expressionless. The royal swords were the greatest of the great symbols of Arra's Folk: blades forged of star-fallen iron, sealed to each arros by blood and fire. Both the smith and the speaker had declared it time Esclin claimed one. But the speaker had added another ill omen at the equinox: *The royal sword made*, she had chanted, deep in trance, *by the arros betrayed*. No matter how she tried to hedge those words after, or how hard he tried to twist their meaning, no one was about to forget them. "I will be careful. As will Talan."

She gave him an impatient look. "I'm always careful."

"Keep Cat Meirin by you," Esclin said, and she nodded. There were more things he wanted to say, more strictures he wanted to lay on her—she was the child he had raised as well as his heir—but she was a woman grown, and responsible for herself. "Then ask Ilgae to see if any of the Exiles will perform the rites for this girl."

"I will," Talan said, and turned away, collecting her witchlight as she went. It receded along the corridor, leaving them with only his own light and the duller lanterns.

"Is there anything else I should know?"

Rota shook her head. "If I do find more, of course—but I don't expect to."

"No more do I," Esclin said, and cupped his witchlight in his open hand, drawing it back to hover at his right shoulder.

Kelleiden kept place at his left as they started down the corridor.

"Cat Meirin will keep her safe," the smith said. "And, more to the point, Talan will put up with her. That was a good thought."

Esclin nodded. Cat Meirin was Talan's milk-sister, her mother Lysse had been Talan's nurse from babyhood. She was six months older than Talan, and a head shorter, small and fierce as the mountain cats from whom she had taken her name. She was deadly with bow and knife and sword, and if her tongue stumbled, her hands did not. "Let's hope so."

"And yourself?"

Esclin gave him a sidelong smile, knowing what the smith was really asking. "When have I ever slept alone? But I'd be glad of your company these nights." As he had hoped, Kelleiden breathed a laugh, and together they climbed back toward the halls.

Huwar Ellemas, the lord of Nen Salter, returned from the hunt to find the nenn buzzing like the beehive it resembled, women and men abandoning their usual tasks to gather gossiping in corners. He scowled at his groom as the man took his horse's reins, and the man bobbed his head nervously.

"Your pardon, my lord. Someone tried to kill Esclin Arros, and we're all at sixes and sevens."

Nonsense. Huwar swallowed the word, as it was patently clear that something had happened, and pushed back the woolen hood. "What do you mean, tried to kill him? Is he wounded? Well?"

"Uninjured, my lord," the groom answered, and Huwar was conscious of a bit of disappointment mingled with the relief. His mother Ellem had been of royal blood, a distant daughter of Arra's house; if Esclin were incapacitated, Huwar doubted he could claim the throne, but he could certainly demand a place on the thegen's council. The arroi of the

Hundred Hills held power by the consent of their people, not by birth alone, and Talan was too young to take her father's place without the support of the great nenns.

"What happened?"

"A girl from the docks tried to knife him," the groom said. "Or so I hear."

"Crying vengeance," a woman put in, and another woman shook her head.

"No, she was sent from the coast, from the Fengal Exiles."

"Maybe he refused her favor," a man said, and when Huwar turned, scowling, the speaker effaced himself in the crowd.

"Were any of you there? Or spoke to one who was?"

There was a silence, sharp after the chatter, and the head groom cleared his throat. "Your pardon, Lord, but I did speak to one of the guards. He said it was a boat-girl, and that she was mad."

It was of a piece with the omens at the equinox. Huwar swore under his breath. He was still a guest here, even if he was a man of rank and station—the next in rank after Esclin himself, as Nen Salter was one of the four great nenns along the Hidden River, but still not one of the arros's household, not his intimate in any sense of the word. He should offer his service, he knew, and see if he could win any advantage for Nen Salter in the process, but could not think how best to begin.

"My lord!" That was one of the thegen's companions, a gangling boy in everyday woolens. "My lord Huwar, I'm glad to have found you. The arros would like a word with you."

"And I'd like a word with him," Huwar answered, and couldn't resist adding, "if he doesn't mind me all unwashed."

"I think the matter's urgent," the boy said, seriously, and Huwar followed him through the hall and up the winding stair to the presence chamber. It was one of the showpieces of the nenn, not large, but intricately dug out from stone the color of a crust of new-baked bread, its ceiling crossed by three great arches carved to look like living trees wound with vines. It was lit by paired sun-shafts and lanterns at the edges of the vaulting, and there was an unlit brazier in the room's center, beneath the point where the arches met in a tangle of carved grapes and vines. Esclin sprawled in his carved chair, not quite a throne in this relatively private space, his black cloak of unshorn lambskins flung carelessly aside. At Huwar's entrance he rose to meet him, and they clasped hands, exchanging the kiss of kinship. Esclin seemed unharmed, but Huwar eyed him thoughtfully.

"What's this I hear about someone trying to knife you?"

Esclin made a sound that was almost laughter. "Sadly true." He waved toward the nearest stool, and Huwar seated himself. The thegen's companion poured wine for him, then refilled the arros's cup, and Ilgae Marshal pushed herself away from the pillar.

"She bore the mark of the Blazing One."

"Which is not a thing I want repeated," Esclin added, and Huwar nodded. The master smith emerged from the shadows to lean against the arros's chair, dark hair and dark skin a startling contrast to the arros's brighter coloring. Huwar wondered if that was the reason Esclin favored him, then put the thought firmly aside.

"As you wish."

"The girl is dead," Esclin went on. Huwar lifted his eyebrows at that, and Esclin gave a wry smile. "Not at my hand, or my men's. But she needs her rites."

Huwar pursed his lips. Even before the autumn prophecy, Esclin had barred the wheelmen, the priests of the Blazing One, from Nen Elin; he himself had been careful not to inquire too deeply into any less formal practice among his people, but it remained a sore point among the southern nenns, where wheelmen had served side by side with smiths and speakers for a generation. "Surely the master smith can see to that, Sire."

"Not my fire," Kelleiden said.

"None of my men know the rites," Ilgae said. "Not to lead them."

"It occurred to me," Esclin said, "that—though I'm sure you wouldn't disobey my direct order and bring a wheelman within my walls—someone of your people might have sufficient standing to direct my steward."

Huwar could feel the ready color rising beneath his skin. He had, of course, obeyed the letter of the arros's command, but his nephew Thedar lacked only the final vow. "There is someone I could ask. If you're sure you want those rites for her."

Esclin shrugged. "I—well, I won't say I bear her no ill will, but she's dead, and I'm alive. It's little enough."

And that, Huwar thought, was one of the reasons he followed the man. Esclin was nothing if not generous. "I'll speak to Thedar."

"Thank you." Esclin took another swallow of his wine. "Tell me, Huwar—I'm curious. Why did you let them in?"

"The wheelmen?" Huwar said, and the arros nodded. Huwar grimaced. "My sister is the consort of Nen Saal—my second sister, Anneth. One of her boys was born with the bone-ill, never could walk and had to be carried everywhere. A little, wasted thing, bright and light as a sparrow, and about as strong. Five years ago, a wheelman came, said he was sent to aid the boy." He stopped there, unable to explain. He had seen only the impossible result: Anneth and her son riding side by side to the gates of Nen Salter, Riold springing down from the saddle as though he had never been crippled, and offering his hand to steady his mother down. His gait wasn't perfect, but it was more than enough that he could walk at all.

"And he did so," Esclin said, after a moment.

Huwar nodded. "Riold limps, but he goes on his own two feet without even a stick to steady him."

"I'm glad," Esclin said, and sounded as though he meant it.

"They mean only good," Huwar said. "They are good men, and they do good."

"They serve the lord paramount," Ilgae said.

"They serve the Blazing One," Huwar answered. "And the Blazing One shines on all alike."

"The speaker has seen, and the Huntress-man and I have both confirmed it, that the day the wheelmen enter Nen Elin is the day the nenn falls," Kelleiden said.

"And you agree?" Huwar knew he shouldn't ask. "The servants of the gods are only human, after all."

"I've seen it," Kelleiden said, with a smile that held no amusement. "Do you call me a liar, Huwar?"

"Anyone may be mistaken," Huwar said. He liked the smith, wished him no ill even if the wheelmen called his fire false.

"It's not a risk I choose to take," Esclin said.

His tone foreclosed further argument, and Huwar bowed. "As you say, Sire."

"I would like your nephew's help," Esclin said, after a moment, and Huwar bowed again.

"I'll tell him." He paused, remembering the arros's words. If neither he nor his men had killed her... "How did the girl die? You didn't say."

"Her name was Meleas," Esclin said, his eye fixed on something in the far shadows. "From Ramnos, they think." He shook himself then, and turned one hand out, not quite a shrug. "She died of a sudden fever. She tried to kill me, she failed, and she burned from within."

There was no mistaking the implication, and Huwar drew a quick breath. "The Blazing One would never do such a thing."

"The servants of the god are only human," Kelleiden quoted, and Esclin laid a hand on his arm.

"That's how she died. I draw no judgment myself."

There was a note of sincerity in his voice that made Huwar dip his head again. "Thank you, Sire. I'll speak to Thedar."

"I'm grateful," Esclin said, with a quicksilver smile.

Huwar bowed himself out, determined to find his nephew—in the stables, most likely, or with the young men in the training hall, flaunting his skills in the hope of finding a bride who wasn't a cousin. *Died of a fever.* The words echoed in his mind. *Burned from within.* There were whispers, of course, there had always been whispers, but he did not believe them, would not believe them. If it was punishment, it was for the crime of attempted regicide, surely, not for its failure.

Thedar was in the hall, laughing with a red-haired girl whose well-cut gown marked her as a woman of substance and birth, but he came to his uncle's side with flattering deference.

"You've heard what happened?" Huwar asked.

Thedar lowered his voice. "That someone attacked the arros? I'd heard."

"The girl is dead." Thedar lifted his eyebrows, and Huwar scowled. "Not at the arros's hand. She died of fever, a sudden fever."

"The Blazing One receive her," Thedar said.

"The Blazing One may have taken her," Huwar retorted.

Thedar shrugged. "That is the Blazing One's privilege, surely."

Huwar stared at him for a long moment, questions trembling on the tip of his tongue. But there was something about the boy's set face that silenced him, that and the fear that he would hear an answer he did not want, and he cleared his throat. "The arros wants her given proper rites. I said you might be able to help."

Thedar's expression lightened. "That's—kinder of him than I would have thought. Yes, of course, I'm more than willing."

"Talk to Maeslin Steward, then," Huwar said, and the boy bowed and turned away. Huwar watched him go, remembering other conversations, other moments when the light of kindness had failed. Perhaps he would not bring Thedar into his council after all, at least not this year.

Talan made her way up the narrow twist of the observatory stair, her companions panting behind her—all except Cat Meirin, who kept pace without effort. She ignored them all, climbing past the ramps that served the forge, tucked near the top of the nenn so that the smoke could escape more easily, past the upper guardroom and the rain-catch and the watchpoints, until she emerged at last at the top of the nenn.

The platform had been hewed from living rock with strong powder, there being no water this high to shape the stone, and the drill-marks still showed despite the masons' attempts to polish them away. Across the valley, the afternoon sun was already sinking between the twin peaks of Atha and Arranme, throwing long shadows. The air was clear and cold, and she could see the smoke of other nenns rising from the distant hillsides. She had done her duty, brought her father's message and seen his orders carried out. If anything, she was following her father's orders in sharing this with her closest companions, and if she chose to do it here where no one was likely to follow them, that was her decision.

She turned back to face the others, Cat Meirin taut as a harp string, without a cloak and apparently oblivious to the cold, Estor towering over her, and Sian staying close to the wall, her fur collar turned up against the wind. She had other companions, the loose coterie who served as royal pages, but these were her closest friends, the ones she could trust with her doubts as well as her certainties.

"Well?" Sian said, hugging her furs closer, and Cat Meirin fixed her with a glare. Sian matched the stare with interest. "She dragged us all the way up here —"

"I wanted to talk to you all," Talan said. "In private. And we don't have much time before we have to go back, so stop arguing."

"Wasn't," Cat Meirin said.

Talan ignored her. "The girl who tried to kill the arros today was sealed to the Blazing One. That's not to go any further—I want your word on it, all of you. The arros will burn her according to her rites, but that's all he wants known."

"You have my word," Estor said.

"And mine." Sian edged back against the wall.

Cat Meirin nodded. "M-mine."

That was promise enough, and Talan seated herself in the

niche carved into the northern wall. The others piled in after her, pressing hard against each other. It was meant to hold the astrologers' instruments out of the way, and the four of them could just fit. For a moment, they heaved and shifted, adjusting knees and elbows and excess fabric; then Sian wrapped her furs around Cat Meirin, Estor drew his knees to his chin and they settled, pressed warmly together like puppies in a basket. Talan felt herself relax just a little, soothed by their familiar presence.

The sun still shone on the platform, the angle steep enough to throw the incised patterns into shadow, compass bearings and elemental symbols and the sun-marks for each time of the year. It was one of the few places in the nenn that she could be sure would not be occupied except at times of ceremony, too high and at this season too cold for most people.

"Do they know who sent her?" Estor asked.

Talan shook her head. "Father—the arros says I'm to keep you close until we know more—especially you, Cat."

She felt Cat Meirin nod vigorously, and Sian said, "None of our people would want to harm the arros. And I don't see the kyra of the Westwood bearing him any grudges, either."

"What about the rivermaster?" Estor said, but Sian shook her head.

"It helps him even less than it helps the kyra. He needs our men to drive the Riders back every spring, he can't afford to antagonize us."

"The master smith suspects the lord paramount," Talan said. "And that's a secret, too."

"That makes more sense," Sian said. "The Blazing One is their god, and they're the ones who send the Riders every spring."

"Why?" Cat Meirin's clumsy tongue couldn't form the rest of the question, but Talan straightened thoughtfully.

"What do they hope to gain, you mean?" Cat Meirin nodded.

"You know, that's not a bad question," Sian said. "Every year they send over a raiding party, and every summer we fight them all across the Dancing Ground, and every fall they sail back again. It seems...unproductive."

"Stealing," Cat Meirin said darkly.

"They can't steal enough to make it profitable," Talan said. "Not anymore." Even the most recent wave of Exiles had all but abandoned the central plain, the wide grassland the harpers called the Dancing Ground of War. It was hard on the common folk, her father said, hard on anyone who farmed or traded along the coast; but the Hundred Hills and the Westwood were still untouched, and the rivermaster patrolled his southern borders and brought his folk in safe to Riverholme when they were pressed too sharply.

"They want to bring us under their rule," Estor said. "They claim our land—they call us 'Manan-Oversea', not Allanoth, they say we're theirs because the Exiles are here and our blood's mixed with theirs. That's what they want."

"That's folly," Talan said. "We're none of theirs." She looked across the valley toward the setting sun, a sliver of molten red against flaming sky, the mountains purple-black to either side. This was her realm, her home, and she was no kin to the Riders.

Cat Meirin stirred. "T-t-tried it." She tapped her left eye, her shorthand for Esclin. "B-b-"

She stuck, and Estor said, "Before? You mean when Audan was the arros?" Meirin nodded.

"When my great-uncle was arros," Talan said, "we'd lost too many men to hold the Riders back." Because her grandfather had gotten most of his army and the Levy of Riverholme slaughtered at Eith Ambrin, which was still a sore point for everyone. Cat Meirin squeezed her arm in sympathy, and Estor had the grace to look abashed.

"You know what I meant."

Talan sighed. "I do. And, yes, the Riders took tribute from us for four years. Which my father ended. But that's not the same as claiming to rule by right."

The sun was down, even the high platform sinking into twilight, and she could see the first brightest stars above the last bands of sunset color. A long way off, across the valley, she saw a light wink from the hillside, flashing twice, and then another: the twilight signal, passing word that all was well. On the watchpoints below, her father's men would be making the same signal, and building up the braziers for the night. Within the nenn, the kitchens would be readying the evening meal while the household servants cleared the hall.

"We should go," she said, and wriggled free of the others.

The arros expected his court to come to the hall clean and decent, and that went doubly for his heir. Talan was just in time to change the well-worn short gown that she'd worn for the day's work for her second-best dress, wine-colored wool trimmed in black and cream. Sian pulled down her braids and brushed her hair out straight and added a plain circlet to hold it in place. By then, Estor was beckoning from the door. Talan looked over her shoulder to collect Cat Meirin, demure in plain indigo with a knife at her belt and another up each sleeve, and made her way quickly toward the hall.

She took her place at the center of the thegen's board, her companions and the junior smiths, senior apprentices and household heirs filling the rest of the places. Most of them she had known from childhood but some were new, particularly among the craftspeople, women and men who'd traveled from as far as the Westwood to learn their art. Many of them were older, some even with children in tow, and it was always hard to know what to say to them outside of the normal courtesies. At least they tended to make their own conversation, and leave her to hers.

One of the understewards beat his staff on the stone floor, and everyone rose for the arros's entrance. And it was an entrance, Talan thought, caught as usual in obscure embarrassment. Esclin was tall and willow-thin and graceful, his pale hair combed sleek and straight over his shoulders, held neat by one of his ornate silver fillets; the blind eye and its scar were hidden beneath black silk and his overgown was of the Westwood's sheerest silk, a silvery gray so fine that the flame-colored lining glinted through. *Shaped of ice and fire*, one of the harpers had said last winter, and she heard one of the land-heirs whisper the line to his neighbor as the table made their bows. They were all more than half in love with him, for all he was old enough to have fathered most of them, a man of more than forty, and she swallowed her annoyance. She was no beauty and never would be, brown as the mother she could barely remember, with a sharp nose and even sharper chin: *You look like my grandmother*, Esclin said, intending to console; but it was little comfort.

The libation bowl was ready on its stand in the open space between the tables, and the speaker and the master smith advanced on it, she with a pitcher, he with empty hands. They bowed to the arros and he put hand to heart to return the courtesy, acknowledging their sacred roles. Rota lifted the pitcher and poured a thin dark stream into the waiting bowl. Talan remembered her with the dead assassin, and couldn't suppress a shiver. Rota served the White Mistress, life and death, healing and harming: an uncomfortable presence at the best of times, and tonight more so than usual. The smith lifted his hands and fire leaped from the bowl, dancing blue and finally gold, until the liquid was consumed. They bowed again, the arros acknowledged them, and abruptly the ceremony dissolved into a scraping of stools and a rush of conversation. The first wave of servers bustled out, bearing bread and wine, and Talan dropped into her place aware that she was thoroughly hungry.

Cat Meirin grinned at her, reading the thought, and at her right hand Perrin Huwaros, the thegen of Nen Salter, turned to offer the best loaf. Before she could take it, the understeward intercepted it.

"The arros's orders, Thegen," he murmured, and drew a nacre disk from his sleeve. He laid it against the bread, whispering an incantation, and Perrin stiffened.

"Do you mean to imply —"

Talan glared at him. "Of course he doesn't, don't be stupid. Someone tried to kill the arros today, it's wise to take precautions."

Perrin dipped his head. "Of course. I beg your pardon, Thegen—and yours, Steward."

Talan nodded, not displeased, and allowed Nisar to test her wine as well. At the high table, she saw Maeslin doing the same for her father's food: pointless, she thought. Who would try poison the very night knives had failed? She turned her attention to her meal, hiding a scowl.

The shallow curve of the harbor at Mal-Manan was crowded with ships, a forest of masts strung with cordage, the air sharp with the scent of melting tar. The broad-bellied transports were pulled close to the quays in the sheltered center, ready for the next draft of horses. No one liked the crossing, the horses least of all, and Sunnlef en Angeiles eyed the ships warily from the top of the shallow hill. His horse fretted under him, eager to be moving and out of the surrounding crowd. The Rider curbed the gelding—this was one of the things he was there to do, to accustom it to the kind of crowds they would encounter once they reached the shores of Manan-Oversea— and waited a moment longer, his eyes sweeping over the swarming port, until he was sure that the gelding knew they were moving only because its master willed it.

He crossed the broad wagon-road that carried the bulk of the cargos down to the port, and followed the narrower track that curved up the low hill crowned by the domed house of the Blazing One. The lord paramount did not reside within it, though by old custom he conducted some business there; instead, the senior wheelmen had vacated their perimeter dwelling-houses, and the lord paramount and his officers were crowded into the narrow quarters. At least the stables were large enough; but then, even the wheelmen understood the value of good horseflesh.

He swung easily out of the saddle and gave the reins to the page who hurried to take them, then made his way up the shallow stairs into the shadows of the hall. The lord paramount's levy had already shifted to campaign manners, the sides of the hall stacked with lumpy bedrolls and untidy packs and piles of gear. The only women in sight were the servants of the house, the impoverished elders who served the wheelmen in exchange for room and board. They scurried past with downcast eyes, carrying baskets of linen for washing or supplies for the kitchens. The camp-women were elsewhere, the wealthy ones and the ones with powerful protectors set up in rooms of their own, the rest in inns and taverns and tents and alleys. Every year the lord paramount made efforts to leave them behind, and every year he was thwarted. Reys en Nevenel might just be the man to change that.

At the end of the hall, Reys had taken over the rooms that had served as the senior wheelmen's withdrawing room, where the walls were lined with shelves crammed with scrolls and board-bound books, and light streamed in through narrow windows topped with bulls-eye glass. At the back of the room, a hastily-hung curtain concealed the lord paramount's bed. He and his closest companions were gathered around the long table, maps spread out and pinned beneath polished stones. A band of sunlight fell across them, a knot of vivid color against the blackened wood and worn leather. There was no mistaking Reys for any lesser man, in spite of the plain madder-red tunic and well-worn boots, the lack of any jewelry except for the heavy torc at his neck. Across the table, the axial Suetrich, the leader of the wheelmen, was bent over the maps, tracing distances with a pair of brass dividers, his gown of undyed white wool bright in the reflected sunlight. The rest of the commanders were in the shadows, their voices blending into a soft muttering like birds in a coop.

Angeiles stepped forward then, afraid of being caught staring, and the lord paramount turned unerringly, a smile flickering across his face. It made him look younger, high-hearted and eager, and then he resumed the mask of his office. "Angeiles. I'm glad you've come."

Angeiles bent his knee in answer. It no longer felt strange to be addressed by his father's name, and he certainly respected the lord paramount's scruples: his own given name was Sunnlef, a name meant in all honor, but treading too close to the prerogatives of the Blazing One. Angeiles supposed at some point he should choose another name for common use, but for now his father's name would do. He joined the others, a company commander moving aside to let him take the place at the lord paramount's right hand. "I'm sorry I'm late."

The lord paramount waved away the apology. "You've only missed us arguing about the camp-women."

"A discussion that is not yet ended," Hennan en Wendar said, perhaps more sharply than he'd intended. He was generally in charge of the baggage train, and the matter concerned him as much as anyone. "Pardon, Lord, but the women perform a needful service, and many of them are honest wives and mothers. They are cooks and laundresses and nurses, and we will not find folk we can trust to take their place in Manan-Oversea."

"It would be better for wives and mothers to stay at home," the axial said, not lifting his head from the map, "and not run themselves into danger."

"Our women have always followed their men," Radoc en Martan pointed out mildly. He was one of the scout commanders, an upcountry man with a solid reputation as a fighter. "And if we plan to winter over, we will need them there more than ever. Surely you can't want our folk to... fraternize...with the locals. Particularly when they have wives at home."

Angeiles swallowed an annoyed response. Radoc had no standing to speak to the question, it was notorious that he and his wife lived separately while he shared his bed with his household steward. And yet both he and Hennan were right as far as they went. The camp-women did perform necessary functions, and some of them were even honest; and even when they weren't, they were at least servants of the Blazing One, unlike the disbelievers of Manan-Oversea. He glanced at the lord paramount—he had no love for unchastity, and could be harder than he needed to be—but to his surprise, the lord paramount was smiling slightly.

"You're wise to remind us of that, Hennan," he said. "For now, the rule will be that any woman who can prove herself a wife will be granted passage with her man, except on the horse-transports. We'll have no distractions there. For the rest of this..." He straightened, waving generally at the spread maps. "We've done as much as we can today, we'll reconvene in the morning." There was a murmur of agreement, the lords shuffling themselves into order, but Suetrich remained still, frowning.

"There is that other matter, my lord."

The lord paramount shook his head. "By your own account, that's over and done with and made no difference. The rest is for battle."

"Very well." Suetrich bowed and turned to join the others.

The lord paramount put his hand on Angeiles's sleeve. "No, you stay, if you would."

"Of course, my lord." Angeiles waited until the door had closed again behind them, then dipped his head again. "I'm sorry I was delayed."

The lord paramount waved away the words. "There was nothing I needed you for, except your company. Will you pour yourself some wine? And you could fill my cup while you're at it."

Angeiles did as he was told, pouring the new autumn vintage into the bright glass cups that stood ready. The wheelmen had brought out all their best goods for the lord paramount. "So they're still agreed, we'll winter Oversea?"

The lord paramount dropped into the room's single high-backed chair, stretching long legs into a patch of sunlight. "Yes, thank the Blazing One, no one's trying to back out. I think they see it as clear as I. If we want to take Manan-Oversea, we'll have to begin as soon as the weather breaks. And that means we winter over."

"The timing's tricky," Angeiles said. "We'll need to get ourselves established before winter hits, but without Esclin Arros or the Westwood's kyra getting word. But if the weather holds—"

"Suetrich promises us good weather," the lord paramount said. "And I'm not worried about the Westwood, they won't have time to act before it's too late to campaign. The Hundred Hills..." He shrugged, and took a long swallow of his wine. "We'll have to make sure no messengers escape, when we take the steadings."

Angeiles grimaced. That was never a pleasant business, hunting down men who were doing their duty as they understood it, and the lord paramount gave a wry smile. "I don't like it, either, but that's our choice. It's that or we go on fighting for another fifty years."

"And we—you—were promised otherwise." Angeiles had been in the hall when Reys was chosen, shuffled to the back with the other younger sons and landless men-at-arms. The old lord paramount, Lieven en Baumal, had limped into the hall, still pale and drawn from the hard-fought campaign and the sickness that had taken him at its end. He had laid his sword and helmet on the Blazing One's altar, renouncing his office and his power in a voice thready with lung-ill. Suetrich had called the Blazing One to witness, and they had all of them expected to see Lieven reinstated. But instead, the flames bent away from him, and Suetrich had had no choice but to accept the resignation. Lieven had bowed deeply, once to the altar and once to Suetrich, then turned his back and limped from the hall. The silence had weight, like the air before the thunder broke.

Will no one step forward in the Blazing One's service? Suetrich cried, and even from his place at the back, Angeiles could see the great lords exchange wary glances. No one moved, no one spoke, and suddenly the clouds that had covered the sun for most of the day split apart, sending a great beam of light streaming through the oculus at the top of the dome. The light had fallen on Reys en Nevenel, standing with his household to one side, the scarlet wool of his tunic blazing like flame. He had looked up into the blinding fall that pared flesh to stark silhouette, and slowly lifted his hand to the light.

There had been a general outcry then, Angeiles shouting with them, naming it the Blazing One's choice and will and a miracle, and Suetrich's voice rose over them all, praising the Blazing One and proclaiming this a sure sign of victory. *Because if the Blazing One has chosen the lord paramount, how can we fail?*

Not everyone had been happy, of course, in spite of the omen, and there had been considerable shuffling in the old levy. Angeiles had fought for a place, along with every other masterless man who'd been in the hall that day, but by some miracle the lord paramount had seen and singled him out for favor.

"So we were promised," the lord paramount said. "The traders from Oversea say that Esclin's omens have been dire."

"One would assume they'd have to be," Angeiles said, and the lord paramount laughed.

"True enough. But my omens continue perfect." He touched the torc lightly, for propitiation. "Even your name— though I think 'Angeil' means something different in the coastal tongues."

"My father was named for the iron in our hills," Angeiles answered. "I don't know another meaning."

"In the mountains, where I was born, *angeil* is an old word for the lesser lights, the lightning-bearers. And though the wheelmen say there's no such thing, I can't help thinking it's a good sign. Just like your forename."

Even now, the lord paramount wouldn't say the name, apply any attribute of the Blazing One to a mere man. It was strange—a little shocking, even—to hear him talk of the old discarded legends, before the Blazing One's teachings had burned out such imperfection. Angeiles ducked his head again. *I would gladly be your lesser light*, he thought, but knew better than to say such words aloud. "You do me too much honor."

"I know you'll earn it," the lord paramount answered, and the words warmed Angeiles to his core.

☾

It was the slack of the mid-afternoon, when even the kitcheners found a moment to rest, a time when all the parts of the royal household would assume Esclin to be elsewhere, closeted with someone else. He knew what Kelleiden would say to see him slipping off alone, but he doubted there would be another assassin so soon after Meleas had failed, and in any case he trusted his own arts to keep himself safe. He was doubly armed, long knife at his belt, smaller blades hidden in boot and sleeve, and as he made his way toward the inward stair, he spun strands of shadow to veil his presence. By the time he reached the stair itself, he moved unseen; his step on the stones was soundless, and not even the movement of the air betrayed his passage. The steps spiraled down into the dark, his hand on the wall his only guide. To his left, arches opened onto the central void, and there was only the faintest of light in the depths to prove that there was any end to them at all.

At the foot of the stairs, he released most of the illusion: he had no right to enter this place unseen. Witchlights burned low along the corridor; the door of the sanctum was shut, but the side door was open, a brighter light fanning out onto the rough-hewn floor. He reached for the iron bell at the foot of the stairs, but before he could touch it, a shadow moved, and Rota appeared in the doorway, her face unpainted, gray-streaked hair loosed over her shoulders, a few tiny skulls dangling among the strands, brighter than the gray. Her eyebrows rose, seeing him, and she made a formal curtsey.

"Sire."

"Speaker. I'd like to talk with you—informally."

"You know that's not how it works." Her stillness eased into a crooked smile, as familiar as his own. They were of an age; he would have taken her as one of his companions had her heart not been given early to the White Mistress, and she was still one of his close council.

"Just a word."

She shook her head, still smiling, and beckoned him into her antechamber. It was brightly lit, a great witchlight lamp in the center of the ceiling, half a dozen standing lamps along the walls, a pair of working lights on the long table beside a half-finished embroidery. A kettle simmered in the hob of the stove, and the air smelled of tea. She poured a cup for each of them without bothering to ask and settled herself on a padded stool, waving for Esclin to take his place opposite her.

"I assume this is about the girl? Or is it the sword? Or this fall's prophecy?"

"All three."

"Which first?"

"The girl." Esclin reached for his cup but did not drink, wrapping his fingers around the thick pottery. "Or maybe it is the fall omens. I was worried she might fulfill that prophecy."

Rota pushed her embroidery aside and rested her elbows on the well-scoured wood. "I doubt it. She was the Blazing One's agent, yes, but not a priest—they don't allow women in that service—so she doesn't count. The prophecy's still open: the day the wheelmen enter Nen Elin is the day the nenn falls."

"You said 'a wheelman' before," Esclin said. "The day a wheelman enters Nen Elin is the day the nenn falls."

Rota sighed. "I think both are true. I've asked more than once, and I get both answers."

"There's a considerable difference," Esclin said.

"Don't you think I know it? 'A wheelman' is the safest version."

"But if I could let one in, carefully chosen..." Esclin let the words trail off. "Which I can't, not without opening the doors to the rest." He gave a crooked smile. "You're right. Again."

Rota dipped her head in acknowledgment, and returned the smile. "For what it's worth, I've never been more certain of a vision. And the master smith sees it, and every wandering fortune-teller."

"And that brings us to the sword," Esclin said. His father and his grandmother had each had one, made by their master smiths, and both had been lost; his grandmother's was drowned in the swamps at the mouth of the Lammard, though its loss had bought a famous victory, while his father's had been broken with his death at Eith Ambrin. "You said that the sword made is by the arros betrayed. What do you mean by that betrayal?"

"If I knew that, I'd be the Mistress in truth, not just her voice." For a moment, she looked tired to the bone, and Esclin looked away. "That's not how this works. You know that. The only other thing I know is that the sword aches to be made."

"Kelleiden says the same thing," Esclin paused. "The sword is as much a symbol of the Hundred Hills as Arra's ring. As the water horse and the arros himself. The sword betrayed is the realm betrayed."

"I know that as well as you do," Rota said. "And I also know why you don't want to do it, which is not the same thing."

Esclin's fingers itched to settle the patch more closely over his missing eye, but he kept his hands still. "That's not—it's not the only reason. If I use the sword to bind the southern nenns more closely to me, and then I betray it—I don't see that ending well."

Rota bent her head again in agreement, the skulls clattering. There was a little silence between them, the fire hissing in the brazier. "So what is it you want of me, Esclin?"

Esclin took a swallow of the cooling tea. "Your advice, for a start."

"About?"

"Let's go back to the girl," Esclin said. "Obviously she was sent by agents of the Blazing One—by the new lord paramount, whoever he turns out to be." Rota nodded. "I doubt the ordinary wheelmen—the ones who've found places in the southern nenns, I mean—had any knowledge or involvement in this, but I don't think it really matters. They'll obey the lord paramount if it comes to a choice. The question is how to prevent them from having to choose, and how to prevent the nenns from following them if they choose badly. I think I've planted some doubts with Nen Salter, and burning her properly ought to win some favor, but what I don't see is how this fits with next spring. The Riders will come, they always do, so why try to kill me now?"

Rota laughed softly. "You know better. I'll gladly give you my opinion, for what that's worth, or I'll scry for you; but if you want that, you'll have to ask. And pay the price."

"Your opinion first," Esclin said, and she shrugged.

"Why kill you now, when Talan would have all winter to consolidate her claim? She'd do it, I make no doubt. A warning maybe, or a threat? To say they could reach you even here, even where the wheelmen are forbidden? That could all be true, and none of it."

"Am I doing right to burn her according to her own rituals?"

"I don't—" Esclin gave her a sharp look, and she sighed. "I think the followers of the Blazing One will respect it, though they won't all take it the way you'd hoped."

"What do you mean?"

"Some of them will see it as weakness, not a gift. Although—" Rota gave a wry smile. "If I had died in a strange land, I would be grateful for that gift. I say it's well done."

"Thank you." Esclin slipped a ring from his finger and slid it across the table. She caught it, turning it in the witchlight so that the stone flashed blue. "Yes, I'll ask for more."

"It's a fair price."

Esclin took a breath. This was not the place for the large questions; those should be brought to the sanctum in their proper time, when he was braced and ready. But a small question, chosen well, could pry loose a piece of the future without committing him to its fulfillment. "Will the sword bind the nenns more closely to me?"

Rota blinked. "That wasn't what I was expecting."

Esclin spread his hands. "It's what I'm asking."

Rota nodded, reaching into the curtain of her hair to free a pair of skulls. She took a box from one of the low cupboards, removed a smaller box and a well-worn leather pouch. From the box she took a generous pinch of incense and tossed it onto the stove. The grains-of-amber caught instantly, sending up thick strands of smoke as the familiar sweet-spicy scent filled the room. She opened the pouch and spilled its contents across the table: carved stones, shells brought from the shore south of Nen Ddaur, crystals and nuts and bones and odd shriveled things that Esclin did not want to examine too closely.

She considered them and the skulls, then chose a handful and swept the others aside. She brought her hand to her lips as though she whispered to the things within, her expression thoughtful, remote and serene, and the smoke reached from the stove to wind itself around her head and shoulders. The air thickened, the light dimmed, and then she opened her hands and tossed the objects rattling onto the table. They fell in no pattern Esclin could read—a bird's skull, the broken jawbone of some small rodent, a gray rune-marked stone, a crystal, a chipped snail's shell, spread haphazardly across the boards. Rota tipped her head to one side, studying them, then carefully separated them with an iron nail.

"They're uncertain," she said at last. "It's not that they don't love you, but they're hard-pressed and their wheelmen do good service. The sword is a kind of certainty. Are you answered?"

"I am answered," Esclin said, though the ritual response sat badly on his tongue.

"I don't think you can twist free of this," Rota said gently, and Esclin smiled in spite of himself.

"I think I mustn't."

The High Forge was little more than a cleared space, the ground beaten flat by use and bounded by stones; its advantage was the clear air and the easy exposure to the influences of sun and moon and stars, though the winds that curved around the mountain's sides always made managing the fires tricky. It was more often used for a summer smelting, but Kelleiden was hoping to reap a greater harvest from the winter's session, and all the signs indicated that the High Forge would be the best choice. There was already a stack of seasoned wood set close against the mountain, carried up by the woodmen as part of their duty, and a clay-scrape lay under a flat stone marked with the royal water horse. He checked it and the wood, found them both in order, and moved to the edge of the plateau.

Smoke rose thick at the base of the Doubtful Scarp, the flames licking ever higher into the stacked wood of the pyre. The wind was less there but it would keep the fire burning hot and strong, to consume the girl's body as quickly as possible. He was grateful again that it was not his fire, not his responsibility: he was sworn to the Mistress of the Forges, whose fire was kindled from flint and steel, never drawn from the burning glass. The followers of the Blazing One recognized no other gods, no other powers at all in the working world, and the mere idea made his teeth clench with rage. They had no right to take the forge from him or any other smith, the fire and the skill and the simple discipline that brought iron from rock and useful things from iron.

Worst of all was the pity, the soft sympathetic voice in which the wheelmen urged, meek and wide-eyed, that theirs was the only way, that their gifts were greater, worth more, than the hard-won work of the forges. And, yes, in time of sickness there was little he could do, any more than any other man, but he had never been promised more. His skill was in metal, in things of daily or of extraordinary use. They needed to keep the wheelmen out of Nen Elin, and if only Esclin would listen to him, listen to Rota, and let him forge a royal sword, they might stand a chance... He had nearly enough raw material, knobs and pebbles of star-iron from the plains north of Riverholme, and he knew he had the skill and the men to make it. He could almost see it, hovering in potential, waiting, wanting to be born, a constant presence like a shadow moving at the edges of his sight. And if the sword was to be a sacrifice—because how else could he read Rota's words, *The sword made, by the arros betrayed?*—it would still be worth the making. Surely Esclin could see that.

Of course he knew why Esclin refused. Kelleiden had been with him at Eith Ambrin and after that in the flight that had ended in the burning tower, had nursed him through the fever after he had lost his left eye. *I've walked through enough fires,* Esclin had said after the fall divination, once they were safely back in the arros's rooms. Kelleiden frowned down at the pyre. There were easily fifty people gathered there, maybe more, and not all of them belonged to Nen Salter. Even in Nen Elin, the people listened to the wheelmen, or at least to their followers. If he left it much longer, Esclin might have no choice at all.

And it would do no good to say any of that—Kelleiden had already said it, bluntly in private and more circumspectly in the arros's council. The last few years had been hard. The Riders had driven far into the Dancing Ground each summer, keeping people from their fields and the harvest of the hunt; all the signs said they would do the same again come spring. There was nothing he could do about it except forge more common swords, more arrowheads and knives and thick-drawn wire for mail; and he looked southwest again, shading his eyes as something moved on the long road.

It looked like a caravan, a plume of dust pale against the pines that ran along the banks of the Aurinand, and he strained to see. Horses and carts, and maybe twenty men? It was hard to be sure, but that should mean a substantial trader, or a consortium of traders. Most of the richer sort came by the Hidden River, but there were things that could only be brought from the Dancing Ground or from the Westwood. It would be worth it to be there when the caravan arrived, and he started back down the long trail.

He reached the gates of the nenn just as the caravan's outriders hauled their horses to a stop under the watchful eye of the arros's guard. Their leader carried a spear strung with half a dozen traders' pennants, and Kelleiden paused to read them as the leader exchanged words with the guard-master and Maeslin Steward came striding from the hall. The largest pennant showed three black stars on a saffron field. That was Croenel Bennialos, out of the Westwood, with his usual last load of dried fruits and spices; if he followed his routine, he'd cross the pass by Nen Gorthen and let winter chase him back down the Lammard to his home in Callamben. Then there was the Old-Man-Moon that was the brothers Daffylt and Arno, the spindle for Wenne Faracinas—she would be buying, not selling—the back-to-back crescents of Prestor Kotaros, the blue and white stripes of Cardys Neissas and the hammer, gold against black, of the smiths. There was no way to tell who it would be, of course, but his heart lifted anyway. It was always good to see a kinsman, and the kinship of the craft was a far greater bond than that of blood.

The next group of riders had reached the gates, and behind them the first wagon slowed to a stop. It was smaller than usual but built for heavy cargo, two sturdy oxen in its yoke. The driver looked familiar, and as he pulled off his broad-brimmed straw hat, Kelleiden broke into a grin.

"Raikin!"

"Kelleiden." The driver lifted a hand in answer, and Kelleiden threaded his way through the gathering crowd to stand at the wagon's near wheel. "I hoped I'd see you first."

"You've got something for me?" Kelleiden couldn't help glancing into the wagon's bed, though all the goods were contained in sturdy chests, only a traveling anvil identifiable under its canvas cover. Raikin Smith dealt mostly in raw gems and rare ores, and if he had come this far north at the end of the season, he must think he had something worth the trip.

Raikin grinned, showing a chipped front tooth. He was a big, brown-bearded man, one of the Deirand Exiles who had settled the plains south of Riverholme. He'd had no particular skill with horses or war, so his father had traded him to the smithy while he was still a boy. "If you're still seeking star-iron."

"Always." Star-iron was the rarest of elements, worth more than its weight in gold, and to have it fall into his lap and yet be denied the chance to use it was intensely frustrating. "I'd certainly like to see what you have."

"Let me get the wagon inside," Raikin answered, "and I'll be glad to show you."

Kelleiden summoned the apprentices from the forge, and under Raikin's eye they hauled the chests up the Wideway that spiraled around the edges of the nenn. In the forge chamber, Raikin unlocked the chests to let the journeymen and apprentices examine the ores and ingots and unset stones. He reserved one small bag for himself and drew Kelleiden aside, handing it across so that Kelleiden could feel the weight. Kelleiden loosed the drawstrings, folding down the worn leather to reveal the silver-gray lumps. The largest was the size of a quail's egg, its surface pitted and folded; the smallest were barely larger than pebbles, but altogether it was a surprisingly substantial haul. Kelleiden weighed it in the smithy scale: half a river-pound. Fortunately the treasury was full this year.

"I want it," he said, because there was no point in pretending otherwise—there was no smith alive who wouldn't want that much star-iron, especially not one who served a royal house. "How much will you take in trade?"

"Only what I'd pay in stabling and housing," Raikin answered, and Kelleiden nodded. That was also expected, and entirely fair. Raikin was on the road to make a profit in coin, not in kind, and there was only so much he could carry in his wagon anyway.

"Hold it for me, if you would, and I'll talk to the steward."

"I have more goods you might like," Raikin offered.

"I'm sure," Kelleiden answered. With this latest purchase, he would certainly have enough to make Esclin a royal sword, if the arros would only permit him to begin. And that was not a problem he could solve immediately. He looked at the long bench where journeymen and apprentices jostled for a look in each of the chests. Raikin would have river-rubies and cats-eyes and salt-tears, the red gold of the northwestern hills and moon-silver from north of the Westwood; fine amethysts and opals and citrine gathered from all across the Three Realms. He saw one of the youngest journeymen turning a piece of emberine in her hand, looking for the inward flame, and made a note to buy at least a small piece for the forge. The girl had a feeling for gems; it was time to let her try her hand. And that teaching was his responsibility, as much as any sword. He turned his attention to the chests, and let Raikin lead him through the contents, determined to strike the best bargain he could.

The Day of the Dead dawned bright and cold, a rime of frost creeping into the great hall before the servants and the sun swept it away. It was a day of feasts, families taking the time to travel down the valley to the honeycomb of caves where the nenn's dead were laid, to brighten their markers and share the year's news. The royal tombs were within the nenn itself, burrowed deep into the mountain's heart, beneath the Hidden River, and Esclin paid them scrupulous honor, laying a great spray of late-blooming aleantis on the narrow table set against the wall where Arra's water horse was carved in strong relief. It rose from a lighter band of stone as though from foaming rapids, crystals flashing in its clawed forefeet and from the coils of its mane as they caught the witchlight.

The shadows were heavy on the narrow niches where the bodies lay—where he himself would lie in the fullness of time, though not, he hoped, any day soon—and the flowers were bright as flame against the rock. Talan held the bowl as he doled out the libations at the mouth of each niche and poured the rest at the feet of the water horse, and then they began the long walk back to the nenn's main level. Rota was waiting there, a wreath of aleantis in her hands. Esclin traded the libation spoon for the wreath, and stepped back into the light.

The speaker presided over the feast, in her Mistress's name, and afterwards unleashed the nenn's children to demand presents from any adults they could catch. Esclin had always enjoyed the game, and had a bag of fancy sweets from the coast to buy his ransom and a ring for the first one to find him. As the children beat drums and a few pots and kettles, joyful cacophony filling the hall, he slipped away with the rest. He climbed along toward the nenn's roof, aware that he should have company after the attack on the docks, but he thought another attempt unlikely. Besides, he would not show himself afraid.

He stopped midway up the Five-Leaf Stair—any higher, and the younger children would have no chance—and turned toward the mountain's heart. The wall curved gently around the northern cistern, full after the summer's spate. The nenn would draw it down again as the water dropped in the Hidden River, and refill it again at the spring flood. He could feel the weight of it, cool and quiet and strong as the stone that contained it, and followed it to the gallery where the cisterns met.

It was a working space, one wall filled with great gears and levers that moved the shutters that diverted water from the cistern through the channels of the nenn. Esclin called a ball of witchlight and let it rise to the room's peak, then settled himself on the ledge that ran along the outward wall. The stone was pierced behind him, and he could hear laughter and shrieks as the first forfeits were claimed.

Something moved in the shadows of the right-hand corridor. It was too soon to be any of the children and he came to his feet, reaching for his dagger with one hand and with the other drawing the ghost of the hidden water into a compact ball, mist seeping from between his fingers. If he had misjudged the risk…

"It's me," Kelleiden said.

Esclin drew a deep breath, opening his fingers to let the mist dissipate. "You shouldn't startle me."

"You shouldn't be alone."

There was an hour's argument lying beneath those words, but they had known each other long enough not to need it. Esclin sighed. "It's not fair that the children get two for one."

"They'll live," Kelleiden said. *And so will you*: the words hung unspoken, and Esclin shook his head. He couldn't say the smith was entirely wrong, and saw the moment when Kelleiden saw his surrender.

He gave a wry smile. "Since you're here..."

Kelleiden moved closer and Esclin caught him by the front of his gown, drawing him in for a long kiss. Kelleiden murmured something, leaning against him, and then they both heard the sound of footsteps in the corridor behind him. Kelleiden sighed, and Esclin grinned as he pulled away, turning to face the entrance. "Who's this?"

It was a child or seven or so, a girl, to judge by the long gown that was kilted to her knee, showing striped stockings above bright red shoes, her hair straggling in elf-locks over her shoulders. "Amila, please you, Sire, and I'm first."

"Indeed you are," Esclin said, and slid the ring off his little finger. The silver gleamed in the witchlight.

Amila reached for it, then stopped short. "The lady told me you were here. Does that still count?"

"Lady?" Kelleiden said sharply, and Esclin frowned at him.

"What lady?"

"By the Five-Leaf Stair." Amila waved vaguely behind her. "She said she'd tell me where you were if I'd bring you a message."

Kelleiden drew breath, but Esclin put a hand on his shoulder. "What message, then?"

"She said you must take the sword." Amila frowned in turn. "I told her you had a sword, you didn't need to take one, but she said you'd know what she meant."

"I expect I do," Esclin said.

"What did she look like, this lady?" Kelleiden asked. "Did you know her?"

Amila shook her head. "Does that mean I cheated?"

For an instant, Esclin wanted to say yes, but that was petty as well as pointless. He held out the ring again. "You kept your bargain, so I think that's fair. Kelleiden, go see if the lady's still there."

"Oh, yes," Kelleiden said grimly, and slipped past the girl.

Amila took the ring, sliding it first onto her forefinger and then onto her thumb. "Do I get a sweet, too?"

Esclin couldn't help smiling at that. "I suppose you do." He handed her one from the waiting bag, and she took it with a curtsey and a gap-toothed smile.

This was an omen, the most blatant one yet—there was no one in the court who'd dare say such a thing who hadn't already said it to his face. And the girl would talk, in all innocence; even if he asked her to say nothing, she was too young to keep a secret. He could hear more footsteps, coming from the Crescent Stair. The group of children slid to a disappointed stop, seeing Amila, and Esclin found a smile.

"Very close! Well done, all of you."

He handed out sweets and the children turned away, drawing Amila with them to hunt for more prizes. He heard movement behind him, and glanced over his shoulder to see Kelleiden at the corridor's mouth, shaking his head.

"No sign of any mysterious ladies, nor much sign that any but the girl had been there."

Esclin sighed. "The trouble with a royal sword is the second part of the prophecy. *By the arros betrayed*—it's no good answer."

"The sword will help hold the southern nenns," Kelleiden began, and stopped. "But you know that."

"It will help hold them until I betray it." Esclin shook his head. "And then—won't it be more trouble than it's worth?"

"That's a question for the speaker, not for me."

"I know."

"The girl will talk," Kelleiden said, after a moment. "At least to her parents, and they'll tell the rest of the nenn."

"I know," Esclin said again. "It's nothing new." He gave Kelleiden a sidelong smile. "Find me a way to avoid the betrayal, and I'll take the sword."

It was late enough now, five days after the Day of the Dead, that the light had started to fail and the lamps were lit in the guest-hall allotted to Nen Salter, while outside in the broad corridors Huwar Ellemas could hear voices calling back and forth, arranging the stabling for a caravan newly arrived from the south. His own party would be leaving soon, returning to Nen Salter before the first snows fell, but all in all it had not been an unprofitable visit. Esclin had been willing to listen to his complaints after the summer's campaign—too many men dead and not enough time or treasure to make up for it—and if there was little anyone could do to abate it, Huwar at least felt confident that he was not unheard.

But there would have to be changes made, and sooner rather than later. The southern nenns in particular were stretched dangerously thin as the yearly fighting washed up the valleys that fed them like an unwholesome tide. Nen Salter was better off than many, located as they were on the Hidden River, but trade would not solve all their problems. He thought they had another three years, maybe four, before the situation became unmanageable, and hoped Esclin could broker some solution by then. Or defeat the Riders, of course, but that was looking increasingly unlikely. Every year the invaders seemed better armed and more numerous, and they always managed to land enough cavalry to dominate the Dancing Ground. The rivermaster raised horsemen among the Deirand Exiles who had settled in his territory, but they were growing less enthusiastic with each campaign. Perhaps if Esclin would relax his strictures on the wheelmen he could persuade the Riders to come to the bargaining table, but the arros showed no sign of softening. This assassination attempt wouldn't help that, either.

He looked up as the door opened to admit his son Perrin, Thedar trailing behind him with a sulky look on his face. Despite the twilight, it was early to dress for dinner, and he couldn't suppress a frown.

"A word with you, Father," Perrin said, and Huwar lifted an eyebrow.

"Of course."

"In private."

Huwar felt his eyebrows rise further at that, but waved them toward the tiny antechamber that he had taken for his cabinet. It was as private as one was likely to find in Nen Elin, which was not to say very private at all, but it would have to do. He leaned against the worktable, watching as Thedar scuffed his feet against the stones and Perrin pulled the door almost closed. If they kept their voices down, they could not be overheard without knowing it. "Well?"

"Thedar has news to share," Perrin said.

Huwar looked at his nephew, who shrugged one shoulder. "It's not certain. I didn't want to trouble you until I was sure. If it ever came to that."

"There's a new lord paramount," Perrin said.

"We knew that," Huwar said.

"Yes, but Thedar can put a name to him." Perrin glanced nervously out the door.

"Is that true?" Huwar bit down on unexpected anger. Esclin had been looking for that piece of information since the first word had come north along the River. He would not be pleased that it had been withheld.

"It wasn't certain." Thedar met his eyes defiantly. "Otherwise of course I would have said something."

"How did you hear?" Even as he spoke, Huwar grimaced, seeing the trap opening before him, and Perrin nodded.

"There was talk at the pyre. But I don't think there were any wheelmen there, just our own folk."

"Are you sure of that?" Huwar asked.

"What does it matter?" Thedar said. "You know there's no harm in them, and great good."

"It matters because the arros has banned them from Nen Elin," Huwar said, holding onto his temper with an effort. "And agree or not, we obey the arros."

"The arros is wrong," Thedar said.

"Wrong or right, he's the arros," Huwar snapped. "Blood and bones! If you flout his word here, he'll have every cause to ban them from every nenn in the Hills."

"He'd regret that," Thedar began, but broke off under Huwar's outraged stare. "I mean that he would lose a good deal of our people's love —"

"Will you mind your tongue?" Huwar shook his head. No, he would not be admitting Thedar to his councils any time soon, not until the boy proved he'd learned a little sense.

"Many of our men have received the fire," Perrin said cautiously, "but none are full initiates. And the caravan will have brought news as well."

That was true, and Huwar made himself relax. "It would have been better to speak at once."

"I didn't know anything more than rumor," Thedar said.

"Even a rumor is of value these days." Huwar folded his arms. "We'll speak to the arros."

"I only know what people have said fifth-hand," Thedar protested. "What if they—what if we're wrong?"

"Better than being right and not sharing," Perrin said.

"And there, my son, you hit the heart of it," Huwar said. "Send a page, ask the arros for an audience. And you, nephew, will give me all the details."

Unsurprisingly, Esclin was willing to receive them, though the chamber was in a disarray that showed he'd been caught between the baths and the hall. Only Ilgae Marshal was present, along with yet another of the thegen's companions acting as a page, and Huwar wondered where Kelleiden had gone.

"Sire," he said warily, and Esclin waved for him to seat himself.

"You said this was urgent." He nodded for the page to pour wine anyway, and Huwar accepted the cup with some relief.

"My nephew has some news to share."

"Thedar, isn't it? Who gave Meleas her rites." From anyone else, that would have been a compliment, but from Esclin it was very much a double-edged sword.

"Yes, Sire." To give him his due, Thedar's voice was steady, his back straight. "I've heard a whisper that says Reys en Nevenel has been chosen lord paramount. Mind you, I've no proof, none at all, just the name —"

"Reys en Nevenel," Esclin repeated. "Ilgae?"

The Marshal shrugged. "Did he command a wing of the heavy horse last summer?"

"He wasn't the lord paramount," Esclin said. "That was Lieven en Baumal. What happened to him, do we know?"

"He died," Huwar said, keeping his voice scrupulously neutral.

Esclin lifted an eyebrow. "And of what, I wonder?"

"The Blazing One withdrew his favor," Thedar said. "Or so they say."

Huwar said, "He laid down his arms in the citadel, or so I heard, an offering against his failures. The Blazing One—the wheelmen accepted them, and not long after he sickened of fever. But I expect you heard that same tale, Sire."

Esclin nodded. "I did."

"They say that Lieven laid down his arms a broken man," Thedar said, "and there was no one in the council who was willing to step forward after the fate that came to him. But then when the fire was kindled and the incense offered, the sun came through the oculus of the hall and the light fell on Reys en Nevenel. And he said if he was chosen, then he would serve, and so they named him lord paramount and first servant of the Blazing One. Or so I was told."

And if that was the story that was whispered among the Exiles and in the southern nenns, it was no wonder people were talking of ill omens. Huwar saw the same thought on Esclin's face, and said quickly, "If that's Nevenel en Carrag who's the father, they have a holding in the Anteral."

"I know the family," Ilgae said. "Not greatly wealthy, but good blood."

"And devout, presumably," Esclin said.

Ilgae nodded. "I would assume so. I can ask about, if you'd like."

"You might as well." Esclin leaned back in his chair, took a swallow of his wine. "When exactly did you hear this, Thedar?"

That was the question, and Huwar was glad to see the color rise under Thedar's tan. "I'm not certain of it even now," he said.

"That's not what I asked," Esclin said.

"I heard it first a week or two ago," Thedar said. "But it was just rumor. It didn't seem worth considering, not without more."

Esclin flicked a glance at Huwar, who spread his hands. "He came to me today, Sire, and I thought it best to come to you. Even without certainty."

Something like a smile tugged at the corners of Esclin's mouth. "Quite." He leaned back in his chair, apparently at ease, and Huwar, who had seen that act before, had the strong desire to clap a hand over Thedar's mouth. "Tell me, Thedar, what do you make of this tale? You serve the Blazing One. Is this how his servants are chosen?"

Thedar's face brightened, and Huwar willed him to hold his tongue. "Not often, Sire, no. But when men are at a loss, the Blazing One does guide them. And this certainly seems to be such—"

"Hardly that," Huwar interrupted. "To choose a man of no experience—it sounds as though cooler heads refused the job, and a young man was handed it when no one else was left."

"That's not—" Thedar began, and Esclin lifted his hand.

"Peace. We mustn't annoy your uncle." He flicked Huwar a dark smile, and Huwar bowed, acknowledging defeat. "I'm grateful for the warning. You've given us much to consider."

"We are your servants, Sire," Huwar said, with another formal bow, and put a heavy hand on Thedar's shoulder to steer him from the chamber. Thedar had proved himself a fool before the arros, though from the look on his face he hadn't realized it, was still basking in the moment when Esclin had spoken to him apparently as an equal. It was only to be hoped that Huwar would have the chance to make his own position clear to the arros and the council before they left for the winter.

Ω

Esclin's bedstead was wide and piled with furs, the posts that supported the canopy and curtains carved with water horses. In the dim light from a single witchlight and a few last wavering candles, Esclin imagined that he saw their hooves quiver, their manes shift. It was late enough that he had dismissed his pages; the fire was banked in the hearth, but there was still wine in the pitcher and he poured himself a final cup. Kelleiden Smith regarded him from beside the fireplace, his expression blurred in the shivering light.

"They tell me Nen Salter's nephew gave the girl her rites. And did a good job, too."

The admission had cost him: Kelleiden rarely had anything good to say about the followers of the Blazing One, and for a moment Esclin was sorry to have to spoil the moment. "He did. And then Nen Salter brought him to me to tell me the name of the new lord paramount."

Kelleiden made a soft sound, not quite a hiss. "That I hadn't heard. Who is it?"

"Reys en Nevenel."

Kelleiden shook his head. "I don't know him."

"No more do I," Esclin said. "Though I've set my people to find out what they can. Ilgae thinks he may have commanded cavalry these last few years? He's young, they say, and has the wheelmen's favor—was chosen by the Blazing One after Lieven en Baumal laid down his shield. Lieven is dead, by the way, died of a fever, or perhaps the withdrawal of favor, take your pick."

He leaned back in his chair, stretching his feet out to the last of the fire, and Kelleiden came to rest one hip cautiously on the chair's arm. "That is not good news. Not at all."

"No." Esclin leaned against him. He was being pushed into a corner, and knew it. "There must be a sword." He felt

Kelleiden shift, looked up to try to read the shadowed face.

"A royal sword? Yes, it wants to be born. I tell you that from the heart of my mystery. It wants it so much that I can see nothing else—" Kelleiden stopped abruptly. "Are you saying yes?"

"I..." Esclin felt his own smile twist out of true. "I had thought I might try to come to some terms with the wheelmen in the southern nenns, but the omens this fall put paid to that. I need some symbol to pull them all behind me, south and north alike. Can you do it?"

Kelleiden breathed a laugh. "The traders who came today, along the Aurinand. Raikin Smith was with them."

"Your forge-brother," Esclin said.

"He brought his usual wares, fine gems and metal ingots. And half a pound of star-iron. It wants very badly to be made."

Esclin closed his eye. To claim the sword, he would have to walk through fire; he knew how it was done, had been there when his father's sword was made, but he had survived real fire, and his muscles clenched at the mere thought of it. And there was the second part of Rota's omen to consider. "What do you make of this betrayal Rota speaks of? Do you see it?"

"All I see is the sword," Kelleiden said. "I'm sorry."

Esclin leaned harder against him, fine wool against his cheek, and Kelleiden draped an arm across him. "Buy the star-iron. Take whatever you need from the treasury."

"I did already."

"Clever man."

"I have enough and a bit to spare," Kelleiden said. "Room to make a mistake."

"You don't make mistakes," Esclin said.

"Everyone makes mistakes," Kelleiden said. "I prefer to know I can recover from them."

"I need it by spring."

Kelleiden sighed. "I was planning to make iron before the winter closes in—we need it, and that way we'll have all the winter to work it. We'll need to use the High Forge, I think, especially if I'm going to smelt the star iron." He nodded again. "I'll do my best."

"That's all I ask." Esclin paused. "You'll stay?"

"Always."

Esclin rose to let him lift the fur-lined gown from his shoulders, then slid between the sheets, the night air chasing after him. Kelleiden pinched out the last candles and joined him, cold skin against cold skin. Esclin shivered, curling tighter under the weight of the furs, the piled featherbeds hollowing beneath them. They had lain together often enough that their bodies knew the dance, fitting limb against limb until the bed warmed.

"A royal sword," Kelleiden said, after a while. "You deserve one."

Esclin shrugged. His father had lost his at Eith Ambrin along with his life, and had deserved that, too. It was dark in his bed, the curtains closing out the last light from the embers in the fireplace, but in the moving dark behind his eyes, he could see the faint shape of his father's sword. "Deep-Biter," it had been called, a broad, slashing blade that seemed to flame with silver where the whetstone sharpened it to a killing edge. It had been old-fashioned when it was made, though it certainly suited Aubrin's fighting style. And it was just that old-fashioned style that had sent Aubrin charging across the ford at Eith Ambrin, into the teeth of the Riders' shield line and the archers hidden on the wings.

Esclin had just turned twenty then, commander of the reserve. He'd thrown it in to try to blunt the defeat, knowing he would lose half his men or more, but even that sacrifice hadn't been enough to bring his people off. On the right, the Guard of Riverholme had shattered under the third Rider charge, and his own people had broken and fled, scrambling to the shelter of the Westwood or back to the Hundred Hills. The Riders and their allies among the Fengal Exiles had held most of the Dancing Ground for five long years. If he had held back, let Aubrin bear the brunt of the counterattack he'd brought on himself—

The calculations never changed, no matter how many times he reworked his choice. He rested his head against Kelleiden, his empty eye socket against the curve of the smith's shoulder. "Have you thought what you'll name it?"

Kelleiden was still for an instant. "Royal swords name themselves. Or earn their names."

"I should have known that."

"Mostly they earn their names," Kelleiden said, drowsily. "You have until you place the grip for it to name itself, the blade is wild till then. I remember my old master said he waited and waited for Deep-Biter to name itself, but it never did."

Deep-Biter was lost, shattered and ground into the mud and stones of the ford at Eith Ambrin—if it had survived, one of the Riders would have claimed it, a trophy for the lords protector to take back to Manan. "I never liked it."

"You wouldn't," Kelleiden said.

"I don't think it liked me."

"The one I make for you," Kelleiden said, "will love you."

CHAPTER THREE

The roads were worse than Leicinna had expected, even factoring in the lateness of the season; and when the band reached what was left of the abandoned steading, she ordered a halt even though the sun still stood a good two fingers'-breadth above the horizon. But the ground was worse ahead, and if the track here was mud-slicked and difficult, within a league the horses would be stumbling ankle deep even before they came to the ford that would take them across the Lammard. Better to do that in good daylight, and shelter here tonight where what was left of house and barn provided some protection from the wind.

They made camp with practiced speed, stringing half-tents from the crumbling walls to the ground while the horsemaster laid out the picket lines and the most junior troopers took the animals two by two to the stream that wound along the edge of what had been the steading's fields. A Fengal steading, the leader thought, surveying the courses of stone and brick, the undecorated sill of the main door. Her kin were Deirand Exiles, the first group to flee Manan for the safety of Allanoth. The plains of the Dancing Ground had been no haven, and they had put themselves under the rivermaster's rule. This was not her place. Nor had any land been since they rode north from Ramnos; she turned her back firmly to the standing stones.

The band knew its business—she had been careful to enlist primarily experienced soldiers, and they'd had a season's hard campaigning to solidify their skills. Several fanned out to collect water and wood, and by the time the sun kissed the horizon the watchfire was blazing, the stewpot ready to receive each trooper's handful of grain and dried peas. There was dried sausage from the common store as well, and a second pot already boiling the night's tea; Leicinna drew an appreciative breath and reached for her pipe.

"Do we plant the standard, Captain?"

That was her second, Gimmell, a sturdy shadow against the firelight. Leicinna lit a long twig from the fire, teasing the shredded herb to light, buying time while she considered. They were a long way from anywhere, here on the Dancing Ground of War where three generations' fighting had destroyed all but a handful of well-fortified holdings along the Lammard. There was no one to impress, and this late in the year there would be only bandits and a few belated travelers sharing the roads. On the other hand, they were thirty strong, well-trained and equally well-armed, ample force to deal with any attack, and the banner-right was new enough to please her people out of all proportion to either effort or danger. All of that passed through her mind in a heartbeat, between the first flame laid to the leaf and the first lungful of sweet smoke, and she dropped the burning twig into the fire.

"Yes, go ahead." She drew in another breath of smoke, warming herself from the belly out, as the bannerman brought the strip of silk on its long pole and planted it in the ground. The last of the light caught on the gold and saffron thread of her initial—she had no house-sign, not yet—and deepened the scarlet background to blood.

Her page, her cousin's daughter Fisk, had already arranged saddle and blankets in a dry spot not too far from the fire, and she lowered herself to their comfort, glad of the coarse wool to cut the chill. They had not ridden in armor, so there was no need to disarm; she shifted her sword out of the way and accepted a cup of tea.

The sun melted into the horizon, red as iron in the fire, spreading along the Westwood's distant trees. She finished her pipe and the tea, one eye following the ordinary movements of the camp, when there was a shift in the familiar pattern. A moment later, one of the watchers at the road's edge called a challenge. She couldn't hear the answer, but she could see her people relax. Something ordinary, then, and familiar: a chapman, perhaps, or a herder. There were more voices, coming closer, and she sat up straighter, adjusting her sword as the figures loomed up out of the purpling dark.

"Captain. The harper begs a place at our fire."

Leicinna smiled in spite of herself, and the harper made a flamboyant bow, drawing off her cap to reveal not her usual club of many braids, but hair cropped short and ragged like a felon. "Captain."

"Viven Harper," Leicinna said, though the cropped hair was already waking concern. "You are always welcome at my fire."

"I thank you," the harper said, but she did not unsling her pack. She lowered her voice. "Though I must warn you, there may be trouble at my heels."

"What sort of trouble?"

"I came north with news for the arros and for the rivermaster, word from Nieve and Reyscant. There were four of us set out from there, and I've found one dead already on the road."

"Gimmell." Her second seemed to materialize from the shadows, as though he'd been waiting for the order. But then, he knew as well as she the risks of the road. "Double the watch. Keep an especial eye on the track from the south."

"Yes, Captain."

He disappeared again, and Leicinna turned her attention to the harper. "Are you being hunted?"

Viven spread her hands. "I think I've lost them? There were as many as five that I saw behind me, but I cut cross-country and haven't seen them since." For the first time, exhaustion flickered across her thin face. "I was afraid for a while that I'd lost myself as much as them. I was never so glad as when I saw the road—except maybe when I saw your standard."

Five men were no real threat to a troop of thirty, and even if they were archers, the shell of the steading would be good cover. "Sit," Leicinna said, and lifted her hand for Fisk. "There's food to spare."

"I'm happy to put in my share," Viven said. She lowered her pack, and went to one knee to retrieve a double handful of grain from a bag tucked into its depths. The page took it and backed away, and Viven settled herself cautiously onto the blankets.

"Will you share your news?" Leicinna asked. She hunched her shoulders under the weight of cloak and tunics, a chill that had nothing to do with the weather spreading through her.

The harper nodded, rubbing her hands together. She was underdressed for the road this time of year, Leicinna thought, and given that musicians of her caliber spent half their lives traveling, it was one more indication, if she'd needed it, of something seriously wrong. "Nieve has deposed their mayor and council, and elected a lord protector instead. They've locked the town gates and won't let anyone in or out. I was in Reyscant when I heard the news—I was there with two of my guild-brothers to play at a wedding—and the next thing I knew, the Council there had declared their own gates closed and called for elections of their own. I made the mistake of talking back to one of the councilmen, that's how I ended up shorn, though in the end they took a fine instead of prison.

"But then another of us—Salemen Mawdas, he's from the Westwood, though he has kin along the coast—he'd been planning to stay the winter with his sister's son, but he heard there was a Rider lord staying with the mayor, and the four of us thought it was best to slip away with the news before the gates were sealed any tighter." She sighed. "But I suppose we weren't as clever as we'd thought, for all we split into three. I knew there was someone tracking me, and four days on I found Salemen dead beside the road, stripped bare and all his goods taken. I only hope Pedder and Amiel got clean away—" She stopped again, shaking her head. "In any case, it's grave news. The arros needs to know, and the rivermaster—"

"And the kyra of the Westwood," Leicinna said, sharply.

"And her, yes, though Pedder and Amiel were headed that way. But the rivermaster can reach her, too." Leicinna nodded. "I left the road after I found Salemen," Viven continued. "He'd been dead some days, and the foxes had been at him. I knew him by his hands and his hair. I didn't—I couldn't bury him."

"You'd have been a fool to try," Leicinna said, but she was already grappling with the more important problem. Neither Nieve nor Reyscant were particularly rich, but they both had sheltered ports, ports that would let the Riders cross the Narrow Sea even this late in the season, and land men and horses unopposed. And if these new, home-grown "lords protector" could keep word of their defection from reaching any of the rulers, they'd have a decent chance of gaining the advantage all across the Dancing Ground come spring.

She reached for her pipe again, only to realize it had gone out. They were still a good week's march south of Riverholme, traveling along the Lammard; it was twice that to Nen Gorthen even if they struck out cross country. And she was willing to bet that there had been more than five men assigned to chase the fleeing musicians—she would certainly have sent more, and the Riders weren't stupid. On the other hand, the group couldn't be so large as to draw notice....

"Tea, Captain?" Fisk said, timidly, and Leicinna looked up, forcing a smile.

"Thanks." She took the cup, and Viven did the same, wrapping her hands around the wood to warm them. "Gimmell!"

"Captain?"

"Ask Finn what he makes of the next week's weather."

"All right." Gimmell backed away again, and Leicinna took a deep breath.

"If you ride with us, we can make Riverholme in a week, ten days at the worst. That's closest. And the rivermaster can send messengers to Nen Elin and the Westwood—the road to Nen Gorthen won't close for another month or so, and from there they can take the Hidden Rivers."

"So I could," Viven said, and Leicinna nodded. "You could. You could go yourself."

Viven shrugged. "The arros has been a good patron to me."

"You'll also stand a better chance with us if the Riders have tracked you."

"I will." Viven nodded in her turn. "Yes, I'll ride with you, gladly."

"Captain?" Gimmell emerged from the dark, and Leicinna gestured for him to seat himself.

"The harper has brought important news," she said. "We'll make all speed for Riverholme in the morning."

Gimmell nodded. "Finn says he thinks the weather will hold until the moon wanes. He makes no promises after that."

"That'll get us most of the way there."

"Should we expect trouble?" Gimmell kept his voice low.

"I was pursued," Viven said, "but I think I lost them."

"We won't take chances," Leicinna said. "We'll ride in battle array."

Gimmell nodded again. Fisk returned, carrying bowls of the night's stew, and they ate quickly and in silence. It was plain and savorless, though filling: they had run low on salt, and only the dried sausage offered spice. The harper ate without complaint, and scraped her bowl clean like a soldier. Gimmell rose to his feet and collected the empty dishes.

"I'll just see to the watch, Captain," he said, and disappeared into the night. The others sat in silence for a long moment. Viven's face was deep in shadow, her back almost to the fire, her expression hidden.

"A cold night," Leicinna said at last.

Viven hunched her shoulders. "They were saying in Reyscant that it would be an early winter."

"I believe it." Leicinna took a breath. "You could share my blankets tonight."

Viven lifted her head, her face coming into the light. She was smiling in spite of everything, and Leicinna's heart lifted. "Did you really think I'd say no?"

"I always ask," Leicinna said, affronted, and Viven leaned forward to pat her knee.

"I expect that's why I always say yes."

Leicinna woke abruptly, every muscle tensed, her ears cocked for a sound that had begun in her dreams. There was nothing, though, only the faint and distant shuffle of the horses on the picket line, the crackle of the fire and the harper breathing deep beside her. The half-tent stretched from the wall nearly to the ground, keeping out the dew and some of the wind; through the gap she could see the dying fire, and her banner, and the night's watch pacing slowly through the camp. And yet there had been something.

She slid her hand sideways beneath the coarse blanket, and found the hilt of her dagger. Her sword lay just beyond it: she could seize it if she rolled and stood, but she wasn't yet sure of her ground. Viven shifted and sighed, and in that moment Leicinna heard another movement by her feet. Her own people would know better than to come up on her like that. She kicked off her blankets, flinging them toward the sound, and rolled away, snatching up dagger and sword to come up yelling. She saw Viven come awake, covering her head and kicking free of the blankets, and then a dark shape rushed her. She saw his dagger just in time to parry it left-handed, and dragged her sword from its scabbard.

"To me!"

The alarm was picked up by the fire, troopers turning toward her, and she put herself between the attacker and Viven. "To me, Leicinnas!"

She swung at the attacker as she shouted, saw him fall back, little more than a dark shape against the night. He was hooded and cloaked and masked, his face invisible in shadow; she saw his blade, a Mananite short sword, and parried again. The half-tent blocked her arm for a moment, and the attacker darted past her. Viven yelled something, and tore the tent loose, smothering him momentarily in its folds. She struggled free, kicking and punching the fallen shape, and a second figure lunged from the shadows. Leicinna leaped to block him, blade ringing on blade. Then Nea and Gimmell and Aylflet were there, and the man went down beneath their swords.

"Don't kill him," Leicinna called, but it was too late.

Gimmell gave a little shrug. "There's this one, Captain," he said, and jerked at the fallen half-tent. The fabric caught and held, and he pulled harder, rolling the assassin against the wall of the ruined house. The man's own dagger was planted in his chest.

"Torches," Leicinna said. The moon was down; from the set of the stars, she guessed it was still an hour or more to dawn. "Secure our lines and look to the horses, then see if you can back-track where these came from."

There was a confused murmur of acknowledgment, and Aylflet pointed to the men nearest him. "You, with me."

Fisk brought a torch and planted it in the ground beside the body. Leicinna looked at the harper, who still crouched at the edge of what had been their bed. "Are you all right?"

Viven nodded, though she was still shaking. "Unhurt."

And that was the important answer. Leicinna went to one knee beside the dead man, plucking at hood and short cape until she revealed his face. A fair man, dark-bearded from days on the road, ordinarily handsome in life, slack now in death: nothing to mark him out in any crowd.

"That's his own knife," Viven said.

Leicinna nodded. She searched the body, looking first for purse or jewels, then feeling along his limbs, and finally opening his clothes in the vain hope of finding some identifying mark. He was dressed in black from the skin out, even his shirt and belt and boots; he carried nothing but his weapons. She straightened, frowning, and picked up the mask. It was thin leather, too, curved to fit the man's face, with wide eye slits and a button at the mouth, on the inside. He had held that with his teeth, she guessed, and looked down again.

"He killed himself because he didn't kill me," Viven said

softly.

Leicinna found a blanket that didn't have obvious bloodstains and draped it around her shoulders. "Evidently. I don't suppose you know him?" Viven shook her head.

Another torch loomed out of the dark, Aylflet under it. "No sign I could follow in the dark. I think he came through what's left of the steading, though, and I may be able to do more in the morning."

"Leave it for now," Leicinna said. An attempt to kill them sleeping argued that the attackers didn't have enough men to take on the entire company, but that didn't mean there weren't more of them out there in the dark, circling like wolves. "Make sure no one goes alone. There may be more of them."

"Yes, Captain," Aylflet said, and beckoned to his troopers.

Gimmell was on his knees beside the second body, searching it as she had done, and he sat back on his heels with a grunt of satisfaction. "Nothing on this one either, Captain, but his masters marked him."

Leicinna turned to look, and Gimmell lifted the man's shirt higher. On the point of his hip, where none but closest kin or lover would see, was the brand of a circle made of flame.

"Well," she said. "If we'd needed confirmation—there it is."

"What now?" Gimmell rose to his feet, wiping his hands on the hem of his tunic.

Leicinna looked at the stars and then to the east, looking for the first signs of dawn. Perhaps the dark was less there, the stars paling. "Get our people moving. We'll ride at first light, straight for Riverholme."

The younger troopers had already built up the fire again and were standing to in arms while several more took up positions along the picket lines. Nothing moved in the surrounding dark, and as the sky slowly paled, Leicinna began to hope that perhaps there had only been the two of them after all. Even so, she armed herself, pulling the heavy mail shirt over tunic and padding, and made sure the rest of the troop was armed as well. They ate a hasty meal as soon as it was light enough to see the road, then mounted up just as the eastern horizon turned gold. Leicinna rose in her stirrups, scanning their surroundings, but the grasslands and the road were empty of everything but the wind.

They had given the harper one of the spare horses and she managed competently enough, her harp cased at her back and the rest of her baggage stowed among the pack horses' loads. For the first hour the road was decent, but as they drew closer to Cielford, the road dipped down into boggy ground and even the beaten surface of the road turned to mud, dragging at the horses' hooves and making them balk and stumble.

Leicinna could see the Lammard clearly, wide and shallow despite the autumn rains, the first low rays of the sun glinting off the ripples. The ruins of Ciel lay to her right, destroyed so long ago that no one could remember if it was an Exile town or one of Riverholme's outliers. There was almost nothing left, nothing more than a huddle of stone on stone, barely recognizable as wall or well or byre. A riot of roses long past their best spilled over what might have been a step, their pink-streaked petals brown at the edges and drifted like snow; last year's leaves still lingered in the angle between two lumps of stone. It was the best place for an ambush along the road, here where the ground was soft and the river required due attention, and she loosened her sword in its scabbard.

"Take care," she called. "Close up."

The troop obeyed, shuffling the harper to the center of the line, and Leicinna lifted her head, scenting the air. For a second, she thought she caught the smell of smoke, of a quenched fire, and she drew her sword before she saw the movement among the ruins. Aylflet saw it, too, and shouted, pointing. "Arms! To arms!"

Leicinna pulled her gelding around in a circle, and ducked her head as she heard the thrum of bowstrings. A horse shrieked, and someone cried out in pain, but she was herself unharmed, and lifted her head to seek out the bowmen. There they were, four of them, rising from where they had lain in the cover of a ruined wall; there were two more among the roses, scattering the last petals as they moved forward, readying their next shot, and three more beyond them. "With me, Leicinnas!"

She spurred the gelding, ducking again as they loosed their second flight. Something plucked at her sleeve and her horse shied; but she corrected him, and then she was riding through the remains of the rosebush, slashing at the first archer. The gelding's shoulder hit another man and the horse tried to rear, but she forced him back down. If one of them got under his belly— She slashed again, pulling the gelding sideways, felt the blade strike home, turned and swung again before a second archer could draw his bow. Another horse screamed and she lunged sideways, catching the man in the gap between corselet and pauldron. The rest of the ambushers were down, she saw, trampled or hacked to death, but then a figure broke from cover and ran, head down. She kicked the gelding into a gallop, Gimmell half a step behind them, and took the man's head half off as he fled. A moment later, she regretted it—it would have been good to ask a few questions—but the body sprawled in the dirt, a great fan of blood spreading from the severed neck.

She turned back to the others, already knowing what she would find, and swore under her breath to see only bodies on the ground. "Well?"

"All dead," Aylflet answered. "We've three horses hurt—they'll all go, but Jemme's bay won't carry him, or anything—and two people, none more than a scratch."

Cielford was the last best chance for an ambush for a good fifty miles. From here, the road north ran along the Lammard's eastern bank, through open grassland that hadn't been well-settled even before the Riders began raiding across the Narrow Sea. And that was eleven dead—she would guess there had been a round dozen, with the last left to carry back the message of their failure. "Tend to our wounded and sort out the horses, quick as you can."

"Yes, Captain," Gimmell said, and Leicinna nudged the

gelding back toward the main group. Viven was still sitting her horse where the others had left her, her face very pale in the rising light.

"Can you ride?"

"Yes."

"Good." Leicinna lifted her hand, raising her voice to carry to the rest of the troop. "Leicinnas! Hear me! We carry news to Riverholme: Nieve and Reyscant have gone over to the enemy, electing lords protector for themselves. Whatever happens, that word must get through." She paused, waiting out the murmur of shock and anger, looking over the troop. The juniors had unharnessed the wounded bay, shifting its saddle to one of the remounts and dividing the remount's load among the pack horses. The human wounded were bandaged and ready; the nearest of them worked his shoulder unhappily, but when she met his eyes he nodded back. She lifted her hand. "We ride!"

❂

Leicinna pushed her people hard, despite the apparent lack of pursuit and the storm that swept over them halfway up the Lammard, forcing them to shelter for a day and turning the ground to mud. They came onto the river road shortly after dawn on the eighth day; and as the sun rose higher, she could see the cliffs of Rhidd and the haze of the Great Fall where Dyre and Saal joined to form the Lammard. Riverholme sat beneath the Fall itself, protected by its embrace, its towers still hidden in the mist. They were well within the Ward of Riverholme, the rich farmlands that stretched a dozen leagues south along both sides of the river, and the land showed it, unlike the empty ruins of the Dancing Ground.

The harvest was past now and the fields were fallow, save for a few patches that had been plowed for a winter crop, but still the farmers were busy at their work, women spinning in their doorways, taking advantage of a clear day's sun. Here and there a gang of men sawed wood for repairs or gossiped

outside the village smithy. They watched the band pass
without concern, though she doubted they knew her banner.
It had been a hundred years since the Riders pushed this far
north, but Leicinna couldn't help eyeing the ground as though
she had been employed to take it. If there were an attack, the
people would retreat to the fortress of Riverholme which had
never yet been taken; on the other hand, one could feed an
army for months off the fruits of the land, even in winter. If
you sent a sizable force up Salkin's Stairs to control the Fall,
eventually even Riverholme must starve.

She shook the thought away. The rivermaster could put a
thousand men in the field—and that was just his own levy,
never mind the dozens of companies like her own that he either
hired or bound by land-right. That was more than enough to
keep the Riders out of the Ward; more than enough to let the
rivermaster choose his battlefields. Still, as they crossed the
Stonebridge to reach the western bank, she couldn't suppress
a superstitious fear. Riverholme was too bright, too perfect.
She crossed her fingers where no one could see, and spat in
the dust by her horse's near forefoot.

The various cavalry bands were housed in the Garth, the
walled town on the Lammard's western bank that guarded the
main bridge into Riverholme proper. They were not expected
so early, and even as Infrid Horse-Marshal came to welcome
them in the stable court, she could see the question in his
eyes. Leicinna swung herself off her horse, and tugged him
sideways so that Infrid was drawn with them.

"We bring news," she said, keeping her voice low enough
that no one outside the yard could hear. "I need to speak to
the rivermaster."

Infrid looked from her to Viven, dismounting stiffly with
Aylflet's help, and she saw him recognize the harper in spite
of the half-grown felon's crop. "I'll send to him at once. In
the meantime—the stables have room for your mounts, or you
can turn them into Leythcop's Field. Your old quarters are
empty, you can have them again. We weren't expecting you
for another few weeks."

"Thank you." Leicinna wanted to follow him to be sure that a page was instantly dispatched, but she made herself turn her attention to the band. By the time she had gotten everything sorted out, men and horses and gear dispatched to their proper destinations, Infrid had returned, his face grim.

"The rivermaster will see you. And the harper. If you'll come with me?"

Leicinna held out her hand to Viven, who had collapsed wincing onto a pile of sacked grain. Viven groaned but dragged herself upright, and Leicinna looked back at the marshal. "We're at your disposal."

For all that she had wintered in Riverholme twice before, she was still not used to the sight of it, the bridge wide enough for three to ride abreast that spanned the roaring water, and then the stone city itself, rising in tiers and towers, pale stone little darker than the mist behind it. It was as if someone had taken the carved interior of a nenn and turned it inside out, building on top of building, towers straining for the sky. The towers were tallest toward the Fall, turning sheer walls to the spray that filled the air; on the downstream side, they showed windows and terraces and walkways carved like lacework through the stone. In the heat of summer, Riverholme was nearly paradise; in winter's depths, the rivermaster worked his magic to slow the Falls and make the stone less damply cold.

Infrid led them through a maze of ramps and corridors—like a nenn indeed, Leicinna thought—and brought them out at last into a narrow room midway up one of the eastern towers. It was plainly furnished, a table along one wall and a carved chair and a few stools, but the brazier was of fine hill-folk work, three fox-headed women holding the fire-bowl, and the cups and wine-pitcher were of the best Riverholme glass. The rivermaster himself, Liulf Nestoros, was settled in the chair, one foot propped on a padded stool to bring it closer to the brazier's heat. He was a big man, broad-shouldered and gray-haired, with a neat gray beard. His son Gelern, who served as spear-hand, commander of Riverholme's Guard, was taller and not quite as broad, but he had the same hazel eyes, the color of pebbles under running water. A woman stood beside the table, her sleeveless overgown not quite straight, as though she'd pulled it on in haste: a wife or a guildmistress, Leicinna thought, until she saw the hazel eyes. She would be Liulf's heir, the shield-hand Melcana, and Leicinna averted her admiring gaze.

"Leicinna Elloras," Infrid announced, "and Viven Harper."

"Infrid says you have news," Liulf said.

"I'm afraid so," Viven answered. She straightened painfully, and Melcana cleared her throat.

"Perhaps the wine first, Father? They've ridden a long way."

"Thank you," Viven said, and Liulf sighed.

"Of course. And sit, the pair of you. No need to keep standing."

Gelern filled each of the cups, serving the guests first, and then his father and sister. Leicinna seated herself awkwardly on one of the stools, Viven at her side. Melcana leaned against the table's edge, her face intent.

"Well?" Liulf drained his cup.

"Reyscant has thrown over its reeve and syndics and called for the election of a lord protector," Viven answered. "I was there and can vouch for the truth of it. There was news came from Nieve that said they'd done the same, and I believe it, for that's what started the trouble in Reyscant." She went through the story quickly but without omitting any useful detail, and when she had done, Liulf sat frowning, turning his wine cup in his hand.

"You were pursued up the Lammard, Captain?"

"We were attacked the night the harper found us," Leicinna said. "Two men crept into the camp and tried to knife her as she slept." No need to explain who was sleeping where, particularly not in front of Liulf's handsome daughter. "The next morning we rode on to Cielford, and they tried an ambush there. We killed them all—which I regret in hindsight, but I'm not sure we could have taken any of them alive. The second ambusher killed himself rather than be captured."

"They didn't follow you further?" Gelern asked.

"I don't know if there were any more with them," Leicinna answered. "We rode hard for Riverholme and didn't worry about leaving a trail. If there had been more, they could certainly have tracked us."

"What sort of men were they?" Melcana asked.

"Trained soldiers. They chose the only spot where they could reasonably have mounted an ambush, and they did it well. If we'd been fewer, I think we'd have had more trouble."

"This is word we must share," Gelern said, and Melcana nodded.

"We can send a messenger to Esclin Arros—by the Hidden River, that would be quickest."

"Agreed." Liulf nodded.

Melcana glanced toward the door, where a stripe of sunlight was just visible on the stones of the corridor, and pushed herself away from the table. "There's still time to send to the Westwood before the towers lose the sun."

"See to it," Liulf said to Melcana, and she swept away. He looked at his son. "Are there any traders going to Nen Gorthen?"

"I'll find out."

"My lord," Viven said. "If you're sending messengers to Nen Elin, let me go with them."

"Why?"

"The arros knows me. He'll take my story most seriously from my mouth."

Liulf nodded again. "Very well. Though the Hidden River is not so pleasant this time of year."

"I know." Viven was grim but determined, and Leicinna stirred.

"Please you, my lord, I can provide her with the gear she needs for the journey."

"Thank you, Captain," Liulf said. "I'll see you're properly recompensed. I'll send the harper to you when we're done."

"Yes, my lord." Leicinna rose, and to her surprise Gelern walked with her to the door.

"I don't think we can gather riders before tomorrow." He gave a wry smile. "I'd spend the rest of the day in the baths if I were her."

"I'll see to it," Leicinna said. She wanted to volunteer for the escort herself, but her horses were worn out from the ride up-river and she couldn't afford to ruin them. Instead, she bowed herself out onto one of the broad promenades, striped with sunlight falling between the buildings. That made her think of Melcana and her mission. She tilted her head back, squinting up at the tallest tower. Somewhere at its crown was a marvelous machine of mirror and crystal and magic that could flash simple messages a hundred leagues, all the way to the Westwood's nearest edge. And then it would be the kyra's business to deal with; hers was to somehow get the harper fit for another week's riding. She looked away, her thoughts already running to gear and goods and her old teacher's best liniment, and started back for the bridge.

Reyscant was a typical port town, small and dirty, the low-roofed buildings huddling close inside the shelter of the walls. But at least the harbor was good, protected both by the curve of the coast and a man-made breakwater, and a good third of the lord paramount's fleet was tied up at the docks. The lord paramount had moved inland, aiming for the crossroads town of Geissa where he hoped to establish his forward camp, but Angeiles remained in Reyscant, supervising the last landings before the weather turned irrevocably toward winter. He had taken over what had been the reeve's house, though the reeve and his family and servants remained crammed into one wing to provide the necessary service, and the axial himself had presided at the rededication of the Blazing One's temple. He could see its domed roof from the window of the upper hall, a thread of smoke rising from its oculus.

The reeve, a graying, bearded man with scarred hands the proclaimed he had begun life as a common sailor, swore that two-thirds of the town already served the Blazing One; certainly the townsfolk had turned out in gratifying numbers, and behaved as though they welcomed the new dispensation. And if the weather held just a little longer... He slid back the shutter, peering through the wavy glass toward the southern horizon. The sky was hazed with clouds, the waves beyond the breakwater sullen and oily. He didn't need to be a weather-witch to know that the storms that ended the sailing season were on their way. Already it had lasted longer than they'd hoped, and the ships crowding the harbor were the proof of it. The lord paramount's plan was well underway.

"My lord Captain."

Angeiles turned to see the reeve's wife standing in the doorway, a neat plain woman considerably younger than her husband. Like all the women in the reeve's household, she wore her hair covered in submission to the Blazing One and, for an instant, he could almost have been back in Mal-Manan. "Yes?"

She bent her knees in a curtsey. "Lord Radoc requests an audience, my lord."

Angeiles felt his mouth tighten and saw the woman flinch. He made himself relax, though he couldn't quite manage a reassuring smile. "Show him up. And fetch us wine."

"Very good, my lord." She curtsied again and disappeared.

Angeiles slid the shutter closed, hiding the view of sea and twilight sky. He had no particular liking for Radoc, but he had to acknowledge that the man knew his business. He wouldn't waste time on idle conversation, unlike too many of the lesser captains.

The door opened again, Radoc holding it for the reeve's wife, whose hands were busy with a pitcher and three glasses. She set it on the side table, dipped a general obeisance, and slipped away. Radoc said something over his shoulder, too soft for Angeiles to hear, but he saw Radoc's steward Linaren stop outside the door and back away again.

And well he should, Angeiles thought, though that explained the third glass. Neither Linaren's rank as steward nor his place in Radoc's bed entitled him to be present. The lord paramount was right to disapprove of such license. "Radoc," he said, and realized with annoyance that the reeve's wife hadn't bothered to fill the waiting glasses.

Radoc seemed to recognize the oversight. "If I might serve you, my lord?"

That was more grace than Angeiles had expected and he managed a nod. "Yes, thank you. What brings you here?"

"I understand my folk are to follow the lord paramount to Geissa." Radoc brought the filled cup to him and they pledged each other formally. It was good wine: the reeve's cellars were well-stocked.

"That was the plan."

"Without waiting to hear if the advance scouts encountered any resistance?" Radoc tilted his head to one side.

"The lord paramount expected none," Angeiles said. "We've taken three towns without bloodshed, and without anyone getting loose to carry the news."

Radoc lifted an eyebrow at that. "That's not what I heard."

Angeiles felt himself flush. "It's true that several harpers tried to flee, but we caught and killed three of them. If the fourth escaped, she still won't reach anywhere in time to warn Esclin. Or the kyra, though she wasn't headed that way."

"You fought last year," Radoc said, and waited long enough that Angeiles was forced to nod in agreement. "So you know what we're up against."

In spite of himself, Angeiles shivered, remembering a dreary summer, cool and damp and always foggy, and the attacks that came out of fog and night. They'd never quite been able to bring the enemy's forces to a decisive battle, though they'd harried the farmsteads in the fringes of the Hundred Hills, and swept back and forth across the Dancing Ground at will. With the damp had come fever and all manner of lesser ills. He made himself smile. "Esclin does not fight fairly, no."

"He's the greatest twister living," Radoc said. "The lord paramount's done a wondrous thing, getting us across in the fall instead of waiting for spring, and we're taking good advantage.

But we mustn't take chances. The moment Esclin hears what we've done, he'll act to counter us. We have to be prepared."

"The lord paramount has accounted for that," Angeiles said. "Even if someone got away without our knowing, word can't reach Nen Elin in time. We'll be settled into winter quarters and ready to move in the spring, and there won't be anything Esclin can do about it."

Radoc heaved a sigh. "I hope you're right."

"The Blazing One has brought us this far," Angeiles said. "The rest must be our doing."

"Let it be so," Radoc murmured, the conventional answer, and straightened. "If we're to march to Geissa straightaway, my lord, we'll need to draw supplies."

"That can be arranged," Angeiles answered, and turned to the table where his maps were displayed.

They found Heldyn first because he was winter's king, and so presently responsible for the Westwood's defense. And also he was easily found, leaning on a pasture fence at the foot of the Carallad while two stead-holders argued about the ownership of an ox, while the animal in question, small and red and liquid-eyed, nibbled contemplatively at his sleeve. He rubbed his knuckles over the heavy muzzle and pushed it away, framing a possible solution to what was essentially unprovable—since the ox showed no partiality for either man—and his eye was caught by movement further up the slope. A youth in royal livery was scrambling toward him, his movement urgent enough that Heldyn straightened before he was in earshot.

"Lord Winter!"

Heldyn saw the farmers exchange unhappy looks. It was on the tip of his tongue to point out that attempting to claim someone else's strayed cattle never ended well—because that was what he suspected was really going on—but instead he said, "Neither of you can prove ownership, and therefore it would be within my rights to claim it for the kyra. Instead, I suggest you share its upkeep and its labor, unless one of you would like to buy the other's claim. Which we'll call four silver marks." That was about what he guessed each of them had put into the animal's upkeep, plus a little more. He saw them exchange glances, and said, "Better decide quickly, though. I'm needed elsewhere."

The farmers eyed each other a moment longer, and then the elder heaved a sigh. "I'll pay you for that share. Though it goes much against my grain."

The younger man sighed as well, but held out his hand. "Four silver marks. Done."

"Witnessed," Heldyn said. That pretty much confirmed his suspicions, as the real owner would hardly give up a nice animal like this for so little. He rubbed the ox's forehead a final time, and turned his attention to the approaching page. "Well?"

"Lord Winter." The page put his hands on his knees and bent double, gasping for breath. "Your pardon, but there's a message from Riverholme. News from the coast."

"Not invaders, this time of year," Heldyn said sharply, all too aware of the farmers' stretched ears and worried eyes, and the page shook his head.

"No, lord."

"Then mind your tongue," Heldyn said. "Lead on."

They wound their way back up the lower slopes of the Carallad, climbing in through the stable outfall—odoriferous, but an effective shortcut, and after a day in the fields, Heldyn hardly noticed. At the edge of the Lower Ward, the page led him along the curve of the wall to the eastern tower. The chief observer was there ahead of him, her long sleeves fluttering in the breeze. Compared to the Hundred Hills where he had been born, the Westwood's winters were mild, and the sun was still high enough to heat the back of his neck, but Savadie's shoulders were hunched as though she felt approaching snow.

"Lord Winter."

"Observer." Not cold, Heldyn thought, his own unease deepening. Not cold, but afraid. "What's this message?"

Savadie stepped out of the doorway, and he followed her into the tower's lowest chamber. It was empty except for a table carved with the zodiac, but she lowered her voice anyway. "We have news from Riverholme, by sun tower. They say they can confirm that Nieve and Reyscant have elected lords protector."

"Confirm?" Heldyn asked.

Savadie nodded. "That was what the message said. Have we had such word?"

"Not to my knowledge." The caveat was pointless; if there were such a threat to the Westwood, he would be told.

"I've asked what they meant, but clarifying any message is a tedious chore." Savadie paused. "The kyra must be told."

"Of course." Heldyn drew a steadying breath. He refused to allow himself to speculate, not yet. "I'll take you to her, if you'd like. And we'll want Lord Summer."

"Thank you," she said, and followed him from the tower.

Summer's king was in the counting house, flipping a dagger idly from left hand to right as a clerk recited a list of figures. "There," he said, as an attending page pushed open the door, and held up his hand to forestall conversation. "That's the error. You've switched the numbers, I'll be bound."

The clerk rustled through a nest of parchment strips, and drew one out frowning. "So we have. Then we're done, Lord."

"And apparently just in time." Rihaleth Ninnandas smiled cheerfully at his fellow consort, and slipped his dagger back into its sheath. "You want me?"

"We do," Heldyn answered. "Where's the kyra, do you know?"

"In the gardens, the last I saw." He was carefully not asking the obvious question, and Heldyn gave the slightest of nods. He saw Rihaleth's mouth tighten in response, but his cheerful tone did not change. "Keep on with the accounts, Berres, I think that's resolved the problem."

"Yes, Lord Summer," the clerk said, and bent over his ledger.

The halls of the royal palace were predictably busy, and

there was no place to stop or to talk without being overheard. Heldyn led them instead straight to the walled garden, where the gate guard touched his forehead and let them in.

"Kyra," Heldyn began, and heard Rihaleth's breath catch sharply behind him.

The kyra of the Westwood stood in the center of her winter garden, the trees' bared limbs showing white and red and gold, while an everlasting vine crept along the edges of the empty fountain, near-black leaves not quite hiding clusters of berries red as blood. The air was full of laughter and the slow beating of many wings: the silk moths had come, and the ladies of the chamber and their children were hanging feeders filled with honey-water to lure them to stay. Heldyn saw his own youngest handing a feeder up to a chamberlain on a short ladder, while the kyra's latest child toddled past, stretching her arms to a low-flying moth. Her nurse caught her before she could do it harm, and the kyra turned to greet them.

Alcis Mirielos was not tall, certainly not by the standards of the hill-folk, her dark hair tumbling in waves nearly to her waist. She wore silk of her own women's weaving, her overgown all shades of pale green like new leaves and unripe apples, falling loosely from her shoulders to reveal a swath of her ivory chemise. A moth the size of a young hawk blundered close, and she lifted her hand to catch it before it landed in her hair, so that it clung for a moment to her fingers, thin legs wrapped tight and its long tongue uncurled to taste her cheek. She laughed and lifted her hand, as though she were launching a hawk indeed, and the moth rose obediently, fluttering toward the nearest feeder.

"My dears," she said, but her dark eyes were already wary.

"A word, if we might," Heldyn said. Out of the corner of his eye, he saw Rihaleth catch a small girl as she stumbled and set her on her feet again with a smile. The toddler swung back to grab her mother's knees with the unerring instinct of a child who knows her mother is about to leave her, and Alcis lifted her, swinging her in a circle to make her laugh. An attendant came to take the child, and Alcis extricated herself without tears.

"This way," she said, and led them from the garden.

The kyra's withdrawing room was not far, a long and narrow space running alongside the more public rooms. The narrow shutters were open to let in the late afternoon sun, the translucent oilskin that blocked the worst of the drafts glowing like white-hot iron. A fire was already burning on the hearth and Rihaleth stirred it to renewed life. There was a kettle ready as well, and he swung it to heat over the flames, then turned his attention to the teapot waiting on the sideboard. It was the out-of-season king's task to mind such things, and Heldyn turned his attention to Alcis. She had already seated herself in her high-backed chair, stretching her feet to the fire, and waved for him to speak.

"It's Savadie's tale," he said, and the observer took a deep breath.

"We received a message today from Riverholme, by sun-tower. It said that it was confirming the news that Nieve and Reyscant had elected lords protector."

Alcis lifted her eyebrows at that. "Have they, indeed? And what's this 'confirmed'?"

"That's all the message we received," Savadie said. "I've asked them to clarify, but that will take until tomorrow."

"I've heard nothing," Heldyn said.

"Nor I," Rihaleth said, still busy with the kettle.

"And we have seen nothing from Riverholme but the weather for the last month," Savadie said. The observers sent messages back and forth to test the sun-towers, Heldyn knew, mostly about the weather or the state of the stars.

"I hope I don't need to say that I also know nothing of this," Alcis said, sweet-voiced, and Heldyn met her gaze squarely.

"I didn't really think so, but I'd hoped you might."

"No." Alcis gave a small, wry smile. "And now we're left with two unwelcome bits of news. First, that those ports have gone over to the enemy, and then that some important message has gone astray."

"Just so," Heldyn said.

"A lovely start to the winter," Alcis said, "though of course that may be what's intended. Savadie, anything you can do to get more answers from Riverholme would be greatly appreciated."

It was dismissal, albeit with silken gloves, and Savadie made her obeisance. "Of course, Kyra."

"What I don't see is what Nieve gains from it," Rihaleth said, after the door had closed behind her. "Or Reyscant, either."

"Hope of safety," Alcis said with a sigh. "I can't protect them, nor can Esclin. I can see how a town might reckon it better to throw in wholeheartedly with the Riders rather than spend yet another year conquered and despoiled."

"It's hard on any of their folk who won't serve the Blazing One," Heldyn said. He had been Esclin's companion before he met the Westwood's kyra—the kore, she had been then, her father's heir; he had no love for either the Riders or their god of absolute and undivided allegiance.

"But most of them will manage it," Alcis said. "And the Riders should be too busy in the Dancing Ground to worry too much about anyone who gives them the outward show of obedience. Fetch the map, will you?"

Heldyn brought out the well-worn parchment, the colors fraying in places, the edges worn soft and blurred. He spread it on the table, weighting it with the polished stones kept ready for that purpose, and Alcis rose to join him, resting one hand companionably on his shoulder. The two ports lay on the eastern edge of the Bay of Mull: more immediate danger to the Hundred Hills than to the Westwood, but still ideal spots to land men and horses. If the Riders didn't have to take the towns first, if they could simply send over the transports as soon as the spring sailing opened... They could muster most of their army before either Esclin or the rivermaster could bring their armies out of the hills.

"So it'll be up to us to hold them come spring," Rihaleth said, and set the teacups on the table well away from the map.

"I'd say so." Heldyn took a careful sip of the scalding liquid, smoky and faintly sweet.

Alcis pressed a finger to her lips. "We can do it," she said thoughtfully. "Especially if we muster here at Drybeck and at Callamben. The Riders won't be able to move any better than our allies until the ground is firm. And if we march from Callamben—" She touched the mark that symbolized the trading town just within the Westwood's easternmost borders. "We can even cross at Broadford and cut them off without losing our own lines of retreat."

They would muster over a thousand men come spring, Heldyn thought. Shield-and-spear men, mostly, but experienced men, men who had withstood a Rider charge before. If they could blunt the Rider advance, then Esclin's bowmen and Liulf's horsemen could sweep down out of the north and drive them back to the shore. "We could make it a short dance, with any luck."

"If we're lucky," Alcis said. She shook her head. "What I'm more worried about—if the Riders have come to Nieve and Reyscant, what's happening in Pen Aman?" She touched the symbol lightly, a dot of blue ink on the western edge of the bay, less than thirty leagues from the edge of the Westwood where it widened in the southeast.

"Pen Aman would never go over to the Riders," Rihaleth said, but his tone was less confident than his words. "At least, I can't think what they could offer that would be better than what you give them."

Pen Aman made a very good business out of being the Westwood's easiest port. Heldyn had been there many times, a stone-built town with walls and guilds and a solid, sober portreeve to manage the place. "Not many Exiles there, either."

"We don't know what reward—or threat—they offered to the others," Alcis said. "And the other matter still concerns me. I'd like to know what message and messenger we've missed."

"Surely they'd be making for Callamben," Rihaleth said.

"I agree." Alcis reached out to touch Heldyn's shoulder again. "Go to Callamben and see if there's any sign of a messenger, or any hint of any trouble. If not, then scout out Pen Aman, too."

A hundred leagues, more or less, from the Carallad to Pen Aman, and for all that winter wasn't biting hard yet, the return journey was likely to be unpleasant. And yet it was unmistakably necessary. Heldyn said, "I suppose we'd better."

"I'm afraid so," Alcis said, and her hand tightened for just an instant. "Be very careful."

Heldyn covered her hand with his. "You know I will be."

He had meant it lightly, but she shook her head. "More than your usual. I... Something is very wrong here."

"Let me ride with him," Rihaleth said. "Just to Callamben. My men can search for the messenger while he rides to the port."

"Yes." Alcis nodded. "And as soon as you can put your parties together. My heart misgives me."

And that was unlike the kyra, who never admitted doubt or fear. Heldyn saw the same sudden worry in Rihaleth's face, and dipped his head. "Tomorrow, Kyra."

Viven had traveled the Hidden River before, though not this late in the season or in this much haste. The narrow boat rode high on the black water, witchfire glowing at prow and stern, and the steerswoman kept a sharp eye ahead and a firm hand on the steering oar. They were in the Long Water now, the last open stretch before they reached Nen Elin, and riding the downstream current. The water here was too deep for the crew to pole them any faster; most of them were resting in the narrow forecastle, worn out from the effort that had brought them this far.

She was tired, too, her muscles still sore from riding, and the sunless cold under the mountain seemed to have settled into her bones. She drew her furred cloak more tightly around herself, sinking her chin into the well-cured leather, and hoped her harp would take no permanent harm. Usually by this time of year she was settled for the winter, warm and well-fed in court or hall or steading, happy to trade song and service for her keep. She had had no ambitious plans this year, but was promised to a wealthy steading a week's journey north of Reyscant. They would be worrying about her, but there had been no way to send them word.

She put that thought aside and rose to her feet, hoping that a few circuits of the deck would drive out the numbness in her toes. On the fourth time around, the light changed and she looked up, blinking as something damp struck her face. Far above, she could see a thin line of sky and what she thought were flakes of snow sifting down through the break in the mountain. Another drop struck her face, and the steerswoman gave her a sympathetic nod.

"Good job we're down here. I'd hate to be out in that."

"Is that snow? Why don't I see flakes here?"

"It's always too warm under the mountain. That's why the rivers never freeze."

Not warm enough for my taste. Viven turned away, intending to take another turn around the deck; but the snow suddenly intensified, a rapid patter of drops striking the deck, and she ducked instead under the canvas that was stretched midships for partial shelter. The tiny iron stove was lit, a kettle simmering, and she poured herself a cup of the weak tea, wrapping her hands around the cup to steal its heat. She had wintered in Nen Elin before and hadn't loved the months spend indoors, below-ground. But there was no choice. She had to carry this message, and there was no place to go once it was delivered, not until the spring thaw.

The mountains closed above them and the rain stopped; she resumed her walk, the chill dragging at her limbs. The steerswoman was right, it wasn't all that cold; but it was damp, and the combination nipped at the very marrow of her bones.

At last the cavern widened ahead, a second channel opening to the right. Lights showed there and the steerswoman shouted for the crew, who dragged themselves from the forecastle to collect their poles. The steerswoman heaved on her oar, the pole men thrust and dragged, and the boat slid easily from the main channel and through the great arch that led to Nen Elin's docking basin. The wharfs were bright with witchlight, great flares of it caged in glass and iron; most of the slips were empty this time of year, so the steerswoman had her choice of anchorage. One of the nenn's stewards came to meet them, and Viven caught his eye and handed over Liulf's token.

"I bear news from the rivermaster, news of the south."

"I'll send to the arros at once," the steward answered, and she busied herself gathering her scant baggage and lugging it ashore.

The steward was as good as his word. Almost as soon as she had unloaded her pack and her harp, the man returned, a page panting at his heels. "The arros would speak with you at once, Harper," he said, his voice apologetic. "If you'd permit, I'll find a room for you—and bespeak a place at the baths as well, for after."

"If the arros will take me as I am, I'm glad to speak with him," Viven answered. "And gladder still of your offer, and gladdest of all of Nen Elin's baths."

The steward grinned. "I'll see to it, Harper. Meiler here will take you to the arros."

She kept her harp with her, though it wouldn't be fit to play until it had had a chance to warm properly, the heavy case thumping against her back as she followed the boy through the maze of corridors. They were going lower into the nenn and crossing toward the hillside gate: heading toward the royal quarters, she guessed, and was not surprised when the boy led her down a final spiral stair to a room that she thought would lie behind the main withdrawing room. A strong fire burned on the hearth, welcome warmth, and the walls had been carved with a frieze of interlocking trees, the few leaves shaped from red and orange and yellow inclusions, as though she stood in a stone garden forever in autumn.

Esclin himself was sitting by the fire, wrapped in a deep blue gown trimmed with fox fur a half-shade whiter than his hair, his wheat-colored skin looking darker by contrast. His steward was there as well, and the master smith, dressed as though he'd been summoned from the forge, and a woman Viven didn't recognize but thought might be the marshal. She made her bow, an apology for her own disarray ready on her lips, but Esclin waved her to a stool that sat ready on the other side of the hearth.

"I can't think it's good news that brings you here at this season," he said. "So I venture to keep you from your rest a little longer."

Viven bowed her head. "I fear so, Sire. Nieve and Reyscant both have overthrown their reeve and mayor and elected lords protector in their place."

Esclin lifted his eyebrows. "Ill news indeed. Is it certain?"

"I was there," Viven said. She took a breath, settled herself more comfortably on the stool, and made herself go through the story one more time. The arros and his counselors listened without speaking, but when she had done they broke out in a babble of comment, one riding over the other. The arros lifted his hand, the firelight catching on a silver-set jewel.

"One at a time, if you please. Ilgae?"

"This goes too well with the woman who tried to kill you, Sire."

Viven lifted her head at that, though she had no right to question this company. She would get the story in the kitchen or the hall instead; but if the Riders were able to send an assassin into the arros's own nenn they were growing bold indeed.

Esclin looked at the master smith as though daring him to speak, but Kelleiden met his gaze squarely. "It also matches the warning your mother sent."

Esclin's mother was from the far north, from Nen Donnea where the old Esmeniade bloodline still ran true. Viven had sung her story more than once, though never in any nenn north of the Dassend Hills: a wild, proud woman wedded to her local god in the ancient way. Aubrin had been hunting north of Nen Gorthen, or so the story went, and seen her and her companions riding through the mist; he had followed her as though she were a river-maiden, wooed and won her and brought her home to Nen Elin in a flurry of haste that was borne out by the son she bore not quite nine months after she stepped beneath the nenn's gates. Esmeny had remained more priest than consort, and she was gone again in a blaze of fury before Esclin was grown. Neither time nor distance had diminished her power, however, and if she had troubled to send a warning south...

"In the very broadest sense, I suppose." Esclin's voice was sharp. "But we need more than warnings now."

Viven closed her ears to the rest of the discussion, the weight of the journey suddenly settling on her shoulders. She had heard what the rivermaster had to say, and Esclin's calculations would not be so very much different, accounting only for different distances and types of men. There would be war on the Dancing Ground in the spring, and a worse one than usual: more deaths and more burned steadings and all the miseries that went with it doubled by the coast towns' treachery. Esclin was a clever man, no one doubted it, for all his airs and graces; but no amount of cleverness could overcome this advantage. She watched him from under her lashes: an elegant, fine-boned man, lovely despite the missing eye that he so casually, so carefully concealed beneath a band of silk. All she could see was a fox sniffing at a trap it could not avoid.

"Well, Harper, I'm grateful for the warning," Esclin said, and she dragged herself back to the moment. "Is there anything more you can tell us? Anything, any little thing at all, that might be of use?"

She shook her head. "Nothing, Sire. You know everything I know."

Talan had dressed with special care, knowing that there would be dancing after dinner no matter what news had come from Nen Gorthen. She had heard little enough of it herself, having been out in the horse-pens for most of the day, and dragged home muddy and cold to be told of the impending feast. There had not been time to see her father, not if she were to make herself decent. Instead she let Sian flatten her hair with oil and hot combs and set a coronet of gold-set garnets on the sleek fall. Her gown was garnet-red, too, worked with a border of golden grapes and leaves, the best thing she owned, and for once she drew eyes when she entered the hall.

Her table was alive with rumor—the Riders had already landed, the coastal cities were alight, the Westwood was attacked, or perhaps attacking, the winter king riding out to drive back the threat before more could land. She met the worst of it with a skeptical stare, and allowed that she had heard that two of the ports had gone over to the enemy: not good news, but hardly a disaster. They would have to move sooner than usual in the spring, but otherwise there was little difference.

When the meal had ended and the stewards had removed the tables to make room for the dancing, she made her way to where Esclin still sat enthroned on the low dais. He danced very rarely, and at the moment seemed content to relax in his great chair, his brocade gown falling in well-planned folds. The harper sat at his feet, tuning her instrument, and the other musicians had found a corner to begin a round of their own. Esclin beckoned Talan closer and she came to stand beside him, as always placing herself in his blind spot so no one else could exploit that weakness. It was a trick she had figured out for herself, and she was proud of it.

"You've heard?" Esclin asked.

"Nieve and Reyscant?" she asked in return, and the arros nodded. "Yes." She paused, and when he said nothing, added, "Unfortunate."

Esclin smiled. "Indeed."

Talan lowered her voice. "There was much talk at dinner."

"I can't say I'm surprised."

No, but what am I to say to them? That was not a question she could ask in public, and she contented herself with a murmur of agreement.

The harper glanced up at her, her face professionally bland: an unremarkable woman, Talan thought, her dark hair cropped between chin and shoulders, and her skin sun-worn. What allure she had was her art, and Talan darted a glance at her father, wondering if that would be enough to tempt him to invite the harper to his bed. That was the one thing his lovers had in common: they were all the best at what they did, or nearly so. Not that she thought the harper would agree. There was a distance in her eyes that she suspected would keep Esclin from ever asking. Or perhaps there was no woman for him but the kyra of the Westwood, who had borne him two children, Talan herself and the brother she had never met. It was a question she had never dared ask, nor likely ever would.

The nenn's musicians struck up a dance tune, and she started to move away, but Esclin caught her sleeve. "Stay."

She nodded, resting one arm against the back of the throne. The harper had picked up the thread of the dance, winding a cheerful harmony around the tune, and Talan was not surprised to see Torrel Engelos, the lord of Nen Atha, make his way around the edge of the dancers. Nen Atha was close enough to Nen Elin—less than seven leagues by a good road—that Torrel had not yet left the court, though he was bound to depart soon. He made his way up the two steps of the dais, stooping to say something in Esclin's ear that made the arros laugh.

"But to be serious, Sire—what's this tale I hear about the cities of the coast?"

"It depends on what you've heard," Esclin said with a wry smile. "But the truth is, I expect, a good deal less dire. Nieve and Reyscant have gone over to the Riders."

Torrel nodded slowly. "Not good news, no. But not as bad as some would have it."

"Oh?"

"I'd heard the Westwood was attacked." Torrel shrugged, and for all the carelessness of the gesture, his eyes were watchful. "But I daresay it's not true."

"Viven Harper was in Reyscant when they elected lords protector," Esclin said. "Certainly it's possible other things have happened since, that was some weeks past—but it's winter. The Riders fare no better than we do in that season."

Talan saw Torrel's shoulder ease just a fraction, and stored Esclin's words to repeat herself later. Clearly the hardest thing now was to keep everyone calm and sensible.

"It's a stroke of good fortune that Kelleiden Smith has begun my sword," Esclin went on. "It'll be done by spring—a royal sword, properly made."

"I'd heard it was intended," Torrel said. "It will be an answer to the Riders."

"Indeed it will." Esclin leaned back, smiling, seeming completely at his ease.

At the foot of the throne, Talan saw the harper lift her head though her fingers did not falter, and wondered abruptly for whom Esclin had intended his words. Torrel would have known of the plan, certainly; more than that, he'd been at Eith Ambrin himself when Aubrin's royal sword failed him. The harper could certainly be relied upon to spread the news as soon as she left Nen Elin, but surely that would not be for some months yet... She glanced at Esclin, seeing him as always glittering and beautiful and utterly impossible to read, and resigned herself to lacking answers, at least for now.

CHAPTER FOUR

They were two days from Callamben when Heldyn became certain the party was being followed. Rihaleth had noticed, too, and it was simple to let summer's king fade into the forest as the group rode toward the clearing where they would stop to water the horses. Heldyn made himself loosen his tack and lead his horse to the shallow stream, noisy over the rocks, without looking back, and was rewarded a few moments later by the sudden drumming of hooves as Rihaleth reappeared, a familiar figure at his side.

"Traher?" Heldyn beckoned to the nearest trooper, handed over his horse, then strode forward to meet them. "What's he doing here?"

"The kyra sent me." Alcis's eldest son swung himself off his horse in a flurry of legs and tunics, his waist-length black hair tangling around him.

"You said you had her permission," Rihaleth pointed out, crossing his hands on the pommel of his saddle, and the boy colored sharply.

"I had a dream." He still sounded faintly embarrassed by his own talents, like a boy not yet used to a new length of limb. "And so she said I should come after you."

"Should or could?" Rihaleth began, and Heldyn shook his head.

"He's here. And I'm curious about this dream."

Rihaleth breathed a laugh and dismounted in turn, shaking his head. "And you'll be hungry, too, I'm bound."

"Starving," Traher said with enthusiasm, and accepted

a handful of the mix of nuts and dried berries that was the troopers' day ration.

Heldyn waited while the youth wolfed that down, restraining himself from asking if Traher had thought to bring food. He was nearly eighteen: if he wasn't capable of planning that far ahead, he could go hungry until he learned. Traher licked the last crumbs from his fingers and twisted his hair back into a somewhat more tidy club, and Heldyn said, "Now. About this dream…"

Traher blushed again. "It wasn't very clear. Just that—I dreamed you were riding into danger. And when I woke, I knew whatever it was, the danger—because I didn't see—I knew I could counter it. When I dreamed it twice, I went to Mother. To the kyra."

Heldyn glanced sideways, saw his own uncertainty mirrored in Rihaleth's face. Traher had inherited many of his mother's gifts and some few of his father's. If he were anyone else's child, he would have been apprenticed to one of the In-Dwellers already. But he showed no particular inclination to any one of them, and he was Alcis's eldest child, though she was free to choose any of her children as her heir. That had left Traher free to learn his art from half a dozen people without any one canon to follow. A child of smoke and mirrors, Heldyn thought, with more airs and graces even than his father, and his mother's fey streak: he would be a man of power when he came into his own, but he would never command a realm.

"And what did the kyra say?" Rihaleth asked.

"She said I should come after you." Traher paused. "And then I was to do as you said."

Well played, Heldyn thought, and then suspected he was being unfair.

Somewhat to Heldyn's surprise, Traher was as good as his word, settling into the company and taking his turn at the juniors' tasks without complaint. If he was sore from the long ride, he gave no sign of it, but Heldyn made a note to be sure the boy spent some time in the baths once they reached

Callamben. He was tired himself, and he was used to a long patrol; youth was no substitute for well-trained muscles.

They stopped that night in a clearing about five leagues west of Callamben. It was a well-worn campsite, though at this time of year unoccupied, and the troop built up a good fire and watered the horses in shifts downstream of the camp. The picket line was in place, the horses muttering and stamping as a pair of troopers served out their grain ration, and Traher and another boy cut more wood to replace the seasoned wood they'd taken for the fire. Sergeant Maud contrived a decent stew for their meal, and afterward Heldyn rolled himself in his blankets with a certain sense of contentment. They would reach Callamben by noon, and they could begin to get a grip on the situation. Rihaleth settled next to him and by wordless agreement they shifted to share their blankets.

"Traher's doing well," Rihaleth said, after a moment, his words already blurring with sleep.

Heldyn nodded. "I just hope his vision's not as dire as it sounded."

"He's but young," Rihaleth murmured, and Heldyn closed his eyes.

It seemed he hadn't been asleep for long when someone spoke his name; but when he opened his eyes, the fire had burned down and all but the watch were rolled in their blankets, a dozen shadowed mounds made almost invisible by the fire.

"Lord Winter," Traher said again, his voice a little louder, and Heldyn sat up, reaching for his sword. Rihaleth woke with him, shaking back his hair, and Traher sat back on his heels.

"What is it?" Heldyn could hear nothing, see nothing out of the ordinary; the watch was unmoving, unconcerned. "Your vision?"

Traher shook his head. "Something else—"

Heldyn got to his feet, not wanting to wake the camp until he had to, and saw Rihaleth string his bow with one quick motion. For a moment there was nothing, just the crackle of the fire and the distant sound of the stream, and the nearest of the watch glanced toward them, frowning nervously. And then he heard it, the sound of something moving in the trees—someone stumbling through the low brush, moving awkwardly, like a man wounded. The watch heard it, too, drawing swords, kicking the nearest sleepers awake; and abruptly a shape lurched into the firelight, coming up from the stream.

Witchlight flared, thrown by Traher and the banner-rider Elian, and in its cold glow the shape was clear. It was a man, stocky and short-bearded, his clothes ragged from the road, his arms tangled in the strings of a harp he held before him. Blood ran down his arms from where the fine metal cut him, dripped from his fingers, and his face was bruised, his eyes swollen shut. A faint, high keening rose from him like a stench, raising the hairs on the back of Heldyn's neck.

"Up! Everyone up!"

Rihaleth echoed him, and the nearest of the watch drew her bow.

"Stand or die!"

The man seemed not to hear but shambled forward, straight for the fire. One of the older men shoved him sideways before he reached the flames and he went to his knees, the harp jangling impossible dissonance as it struck the ground.

Traher cried out in answer, a wordless note that froze the stranger on his knees, one hand still braced to thrust himself to his feet again. "He's dead," Traher said, his own voice tight with fear, and all around him the soldiers made wards against evil.

"The harper's revenge," Rihaleth said, half under his breath, and Heldyn nodded. The harp and its masters were sacred in their way; kill a harper without due care, and his instrument would take its own revenge, drive a man to bloody death, unable to cease until there was no breath left, no flesh nor bone to carry him further. Heldyn had thought it a legend until now.

"What now?" he asked Traher, who was trembling like a harp string himself. "What does it want?"

"Revenge." The boy closed his teeth hard to keep them from chattering, for all that the night was fairly warm.

Heldyn shivered himself. He could see a name carved into the harp's upright, the Westwood's curved letters tangled in a twist of vine-leaves. "Pedder—" The dead man groaned, his mouth falling open, and Heldyn drew his sword.

"Pedder's I am, Pedder Annos, foully murdered on the road from Callamben. Robbers and bandits and thieves of life, the harper's curse lies on you all!"

"End it," Rihaleth said sharply.

Heldyn swung his sword two-handed and carved through the corpse's neck, the blow jolting him to the elbows. The harp gave a final discordant cry and its frame shattered beneath the falling body. The strings stayed wound in the man's arms, the blood black in the mingled light. He remembered Pedder Annos, stocky, cheerful, neat-bearded; his voice was more pleasing than great, but his hands wrought glory from the strings. "Pedder Annos, you will be avenged."

"So far as we are able," Rihaleth said, precise as always, and Traher breathed a word that seemed to be agreement, then stopped abruptly.

"There—what's that?"

Heldyn looked where he was pointing, and in the uncertain mix of fire and witchlight saw a fleck of something white beneath the crumpled body. He stooped reluctantly and turned the body onto its side. Beneath it was a slip of paper, creased as though it had been fitted into the frame of the harp itself. Words were written on it, straggling and ill-formed as though written in haste and poor light with a bad pen, but clear enough: Nieve and Reyscant gone over to the Riders.

"Our missing messenger," he said aloud, and handed the paper to Rihaleth, who nodded.

"So it seems."

Traher looked silently over his shoulder, suppressing another shiver.

"Maud," Heldyn said. "See to the body."

The sergeant grimaced, but he and another man lifted it

by its clothes and hauled it off out of the circle of firelight. A third trooper picked up the head, holding it at arm's length by its tangled hair, and followed them into the dark. Traher swallowed hard, and Heldyn rested a hand on his shoulder for a moment.

"We should backtrack him in the morning," Rihaleth said. "See if we can find where this attack took place, and what we can about what happened. I'd like to know if it was Riders who killed him, or ordinary bandits."

Heldyn nodded and stooped to the nearest supply basket, coming up with a flask of honey water. He took a swallow, tasting lemon and orange and mint, and handed it to Traher who took it gratefully, then passed it to Rihaleth.

"He said—that—I suppose he was one of the murderers?" Traher shivered. "And it was the harp, anyway. The harp said, bandits and robbers and thieves of life. Why 'thieves of life'?" He saw Rihaleth's eyes on him, and shrugged. "It just seemed odd."

"It's what the coastal Exiles call the servants of the Blazing One," Rihaleth said.

"Pedder was of Exile blood," Heldyn agreed. He took the flask from Rihaleth and took another swallow, letting the sweet liquid clear his mind. "We'll ride as soon as it's light enough to see."

It wasn't hard to find the man's path once the sun was up. He had passed through brush and scrub, flattening both and heedless of the road he could have followed with less pain. They were in open ground now, well clear of the Westwood, and Heldyn kept his people mounted, scanning the horizon himself for any sign of trouble. It was just past noon when they crossed the road for the third time, and the banner-rider Elian rose in her stirrups.

"Look there!"

Heldyn shaded his eyes, squinting. She was pointing toward a stand of young trees a little away from the road, the sort of place a man might camp for the night—or, if worst came to worst, make a stand with at least a tree to put his back against. The grass was churned and beaten down, and there was a patch of fresh-turned earth just beyond the trees.

They approached with care, on foot and roundabout, but it was hard to read the marks that were left in the hardened ground. There had been a struggle, that much was clear, and some of the combatants had been mounted, but there weren't enough clear prints to see if the horses wore the Riders' distinctive studded shoes. Heldyn straightened, shaking his head, and saw Rihaleth looking unhappily at the disturbed ground.

"I suppose we'd better," he said, and Heldyn nodded with equal reluctance.

At least the body had not been buried long, or very deep, though there was enough of a stench to make the troopers cover their mouths and noses as they dug. The body lay on its side, and it didn't take long to uncover enough of the face for Heldyn to wince and nod. The cause of death was equally visible, a blow to the side of the head that left the skull dented and broken, and Heldyn backed quickly away, scrubbing his hands on the skirts of his tunic. The air smelled of death.

"Why did the curse fix on one man? He wasn't even dressed like a leader."

"They set it on him deliberately," Traher said suddenly. His eyes were very dark, as though he looked into a cave. "The men who killed the harper. They chose one and gave him to the harp."

"Riders," Heldyn said. It had to be; no one else sacrificed their men that way.

"Cover him," Rihaleth ordered, and Heldyn backed away, spitting to get the taste of it from his mouth. Traher offered him the flask of honey water and he took it gladly. "What now?"

Heldyn looked at his fellow consort, seeing the same knowledge in Rihaleth's face. "One of us goes back to Callamben, to send word to the kyra—that's you, I think, 'Haleth. I'll ride for Pen Aman."

"There's where I'm not so sure," Rihaleth said. "If there are Riders about—"

"We need to know that," Heldyn said. "And we need to know if Pen Aman is taken. A small party, I think, just me and Elian—" A prickle went down his spine, the ghost of a warning. "And Traher. If you're willing."

The boy nodded. "Yes."

"You can explain it to the kyra, then," Rihaleth said, and turned to gather his people.

It was three days to Pen Aman from where they had found the body, traveling by the road, but Heldyn took a more cautious path, following a hunter's track that only roughly paralleled the road. The weather was with them, too, cool and damp, with a grudging fog that rose at twilight and did not disperse until noon or even later. They saw no sign of other travelers, either on the track or on the road itself when the track came close enough for Heldyn to look for sign, and by the second day he wondered if he were being overly cautious. They would make better time on the road... He shook himself. Better to travel more slowly and with greater care.

After a bit of thought, he aimed for a steading near Willowsford held by the sister of one of Alcis's counselors. He timed their arrival for late afternoon, the end of the working day but still full light, though the fog that curled up out of the damp ground cut visibility to a worrying degree. He heard the dogs barking before he saw the new stockade loom out of the mist, and reined in before he heard the bow drawn to full stretch.

"Who's there?"

"Heldyn Dorthinos is my name. I'm seeking the house of Dala Pelattas." If there were Riders there it might take them a moment longer to connect the name with the winter king.

The bowstring creaked again as the bowman loosened his hold. "Lord Winter? Come within, my lord, quickly."

Heldyn lifted an eyebrow at that and saw Elian loosen her sword, but shook his head at her. "Gladly."

There was a rustle of brush as the guardian drew the makeshift gate just wide enough to let the horses through. Heldyn eased his gelding past the barrier and the others followed, Elian's horse blowing unhappily. There were two guards within, both armed with bow and spear and torches, one already lit thrust into the soft ground, and a pack of five or six big deerhounds, relaxed now that their masters had approved the strangers.

"Our holder's at the house," the first guard said, pointing, and Heldyn could see the long low line of the house through the gathering mist. "You can go straight up."

Heldyn hesitated, but the second guard lifted a hunting horn and blew a quick five-note call. He repeated it, and the first guard nodded. "She'll be expecting you, my lord."

"Good enough," Heldyn said, and nudged his horse to a walk.

More of Dala's people were waiting at her door, along with three more of the big deerhounds. Dala herself held the collar of the biggest of them all, but she relaxed as Heldyn swung himself down off his horse. "It is you. I wasn't sure."

Heldyn nodded. "And my companions, Elian Farros and Traher Esclinos." He saw Traher blink at the unfamiliar form of his name—anything he inherited, including his name, would come from his mother, not the father he couldn't remember—but the boy had the wit to say nothing.

"Come in," Dala said, and her eyes strayed nervously to the stockade. "Come in while the light still holds."

Within the hall was crowded, lit by a hasty mix of candles and witchlight, and even through the gloom Heldyn guessed there must be fifty people there. And there were children, and old men: it looked as though Dala had brought in everyone from the outlying farms. Dala led them through the milling crowd to the high table at the hall's far end—hardly private, but at least allowing her the option of pretending that things were more or less normal. She sent for water for them to wash hands and faces, then for wine. Heldyn could feel Traher's tension building as they moved through the ritual, and put a hand on the boy's shoulder to keep him quiet. At last they each had a cup in hand and he could risk a cautious question.

"It seems you've had trouble here? The stockade is new."

Dala's mouth thinned. "We have. I'd hoped you might have come in answer, though we've not dared send a messenger. Not since the harper died."

"Harper?" Traher repeated, and Heldyn put his hand on the boy's arm again.

"Which harper was this?" he asked. "And—died, you said?"

"Amiel, his name was," Dala answered. "Amiel Harper, he didn't use a family name. He traveled with Pedder Annos, most years, though he was alone when my man found him. Two arrows in his back, and his harp missing, and him burning with fever. He died that night, never said a word. But the arrows were Rider arrows."

"Were there any papers on him?" Heldyn asked. "We are missing a messenger."

"Nothing that we found. His clothes were ruined, we burnt them before we buried him."

It had been a forlorn hope, Heldyn thought. Most likely the message had been hidden in the man's harp, as it had in Pedder's, and was lost with the instrument. "You built the stockade before that."

"We did." Dala nodded. "There's been trouble since Midsummer, bandits on the road between here and Pen Aman, and now Riders when they should have sailed back to Manan long ago."

"As far as that goes, I have news to share and some questions to ask." Heldyn took a long swallow of the rough wine, grateful for its heat. "We have news, solid, we believe, that Nieve and Reyscant have gone over to the Riders—that, I think, is where your Riders here are coming from. And so I am here to ask what's the state of things in Pen Aman."

Dala hissed through her teeth. "Ill news indeed."

"The harper was probably carrying that message," Heldyn said. "We found Pedder Annos dead, buried by the road, and saw his harp-curse at work on one of his murderers. Whether Amiel escaped or if they'd separated before, I don't know."

"Pedder would have given him a chance to run," Dala said. "They were lovers all the time I knew them. I hope that curse bit hard."

"It did," Traher said, almost in spite of himself, and buried his face in his cup.

"Good." Dala shook herself. "But you were wanting word from Pen Aman. The Riders have no hold there, at least not as of last week. But you'll want to hear that from the man who was there." She lifted her hand, waving to someone in the crowd gathering for the evening meal. "Huitt!"

A medium-sized man in a fur-trimmed open gown detached himself from a group at the head of the long table, and came to join them. "Holder?" He stopped, visibly recognizing Heldyn. "Lord Winter."

Heldyn nodded, and Dala said, "He wants to hear about Pen Aman. Huitt just came back from there yesterday, I'd sent him with a last pair of yearlings to trade for the winter's goods."

"We've reason to think the Riders are trying to take the smaller ports," Heldyn said. "Is Pen Aman still free?"

"Certainly it is, my lord." Huitt sounded shocked by the very idea, which Heldyn found comforting. "The Portreeve raised the chain at the harbor mouth, so no ships are coming in even from along the coast without being searched first; and the town voted—by acclamation—to pay the militiamen through the winter to keep the walls protected. From what I heard, there was a man who tried to talk some of the lesser folk into following their Blazing One, but most people would have none of it."

"That's good news, at least," Heldyn said, and Elian nodded.

"The trouble is, the Riders are between us and Pen Aman," Dala said, "and between us and Callamben, too. And they raise this fog at will. A house was found stripped bare, the people missing, and then another burned, and I brought my folk inside the walls."

"That was wise," Heldyn said, though he knew what it would cost them in terms of lands abandoned to the winter, with no guarantee anything could be recovered before the fighting began again in the spring. This side of the Dancing Ground had been spared in the last few years, as close under the eaves of the Westwood as it was; there was more to lose now than there had been. "The kyra will offer what support she can."

"I'd be grateful," Dala said quietly. "We've done our best, but a lot was left behind. Of course you're welcome to share what we have."

He would have known as much from the meal, hearty and filling and carefully rationed, a little meat portioned out along with a great deal of root vegetables and coarse bread. They were treated as guests, given an extra cup of wine each and mattresses in the western wing next to the fire, with warm water for washing and stout blankets if not much privacy. Heldyn had had worse many times and he settled himself comfortably, his pack arranged to make a passable pillow, while Traher splashed cautiously in the basin and Elian braided her hair for sleep.

"Where do we go now, my lord?" she asked.

Heldyn considered. He had his answer about Pen Aman; there was nothing to be gained by pushing further, particularly if the Riders were blocking the road. "Back to Callamben— back to the Westwood, at any rate, by the straightest line. We can send word to the kyra from Callamben."

Traher burrowed into his blankets, drawing them tight around himself, while one of Dala's maidservants cleared away the basin and towel. Elian settled herself as well, saying quietly, "Not by the road, surely."

"No." Heldyn shook his head. "There are tracks, but I expect they'll be watched. I'm inclined to follow the little river—Pallis, they call it here. The ground's not too bad and we shouldn't get lost, fog or no." Elian nodded sleepy agreement and Heldyn drew his blankets over his head. They would rest the horses for a day and strike out the next morning.

In the end they stayed two days, resting the horses and collecting as much information as they could about the Riders. From the stories he pieced together, Heldyn gathered that there were scattered bands busy all along the coast of the Great Bay; Pen Aman and Falkaynshold were still free, but there was no knowing what had happened to the dozens of smaller towns and steadings that lay along the trade roads. Most of them were used to surrendering to whoever came ashore and paying tribute to keep themselves unspoiled, and Heldyn hoped they were doing the same this winter. He borrowed pen and ink and paper and wrote out his summary three times, keeping the letters as small as possible, and handed a slip to each of his companions.

"Whatever happens," he said, "one of us must get through. The kyra has to know how things stand."

Elian nodded matter-of-factly and slipped the paper beneath her clothes. Traher's eyes went wide, but he tucked his own copy away in silence.

They rode out the next morning a little after sunrise, horses rested and waterskins full. Heldyn had asked for little in the way of supplies, knowing Dala could not spare it, but there was enough of the dense, sweet-salty journey-cake to take them to the Westwood. After that they could resupply in Callamben.

The Pallis was low this time of year, a few yards wide at its largest, and the ground along its banks was broken but passable. They let their horses pick their way through the worst of the brush, not trying to make time, and at nightfall made a fireless camp in the shelter of a stand of young willows. It was cold enough to make the sleepers huddle together, while the one on watch stamped feet and swung arms to keep from freezing, and in the morning they risked enough of a fire to heat water for tea. The hot liquid was reviving, and they set out again along the Pallis's banks.

It was another day of mist and drizzle, not quite enough to soak through the boiled wool of their outer layers, but enough to leave a film of damp on faces and chill their fingers even within their gloves. They were coming up on one of the Pallis's fords, as nameless as the track that crossed it, and Heldyn rose in his stirrups to survey the landscape. He had fought over these fields and pastures for nearly twenty years, first in the service of the then-thegen Esclin, afterwards as Alcis's consort; even with the distorting mist, he could make out the copse of trees that was the Westwood's first outlier, and the dark line where the Pallis bent away from the road. Two more leagues of open country before they could reach the borders of the wood, but at least there was no sign of other travelers. He lifted his hand to wave them forward, but to his surprise Elian slid from her saddle, stooping to examine the frozen ground.

"There's been people along here," she said after a moment. "Before the last freeze, but I think after, too." She led her horse a little further along the track and Heldyn walked his own a few steps after her, not liking to separate too far in the chancy weather. "Yes, see here?"

She pointed with her toe to a pile of horse droppings, a bit decayed, as though they'd been left before the freeze and had frozen and thawed a few times after. And that should make it five or six days ago, Heldyn thought, but asked anyway. "How long do you think?"

"Five days?" She prodded the pile, watching the balls tumble and split. "No less, I'd say. Maybe a day or two more. The tracks before the freeze were Riders. You can see the print of their horses' shoes. Only the Riders use studs like that."

"No real surprise," Heldyn said. And if they'd passed five or six days ago, perhaps they could hope this part of the Dancing Ground would be free of them.

Elian's horse lifted its head, ears pricking forward, and she swore and flung her cloak over its eyes to keep it from calling. Then Heldyn heard it, too, the neigh of a distant horse and the sound of hooves.

"Off the road," he ordered, and urged his own horse forward. "Toward the wood—"

The others obeyed, Elian still on foot to keep her mount quiet. She was looking for a chance to mount, pushing the horse forward, but there was no cover. Even if they ran, the odds were they'd be seen and chased down, even with the fog. He looked at Traher, meaning to order him to flee, but the boy had dropped his reins, turning his palms to the sky.

"My lord," Elian began, but Heldyn waved her to silence. Traher had his father's gift of illusion; there was just the barest chance he could conceal them even in this unpromising country.

"Keep the horses quiet if you can."

"Yes, Lord Winter." Elian pulled her own horse closer, so that they stood nose to nose with Heldyn's gelding. Traher's horse stood quiet beside them, but Heldyn reached carefully across to take its reins. The fog was thickening around them, swirling up out of the ground, and he realized abruptly that Traher was singing, a weird, wordless, unmelodic thread of sound that was like a counterpoint to several different unheard songs. The fog rose, filling the air, thicker strands draping themselves across Heldyn's shoulders, along the flanks of Elian's horse. The animals stood silent as though charmed, and beyond them, on the road that was now invisible through the fog, he heard the sound of mounted men.

Traher kept singing, the wordless tune repeating itself, drawing the fog and deflecting the eye, weaving itself and them into the land around them, so much a part of it that they were entirely invisible. The sound of hooves grew louder, and with them came a grumble of men's voices, cursing the fog and a long patrol. Traher's voice was like the wind in the chinks of the wall, like the stream running, like nothing at all.

The horses reached the ford, their hooves splashing, clattering against stone; one shied and shook itself, all its gear rattling, and there was a slap as someone urged it on. A voice called them to order and at last the sounds began to move away, fading slowly into the mist. Still Traher sang, until they could hear nothing more. Heldyn drew a deep breath. Esclin could weave illusion, he'd seen it during his boyhood at that court; Alcis could bend the weather to her will, could bring on and hold off and tilt the wind against itself for good and ill. But this...this was both gifts and neither, a greater illusion, a greater power than he had realized the boy possessed.

Traher's song changed, slowed and softened, untangling itself and them from the fog and the grass and the ground. The fog eased a little, the song faded, and suddenly Traher slumped sideways in his saddle. Heldyn caught him, swearing, and Elian grabbed both horses' reins, keeping them close until Heldyn could steady them.

"My lord?" Elian's voice was full of the same fear, and Heldyn fumbled one-handed with Traher's cloak until he could be sure he felt him breathing.

"He's all right. Overdid it, I think..." And what to do now, with two more leagues to go. "Hold the damned horses, they're fretting."

"I have them."

Heldyn dragged the boy across to his own saddle, a limp, ungainly weight. Elian pulled the other horses away, and, moving very carefully, Heldyn managed to get Traher settled safely in front of him. His horse shifted, protesting, and he controlled it one-handed. He hadn't ridden with Traher like this since Traher was a child too small for a pony; this great gangling youth felt for a moment like a stranger. But he was Alcis's son, and Esclin's, and he had saved them all.

"Mount up," he said, to Elian. "Lead Traher's horse until he's recovered enough to ride. He's bought us the time we need."

Nen Poul lay at the southern end of the Hundred Hills, at the tip of a meandering spur of rock that stretched some miles into the Dancing Ground. To its south was the entrance of the Vale of Deulecresse and the road to Nen Ddaur, and to its north the Maillard Vale spread east to the main line of the Hills: both important factors, Angeiles conceded, but still not what he would have made his first target, particularly for a winter campaign. Still, it was not his place to question, and when he was told to bring up the heavy footmen kept in reserve for just this purpose, he was quick to obey.

It was not until they rounded the last ridge, following what was left of the old royal road, that he understood the lord paramount's intention and then it was enough to make him stop and grin, hearing the sergeant at his flank swear appreciatively. Nen Poul sat at the end of the hill, yes, but it was a meager, narrow outcropping compared to the hills that rose in the distance. The builders had delved into the hill, certainly, but they had also built atop it and around its flanks, so that the heap of stone looked more like a bee-skep than a fortress. The stream had been diverted into a moat and there were stone walls behind it, but the equivalent of a good-sized village huddled on the outside of the moat, smoke still rising from burned roofs and walls. Nen Poul was far more vulnerable than anyone would have guessed: take it now, and the lord paramount had a base from which he could control the southern valleys. He could spend the winter raiding and in the spring be ready to split Esclin's army, or even force him to abandon the south. And the south was already more than halfway loyal to the Blazing One.

The lord paramount's army was settled in good order on the flat ground outside the nenn's main gate, with his own men on the walls and patrolling the outskirts of the camp. As they drew closer, it became clear that only parts of the outer town had burned and that the nenn itself was mostly undamaged. Presumably that meant that Nen Poul's lord had surrendered quickly: another good omen for the coming season.

Angeiles left his sergeants to settle his men into their camp and made his way to the lord paramount's tent. The sun was setting now, all colors shifted to amber, and the last of the light just caught the gilded frame of the burning glass set up like a standard outside the tent. To his disappointment, the lord paramount was elsewhere but Lord Radoc beckoned him inside.

"He should be here any time. He went into the city with the axial to discuss the rededication of the Blazing One's temple."

"They're willing to do that?" Angeiles couldn't hide his surprise and Radoc gave a wry smile.

"They're believers here in the south, or so they claim."

"Then there wasn't much of a fight?"

"Not after we broke into the outer town," Radoc said. "Once we set a few roofs alight, the holder sent out parley flags. She begged for terms."

"She?"

Radoc nodded. "It's a woman rules in Nen Poul. Her daughter's dead, died in childbed, and the son-in-law's been her commander. There's no love lost between them, and he's to be sent back to Reyscant in chains. I hear the lord paramount will take her oath as regent for the grandson."

"That's an easier ending than I was expecting," Angeiles said.

Radoc gave him a crooked smile. For all his vices, he was easy to talk to—and a good commander, Angeiles reminded himself. The lord paramount wouldn't tolerate him otherwise. "You and all of us. I thought the lord paramount was mad to set us down at the door without siege engines to back us. But I was wrong."

"How did he manage it?"

"We came down on them at evening, before they knew we were here," Radoc said. "They got a company out to meet us but we hit them before they could form up, drove them back on the moat and into the walls. And we got lucky, too: their commander, Nen Poul's son-in-law—Ferris, he's called—he stayed to fight, and the lord paramount took him. After that, the holder had no choice but to surrender. Only a handful of our men were even wounded."

Angeiles smiled. That was the lord paramount for you, careful of his men when he could be, and clever enough to seize every chance. It was no wonder the Blazing One favored him. He saw Radoc's gaze shift, his posture straightening, and turned himself to see the lord paramount approaching, the axial Suetrich and a cluster of wheelmen at his back. "My lord," he said, bowing. "The heavy foot—"

"Are here and settled, and in better time than I expected," Reys answered, smiling. "That was well done."

Angeiles bowed again, the words warming him. "Thank you, my lord."

"Radoc?" Reys asked.

"Our patrols are in place, and no one has passed them. We've turned back a handful of folk—refugees, mostly, but no messengers. I think there's a chance none were sent until too late."

"That's good news, too," Reys said. "Though we won't rely on it. Keep me posted."

"Yes, my lord." It was a clear dismissal; Radoc bowed and withdrew. Angeiles made to follow him, but Reys caught his shoulder.

"Stay. I want a word with you later. Can I ask you to pour the wine?"

"Of course, my lord." Obscurely pleased to have been asked, Angeiles filled and fetched the cups that were waiting on the side table, while Reys and Suetrich gave orders to the hovering wheelmen and finally settled into the chairs that waited around the brazier. Suetrich's clerk waited at his shoulder like a shadow, and Angeiles was almost surprised when the clerk accepted his cup of wine.

The lord paramount tilted his head back to look at Angeiles. "We're going to rededicate the Blazing One's temple the day after tomorrow. I want you with me."

"Yes, my lord," Angeiles said, and then the meaning registered. "Are you expecting trouble?"

"The folk of Nen Poul seem surprisingly devout," the clerk offered.

The lord paramount ignored him. "Let's say I don't want to leave things to chance."

"I've spoken with the wheelmen here," Suetrich said. "Holder Jiala has been a faithful servant and a generous patron, even against Esclin's wishes. The removal of the other temples is a welcome change."

"I believe she is," Reys said. "And the nenn's smith and their speaker for the Mistress of Death and all the other hedge-priests have made due surrender, for which we gave all honor to the Blazing One. But not every man in this nenn agrees with Jiala, and we should take precautions."

"I agree," Angeiles said, though he knew he should keep silent. Reys smiled, but Suetrich shook his head.

"If we want to win these folk peaceably—"

"Suetrich." It was rare for Reys to use the axial's given name, rare enough to silence him. "There will be guards—there must be. Angeiles will be discreet."

Suetrich sighed, and Angeiles dipped his head. "As my lord commands."

The day of the dedication dawned cloudy, but as the morning wore on the sun broke through the haze of clouds: an excellent omen, everyone agreed. The Blazing One's temple lay within the walls, but its builder had obeyed the letter of Esclin's prohibition by keeping it separated from the other structures that had been built out from the cliffs that faced the hill. Unlike nearly every other building, the temple stood in its own narrow yard, with a gap of a half dozen ells between it and the blank face of the warehouse behind it, and twice as much or more in front of the main door. It and most of the streets that led to it were overlooked by windows and balconies and roofs, and Angeiles did not envy the guardmasters set to secure them.

The procession went on foot, in honor and submission to the Blazing One, and Angeiles walked at the lord paramount's left hand, sweating despite the chill of early winter. They all wore mail beneath their outer robes—the Rule did not require them to take unnecessary risks—and the lord paramount himself went bare-headed except for a wreath of gilded flowers. Ahead of him walked the axial and four other senior wheelmen, each carrying a burning glass on its tall pole, the light glinting from the frame, the lenses scattering flecks of light across the crowd. Behind them walked the Rider lords and a contingent of their men in their best array: more than enough to ward off an outright attack, Angeiles thought, but not enough to stop an arrow loosed from above. But that wasn't his concern, and he would have to trust that the guardmasters had dealt with it; his worry was the madman with a knife, and he let his eyes roam over the crowd even as he matched the procession's decorous pace.

To his surprise, the crowd seemed in a good mood, for all that they'd just lost a battle and seen their nenn defeated. Perhaps it was because the lord paramount had strictly forbidden looting, or perhaps the folk of the southern hills were as sick of the endless war as the folk of the coastal towns had been. Certainly there were troops lining the streets ready to hold back any trouble, but there were cheers as the burning glasses went by and Angeiles thought they were genuine.

The cheers were louder as they reached the temple yard, and Angeiles could see that there were more than wheelmen waiting at the temple door. The priest and his acolytes were ready, robed in white and pale blue, but beside their senior man stood a woman in gray, a child of four or five held close in front of her. It—he, presumably; surely it had to be the grandchild—was also dressed in gray, and fidgeted in spite of the woman's iron hold on his shoulders.

At the gate, the Riders clashed arms and cheered, and the townsfolk behind them cheered as well, calling praises on the Blazing One. The nenn's senior wheelman went to his knees before the axial, his words lost in the noise around them, but he bent to kiss the hem of Suetrich's robe. Suetrich stooped to raise him, kissed him on both cheeks, and the woman in gray dropped into a low curtsey, her skirts pooling around her. She tugged at the child's coat and the boy went to his knees as well, though his frown suggested he didn't understand.

"Welcome you...representative of the Blazing One... hallowing our house..."

Most of her speech was lost in the scuffle and shouting, but the axial raised her as well—one-handed, Angeiles noted, and without the kiss—and turned to give her hand to the lord paramount. She curtsied to him as well, perhaps not quite as deeply as to Suetrich—as was fitting—and he raised her as well, inclining his head in acknowledgment.

"Holder Jiala." His voice didn't seem particularly loud but it was pitched to carry, and the crowd quieted to hear. "It is good to stand with you on this auspicious occasion."

"It is my honor and duty, Lord Paramount." She had covered her hair, Angeiles saw, Rider-fashion, though the fabric was gray silk embroidered with silver.

"And I am pleased to acknowledge you as Regent for your grandson Imenor," the lord paramount said. "Is this he?"

"Yes, Lord Paramount," Jiala answered, and Angeiles saw her hands tighten again on the boy's shoulders. Thus prompted, the boy made another bow to the cheers of the crowd, and the lord paramount ruffled his curls.

"I'll be pleased to see him take his place at the head of this nenn, in due time."

"My lord is gracious," Jiala said, and let the wheelmen move her and the boy aside. Suetrich lifted both hands in adoration, and the sunlight seemed to strengthen on the temple's domed roof. Acolytes threw back the double doors and the procession moved on into the temple.

It was like most others of its kind, a great round room with a central altar beneath an open oculus; there were rooms off to the sides, living space for the wheelmen who served there, but Angeiles's eyes were drawn to the pile of wood that waited on the altar. Suetrich lifted his hands again, beginning the long chant that carried praise to the Blazing One, while his wheelmen moved to position themselves and their burning glasses at the four points of the compass. Nen Poul's wheelman was among them, Angeiles saw: a sensible choice. He glanced quickly around, making sure that no one was waiting for a moment of distraction to attack the lord paramount, and realized that he was standing next to Nen

Poul's holder. She gave him a quick glance, and when he bent his head politely she nodded in return.

"You're the bodyguard?"

"Holder?" He pitched his voice low, to keep their words beneath the general sound of the chant.

"The lord paramount's bodyguard, the one he was waiting for. That's you?"

Waiting for me? The words struck warmth in his chest like the sparks from a burning glass. "I serve the lord paramount," he said carefully. "I'm called Angeiles."

"That was the name." She gave him a hard look. "Will he keep his promise to my grandson?"

That question was easier to answer than several others might have been. "He keeps his word, Lady. If he's promised to protect your grandson, he'll do it."

She eyed him a moment longer, not visibly convinced. "I pray so."

There was a shout from the altar, the wordless adoration as the burning glasses were thrust into the column of light that fell from the oculus. Angeiles saw the practiced shift, the moment that each glass caught the Blazing One's fire, not quite simultaneously but within a heartbeat of each other. Smoke began to curl from the readied kindling, and then the first flames leaped up. The dry wood caught, crackling, and Angeiles smelled herbs and sweet oils as the flames rose higher. The wheelmen pulled the burning glasses back, the chant changing to the Hymn of Thanksgiving, and the flames rose higher still, reaching for the oculus as though they, too, offered adoration to the Blazing One. Angeiles lifted his hands with the others, summoning gratitude for the victory and a prayer for continued success, but it was a different thanks that filled his heart. *The lord paramount waited for me.*

The three days' forging was over, and evidently a success, in spite of the storm that had blown in and buried the High Forge

and the paths that led to it. Esclin had acknowledged word of
Kelleiden's safe return with a nod and a word of praise for
the guards who'd helped dig through the drifts, but he had
made himself focus on his own work. After all, Kelleiden had
work of his own to get through now that the iron had returned
to the forge. Only in the late afternoon, when Kelleiden had
had time to sort out men and metal, did Esclin allow himself
to venture to the baths, Talan and her companions trailing
behind for an escort.

The baths lay deep in the mountain, where water welled
from hot springs and careful channels had been carved
to bring cooler water from the Hidden River to temper the
pools' heat. The low-ceilinged chamber was thick with steam,
the witchlights that floated at the ceiling reflecting from the
seven pools. From the sound of things, the main bath was well
occupied, cheerful voices and splashing and a group singing a
round; Esclin stripped in the cooler antechamber and let the
attendant bring oil and hot water. As he scrubbed himself,
shivering, the attendant gave a sly smile and offered, "The
master smith is here before you, Sire."

"I'm glad to hear it," Esclin answered—there were no
secrets in a nenn—and stood over the drain to let the woman
sluice him down before he entered the main chamber.

The largest pool was crowded, the guards who had dug
out the path and the younger smiths mingling with others of
the household, loud with the relief of a job that would not
have to be done again for months. Not all the other pools were
occupied, and Talan was quick to claim the largest remaining
for her group, splashing down into the water with shrieks and
laughing curses. Esclin glanced around and saw through the
steam that Kelleiden had claimed the smallest of the pools.
He was leaning back in the water, head tipped back and
elbows resting on the smoothed stone edge, and Esclin was
unsurprised to see a pitcher and cup in easy reach.

"Are you getting warm?" he asked, and crouched to refill
Kelleiden's cup.

The smith opened his eyes with a wry smile that widened

as Esclin drained half the cup. "Better than I was. I didn't see that storm coming."

"No more did anyone." Esclin slid into the water beside him, hissing softly as the heat bit at delicate skin. "Are you all right? And your people?"

He could see a bruise rising black and angry on Kelleiden's shoulder. The smith saw where he was looking and shrugged the other shoulder. "It's not bad, just sore. The wind blew our tent down this morning. Kesa was thrown against the furnace and Elyon took a knock to the head, but they'll both be fine." He reached for the cup and drained it. "We're short in the main firing, that's the bad news. We were short with the star-iron, too, but I told you, we had a bit more ore than we actually needed. I can still make your sword."

Esclin nodded, letting himself relax into the steaming water. Kelleiden poured the cup full again, then handed it across. Esclin took it, glad of the sharp sweetness of the cider, and handed it back again half emptied. "What does it mean, that you're short in the main firing?"

"I'd hoped to spend the winter crafting new swords and better mail," Kelleiden answered. "I've men enough, and the Mistress knows they've had the practice these last few years. But instead I'll have to mend what we have, and make the best of it."

"The dance will be early this year." Esclin leaned back, letting the water fill his ears and lap at the scar beside his missing eye. He straightened, shaking his head in a spray of droplets that caught the witchlight, and saw Kelleiden nod.

"If the Riders already hold two ports, yes, certainly." He paused. "You'll need to claim the steel at midwinter."

Esclin grimaced. At least this was a relatively private place for this conversation: everyone's attention would be on the louder groups in the main pool, on Talan and her friends splashing and shrieking and not on a quiet conversation between acknowledged lovers. "I know." He had seen it done before, in his father's day, had handed him the knife for the blooding. Of course, then he hadn't feared the flames. But the rite itself was simple enough. They were Arra's children, kin of the water horse, and that blood gave them mastery over its element and its opposite. He remembered his father drawing a knife blade across the heel of his hand, then walking practical and commonplace as ever through the flames to let the blood from the cut fall onto the molten iron. Esclin knew he possessed the strength and the will to do the same, even if the smell of hot metal made his cheek ache and flames drew sparks from his missing eye. "With winter here—there's too much snow in the gate-yard."

"We can do it within doors if we must," Kelleiden said. "In the hall, or in the forge, even. The forge might be better, though you won't have as many witnesses. Of course, if we get a thaw, we can clear enough of the gate-yard. Most years we get a warm spell before the year turns."

"Doesn't seem likely, given the weather so far." Esclin rested his elbows on the pool's edge, drawing himself a little way out of the water. "How much trouble will there be if the nenn in general can't bear witness?"

"This year? The more who see it done, the better."

Esclin gave a wry smile. "Well, yes. Can it really be done in the hall? Without setting the ceiling beams afire?"

"It's been done before," Kelleiden answered. "Or so they tell me. I'd rather see if we get a break in the weather first, though."

"We'll wait, then," Esclin said, and was secretly, shamefully, relieved.

The smiths drank deep that night, after the long hours on the mountain and a few snatched hours of sleep in the middle of the day, though Kelleiden kept his cup half-watered and sent the apprentices off to rest before they could drink themselves incapable. The journeymen had earned their indulgence, however, and Maeslin's feast was everything it should be. After the servants had cleared the hall for dancing, he took a turn in the lines, then stood aside and watched Esclin make his way through the court. The arros did not dance except on the most important occasions—the blind eye made him clumsy in the figures, and he would not endure that—but he managed to exchange smiles and laughter and a few words with nearly all the nenn. He listened, too, his sleek head bent to catch words barely audible over the noise, and Kelleiden saw the thegen watching him from among the circle of her friends, studying the art.

It was late enough that he could relax a little; so the next cup he poured without water, the soft new wine easy on his tongue, and as he made his way back through the crowd, the arros caught his sleeve. "Come to me after."

Kelleiden had been expecting the invitation, but even so, even after all these years, the old excitement jolted through him. He bowed, hiding his smile. "Of course, Sire."

Esclin turned away, his fingers trailing deliberately across Kelleiden's hand, and let himself be drawn into yet another conversation. Kelleiden turned back to the dancing himself then, partnering Ismenia's daughter Annora through a round dance, then the spinner Pennela in a four-in-hand. When the pattern fell apart in cheerful laughter, she leaned against him, breathing hard, and fanned them both with the silver-mounted feathers she wore at her belt.

"Ah, that was fun." Kelleiden nodded, still out of breath himself, and she gave him a sidelong glance. "We match well, I think."

"We do." They were old friends, had slept together a few times since Pennela's husband had died, without, he thought, going beyond the bounds of friendship, but now she laid her hand on his arm.

"Come home with me."

"I've...other arrangements."

Something flickered in her eyes, between pity and anger, and she shrugged one shoulder. "Ah, well."

"Don't think I'm hard done by." Kelleiden winced—he should have watered the wine—but her face softened.

"No. Not you."

Not anyone the arros chose to share his bed, but Kelleiden knew better than to make that argument. "Another dance?" he asked instead, and she let him lead her into the next figure.

By the time the music stopped he had had enough of both wine and friendship, and was glad to make his way through the back corridors to the arros's rooms. Esclin had left orders for him to be admitted at once, and dismissed his page as soon as the boy had poured them each a final cup. Kelleiden set his aside without tasting it, watching the arros pace the length of the narrow room. He had discarded gown and overgown, was left in his shirt and an enormous night-robe, a great sweep of black-on-black brocade that made his hair shine like silver in the witchlight.

"You're overdressed," Esclin said.

"Am I?" They had played this game many times before, every step of the dance well-known yet still exciting.

"I say you are." Esclin circled him, trailed one long hand across his shoulders.

"As my lord commands," Kelleiden answered, and loosed the collar of his own gown, content to let himself be ravished.

Later, they lay sprawled in the great bed, Esclin at last unstrung, already three-fourths asleep. Kelleiden smoothed his hair in wordless apology. He knew what he was asking— he had been at Esclin's side at Eith Ambrin and the long week after—but there was no other way to make a royal sword. That Esclin hated fire was not a problem he could solve.

The tower loomed in memory, pale stone that almost seemed to glow in the fading light. He could remember the shouting at their heels, and the sound of horses, the way the breath burned in his chest and the rasp of Esclin's voice as he gasped and pointed.

"In there."

It was better shelter than rock and scrubby trees, and Kelleiden forced his legs to move again, dragging himself the last fifty paces into the tower's doorway. He heard Heldyn curse, glanced over his shoulder to see the first of the horsemen breaking from the wood, spears raised, and then Esclin caught his shoulder, pulling him into the tower's dubious shelter. Heldyn followed, and together they raised the heavy bar into its brackets. It was as thick as a man's arm: the Riders would need to cut timber for a ram before they could breach that, and there were no windows on the lowest floor.

Esclin drew witchlight spilling from his fingers, turned in a full circle in the center of the six-sided room before releasing the cold flames to float toward the ceiling. In their flickering light, Kelleiden could see their situation as well as the prince. The ground floor was empty, long-abandoned, leaves and dirt drifted across the flagstones; there had been a second floor, but the timbers had rotted in the center—a leak in the roof, he guessed, and thought he saw sky through a gap in the leads. No water but what they carried, no food either, and only the weapons on their five bodies: it was better than facing the Riders on foot and in an open field, but not by much.

"There's a window above," Ilgae said, and Esclin nodded.

"Take my arrows—all of you, give Ilgae your arrows."

Ilgae was far and away the best shot of all of them. Kelleiden handed his across—half a dozen, and the others were no better, but Ilgae fitted them one by one into her quiver. The ladder still stood, and she shook it, then climbed cautiously up to the next level. The section above the door seemed more solid and she eased the shutter back, peering out into the rising night.

"There's usually a way out," Jornard said. "These towers—they were built for watchers, not for defense. Someone had to get out with a message. There should be a tunnel, something."

"Look, then," Esclin said. "Ilgae?"

"There's fifteen, maybe twenty of them—" Her words were cut off by a thump against the door. Kelleiden jumped and spun, but the bar held. There was a brief rattling of blows, but the Riders did not carry axes and the heavy timbers were proof against swords. "They're pulling back," Ilgae said. "Talking." Kelleiden looked at the thegen, who managed a shrug.

"Rabbits in a trap," Heldyn muttered.

"Not if there's a tunnel," Jornard said, still sweeping a foot across the floor. So far, she'd revealed nothing but cracked stone.

Kelleiden kept his eyes on Esclin. "And if there isn't?"

"It's better to bargain from in here than out there."

That was true enough, though not particularly comforting. Kelleiden scanned the stone walls, searching for any sign of smithcraft or witchwork, but saw none of the small betrayals that would indicate either had been in use.

"Esclin!" Ilgae leaned away from the window. "They're showing parley."

"Are they, now?" Esclin said. He hauled himself up the ladder, lithe as ever in spite of the long flight, his straw-white hair bound back in a twist of braids that fell almost to his waist. They had all discarded shield and helm days ago when they were forced west across the Lammard; Esclin and his smith still had their shirts of light mail, but the others had only leather. Kelleiden followed unbidden, stepping carefully on the creaking beams.

Through the narrow gap in the shutters, he could see the Riders' leader riding slowly toward them, a strip of scarlet fabric trailing from the tip of his spear. "Aubrinos! Come down, and we'll talk terms!"

Esclin pushed the shutter open another finger's-width. "We can talk terms from here."

"Your father's dead," the Rider answered. "Aubrin is dead. The lord paramount says to you, all he wants is what he asked of your father. To cross these valleys without hindrance. Grant us that, and we will let you go."

Esclin laughed softly but, when he spoke, his voice was convincingly uncertain. "Dead? I don't believe you."

"I give you my word."

"And I don't doubt you believe it," Esclin answered. "But in the heat of battle, it's easy to be mistaken."

Kelleiden could read the hope in his stance: if the Riders were even halfway serious about trying to talk them out, that would buy them time to find the tunnel—assuming there was one—or for rescue to arrive, or something else, anything else, that would let them get away.

"Aubrin is dead," the Rider repeated. "Audan is pursued. And you are trapped here. We ask very little for your freedom."

"What you ask may not be mine to give," Esclin answered. "Nor my uncle's."

"We don't care who rules in the Hundred Hills," the Rider said. "You can be of use, or you can die."

Esclin glanced over his shoulder, and Kelleiden saw Jornard spread her hands: nothing yet. Esclin bit his lip and peered out the window again. "You'd be wise to care a little— not just on my account, but because the people will choose their arros. You can't just name a name and say 'He has said we may pass here.'"

"They'll follow the leader that's left," the Rider said. "Choose quickly, little man. This is the only chance you'll have."

Kelleiden shook his head. "He's lying..."

"Of course he is." Esclin glared at him. "We need time." He raised his voice to carry to the men outside. "How do I know you'll keep your word?"

"Unlike your kind, we answer to our god for our honor," the Rider said.

"That's not much inducement to come down," Esclin said, but not so loudly that the Rider had to hear. He raised his voice again. "There are my people to consider as well."

Kelleiden looked back at the lower level, where Jornard and Heldyn were still probing the stone floor. They'd disturbed leaves and dirt in plenty, but there was no sign of any secret entrance.

"They're bringing torches," Ilgae said.

Esclin's mouth tightened, and Kelleiden craned his neck to see past them both. Sure enough, men were emerging from the woods on foot, each one carrying a torch whose flames streamed tall as a man's arm. The flickering light drove back the shadows: even if they could find the tunnel, it would be harder to evade pursuit in that growing light.

"Your people will be treated fairly," the Rider said. "Come out, and we can make a deal."

"I'd like more security for my friends," Esclin said.

"You have no security where you are," the Rider said. He moved his hand and there was the sudden twang of bowstrings, followed by a series of thuds from the timbers overhead. Ilgae jerked back, swearing, and Esclin looked up at the roof, fear for once written plain on his face.

"Fire arrows." Ilgae reached for her own bow, taking aim on the leader, but Esclin caught her arm. "Wait. Don't waste the shot."

The bows sang again, a more ragged volley this time, and Kelleiden counted another half dozen hits above them. He could smell smoke, too, the first thin whiff of disaster. There was no well, and they carried no more water than what was left in Ilgae's waterskin.

"Consider that incentive for making a quick decision," the Rider called from below. Esclin slammed the shutter closed without answering.

"Let me just take one," Ilgae said.

Esclin shook his head. "Not yet. If we have to fight—"

"If we have to fight, we'll all be dead," Kelleiden said bluntly. He dropped down the ladder to join the others, trying to ignore the rising smell of fire above them. Those torches had been dipped in pitch; the arrows would have been, too, and a dozen of them would be enough to set the second floor alight. "Anything?"

"Maybe here," Heldyn said. He tapped the butt of his spear on a flagstone perhaps an ell from the western wall, then tapped the one next to it. "You hear?"

The two did sound different. Kelleiden nodded. "How do we lift it?"

"That's the question." Heldyn went to his knees, scraping at the edges of the stone, and after a moment Kelleiden joined him. He imagined he could feel heat on the back of his neck, but refused to look up. Jornard dug the tip of her sword into the crack on the other side and heaved; the steel bowed but the stone did not move, and she released the pressure, swearing under her breath.

Kelleiden ignored her, concentrating on the seams between the stones. If this was a hidden door, there would be a catch, and probably some sort of handhold and counterweight system. The builders would not have wanted to betray the tunnel's entrance even after they had escaped. The smell of smoke was stronger, wood and the bitter stench of the tar that sealed the cracks in the walls and roof, and he couldn't stop himself from looking up. Above the window, the wall was well alight just beneath the roof, and flames were starting to lick their way along the beams and into the conical roof. The hole at the top was acting as a chimney, drawing air in to feed the flames.

Esclin slid down the ladder, and a moment later Ilgae joined him. "You've found it?"

"Maybe," Heldyn said again, still scrabbling in the dirt. Something cracked overhead, and they all ducked as a piece of wood fell, smoking, to shatter on the stone, spreading a fan of embers.

Jornard licked her lips. "If we were to surrender—"

"They're not likely to keep their word," Esclin said. "Me they'll keep alive, but they've no reason to spare the rest of you."

Kelleiden grinned in spite of himself. "That's good for morale."

"Well, I won't last much longer than it takes for me to sign their charters," Esclin answered. He glanced nervously up at the roof. "Gods, that was quick."

The summer had been viciously dry. Kelleiden refused to look, instead working his fingers under the edge of the stone. It felt almost as though the stone had been cut away, there in one spot, a gap comfortably sized for a man's hand. "I've found a handhold, no, wait, two of them. Heldyn, are there any on your side?"

The other searched for a moment. "Yes—yes, just here.

Two of them."

Kelleiden considered what the mechanism might be. "On three. Lift. One…two…three." He hauled up sharply on the last word, and Heldyn did the same. The stone rose with them, something clicking beneath it, and Heldyn cried out sharply in triumph.

"Turn it! Turn it sideways!" Kelleiden called. Heldyn did as he was told and the stone turned smoothly on a pivot, revealing a dark opening into the earth beneath.

"Well done," Esclin said, and sent a ball of pale flame floating down into its depths.

"There's a ladder," Jornard said, and lowered herself down without waiting for orders. "It's a cellar—but I don't see any way out."

"Keep looking," Esclin ordered, and at his nod, Heldyn dropped down to help.

Swords thudded on the door again and Kelleiden looked around, his hand going to his own sword until he was sure the bar still held. "Little man!" the lead Rider called. "You'd better come out soon. Your roof's aflame."

"Let me take a shot," Ilgae said, and Esclin looked longingly at the window before he shook his head.

"Too risky. The fire's too close."

"It'd be worth it."

"Not to me." Esclin touched her shoulder. "Help Jornard." Ilgae made a face but scrambled down into the hole. Above them, the fire had taken solid hold. Almost half the second story was in flames and fire was creeping along the beams, the roof above it groaning softly.

"That won't hold much longer," Kelleiden said, in spite of himself, and Esclin gave him an unhappy glance.

"I know." He leaned into the hole. "Any way out?"

"Nothing yet." Jornard's dirt-streaked face appeared at the base of the ladder, drawn with worry. "I'm afraid it may just be a cellar."

"It's still shelter," Esclin said, but his tone was dubious. He looked up at the roof again, wincing as a shower of sparks fountained down the wall.

"Not if the roof falls on the trap door," Kelleiden said. Something fell from higher up in the roof, a flame that flared and died as it fell, and he flinched away. Or if the fire drew all the air—they all knew of miners trapped by the mountains' shifting fires, dead without a mark on them.

More gouts of flame were falling now, soft as flowers, and the sound of burning grew louder. Esclin tipped his head back, tracing the line of the roof beams. "Won't it fall clear?"

"Can you make it fall where you choose?" Kelleiden asked. "Otherwise—I can't tell."

"Not unless I can see what I'm doing," Esclin said. "Jornard!"

There was no immediate answer, and Kelleiden peered into the hole. Esclin's witchlight was faint compared to the flames; he had to blink and frown before he could make out the shapes in the corner of the cellar. They were clustered around something toward the back of the squared space, and Heldyn turned to face him. "We think—maybe there's something—"

Kelleiden turned back toward Esclin, and something snapped overhead. He saw a piece of roof fall toward them, a waterfall of flame and spark, and he caught Esclin around the thighs, flinging them both down and to the side. The main section fell on the far side of the opening, but bits of flame and wood and metal rattled around them like a shower of hail. Kelleiden rolled to his knees, swiping frantically at hair and clothes until he was sure no spark had caught, and saw Esclin come upright more slowly, his hand to his face. Kelleiden reached for him, ready to smother any flame, and Esclin elbowed him away. "I'm all right—"

His hand still cupped his left eye, and Kelleiden seized his wrist. "Let me see."

"There's no time," Esclin answered, but let Kelleiden pull his hand away. At the outer corner of his eye was a smudge the size of his thumb, too dark for blood, the flesh already swelling around it. "Something hit me."

Overhead the beams creaked again, and Kelleiden released him. "Down."

Esclin obeyed without complaint and Kelleiden followed him, dragging the stone half-closed behind them. There was no time to do more. Already the roof was groaning, more and larger pieces falling in flames, and Kelleiden jumped back as a chunk of board dropped to lie burning at his feet.

"We've got it," Jornard called. "I don't know where it goes, though."

"It doesn't matter," Esclin said. "Go."

They should stop and tend Esclin's face, Kelleiden thought, but there was no time. Something heavy struck the stones above them, and the air grew sharp with smoke.

"Go," Esclin said again, and grabbed his sleeve to shove him on.

The tunnel was dank and dark and not in good repair, the timbers that had supported the roof and walls sagging and cracked and occasionally missing altogether. Esclin conjured another ball of witchlight, though it wavered and faded for a moment before he could force it into shape. The tunnel curved gently away—toward the southwest, he thought, where the trees ran closer to the tower. Another blow struck the stones behind them, and another; the air around them got hot.

Jornard swept the first witchlight ahead of her and the others followed, ducking now and then as the beams bellied low. It had never been intended to be very tall, Kelleiden told himself, but he couldn't ignore the places where the tunnel narrowed, the worn side supports spilling great fans of earth into the tunnel itself. There were fewer supports in evidence the further they went from the tower, and no real sign that the quality of the ground had changed: he had put in his term as a pit-boy, and he couldn't say he liked this work.

"Do we know where this comes out?" Ilgae asked.

"Not exactly," Jornard began, and was overcome with coughing. Heldyn pounded her back, and after a moment, she went on, "Probably well into the forest. They built these so that messengers could get away."

"'Probably' is not odds I like," Ilgae muttered, and Heldyn turned to glare at her.

"Better odds than facing the Riders."

"We could have held them."

"Not with the roof on fire."

Normally Esclin would have shut them down by now, and Kelleiden glanced uneasily over his shoulder. Esclin still had one hand up, covering his eye, the witch light bobbing ahead of him to throw him into shadow.

"I'm all right," Esclin said again, soft and fierce, but when Kelleiden held out a hand to steady him over the next pile of rubble, the thegen took it, clinging painfully tight. The air was growing worse, the smell of the fire following them. Or perhaps it just clung to hair and clothes; perhaps it was all a fear-born illusion, but he could not bring himself to believe that.

Jornard swore, her witchlight coming to an abrupt halt. Kelleiden peered past the others to see that a support had collapsed outward, falling across the tunnel. It had brought the beam partly down, too, and with it enough dirt to choke the tunnel. There was a gap, a dark hole like a fox's earth and only a little bigger, but it was hard to see what lay beyond.

"I'll go," she said, stripping off her leather shirt. She was considerably the smallest, a hand's breadth shorter and a good ten pounds lighter: no one argued. Ilgae waved the witchlight into the hole ahead of her, and Jornard eased herself after it. After a moment, she backed out far enough to say, "It goes through."

Heldyn pulled off his belt. "Here, take this."

"It's too short." Jornard shook her head. "I'll be fine."

Kelleiden glanced sideways again, but Esclin was leaning against the tunnel wall, pale and silent. Jornard pushed herself back into the hole, head and shoulders disappearing first, then drawing her legs in after her. The others waited in silence, broken only by Ilgae's stifled coughing. *If she gets through,* Kelleiden thought, *if she gets through, we can all manage—we can pull Esclin bodily if we have to.* If. If what was left of the passage had collapsed...but he wouldn't think of that.

"I'm through!" Jornard's voice was damped by the narrow passage. "And I think we're at the end."

Kelleiden looked sideways again, and Esclin straightened. "Good news. Ilgae, Heldyn, you go first. Push your weapons ahead of you. Kelleiden and I will follow."

For an instant it looked as though Heldyn would protest, but Kelleiden shook his head minutely and the other relaxed. "I'll go first," he said, and Ilgae made no protest. They vanished into the narrow passage. A few clods of dirt fell but the tunnel otherwise seemed solid.

"Now you," Esclin said.

Kelleiden shook his head. In the dim witchlight, it seemed as though the mark on Esclin's face had spread. His eye was swollen shut, pink-tinged tears oozing from the lid to leave tracks on his dirty face, his body braced against pain. They needed time to tend him, but that was something they wouldn't have until they fought their way clear of the Riders. "No. You next, and I can push you if need be."

For a moment he thought Esclin would object, but then the thegen nodded. He unbuckled his sword belt and pushed it ahead of him into the gap, then pulled himself after it. The last witchlight flickered and faded, then strengthened again. Kelleiden counted to a hundred, and then again, and finally took a deep breath and pushed his sword ahead of him into the opening. The gap was tight, his shoulders and back scraping along the top of the tunnel as he crawled, and he could feel little showers of dirt against his legs and working their way down his shirt.

He had left the witchlight behind, stupidly; but there was light ahead, and he broke gasping from the tunnel, his sword and belt falling to the ground ahead of him. Heldyn tipped his head toward where Esclin sat with his back against the wall. One of the others had found a scrap of fabric—it looked like the hem of someone's shirt—and tied it around his head, hiding his burned face. They were at the tunnel's end, in a wider, taller chamber; and even as that registered, Kelleiden smelled fresh air and forest damp, and Jornard looked down from the top of a rickety ladder.

"We're in the forest," she said softly. "A hundred yards from the tower, on the western side, and the Riders look to be on the other side. They're riding round but nobody's looking our way."

"That's a mercy," Ilgae said, and Heldyn clouted her before she said something ill-omened.

Kelleiden closed his eyes. They had been driven west every time they tried to get back to the Lammard, so by now they should only be a dozen leagues from the outer edges of the Westwood. If they could reach that, there were settlements that could take them in and the Riders would not dare cross those borders, at least not on pure suspicion. And there were good healers there, too.

"We make for the Westwood," he said, and saw from the unsurprised nods that the others had made the same calculations and come to the same conclusion. "Esclin. Can you walk?"

For a heartbeat he thought there would be no answer, but then the thegen managed a crooked smile. "If I have to." He took Kelleiden's hand and hauled himself to his feet.

"Right, then." Kelleiden gathered the others with a look. "We go while they're distracted."

They had made the Westwood unmolested, though by the time they'd reached its edges Esclin had been alight with fever, the fleck of molten metal from the roof sunk deep into his flesh. Miriel, the kyros of the Westwood, had managed to carve it loose without doing further harm, but neither he nor his daughter had been able to save the eye.

They'd spent two years in exile there, two years in which Esclin did his best to serve as consort to the Lord's black-eyed daughter, the Kore Alcis Mirielos, fathering her first son. When he had claimed his throne again she had followed him, but she was no more suited to second place than he was. After Talan was born, she had gone gladly back to the Westwood, though she had taken Heldyn with her as a more biddable consort. Jornard was dead, her daughter studying lithomancy in Nen Gorthen. Ilgae was marshal now, and Kelleiden... He stretched against the pillows, settling himself against Esclin's solid warmth. He was the master smith, but this, at least, had not changed.

CHAPTER FIVE

The lord paramount moved on from Nen Poul in good time, overrunning a series of steadings on the eastern bank of the Lammard. The largest, Mag Talloc, held out for three days and only begged for terms when half the outer ward was alight. The lord paramount was disinclined to grant them, with which Angeiles sympathized, but it was the best location for the Riders' winter base, and the lord paramount allowed himself to be swayed by the pleas of the place's wheelman.

They dined uneasily that night, while the steading's folk pulled down the smoldering outbuildings under the eye of a well-armed Rider company and the lord paramount's own cooks claimed dominion over the kitchens. The axial led them in the Service of Thanksgiving, supported by the steading's own wheelman, and the lord paramount presided over the high table with a few of the steading's officers who had given their word grouped nervously among the Riders.

One person was conspicuously missing: Verwin Gressandos, the steading's lord, though Angeiles gathered from whispers among both the steadings' folk and their own people that he was currently held in the hall's counting house, and would be brought out to make his peace when the meal was over. His consort was already present, a thin, tall girl seated between the axial and the steading's wheelman, a few strands of fair hair peeping out from under an inexpertly-pinned blue veil. She picked at her food and said little, and Angeiles could find it in him to feel sorry for her.

When the last dishes had been removed, the hall doors

opened, and Radoc en Martan led Lord Verwin into the hall. The steading's lord was older than Angeiles had expected, a barrel-chested, gray-haired man with a neat gray beard, his short gown stained from his armor and dabbled with blood at hem and sleeve. He looked old enough to be the girl's father, Angeiles thought, seeing him stumble as Roudon urged him toward the high table.

"Lord Verwin," the lord paramount said. "You've wasted my time considerably."

Verwin shook a lock of hair out of his eyes. "You've won. I'm not sure you've cause to complain." Out of the corner of his eye, Angeiles saw the girl straighten, her face if anything more blanched than before.

"You have a choice," the lord paramount said. "Swear allegiance to me here and now, or I will drive your people from the steading. This is no good time to be on the road, and I hear you are a man who cares for your folk."

Verwin's mouth tightened. "My oath is given, Lord Paramount. I cannot unsay it. But I ask your mercy on my people."

"There can be no mercy to an unregenerate enemy," the lord paramount answered.

"You know what strength is left in my hall," Verwin said. "At least spare the women and children. There's not much they can do, and I'll answer for them."

"Your head's no use to me," the lord paramount said. "And I have your hall and holdings. Perhaps I should keep some few to serve me and kill the rest."

"My lord!" The girl shot to her feet, nearly overturning her stool in her haste. She swept forward, evading the wheelman who would have grasped her sleeve, and fell to her knees before the lord paramount's place. "Lord Paramount, I ask mercy for our people, for our house. You have defeated us, there is nothing left here but to serve you—to serve the Blazing One as we have long known we must."

Verwin scowled at that, and the lord paramount rose to his feet. He came down from the high table, holding out both hands until she reluctantly took them and let herself be brought upright. "It has been made known to me and to the axial that you are a devout daughter of the Blazing One. But this is your husband's steading. You cannot promise for him."

The steading's wheelman came forward then, plucking at her sleeve until she took a step back. Verwin said, "My lord. You came here with your army, and I have but a handful of men—of course we couldn't hold. But I will meet you man to man and ransom my folk with my body."

"Your body's already forfeit," the lord paramount said. "Your life is in my hands, yours and everyone's within these walls." He paused, a slight smile playing over his lips. "But if this is how you want to meet your end, I won't deny you."

Angeiles started to his feet, a protest bursting from his lips and hastily swallowed. Suetrich had no such restraint, was saying something vehement that was lost in the sudden uproar. The lord paramount's smile widened and he shook his head. "Have faith," he said to the axial. "Angeiles! Fetch my sword and a leather coat."

"My lord—" Angeiles bit off the words, and ducked his head in obedience.

The lord paramount's arms were in the solar above; Angeiles found them and the page busy cleaning them and brought them down the stairs, driving the boy ahead of him with the heavy leather coat. The hall had already been cleared, the tables pulled back to create enough open space for two fighters. Someone had freed Verwin's hands and found coat and sword for him. He stood rubbing his wrists, lips pressed tight, and Angeiles shouldered through the crowd around the lord paramount.

"My lord. Your arms."

"Thank you." The lord paramount gave him an almost mischievous smile and shrugged out of his long overgown. Beneath it he wore a serviceable short gown; Angeiles moved quickly to help him settle the leather coat over it and began doing up the buckles.

"My lord, is this wise?"

"Where's your faith, man?" The lord paramount worked his shoulders inside the light armor and nodded approval. Angeiles handed him his sword and the lord paramount drew it, steel hissing against steel.

"I have faith," Angeiles said. "But we've already won."

"Have I not said so?" Suetrich exclaimed, and the lord paramount stepped past them into the open space.

"Verwin! Are you ready?"

The older man turned, grimacing. The coat fit him well enough; he swung the sword experimentally a few times and nodded. "Ready as I'll ever be."

"Then take your place." The lord paramount walked lightly out to meet him, hair gleaming in the torchlight. Verwin snorted and backed away, turning so that he passed his wife, standing with the wheelmen, her hands pressed to her mouth. He said something, the words sending the color flaming to her cheeks, then lifted his sword in salute. He moved stiffly, as though he was wounded somewhere, or maybe it was just the weight of the day's fighting.

Either way, he settled into wary guard, turning slowly as the lord paramount came toward him, the torchlight glittering on his naked blade. The lord paramount took one step, then one more, and launched abruptly into an attack that Angeiles was sure would take Verwin completely off guard. Verwin managed a desperate, two-handed parry, staggering sideways under the weight of the blow, and the lord paramount struck again, a glancing blow along the outside of the other man's arm. Verwin cried out, and Angeiles caught a glimpse of bandage and bright new blood beneath the torn coat: a lucky blow, to have hit him where he was already wounded.

The lord paramount grinned, showing teeth, circling again to force Verwin back against the line of the tables. Verwin gave way reluctantly, feinted at an attack, but pulled back, wincing, before the lord paramount had even countered. The lord paramount attacked, and again Verwin managed to counter, metal ringing on metal. Again an attack, and again the flailing parry, and this time Angeiles saw the blood running down

Verwin's arm. The lord paramount saw it, too, and beat aside Verwin's blade. The bloody hand slipped, the sword falling out of guard, and the lord paramount thrust hard, sinking the blade deep into Verwin's chest.

The steading-lord staggered, his sword clattering from his hand, and in a single graceful movement the lord paramount withdrew his sword and swung it in a whistling circle, slicing cleanly through the bones of Verwin's neck. The body collapsed silently, blood fountaining over the battered floor—the servants would have to sand the boards to nothing to remove that stain, Angeiles thought. There was an instant of shocked silence before the cheering began.

Beside Angeiles someone swore and someone else shouted for servants to deal with the body. Angeiles found the lord paramount's cup, filled it to the brim, and brought it to him, bending his knee in homage.

"My lord."

"Yes," the lord paramount said, and accepted the cup from Angeiles. "Thank you. I needed that."

"My lord." That was the axial, pushing through the crowd, and Angeiles would have begged for a moment more, just to let Reys breathe a moment, if only it had been his place.

"Yes?" The lord paramount drew a heavy breath.

"You should look to the lady."

"Lady?" The lord paramount looked past Suetrich, and Angeiles saw him recognize Verwin's wife—widow, now.

"She awaits your judgment," Suetrich said, his tone faintly reproving.

The lord paramount clapped a hand on his shoulder, leaving a faint smear of blood, and handed the cup back to Angeiles. "I'll speak with her. Angeiles, pour me another, if you love me."

"Of course, my lord." Angeiles took the cup, found a half-full pitcher and poured again, sliding back through the crowd to the lord paramount's elbow. The lord paramount took it absent-mindedly and drained half of it. Verwin's widow faced him, her skin even more blanched than before, the steading's wheelman hovering at her shoulder as though waiting to catch her if she fainted.

"Verwin's widow—Aelin, is it?" the lord paramount asked.

She bent her knees. "It is, my lord. Aelin Anstellinos."

"I am sorry you were here to witness that," he said, "but it was his choice."

"Yes, my lord." She kept her eyes downcast, unusual modesty for a woman Oversea, and Angeiles could hear the faint tremor in her voice. "My lord, now that Verwin is dead— it's my place to plead for our people—"

"Your folk are free to go," the lord paramount said. "I cannot let them take arms or livestock, but they may take carts and some food. If there are any who wish to join us, we will consider it."

It was not a good time to be turned out of doors, even if they were able to bring some of their goods. Angeiles grimaced and Aelin dropped her head even further. "As my lord wills. I will tell my women—"

"You'll remain," the lord paramount said. He gave her a smile that was almost normal. "It's your steading, as you say. And perhaps we will find a better husband for you, in due time."

Aelin swayed slightly, then steadied herself to curtsey again. "As my lord wishes."

"See to her," the axial said to the hovering wheelmen, and they turned her gently away. Angeiles watched her go, hoping she was in fact as modest and devout as she appeared. The lord paramount's offer had been well meant, but perhaps it was not the time yet for it to be a comfort. He shook the thought away, returning his attention to the crowd around him. In the meantime, there was work to be done.

Viven was known to Esclin's harper Tevin, so all the courtesies were scrupulously observed. The weather had eased since the early storms, only the occasional flurries to whiten the hills, and the Hidden River still ran south though the way north was closed, the water running too low to carry a laden barge beyond the mouth of the Vine. A few barges remained in the docks, but most of them would stay the winter and make the perilous run south with the spring floods. There was no particular reason to hurry herself, and after the ride and the river journey she was glad to rest and enjoy the nenn's hot baths.

It was easy to relax into the pleasure of weaving harmonies with new talents, and Tevin gave her a turn at the hall-harp as well. It was a massive thing, taller than she by a good foot— taller even than Dinne Brass, the nenn's lanky trumpeter—and a good seventy years old by Tevin's account, but the wood was sound and the strings were only a year old. A lovely instrument, she thought, with a voice that could cut through a quintet in full song or whisper to break the heart.

She had not been asked to join the consort that would play for the dancing that would celebrate the Water Moon and the nenn's founding, though she heard them practicing, strange snatches of music that sounded older than the nenn itself. Nor had she expected to be: that was for the hill-folk, the dwellers beneath the stone, who had the hidden waters in their blood. She was welcome enough at the feast, but as the hall was cleared she slipped aside with the other strangers while the lights were extinguished, until there was only the blaze of flames in the great hearth at the opposite end of the hall from the dais. Someone struck a drum, the deep, resonant drum of the hills, and the beat was taken up by another, and another, two slow and three quick. People joined hands, forming a chain in the dark, pacing a circle that wound around the hall's outer edge, growing more like a dance with each quickened step. Someone, she could not see who and did not recognize the voice, began a chant.

"Arra howd in monten, Arra quen by alles kind, Arra ridden arros, gallas mis al montenen."

It was an old song, a hill-folk dialect so old she could barely understand the words, but the dancers took it up, flinging the words back at the singer. Someone else offered a verse as the dancers circled, and they answered with the chorus; another verse, and the chorus again, the dancers losing breath as they moved faster, winding in toward the hall's center, the drumbeat building.

"Arra howd in monten, Arra quen by alles kind—"

The dancers knotted at the center, circling so tightly around each other that it seemed for a moment they would trip over each other's feet, pressed breast to breast and back to back.

"Arra ridden arros—"

And then, as suddenly as it had begun, the line flicked out again, winding away from the center toward the fire on the hearth. The singer's voice took on a note of triumph, for all that it was the same five verses, and the drums quickened again, the chorus ragged as the dancers struggled to keep up. She saw Esclin swing past her, the astrologer Ismenia clinging to his hand and Talan to hers—Esclin who danced so rarely— and there was Kelleiden a dozen men behind them, head back and laughing. Three of the knitters whirled past, skirts flying, one of Talan's companions struggling red-faced to keep their pace. Then they were lost in the shadows, among strangers— strange to her, not to each other—and the stamping feet, and the drums hammering the chorus. The line had made its way to the center and back out again, the dancers at the end stumbling and laughing as the drums picked up the beat a final time.

"—gallas mis al montenen!"

The dance fell apart, the dancers laughing and leaning on each other's shoulders; and after a moment, witchlight sprang up along the edges of the hall, bringing a semblance of the ordinary. Someone touched her shoulder, said something in her ear about joining the quartet, but she shook her head, murmuring some excuse, and slipped away into the shadows. She did not belong there, for all she would have been welcome: whatever magic lay there, it did not touch her bones.

The corridor was blocked, the kitcheners suddenly busy, bringing in the after-feast, trays of gingerbread and shaped nut-pastes, and she flattened herself against the wall until the path was clear to the guests' stair.

"Harper. A word?"

She turned, recognizing neither the voice nor the man: a middling man, middle height, middle shape, his coloring middling brown over clothes neither good enough nor plain enough to draw notice. "Yes?"

"I've a message for you."

He held out the folded slip of paper before she could question and she took it warily, feeling the stiff blob of a wax seal on its underside. Her name was written on the face, neat letters in a plain unmemorable secretary's hand, and she drew a careful breath. No one who would write to her could know she was here. There was something folded into the parchment, small and hard like a bead, and she broke the seal with a gasp. The thing it contained slithered free, a coil of dark hair unwinding, a flash of silver at one end dragging it toward the floor. The stranger caught it, alarmingly quick, and held it out with a bow. Viven took it, fear freezing in her belly as she saw the words within.

The Riders have Gemme, and also me.

There was no need for a signature, Viven knew the hand, and in any case had there been any doubt there was the curl, black as her own hair and bound with one of the beads she had left with her daughter. Nichita was a weaver in Nen Poul, her husband was a guard sergeant, she had been sure Gemme would be safe tucked in among their children... She opened her mouth, and found no voice; she shook herself, swallowed hard, and managed to produce a sound. "What do you want?"

"A word," the stranger said again. "In private."

There was little privacy in any nenn in winter, when the hunters and herders came home to their hollowed hill. "Where?"

"Follow me."

Viven nodded, though every nerve shrieked a warning, and she regretted the knife she had not worn to the feast. But she was still a harper, still under her harp's protection, and she walked at the stranger's heels past the well-lit antechambers and down a curling stair that led into the nenn's grand entrance. It was mostly empty at the moment, the temporary stalls that would house the livestock in the coldest weather still only half-built; witchlights flared by the main gate, but the interior was dark, and shadowed enough to be private. "Well?"

"You've seen the letter," he said. "I assure you it's true."

"I don't doubt it," Viven answered. "And I ask you again, what do you want?"

"Esclin's smith is making him a sword."

"The world and her sister know that," Viven snapped. Something moved in the shadows toward the stair, but she didn't dare look more closely. If it was one of the guard— if it was anyone, anyone of the household or of the nenn— perhaps she could turn the tables, have the stranger taken.

"I want it spoiled." The stranger lifted a leather bag the size of a child's fist. "There is ore here, crafted to seem like star iron, and you are a licensed harper, you have the run of the nenn. Replace two pieces of the star iron with this, and we will free your daughter."

"I can't." Viven shook her head, despair scything through her.

"If you don't, she'll die. Your friend with her."

"You don't understand. I can't." Viven fought for the words that might convince him, though she was all but certain now that he was either Rider or new-come Exile, to have even tried this tactic. "I'm a harper, I've sworn blood oaths to stand outside war and policy."

"You can be released from those oaths," the stranger began, and in spite of herself Viven laughed aloud, the sound ringing in the empty hall.

"Quiet!" The stranger glared at her, grabbing her sleeve to tug her deeper into the shadows, and Viven mastered herself. One of the guards by the door shifted as though he was looking for the source of the noise, but made no move to come closer.

"You're a fool," Viven said, too angry now to care. "I'm a harper, man, I am bound to my harp and to my oath, and my harp itself will kill me before it lets me betray it. Why do you think harpers generally have no children, why do you think I hid my daughter away after her father died? You're not the first to think that's a clever plan, but all you've done is kill us all."

The stranger scowled, angry but impressed in spite of himself, and another man stepped from the shadows. "By the—what do you think you're doing, Cres? I told you to wait—"

His voice was familiar enough, and there was enough light to see to confirm it: Thedar Daranos, nephew of Nen Salter's lord. Viven's breath caught. He would surely believe that she was harp-bound; perhaps the harp's curse might protect her, but if Cres killed her, the curse would fall on him... "If you harm me, you will suffer—"

"Fool," Thedar hissed, and seemed to encompass both of them in the word.

"Her oath could be broken," Cres protested.

"Not here, and not with the men we have," Thedar answered. "I told you to wait!"

"She was there, and unwatched," Cres said. "What harm?"

"This harm."

Thedar switched his stare from Cres to Viven, brows drawn together in a frown. He looked more thoughtful than Cres, more dangerous, and Viven said, "Kill me, and the harp will kill you."

"I know what the harp can do." Thedar rubbed his chin. "But. We have your daughter—"

"Let her go free, and I'll say nothing." It was a desperate chance, and Viven wasn't surprised when Thedar snorted.

"No. You have other uses. You'll go south with Cres. Pass on what you've seen to the lord paramount, and we'll let your daughter go."

"I can't," Viven said again. "You're hill-born, you know that I'm bound to keep any secrets I've been told."

"You'll have seen some things that weren't secrets," Thedar said. He sounded more confident and Viven swallowed a curse. "And it's as Cres says, such lesser oaths can be broken. No, the barge leaves tomorrow, and you'll be on it. Or your daughter will die."

"If I tell the arros, it's you who'll die," Viven said. She was sure they had some plan to prevent that, but she wanted to know what it was.

"If no one returns from Nen Elin, the lord paramount's men have orders to kill the child." Thedar spread his hands. "It's your choice, harper."

So it was, and none of them good ones. Viven swallowed those words, considering. She knew little that the lord paramount couldn't find by other means, and the harp would keep her honest—and surely that bond could not be broken without her consent. She assumed that they intended to kill Gemme and Nichita—and herself, of course, but that went without saying — but if there was any chance that her capitulation could keep them alive... "Yes," she said, on a rush of breath, and nodded. "Yes."

They sent a woman with her to watch through the night and into the morning, while she packed and made her excuses to the steward. Cres's wife, Viven thought, though the dark-haired woman gave no name. Or perhaps she belonged to the boat, the last one leaving Nen Elin before the Hidden River closed. It didn't seem to matter, either to the people of the nenn, who wished her well just when Viven would have been glad of curious attention, or to the others who were scrambling to depart before the weather turned at last. There was a caravan leaving for Nen Salter, and a party going on from there to the southern nenns and the Exile steadings at the entrance to the Aurinand Vale. Her presence on the last boat aroused no interest at all.

At least the harp would be some protection, though she

misliked Thedar's remark about breaking lesser oaths. If she could persuade them to free Gemme and Nichita, there was a chance she might herself survive. Or if not, at least not betray Esclin to his enemies. Not that she had much to betray: she was a harper and the price of her safety was that she carried news to all impartially. The arros's people had shared little with her, either of their plans or the state of their armies, and though she could tell the Riders the current state of the nenn—and was obliged to, if asked—it was no more than Thedar or any of the others could say. Or so she hoped. Though she could also speak of Riverholme, and of the northern plains, should the Riders think to ask. Impartiality did not require her to volunteer information.

She had carried little away from Reyscant, little more than her harp and a change of linen, and had acquired little more in Nen Elin, but even so her pack seemed heavier as she carried it and her harp down to the docks. The witchlights were in full flame, casting flicking shadows; when she glanced up at the sun-traps, they were occluded as though by clouds. And perhaps it was a cloudy day outside the nenn's walls. She would never know.

The docks were crowded, the last boat to make it up the Hidden River still unloading, while two more rode high beside it, fendered and covered for the season. Cres was waiting at the foot of the plank that led aboard while a stocky man, presumably the boat's captain, directed a gang shifting barrels in the boat's middle section. Viven's steps slowed in spite of herself. If only there was some way to warn the arros, to trap Cres and Thedar—the dark woman prodded her shoulder ungently; Viven shook herself and moved on.

"Harper! I had hoped you would stay the winter."

That was Esclin's voice, and Viven turned with sudden relief only to feel the dark woman's elbow in her ribs.

"Mind what you say," she whispered. "Or your daughter dies."

"Sire." Viven scraped a bow, awkward under her load, all too aware of how close the other woman pressed. If she had a knife, she could drive it home before Viven could call a warning. "I had made arrangements in the south, and when I realized I could still make them—thanks to *Cailtie*'s captain—I had to try."

"It's our loss," Esclin said. He was dressed, for him, in near disarray, a plain dark gown over plain hose and well-worn boots, his missing eye hidden beneath a strip of what looked like black silk. "Can't I persuade you? Surely your hosts would understand."

Viven heard the woman's soft intake of breath, felt something sharp as a needle prick her ribs. "The harper gave her word, Sire."

Esclin's visible eyebrow flicked up. "The situation is hardly usual."

The pinpoint dug deeper into her ribs, the woman leaning close as a lover. Viven said, reluctantly, "I am promised, Sire. I would stay if I could."

"You're likely to be stranded at Nen Salter," Esclin said. "Or Nen Brethil." His gaze strayed past her, taking in the *Cailtie* riding low at its moorings. "They say the River's already low this year."

Viven hesitated, struggling to find words that would not end with Gemme dead and that thin dagger in her own ribs, but none rose to her tongue, her harp equally silent in its case. "I'm afraid I'll have to take my chances, Sire."

"We'll miss you at midwinter," Esclin said, and slid a ring from his finger. "Take this in some recompense for the news you brought."

Viven froze. It was gold, etched with a design of twisting leaves: not a ring she had seen before on the arros's hand, and possibly made to be given away. Even so it was too close a connection to be safe. She opened her mouth to refuse but the woman at her elbow dipped a curtsey. "So very kind, Sire."

"It's too much," Viven said, but the gold was already heavy in her palm. "Sire—" The point dug deep again and she gasped. "Thank you."

"I wish you a safe journey," Esclin said, with a nod that

encompassed both women, and turned away.

The dark woman hissed with delight and turned her bodily toward the boat. "The Blazing One smiles on us—you see how we are favored."

I should have spoken. Viven shivered, the harp silent and reproachful on her back, and let herself be shoved toward the boat. At the edge of the gangplank she slowed, hoping to find an instant to lose the ring in the still water, but the woman grabbed her hand. "Give it to me."

"No." Viven tightened her fist and Cres came down the gangplank to meet them.

"What's the trouble?"

"Esclin gave her a ring for a parting gift," the woman said and Cres nodded.

"Hand it over, or I'll break your fingers."

"What, here in front of everyone?" Viven took a half-step back, hoping against hope to find an opening.

"Here in front of everyone I could kill you," Cres said, so quietly that his words could not be heard more than a pace away, "and that will doom your kin. Are you willing to pay that price?"

And that was why harpers did not marry, did not have children of their body—or if they did, they hid them away. Only she hadn't hidden Gemme well enough. Viven opened her hand and Cres plucked the ring from her palm.

"Good. Now get aboard."

Viven hauled herself and her packs into the center of the boat, where a canvas roof was stretched to break the wind. There was a small iron stove at its heart, as there had been on the other boat, and the dark woman dropped her haunches beside it, building up a tiny fire.

"Sit there and be still," she said, distracted, and Viven arranged her pack so that she could lean against it and—if she were careful enough—slide her hand within and reach the dagger that was her only weapon. What good it would do, she didn't know, but it was more comfort at the moment than her silent harp. Behind her, Cres and the captain—his name seemed to be Brito—organized the crew to pole them away from the dock, and she felt *Cailtie* rock as they steered toward the main stream. She glanced back, watching the crowds fall away, the boat sliding into shadows. For an instant she thought she saw Esclin, pale hair gleaming in the witchlight, but a gang of loaders intervened, rolling barrels across the stones with a noise that carried like thunder, blocking her view. The boat kicked again and they were in the main channel, *Cailtie* picking up speed as though they were in a wagon going downhill.

An hour out of Nen Elin, the sound of the water changed and she could see that ahead of them the walls narrowed again to a passage perhaps three times as wide as *Cailtie* herself. The captain called out orders from his place at the steering oar, and Cres and another man came clattering back along the catwalks to drop two more steering boards to hold the boat steady in stronger currents. At the mouth of the passage the water showed broken, streaks of foam swirled into intricate lace by the current. The men in the bow dropped the fenders, letting the heavy cylinders of oiled canvas fall into place along the outside of the rails. They were meant to blunt the impact of wood on stone, Viven knew, but they seemed very small for the task.

She glanced at the dark woman, who prodded at the coals in the stove before closing the fretted lid and setting the teapot back in place. "Don't worry, this is nothing."

"If you say so." Viven couldn't help a nervous glance at the rising water, loud now against the stones and the sides of the boat.

The dark woman snorted. "We're more likely to run aground than to wreck."

"Starboard," the captain called, and leaned his weight against the oar. Viven clutched at her harp as *Cailtie* tipped sideways, and two of the pole-men stabbed into the frothing current. There was a thud and a scraping sound, and *Cailtie* settled again into the middle of the channel.

"This is nothing," the dark woman repeated. "You should

make this run in spring."

"This is rough enough for me," Viven said. She should make friends with the woman, find some kind of common ground, something that might be the beginning of a connection, and she made herself smile. "I've not traveled the Hidden River very often."

"I could tell."

Her tone was not actively contemptuous, and Viven took a careful breath. "I never did hear your name…"

The woman looked up sharply and Viven did her best to look harmless. "You can call me Netta."

Viven nodded, not daring to do more, and settled back against her pack.

They stopped for the night in a cavern where the River widened and slowed, the crew poling *Cailtie* into a pool where a broad ledge of rock lay exposed to the air. Netta lighted a cooking fire there, and one of the crew renewed the witchlight so that they could see the full length of the ledge. Craning her neck, Viven thought she could see a thread of lesser dark at the tunnel's highest point, as though there was another gap between mountains, but it was too faint for her to be certain. She was permitted to leave the boat and walk along the ledge, but when she strayed too close to the water's edge one of the crew moved to turn her back. Not that there was anywhere she could go except into the river, but clearly they meant to take no chances.

Nor were they taking chances with the river itself. They all slept on board, pillowed awkwardly among the cargo, with a watch set and the mooring ropes left slack in case of a sudden surge, and in the morning poled back into the center of the stream, letting the current sweep them on. It was easy to settle into the boat's routine, here where there was no chance of escape, and Viven found herself clinging closer to her harp, as though its magic might save her.

As they approached Nen Salter, she braced herself, hoping for some chance to warn someone; but, to her surprise and disappointment, Cres ordered the witchlight dimmed and *Cailtie* slid past the docks without attracting attention. They passed Nen Brethil the same way, as well as the tiny port that served Nen Espelt, and the next afternoon Cres ordered the boat to turn into another of the broad pools. The ledge was narrower there, but as *Cailtie* eased into the confined space, she saw crudely carved steps curving up into the shadows: a smuggler's hide.

"We'll tie up here for now," Cres said, eyeing Viven with satisfaction. "Lord Radoc's man should be watching."

And that, Viven thought, as she settled herself back into the nest she had made for herself in the boat's midsection, should have been her cue to escape, either up the stairs or into the river, regardless of what it cost her. But fear for her daughter held her bound as surely as if she had been chained.

Netta stirred her awake in what she guessed was early morning, though with only the fire and the witchlights for a guide it was hard to tell. There were strangers with the crew, tall men, Exile-fair, and Cres beckoned impatiently. "Bring her! And her goods."

"I'll carry my own harp," Viven said, and thought she saw relief: a harp was a chancy thing in unpracticed hands. The man shrugged one shoulder.

"Suit yourself."

"This is the harper?" That was the best-dressed of the strangers, a light-built man with autumn-leaf curls escaping from his felted cap.

"Yes," Cres answered, and in the same instant, Viven said, "I am."

For a heartbeat, she thought she had overstepped, but the red-haired man merely lifted an eyebrow. "I'm Linaren en Gratoc. I serve Lord Radoc."

And the lord paramount, Viven guessed. She tilted her head in acknowledgment. "I will point out, my lord, that I'm no willing guest."

To her surprise, Linaren grinned, though he controlled himself instantly. "I take that as understood, Harper. But you're our prize nonetheless."

There was no answer to that, and Viven settled her harp more comfortably on her shoulder as they started up the crude stair. She looked back once to see the captain and crew pushing the emptied boat toward the end of the ledge. Setting it adrift? Heading further south themselves? The stair turned before she could be sure. Someone set witchlights ahead and above, but even with that help the ground was rugged and nearly everyone slipped once or twice on the loose stones.

They wound upward for what seemed like an unreasonable time, the stair turning back on itself every dozen ells, but at last light showed above them and they came blinking into the morning. There were horses waiting, and Riders, elegant in bright mail, though they carried no banners. Viven let herself be hoisted on a brown gelding, balancing her harp behind her, and was unsurprised when one of Linaren's men took its reins. They were not going to risk her attempting to escape.

"Where are we going?" she asked, not expecting an answer, but one of the Riders gave her a startled look.

"To join the lord paramount." It was the answer she had feared. She braced herself as Linaren waved the troop into motion.

They reached the Rider army just at sunset. It had taken over a mid-sized steading, though Viven couldn't tell which one it was. They were south of Nen Espelt, which put them into the vale of the Darbuin, but there were half a dozen settlements that matched this one, with its wooden palisade and cluster of smaller buildings around a two-story hall, and the banners by which she might have known the holder were all gone. Instead, there were Rider banners at the hall's peak, and Riders on the walls. The sunset light leached all color from them, dying them and the tents and the moving men a uniform scarlet. There were at least a hundred men and horses in easy sight as the gate opened for them, a far bigger army than she had been expecting this late in the year: they had to have come through Nieve and Reyscant at the last of the sailing season, or perhaps some of them had never gone home at all.

The lord paramount was housed in the hall, of course, with guards at the main door and again at the entrance to the steading's solar. All the work seemed to be gettng done by Riders, and Viven wondered with a shiver what had happened to the steading's folk. There was a page at the door who ducked inside at their approach and emerged again with a sandy-haired man in tow. Linaren bowed.

"Lord Radoc."

The man's eyes moved from Linaren to Viven and then to Cres, one eyebrow rising. "This is the harper of whom you spoke?"

"I am," Viven said, and grimaced as one of Linaren's men slapped her shoulder.

"She is," Cres said. "You should have had word from Lord Thedar."

"The lord paramount has received his message." Radoc's tone was dry, and Viven wondered exactly what Thedar had said.

"She has information that my lord can use," Cres said.

"She's a harper," Linaren said, and Radoc grunted.

"Customs change. The lord paramount will see you."

He pushed open the door without waiting for an answer and Viven straightened her back as Cres shoved her forward, drawing herself up as though she had been invited to play. The room was small and plain, and there were only a handful of men around the table, its surface covered with maps of leather and parchment weighted down with wine cups, a pitcher and a handful of washed stones. Some of the men looked to be of an age with Radoc, solid commanders who probably had holdings of their own back in Manan. They worried her less than the younger ones, who had come to carve their fortunes out of other people's land. And the man who relaxed in the room's only chair worried her most of all. He was, she guessed, the youngest, brown-haired and clean-shaven, neat in a plain brown tunic and unremarkable boots, with only the great gold torc at his throat to mark his rank. There was a circlet, she saw, but he had set it aside among the maps. The Lord Paramount Reys en Nevenel had no need of ceremony.

"So, Harper." His voice was pleasant, neither notably deep nor light—unremarkable, one would have said, except that she could feel the leashed power in it. Had he trained in her art, he could have had the hall at his feet before he finished the first verse. "Thedar Daranos says you may be able to help us."

"I am a harper under the law," Viven answered, and was pleased that her own voice was strong and steady. "I am bound to no lord nor city, and under the law I walk unmolested throughout these three realms—all of Allanoth. It's your men who have made threats and dragged me here, and I pray you, make them answer for it."

There was a startled mutter, and a man rose from the shadows in the back of the room. Like the lord paramount, he wore a torc, though his was silver wound and tipped with gold, and his graying hair was cut close to his scalp, the mark of the wheelmen who had made their oaths in Manan: the axial had come with the lord paramount's army. "This, I believe, is one of the harpers who fled Reyscant at the beginning of autumn, carrying messages for the rulers of these lands. I can't see how that counts as neutrality."

"I am not obliged to stay trapped within walls to suit your politics," Viven said. She was on thinner ice there and, knowing it, attacked before they could pursue the question. "This one says you have my daughter and kinswoman as your prisoners and will harm them if I don't obey your wishes. How is that within the law?"

"Laws change," one of the younger men said, and Reys lifted his hand.

"Yes, I have your daughter, and your—sister, I believe she is. They were taken when we took Nen Poul, and one of my folk from Reyscant recognized who they must be. You serve my enemies, I will do what I must to keep you in check."

"I am a harper. I may carry news—I do carry news, I admit it freely—but I'm no one's servant."

"I had you brought here because there are many things you can tell me about Nen Elin."

"I am no one's spy."

Reys lifted an eyebrow. "You were much in company with Esclin Aubrinos."

"I am not your spy," Viven said again. "If you're asking me what the arros is planning, I don't know."

"Oh, this is pointless," one of the younger men said. "Hang her and be done with it."

"You don't hang harpers," Radoc said, through clenched teeth, and another of the young men shrugged one shoulder.

"One hangs spies."

Viven kept her back straight, disdaining to move, though fear coiled in her guts. She had never heard anyone disregard the harper's right so thoroughly—take precautions, yes, she had spent an unintended summer in the reeve's hall in Callamben once when she was young, but she had been treated as an honored guest, and the kyra had paid generously for her services when the fight was over. No one in Allanoth would make such a threat, not casually. Her harp would not stand for it.

As if he had heard that thought, the axial said, "There is a great deal of talk in Allanoth about the powers of harpers, or at least of their harps—though there is very little said about that power's origins."

That power comes from song and will and the customs of our folk. Viven swallowed what the Riders could only take as blasphemy, and forced herself to stand expressionless.

"Perhaps the less said the better," the axial continued, "but the power of the Blazing One overcomes all others."

Someone moved uneasily in the group to her left, an unhappy intake of breath that had the force of a protest. Reys raised his eyebrows. "Do you disagree, Hennan?"

Viven glanced sideways to see a stocky man scowling. He was one of the older men, gray already showing in his beard. "I saw what a harp can do. It's no illusion. My man is dead."

"A greater faith would have saved him," someone said.

"Not all men are given that gift," Hennan answered. "I say that with all respect, my lord. We are an army of ordinary folk."

"Come," Reys said. "We're better than that. Or at least we can be." He smiled then, like sun breaking through clouds. "But I agree with you on one thing, Hennan, we can't rely on that to win battles." There was a murmur of relief, half laughter, half words, the axial joining in with the rest; and as the laughter faded, Cres took a step forward.

"With respect, my lord, there's one thing more the harper brought us." He reached into his purse and brought out the ring Esclin had given her when they left Nen Elin, holding it up so that it caught the light.

"What's this?" Reys took it, turning it in his fingers. "Harper?"

Viven flinched in spite of herself. "Esclin Arros gave me that as a parting gift."

"He took it from his hand," Cres said, "and gave it to her. I saw it myself."

"Is that true, Harper?" Reys set it carefully in the center of one of the maps.

"Yes." They all knew what that meant: a tie between the arros and the ring that could be turned against him.

"Well." Reys smiled. "That is useful, indeed, and a reason to keep you alive, beyond what you could tell me. Radoc, you'll have the keeping of her."

Radoc dipped his head. "Very well, my lord."

"I want to see my daughter," Viven said. "I want to know that she's alive and unharmed."

"She's not here," Reys said. "Never look at me like that, would you want her in the heart of what fighting there will be? Cooperate with me over this ring, and I'll have you taken to her."

"As far as I can," Viven said. "My harp binds me as much as any other."

"Perhaps I might ease that," the axial said. "If the harper will permit—" He reached for the harp case still slung at her shoulder.

"No." Viven didn't move, didn't swing the harp out of reach, but the axial stopped abruptly and her heart leaped. They had all seen, she thought, though she kept her face frozen, they had all seen that even the axial did not care to touch a harp without the harper's permission.

"My lord," the axial said. "If she is obstinate—"

"I give my word freely that I'll harm no one who doesn't harm me. Nor will my harp." That was the harper's oath anyway, nothing she had not already promised. "For the rest— my oaths are precious to me, they have been the scaffolding of my life's work. I don't know if I could abandon them, even if I wished to."

For an instant, she could feel her fate trembling on the knife's edge: it would be hard to force her to recant, hard and possibly dangerous, with the harp to back her. They had Esclin's ring already, it might be simpler to kill her outright, and Gemme and Nichita as well. She held her breath, and at last Reys shrugged and waved a hand. "Radoc, she's your responsibility. See if you can bring her to see reason."

"Yes, my lord." Radoc put his hand on her shoulder— careful, she noticed, to keep his fingers well clear of the cased harp—and turned her toward the door, Linaren trailing them both. Viven went willingly, glad to have gotten off this lightly, but she knew she had made an enemy.

Four days before Midwinter, the clouds broke and the temperatures rose, melting much of the snow in the gate-yard and opening the trails into the woods. The council met, gathering silent and expectant as Ismenia made her calculations and declared that the weather would remain fair through Midwinter itself.

"A clear sign," Esclin said, with a wry smile for Rota, perched on a stool by the fire. "Kelleiden? Can you be ready?"

"Oh, yes."

"I'll need three days," Maeslin Steward said. "Unless you

intend to forego the feast. And there is Midwinter itself to consider."

"Midwinter itself is the best day for the blooding," Kelleiden said, and Rota nodded.

"All the stars agree," Ismenia said.

"But surely the blooding should have its own feast," Maeslin said, "and so should Midwinter."

"Make it one long feast," Ilgae Marshal said impatiently.

"I agree," Rota said. "The two are linked, one feast won't harm either one."

"One feast. Three days to hunt..." Maeslin frowned.

"Can you do it?" Esclin asked.

"If the hunt goes well," Maeslin began, then stopped. "Yes. One way or another—yes, of course, Sire."

And that was yet another sign, if Esclin had needed it: even the steward was willing to give up his concerns, if only the sword was born. "Then I'll claim my sword at Midwinter," he said, and felt the relief that filled the chamber.

Over the next few days Maeslin sent out hunting parties, while Kelleiden and his men cleared the gate-yard down to trodden mud and built the temporary forge at its center. Esclin watched and approved, testing the power he could draw from the Aurinand as it ran from beneath the mountain. It was enough, more than enough, to keep him safe and whole, but he could still feel the sear of molten metal on his face, biting to the bone. The smiths lit the forge at sunset on Midwinter Eve and fed it through the night; Esclin lay alone, the smoke seeping into his dreams.

The morning dawned clear and cold, though the page who brought hot water and the barber said the sun promised to be warm. Esclin dressed with care, two shirts beneath a gown of scarlet wool and a sleeveless overgown lined in white fox-fur. The barber braided blood-amber beads into his hair, and smoothed the rest into place under a silver circlet set with a single river-ruby the size of a pigeon's egg. His image in the mirror's polished bronze smiled knowingly back at him, but his skin crawled beneath the fine linen.

Talan pushed in at the door, Cat Meirin at her shoulder. She had dressed in her finest gown for the occasion, her hair for once down and flowing, dark and thick as her mother's, the gold at her throat and wrists bright against the wine-red of the gown.

"Father—" She checked herself, settling into the moment. "Sire. The fire is ready."

The halls were crowded; everyone who couldn't find a place in the gate-yard had stayed behind to see him approach the fires. He passed them as though in a dream, already reaching for the waters beneath the stone, their voices and the bending of knees as they acknowledged him blending into a shifting veil that walled him from the world. The main hall smelled of smoke and hot metal, and in the temporary stables, the horses shifted unhappily. One called a challenge as he reached the gates, and was answered by two more.

Kelleiden was waiting in the yard, also in his best gown, though his hands were filthy and there were smears of ash on the cuffs of his shirt.

"Master Smith." Esclin lifted his voice to carry to the waiting crowd. They had left him only a narrow path to the fire, and he could feel the anticipation like the heat of the flame. And that was the entire reason for this: the sword would unite them, help them forget about the wheelmen and their whispered promises.

"Sire." Kelleiden bowed. Behind him, the flames were pale in the sunlight, the air shimmering about the veil of smoke. "Esclin Arros. The steel is waiting."

Esclin could smell the hot metal. A sharp pang shot through his skull, and he laid two fingers against the silk patch. "I claim it."

Kelleiden bowed again. Esclin followed him across the gate-yard, the mud almost solid beneath his boots. The sun was almost at the zenith, dazzlingly bright in his good eye; he saw the forge and Kelleiden through a sudden haze of green, and blinked hard to clear his sight. Talan was at his left hand, though he couldn't see her, only heard her breathe in sharply as they stopped before the fire. The senior journeyman came forward to take the furred overgown, and the rest of the smiths drew back, leaving him to face the flames.

"Talan. Give me your knife."

Talan drew the blade she carried in her sleeve, and turned to present it hilt-first. Esclin took it and drew the well-honed blade across the heel of his left hand. The skin opened to its touch, blood and pain blossoming together, and he closed his fingers tight over both. He handed the knife back and Talan took it wordlessly, her hands for an instant almost clumsy. The tower rose in memory, the burning, falling roof and the weeks of fever after; he acknowledged them and put them away. He was Arra's kin, the lord of Arra's Folk; the flames would not touch him.

The blood was pooling in his hand, hot and sticky. He took a breath and reached for the water that lay beneath the nenn. The Hidden River was strong and cold even at this slack time of year, the Aurinand just as present, winding out from under the hill to spring to life beside the great gates, a dozen lesser, nameless channels. Water horses were born and bred in such streams, lay sleeping beneath the ice, curled among the stones and swelling springs; he drew that power to him, river upon stream.

He reached finally into the heart of the nenn, into Rota's sanctum, the White Mistress's well, where a thread of water fell into a bottomless pool, and drew that darkest of waters to him as well. He wound himself in water, drawing its strength around him like a cloak, like cold shadow. The sunlight faded and the flames recoiled, bending away so that the coals cooled and blackened at his feet. The raised platform of the forge shimmered beyond them, and a sudden twist of wind drove smoke in his face, tasting of the hot metal.

He took one step forward and then another, and the flames cringed away from his feet and ankles, a path opening into the fire. Two more steps, and he would reach the forge, and the waiting steel, but the flames rushed back, blocking the path and snapping at his legs. He could feel their heat through the layer of enchantment, could feel the spell boiling away like steam from a pot. He choked on the smoke, and reached for the Aurinand, its waters just across the gate-yard. It was there, but the ice lay heavy, blocking him from the flowing cold beneath it. The flames licked across his foot, and he forced them back, wincing as the heat bit home.

The sun was suddenly in his eye, a shard of white-hot light driving into his skull. The flames leapt higher, long tongues snapping at him like whips. He reached for the Aurinand again, for the Hidden River and the White Mistress's well, but the sun beat down on him, drying those streams. He could feel himself weakening, trapped by the power of sun and fire.

He was a child of the water horse, he was water, and if one stream is blocked, another will open. He uncurled his bloodied hand: Arra's blood is thicker than water, but it is water nonetheless. He let it spill into the fire, hissing to steam, worked his hand to open the cut even further, smearing more blood across his face, heedless of the pain. The flames recoiled, and he focused on them, using all his strength not to shield himself but to drive them back, to smother them, to suffocate them unborn. The flames roared, resisting, and then winked out, sucked back into untouched coals as though they had never been.

This was not how the ritual was supposed to end, but that didn't matter. There was still the steel to claim, and whatever happened—whatever had happened, whatever he would have to do about it afterward—he had to finish. He took the last steps that brought him to the edge of the forge. Those flames still leaped, untouched by what he had wrought, and he closed his hand again, wringing more blood from the throbbing cut.

"I claim this steel, by Arra's blood in my veins, and I claim the sword to be."

He turned his hand and let the blood fall onto the red-hot metal, saw it flash into steam. The metal darkened for an instant, flushing a deeper shade of cherry, and he stepped back, retracing his steps across the dead coals.

Kelleiden was waiting, his own eyes wide. "The steel, the

sword, by blood and fire and all the strength of my art—all are yours, Esclin Arros."

"Thank you, Master Smith." Talan offered a strip of clean cloth and Esclin took it, wrapping it around the still-bleeding cut. The crowd cheered, but he could feel their unease—could taste his own blood on his lips, copper and salt. He had won, yes, but there should not have been a struggle. "Arra's Folk! The steel is claimed, though as you saw that claiming was difficult and opposed. But the sword that is born from such a blooding will be all the stronger."

"And do you believe that?" Ilgae Marshal asked.

They had retired to the arros's private chamber, where Talan mulled wine while they waited for Kelleiden to finish with the steel and join the discussion. Another page had brought a basin and cloths, and Esclin scrubbed his face and neck, the collar of his shirt stiff with drying blood. He could feel himself shaking, but he couldn't bring himself to move closer to the brazier.

"It might well be true," he answered. "I don't know either way."

"I've never heard of anything like this happening," Talan said, tentatively.

"Nor I," Maeslin Steward said. He should, Esclin knew, be supervising the preparations for the night's feast, but instead he was here with the rest of the arros's council. Esclin was glad enough of his presence to want to wrap an arm around him, but knew that was delayed reaction, too.

"Nor has anyone, I should think," Ilgae said. "Unless you, Speaker?"

Rota shook her head. "It's not my art, of course, but no. Though there are…troubling implications."

"You can certainly call them that," Esclin said. He waved away Talan's mute offer of wine and paced the length of the chamber, unable to stay still. Now that the ritual was over, his hand ached fiercely, and there were spots of pain on his feet and legs that he didn't particularly want to examine.

"You were opposed," Rota said.

"Yes." Esclin paused. "I think. No, I'm certain. But by what—" He shook his head.

"Let me see," Ilgae said, and reached for the arros's bandaged hand. Esclin submitted, wincing, as the marshal washed the long cut and found a better bandage, drawing the cloth painfully tight to keep the edges of the wound closed.

"Fire contraposes water," Rota said. "And fire is the Blazing One's tool."

"Those were my fires," Kelleiden said, from the doorway. "Kindled with flint and steel. The Blazing One had no part in them."

"The steel?" Esclin asked, and the smith's expression eased slightly.

"All's well. You may be right, it might even be better for being born this way."

"But that leaves us with the same question," Maeslin said. "If not the Blazing One, who?"

"The lord paramount," Esclin said. "Talan, I'll take that cup after all."

She handed it to him, frowning. "Surely that's the same thing? The Blazing One acts at the lord paramount's will?"

"It's not quite that simple," Rota said, and in the same moment Ilgae said, "It's more the other way round." She blushed at Esclin's raised eyebrow, but went on determinedly. "At least that's what the Exiles say, what they're taught in Manan."

"I made those fires," Kelleiden said again. "No one else should have been able to touch them."

"And yet someone did," Ilgae said.

Kelleiden bridled, then relaxed with an angry smile. "Not through my negligence."

"But that's the question, isn't it?" Talan said. "How?"

Esclin drained his cup and set it aside, rubbed the back of his hand as though it would soothe the stinging pain. The wine would help, too, though he needed to keep a clear head. "Exactly. And I think we can take it as given that there was no neglect of those fires."

"Thank you," Kelleiden said stiffly, and Maeslin sighed.

"So. If we assume the lord paramount is the actor—how could he know, first of all, never mind how he could act?"

"Someone must have told him," Talan began, but shook her head. "No, that doesn't work, does it? All the travelers have been known and accounted for."

"There are other ways to send a message," Ilgae said.

"The wheelmen can do that," Maeslin said, "I've seen them. But not ordinary folk."

"There are no wheelmen here," Esclin said, and Kelleiden gave him a sharp look.

"As far as we know."

And that was always the null card, the blank face on the dice. There was no good way to control what anyone could do with will and blood and bone. He could not read hearts or thoughts, and disdained to do so even if he could. He shook his head slowly. "This is Nen Elin. Not many of our folk are drawn to the Blazing One or have ties to the wheelmen."

"Plenty of us have Exile blood," Ilgae said. "And the Fengal Exiles—"

"Most of the Exiles here are Deirand Exiles," Maeslin said, "and they hate the wheelmen worse than anyone."

Esclin ignored the old argument. The Deirand Exiles had arrived when the first lord paramount was proclaimed, and mostly foreswore the Blazing One; the Fengal Exiles had come later and with reluctance, and the two groups spent nearly as much time quarreling with each other as they did fighting the Riders. He had not, so far, been able to turn any of it to his advantage. "What I expected was that they'd try to sneak in with someone's train; but as far as I know, none have succeeded."

"But if there couldn't have been a messenger," Talan said, "and there aren't any wheelmen here—that still doesn't explain anything."

"That would be the question," Esclin agreed. "Rota? How would he do it?"

Rota had been staring into the brazier's flames, and answered without looking up. "If they had something of yours—a lock of hair, the parings of your nails, even something you had worn—the lord paramount and his men could use that to reach you."

"I'm more careful than that." Esclin hesitated. "Though I've given away favors enough. Nothing that I cared for, nothing that wasn't made to be given, but—rings, a brooch, a gem here and there, when coin wouldn't serve. That's how it's always been done. Surely you don't mean that."

"It's possible." Rota sighed, and turned away from the brazier. "I should have considered that before now, but I saw no reason for the lord paramount to strike directly. But, yes, a token given even in payment could carry enough of a correspondence. The wheelmen would have to put a good deal of their own energy into it to reach you, but I think we can agree that's one thing they have to spare."

Esclin looked away, feeling the flames licking at his legs, the sun beating down like a hammer. It had taken all his will to defeat them, and if that was the wheelmen working at a distance... They had had surprise on their side, but their strength was worrisome.

"So you mustn't give away any more things like that," Talan said. "At least not ones that you've worn—"

"The hound's already loose," Maeslin said, and looked at Rota. "Unless—?"

"No, you're right about that," she answered. "Though there's no point in tempting fate. You'd be wise to give away unworn tokens from now on, Sire."

Esclin nodded. That would be easy enough over the winter: most of the nenn's folk would rather receive the rarer coin than a ring from the arros's hand. Once the armies were out, it would be another matter, but there was time to work out alternatives.

"If you'll let me take some coin from the treasury,"

Kelleiden said, "I can make some nice gifts that you'll never need to wear."

"Yes." Esclin reached for the pitcher but Talan intercepted him, filling his cup with neat grace. "That would be useful come spring."

Maeslin said carefully, "And now I have to wonder—what more can the lord paramount do, if he has this connection?"

"The nenn is warded," Rota said, and nodded to Kelleiden. "By both our powers. But once the levies are out..."

"He'll be able to find us," Ilgae said, with a sigh.

"Possibly," Rota said. "Though it's also possible we can find a way to obscure our progress."

Esclin suppressed a shudder. That was all they needed, one more disadvantage when it came to the dance. If the lord paramount could use—whatever it was, however he'd gotten it—to find the army, while they were still trying to link up with the troops from the other realms... It didn't bear thinking of. "See what you can do," he said, and plucked at his shirt. "In the meantime, I want to be rid of this."

It was cold in his rooms, the fire quenched, but he shook his head when the servant offered to light it again, sent her instead to find a clean shirt. He was tempted to tell her to burn the bloodied one, but that would be a waste; instead, he had a page bring more hot water and washed again, scrubbing away marks that only he could see. There were scorched spots on the legs of his hose, and burns like fingermarks beneath them. A small price for a royal sword, he told himself, and did not entirely believe it.

CHAPTER SIX

The feast went well that night, and in the days that followed there were no further strange omens. Talan watched with relief as the nenn settled back into the routine of winter. There was plenty of work still to be done, all the preparations for the dance, but at least this had bought them time. After the thaw the winter set in hard, the passes and valleys filling up with snow that seemed to fall nightly, softening the rocks so that only the trees stood sharp against the rounded hills. The livestock came into the hall at night, adding warmth and the barn smells of hay and dung, and everyone not employed at something else took a turn to clean the pens. Talan joined in gladly, grateful for work to leave her tired at night, and only then realized that she had done everyone a good turn: no one would be seen to shirk what the thegen did willingly.

There was always something to do, and always gossip and quarrels, with everyone packed tight within doors. The arros had taken a new lover, the captain of the last barge to make it up the Hidden River from Nen Ddaur. He'd brought a last light load of distilled wine, and planned to take the first boatload of the winter's crafts as soon as the river opened up again: it was a bold plan, and clever, and the captain was dark-eyed and handsome and not yet thirty, and no one was surprised to find him at the arros's elbow at the feast, or in his bed after.

Talan thought it hard on the master smith, who was busy with the royal sword, but she had more sense than to say such a thing aloud even to Cat Meirin. Anyway, she had enough to do herself when Isilde and Sian quarreled over who would court the stablemaster's son, and then to comfort them when the boy came nervously into the hall hand-in-hand with Adasta Pennelas to declare himself father of her child. It was a relief to turn to sword drills and stable work and the occasional hunting party, though even in the best weather they didn't dare stray far from the nenn. This was the Time of Tales, when Arra's Folk turned to indoor work and kept each other company, with music and dancing and the old stories repeated around a hundred hearths when the light failed.

Talan had moved to the thegen's chamber two years before, on the same level as the arros's rooms but off a corridor that overlooked the rear of the hall. She had gotten used to it, though a part of her still missed the smaller room high on the nenn's outer slope, where she could open a shutter to the snow and night. Certainly the extra space was useful, an outer chamber with three anterooms; she had taken one for herself, and her companions slept in the others, and if they didn't keep the divide strictly between boy and girl, she made sure not to see.

Tonight they were huddled close around the brazier, witchlights floating overhead to light their tasks, while a flask of warmed and watered wine made its way around the circle. It was snowing hard the last she had seen, a great curl of flakes swirling in the main door as the watch changed, and she slid her toes closer to the fire.

"I doubt we'll hunt tomorrow."

Oriol looked up from the bowstring he was waxing. "We'll have to go soon. The larder's running low."

"Not in this weather," Isilde said. "The steward will have to manage." She was Maeslin's cousin, and had an eye on his place. Talan thought she'd make a good steward, if she could curb her sharp tongue.

"We'll do well enough," she said aloud. "At least for a week or so." The supplies would be counted with care, but the kitcheners worked small miracles with a few scant eggs and spices, making one meal different from the next. "The weather will turn by then."

"It'll be spring before we know it," Estor said, looking up from his carving with a flashing grin. That was what the bath-mistress always said, every day in the same bright voice, and a ripple of laughter ran round the circle.

"And we'll go to the dance this year," Celein said. "That's settled."

Talan nodded. "The arros has said so."

"And what then?" Sian asked. Her fingers moved without thought, the nest of polished brass needles winking as they caught the firelight, as much a proof of her skill as the length of lacy stocking that dangled from them. She was no fighter, no matter how hard she practiced, would come no further than Nen Salter. "We've done this every year since I was born— longer—and nothing ever gets better. My father says we used to have farms all down the vale of the Aurinand, but nobody dares live there now."

"We have to drive them back," Estor said. "That's all. Teach them not to try."

"That hasn't worked so far," Sian said. She fixed Talan with a stare, shadows flickering across her face. "We need a new plan."

Cat Meirin bristled, lips working as she fought for words, but Isilde spoke first. "I expect the arros knows that better than you."

"And so I'm sure he does." Sian spread her hands in apology, the stocking dangling from the circle of needles. "And he's a clever man, and he always has answers, yes. But I'm not the only one who'll be saying this."

Talan nodded slowly, and saw Sian relax. She would take that message to the arros, though she doubted it was news. The flask had come round to her again and she took a long drink. "The founder of our house was Arra," she said, "and like the Exiles she came from beyond the sea, though Manan was not even a kingdom in those days." She glanced around the little circle, taking comfort from the familiar faces. She had no craft but story and this was the tale that came to her, hard on the heels of the blooding and Sian's worry.

"Arra followed the Lammard into the heart of Allanoth and turned east toward the sunrise. She came to the feet of the Hundred Hills and looked up at them and said, 'This is a place for a fine realm! Who holds this land?' But all the locals answered, 'No one holds it, nor ever will! It is no place for any person, and least of all a maid alone.' When she asked why, the first four would not tell, but the fifth was an old grandmother, and she said, 'The hills are held by a Water Horse, and he kills and eats anyone who comes into his realm. Especially maidens.'

"Arra thought that was strange, and resolved that she would go at least a little way into the hills, to see what she could make of these tales. So she took her own horse and rode out, telling no one where she went so that they couldn't stop her; and for three days she threaded her way up into the rolling hills, through gorse and sweet brush and scrub pine, over granite scree and meadows starred with flowers bluer than the sky and drifts of golden leaves as the trees turned toward autumn. She found a little stream, and, though she had been warned to avoid running water, because that is where the Water Horse makes his home, she thought it was so small and shallow that she could take the chance, and she and her horse could drink deep that day.

"And so in the afternoon she came to a broad ford, and sighed because she would need to leave this friendly stream to find a safer place to sleep. One last good drink, she thought, and dismounted, and in that moment the water boiled up, foam and water and the very stones shaping themselves into an enormous stallion. Her own horse screamed and bolted. Arra drew her sword, but the Water Horse reared, and struck her down.

"When she came to herself, there was no horse, just a naked man with one foot on her chest, pressing her down into the gravel. He was testing the edge of her sword with his thumb, and when he saw her eyes open he nodded to her quite politely. 'You should have stayed out of the hills, girl, for now I will kill and eat you.'

"Arra looked him up and down, hoping to find some way out of her trouble, but he was big and strong, and his weight held her pinned. And then she saw he was erect and straining, and she cleared her throat. 'One question, Water Horse?'

"He tilted his head at her, and she went on as though he'd agreed. 'Have you found the devouring of maidens to be particularly satisfying to your hunger?'

"The Water Horse stopped feeling the edge of her sword. 'No,' he said, after a long moment's thought, 'no, I cannot say I have. Their flesh is without savor, and still I burn for them.'

"'I can show you another kind of feasting,' Arra said, 'and I think you'll like it better.'

"'You will flee,' the Water Horse said, 'and then I'll have to chase you down, and I'm in no mood for games.'

"'I give you my oath I will not flee,' Arra said. 'And as for games, I know one or two you might like quite well.'

"So the Water Horse released her, and she rose, shedding her clothes as she went. The Water Horse made a sound in his throat and lifted her sword, but she stepped inside the arc of his swing. 'That's not the sword you want,' she told him, and seized him by the root. He cried out and dropped her sword, and she pulled him to her, and it was she who rode the Water Horse until at last he lay limp beneath her.

"'There,' she said, 'is that not a better feast than the other?'

"'It is,' he said, and at that he wept, turning his face from her. She stroked his cheeks and wiped his eyes.

"'Why do you weep?' she said.

"'I have found what I desired, and you will go from me, and I will never satisfy that hunger again.'

"And Arra smiled. 'Let's not be hasty,' she said. 'I've come to the hills seeking a new home for me and mine, and a Water Horse would be a fine addition to my household. If I were to build my house at the head of your stream, you could come and go, and we could both satisfy our desires.'

"And so Arra rode the Water Horse along the stream by day, and at night she rode him in her blankets, and at last they came to the place where the stream broke from the highest hills. It was a fine clearing, with a pool and a cave and a meadow starred with flowers. 'This is the place,' he said. 'I can go no further.'

"'It's a fine place,' she said. 'I believe I will stay.' And stay she did, though first they rode back down the stream to find her people, and together they built Nen Elin. And the Water Horse lived in the stream, though as the nenn grew, it grew shy of people and was seen less often. But that is why we are the house of the Water Horse, and lords of the Hundred Hills."

As winter settled in, the troops at Mag Talloc dwindled: sent away to other captured steadings along the line of the Dassend Hills, Viven guessed, though she was careful not to ask outright. As the troops moved away they brought her into the hall, an improvement on the tents at least in terms of comfort, but with even less chance to either escape or to reach Gemme. She had spent many winters in steadings all across the Three Realms but Mag Talloc seemed colder than most, and the wind found every crack in the timbered walls. The drafts nipped at her ankles as she climbed the stairs to her new quarters, her harp heavy on her back.

Her new room was tiny, not much larger than the box-bed that stood as far from the window as possible, and the snow had pierced the joints of the shutters to scribe strange symbols on the floorboards. The space had been walled off, she guessed, to give some adult child space for a household: there was an outer room between her door and the hall, with three camp-beds in it lined up feet to the fire, and she saw one of Radoc's sergeants kneeling beside the hearth, coaxing a better flame from his meager stock of wood and charcoal.

Her own room had no hearth, but at least they'd given her a good-sized brazier and a basket of fuel, plus a chair and a close-stool, and the bed curtains were patched but whole. She wouldn't freeze and so far they'd fed her, and she set the harp gently on the bed while a soldier moved to light the brazier.

"I would like to see my daughter," she said to Linaren, as she had said every day since she had been taken, sometimes two and three times, and the Rider gave her a pained look.

"There's no one to spare to take you there, and I won't risk my men in this weather anyway. As I've said before."

"Then how am I to know she's alive? Better I should throw myself out this window than let you use me, if she's dead."

Linaren blinked, his eyes moving from her to the window and back again as though he was trying to judge her determination. She folded her arms, and he sighed. "I will ask the next messenger to bring back word. Will that content you?"

"Not really," Viven answered. "But I'll take it."

"I'll see what can be done."

The fire was crackling in the brazier, a welcome point of warmth, and Viven rubbed her fingers together. "I also want your permission to practice. My music is my living, I can't afford to let myself go stale."

Linaren gave a wry smile, as though he suspected she'd asked the impossible question first on purpose. "Swear on your harp that you'll attempt no enchantment."

Viven hesitated, remembering old tales, harpers who'd sung an entire hall to sleep, or made themselves invisible, but she'd never had that kind of power. "Very well." Linaren waited, and reluctantly she loosened the ties of the harp bag, laying her hand on the polished wood. Just to touch it again made her feel stronger. "I swear on my harp that I will attempt no enchantment."

Linaren bowed. "Thank you." He nodded to the soldier by the brazier, and the man let himself out. "You'll take your meals here unless otherwise informed, and I'll try to find someone to wait on you. Until then, I'll send one of the pages."

They were no threat—indeed, no one had shown her anything but remote courtesy, whether under orders or from fear of her harp. "Very well."

"Then I bid you good evening."

Viven called after him, "Wait, a candle—"

The door closed and she heard the key turn in the lock: there was no other answer. There was light enough still, seeping in through the shutters and from the brisk flames in the brazier. She seated herself on the bed, the straw mattress crackling beneath her, and worked the harp free of its case. It would take some hours yet to warm enough that she could tune it properly, but already the wood was a comfort under her hands.

She had made a few tentative adjustments to the tuning pegs when there was a knock at the door. She looked up, wary, and it opened to admit a pale woman in a fog-gray gown almost as colorless as her eyes. She carried a tray, and a page followed her with a basin, the towel draped over his arm. "Harper."

"Lady." Viven set the harp aside. The lord paramount had no wife, but that didn't mean the stranger was insignificant. "My name is Viven, and I am at your service. As much as I'm allowed to be, at least."

The harper's practiced courtesy seemed to strike a spark. "Aelin Anstellinos. I am the holder of the house, by my husband's death."

"My condolences on your loss."

Aelin's eyes flicked toward her at that, and her lips tightened. "Verwin opposed the lord paramount. He has met his just end."

Viven bowed, hiding her own uncertainty. Did Mag Talloc's new holder regret the death, or did she support the lord paramount? There was no reading that blank, blanched face. "As the holder says."

"There are few women in the steading now," Aelin went on, "as the lord paramount does not wish to encourage immorality. You'll take your meals here, or with me and my woman; we have the use of the bathhouse three days a week if you'd care to join us."

"I'd be grateful," Viven answered.

"In the meantime, here's water for washing, and I've

brought your dinner. I'll wait with you and bring the dishes back."

Viven accepted the tray, with its covered bowl and spoon and cup of cold, thin ale. There was a half-loaf of bread as well, the common brown bread of winter commons. "Thank you, Holder." The soup was barely warm, though there was not enough meat in it for any fat to have congealed on its surface; she tasted barley and onion and perhaps a few carrots, and made herself chew and swallow. "Will you not sit? Make yourself comfortable?"

Aelin settled herself in the chair without answering, and Viven broke off a bit of the bread, sopped up some of the soup. "Is this the lord paramount's main camp?"

"He is here sometimes, not always. I hold Mag Talloc for him, under Lord Radoc's advice."

And that was that, Viven thought. "Are you regent, then? Or hold in your own right?"

"I have no child."

There was nothing to say to that. Viven bent her head and concentrated on finishing her meal. Aelin wore neither widow's band nor wife's ring—nor any jewelry at all, not even the simple circle pin that the Blazing One's followers often wore in token of their allegiance. Perhaps she was not as loyal as she pretended? More likely she was simply beaten down, by defeat and loss and whatever grief she felt for her dead husband. Viven could not look to her for help.

She played herself back into form over the next weeks, as the cold deepened and Radoc's men worked to raise the height of the wooden palisade. They were adding a gatehouse as well, and when it was warm enough to look out, she could see Riders chipping great stones to shape. She spent most of her time in the little room, though Aelin asked her to dine more nights than not, and Viven generally agreed just to gain a change of scenery. She visited the baths as well, bundled against the winter wind, but whether at table or in the baths Aelin said little beyond the needs of the moment. Outside the rising walls the Dancing Ground stretched empty to the horizon, the long grass beaten down by wind that would soon bring lasting snows.

She practiced, scales first and simple tunes as she waited for broken nails to grow again and calluses to harden, and then more complicated tunes—dances to set the hall moving, rounds where she played all the parts, left hand against right, Exile tunes that sang of stallions and mares and the coming spring, songs from Riverholme that echoed the rhythms of the lithomancers who had danced it into shape. She sang harvest songs from the Westwood and the Hundred Hills, love-songs written last winter in Nen Ddaur and ones so old that the words were awkward and twisty on the tongue, rhymes that no longer chimed together because the tongues of hills and plain had changed. At first she feared someone would silence her, but no one said anything; and both Aelin and the boy who fetched and carried would dally if she played.

To have the harp in her hands, to feel the strings taut and sharp beneath her nails and the sounding box warm against her shoulder, was more comfort than she had hoped for, and she would have flayed her fingertips had she not long ago learned patience. There would be time, the harp whispered in its silences. There was time still, while Gemme lived.

She had worked her way up to The Baker's Wife, playing as much of the harmony as she could manage, but the chorus was weak without at least another voice and she set the harp aside, working her fingers as she went to the window. It was the middle of the short afternoon but already the light was curdling toward dark; and when she opened the shutter, she was unsurprised to see a line of darker clouds rising over the plain. The men working on the gatehouse had seen it, too, and there was more noise and confusion than usual, hammers on stone and wood and iron and men shouting what sounded like contradictory instructions. As she closed the shutter there was a sudden rattle of stone, far too loud, and shouts and a single ragged shriek of pain. She flung the shutter open, heedless of the wind, and craned out. The waiting pile of stone had collapsed and a young man lay half buried, thrashing against the blocks that pinned his legs. There was already blood on the ground, and the others heaved ineffectually with pry-bars and shovels.

She slammed the shutter closed again and seized her harp, whirled to pound on the door. "Let me out! Let me out, I can help—"

For a moment, she thought there would be no answer, but then the door fell open under her hand. The senior sergeant looked back at her. "How can you—"

"I know the lifting songs," Viven said. "Oh, hurry!"

He caught her free arm and dragged her down the stairs and through the hall, then out into the yard. Radoc and Linaren were both there and a wheelman knelt beside the injured man, a blue flame dancing at his fingertips. Aelin hovered over him, faded skirts caught up in haste, her arms full of cloth for bandages.

"We have to get it off him," Linaren said but, even as he spoke, the lever slipped, and the boy who had been waiting to shove a block of wood beneath it flinched back wailing in fear.

"What are you—why is she here?" Radoc began, and Viven clutched her harp more tightly.

"I know the lifting songs," she said again. "Let me help."

Linaren and Radoc exchanged an unreadable glance, then Radoc shook his head. "The lord paramount—"

"Would surely want this man's life saved," Aelin said, her voice too shrill. "Surely."

The two men looked at each other again and Radoc sighed. "Right. You, Gorshen, put three men here—no, start with the top stone, the one that's leaning."

"If we push on that, it'll make things worse," Gorshen protested, but one of the others shook his head.

"No, I've seen this. Do it."

"My lord," the wheelman said. "My lord, are you sure?"

"Keep him from bleeding to death," Radoc said. "There's work enough there for ten of you." He looked at his men, and then back at Viven. "All right, Harper. Do what you can."

Viven took a deep breath and struck the first notes, her fingers already numbed by the swirling wind. It was a strange progression and she'd not had time to tune perfectly, but she could make it follow, could find the notes that woke the stone and the rhythm that made it rise and dance. She circled through the tune once, twice, and felt the leaning stone quiver. She matched her voice to the notes and sang the orders, "Heave and push, now, heave away. Lift and heave, push it away."

The doubled music seemed to help, the stone grating now against the other blocks, and then with a sudden rush it tipped and fell away, leaving only one stone trapping the injured man. Viven winced at what she might see—there was every chance he was beyond saving and, even if he lived, he probably wouldn't walk again—but she kept singing, matching nonsense syllables to the harp-notes. Radoc's men repositioned their levers, quick but careful, and this time when they pried at the great block it came up in a rush. Linaren was the first to shove a length of timber beneath it and then the others copied him, and the wheelman drew the young man screaming from beneath the stone, his legs covered in mud and blood and leaving a nasty trail behind. The wheelman laid his hand on the man's face and the screams faded into whimpers. He reached for the man's legs without hesitation, his face screwed up in concentration, while Aelin knelt beside him with the bandages. By the hall door, someone bellowed for staves and a blanket.

Viven swayed, feeling the last of her strength run out her fingertips, and clutched the harp closer to her, the strings jangling in warning discord. Someone steadied her, and then Gorshen lowered her onto the nearest stone—not she thanked all the gods of music, not either of the ones that had pinned the poor man. She was no lithomancer to dance the stones into motion, but a harper could manage some of their art.

"Are you all right?" Radoc asked, and she managed a nod. Then the gates swung open and a group of horsemen swirled into the yard, the lord paramount in their midst. The horses checked and started among the fallen stones, and the lord paramount swung down from his saddle, scowling.

"Radoc! What's going on here?"

Radoc straightened, a mask of calm settling over his features. "We've been working on the gatehouse and the stones slipped. One of my men was caught; we've just got him free."

"I heard music. Did she do it?"

Viven looked up at that, shivering now as the cold took hold, and started as one of the men draped a rough blanket over her shoulder. It smelled of horses, but it cut the wind and she huddled into it, wrapping both arms around her harp. Usually there was time to prepare, to tune the harp and gather support; she had never worked that magic alone or given so much of herself to it.

"She raised the stones," Aelin said. "When they couldn't."

"She swore to use no enchantments," Reys said.

"She saved his life," one of the sergeants said, and effaced himself as the lord paramount glanced his way.

"He's not saved yet," Radoc said, "but he's got a chance he didn't have."

"Surely it didn't require her magic." Reys frowned at the wheelman, who looked up from bandaging the injured man's legs. Blood still seeped through the wrappings, but there seemed not to be quite so much as before. Viven wondered tiredly if he'd thank her after all. "Our own would have done as well, or better."

"There is only the one of me," the wheelman said. "My lord. And I have enough to do to keep him alive. I welcomed her help. And now, with your permission, I must get him within."

"Go," Reys said, and the men bore him away on the improvised stretcher, Aelin hurrying ahead to open the hall's doors. "Still, she swore to use no enchantment, and she has broken that word. I will not take her harp, but she cannot be allowed to play."

Viven looked up sharply at that, unable to believe what

she had heard. She tried to struggle to her feet, but her knees gave way and she sat down hard, her skirts dragging in the mud.

"My lord," Linaren said, and put himself between Viven and the lord paramount. At the same time, Viven felt Radoc's hand on her shoulder, pressing her down again. "Certainly she broke her word, but with good intentions and a great cost to herself. Perhaps there's another option?"

Reys smirked, though Viven couldn't guess what had amused him. "Very well, I'll hear it."

"Her choice was for the good," Linaren said, "and argues she might be persuaded to the light. To that end, perhaps I could teach her some of our songs, and then any music she makes would be to the greater glory of the Blazing One."

Reys's smile widened. "And you'd be willing to teach her yourself?"

"I would." Viven bristled, and Radoc's hand tightened again on her shoulder.

Reys laughed. "In that case, I can hardly refuse you, not when you are showing a decent interest in a woman. Very well, you may teach her, and she may play as much as she needs to learn. I hope it will do you good, Harper."

Viven dipped her head, not daring to voice an answer, and Reys fixed his eyes on Radoc. "And you, my lord, will not interfere."

"I wouldn't dream of it, my lord," Radoc answered, and Reys turned away. Radoc and Linaren exchanged a rueful look, then Linaren held out his hand.

"Let's get you within before you freeze. I'm grateful for your help."

"As am I," Radoc said, though his voice was less enthusiastic.

Viven accepted the help to haul herself to her feet, still clutching her harp close to her body. "I don't understand," she began, and Linaren shook his head.

"Better than you don't," he said, and she had no choice but to follow him inside.

◖

They returned her to her room and locked the door on her. Reasonable and expected, she told herself, there was still everything to do, both to save the man's life and to clear the stones and wreckage, but still she sank onto the bed filled with unease. She pulled the harp closer to her, stroking the polished wood for comfort. *Yes, I used enchantment,* she thought, *but to save a man's life, and only to help them raise the stone. That hardly counts as enchantment.*

An emptiness answered her and her heart stuttered. Surely her harp would understand that she couldn't see a man die when she could help, not even a Rider… She held her breath, waiting, new fear coiling in her belly. If she was truly forsworn, if the harp did not acknowledge the greater obligation—an obligation sworn to it as well, to help and never harm—well, she would save Gemme if she could, and then—she couldn't find the strength to go on.

A note sounded, softly, clear and comforting, and she rested her head against the post, tears running on her cheeks. She trusted her harp, had been sure she was doing right, but it was a relief to have that confirmed. She plucked the strings, shaping a phrase that had always sung to her of adoration, and felt the power waiting, still present to her touch.

The key turned in the lock and she looked up sharply, scrubbing her face with one sleeve. Linaren pushed the door open, admitting one of the pages with a tray that held a steaming bowl and a stone bottle of wine. He followed the boy in, letting the door close again behind them.

"Thank you. That was well done."

"It's my oath," Viven said. Her throat was rough from both the song and her tears, and Linaren held out a cup of the wine.

"Here, it's still warm." Viven took it gratefully, sipping at the honeyed liquor, and Linaren nodded. "That'll be all,

Pers." The page bobbed a bow and let himself out. Linaren seated himself on the three-legged stool. "Are you all right?"

Viven nodded. "What about the boy?"

"Too early to tell."

"I was afraid of that." Viven sighed, thinking of the injuries she had glimpsed before the wheelman had begun his bandaging. "I hope he'll thank me."

"Better to be alive," Linaren answered, with a sideways smile. "About this promise I made..."

"Yes." Viven drew herself up straight, resting one hand casually on her harp. If she was forbidden to play anything but songs of praise to the Blazing One—she wasn't at all sure what the harp would think of that, never mind what she liked or didn't like. "I'm not sure I understand."

Linaren gave another of his wincing smiles. "Ah. The lord paramount has agreed that you are not to be forbidden your craft, as long as I am willing to teach you to use it in the greater service. Which means, in plain words, most of what you play or sing would be our music, not Allanoth's."

Viven considered that. It would be good to seem compliant, might get her closer to seeing Gemme, and in any case she couldn't afford to let her skills go slack. "If the harp agrees, I'm willing."

"I hope you can persuade it," Linaren said. "The lord paramount takes these things very seriously."

"*Not even the harper is the harp's master,*" Viven quoted. "But I'll do the best that I can. Why does he want you to teach me—you in particular?"

This time Linaren did flinch. "He—the lord paramount believes that it is time I made some more permanent sort of arrangement. For my household."

Viven tilted her head to one side. "I don't—are you talking about marriage?"

"Yes." Even in the brazier's light, she could see that Linaren's face was red.

"He would want you to marry an Exile harper? A Deirand Exile at that," Viven began, watching the color deepen. "I thought you and Lord Radoc had an understanding."

"We do. Or we had," Linaren said. "The lord paramount disapproves."

Viven blinked. "I'd never heard that the Blazing One prohibited any honest love."

"The Blazing One does not, and never has," Linaren said. He glanced at the door, the went on more softly. "Reys en Nevenel dislikes it. He believes that desire is weakness, and its consummation should be reserved to one man with one woman and only when they want a child. All else should be offered to the Blazing One and be consumed in the Blazing One's fires. And it's hardly the case that anyone is denied by my choice. I'm the fifth son by a second wife, I've neither land nor craft nor coin to buy a marriage. I wanted Radoc and he wanted me—" He stopped abruptly, slanting a glance at her as though he'd said too much. "Well. It's a harper's tale."

"Too common for that," Viven said. "Unless—has Lord Radoc no wife and heir?"

She knew she sounded doubtful—Radoc seemed entirely too commonsensical to fail in that duty—and Linaren snorted.

"He is wed, Harper, with a son and two daughters by a wife who has a woman of her own. It was an entirely amicable arrangement. But the lord paramount dislikes it."

"Then why do you follow him?"

Linaren stopped as though she had struck him. "I follow— we serve the Blazing One."

"But why?"

"Because the Blazing One is good and true, whatever Reys en Nevenel claims for or about the Blazing One," Linaren said. "The wheelmen came to our steading in my grandmother's day. They healed the sick, man and animal alike, they worked in the fields beside us at the harvest and the planting, they offered judgment when we asked, and gave good measure. We know the Blazing One by those fruits."

"Reys en Nevenel is no wheelman."

"The Blazing One chose him." Linaren's voice was bleak.

"I was in the hall when Lieven resigned his office, and the wheelmen called for candidates to take the post, and no one moved. And though it had been cloudy all day, the clouds opened at the wheelmen's third call, and a shaft of light came through the oculus and struck Reys en Nevenel where he stood. There was no mistaking it."

Viven touched the wood of her harp for reassurance, the chill from the shutters suddenly strong enough to make her shiver. If that was how Reys had gained his office, it was no wonder the Riders followed him so willingly. "Esclin Arros could call down a light like that," she offered. "The kyra of the Westwood, too."

"In the house of the Blazing One, in Mal-Manan where the fires were first kindled? I doubt the Blazing One would permit it. I know what I saw." Linaren rose to his feet. "In any case, that's the lord paramount's decree, if you wish to play. For my part, I'm willing to teach you what I know."

Viven nodded. "I'll do my best to learn."

Winter had reached the heart of the Westwood and sleet rattled against the roof of the Carallad, driven on a wind that tugged at the shutters and sought every gap in the walls. Heldyn burrowed deep beneath the furs of the kyra's bed, Alcis pillowed on his shoulder, and watched as Rihaleth brewed hot punch in the wavering firelight. Summer's king wore a fur-lined gown, but by the time he had finished and filled the heavy cups, Heldyn could see him shivering. He nudged Alcis and she stirred, blinking.

"Spiced wine?"

"Mm." She sat up, drawing another fur around her shoulders, and Heldyn took the cups while Rihaleth slid beneath the sheets, spreading the robe over all of them for added warmth. He winced as Rihaleth dug cold toes beneath his calf, and then the three of them were balanced again, body to body beneath the weight of linen and wool and fur.

Another blast of sleet struck the roof, skittering along the tiles: the Carallad would be deep in ice before sunrise, a fairy landscape of glass and glitter until the trees started to fall.

"It won't be that bad," Alcis said. "Ice, yes, but last winter's winds took down most of the weak limbs."

Her hair smelled of storm, sharp and cold, and when she moved, tiny sparks showed among the heavy strands. Heldyn frowned. "Is this your doing?"

"Not directly." She wriggled against the piled pillows and Rihaleth adjusted them for her, winning a smile.

"What exactly did you do?" he asked, warily, and for a moment the answer hung in the balance between annoyance at being questioned and amusement at his unease. Amusement won, as both men had guessed it would, and Alcis's smile was faintly smug.

"There was a storm on the Dancing Ground, moving east, I could feel it from the tower. A big one, its clouds heavy with snow—so heavy I could smell it from the Carallad. And there was another storm coming from the sea. I hurried it on to join the other. This is the edge of it, and the ice should melt tomorrow."

Heldyn nodded slowly, sipping at his wine. The open plains of the Dancing Ground had always been swept by winter storms; in his great-grandfather's day, they said, the steadings there had strung ropes and withy fences to try to shape paths between the hall and the outbuildings, planted stands of quick-growing trees to break the wind, and used magic and harp-song to keep the household safe. Since the Riders had driven most of those families back into the hills or north toward Riverholme, most of the trees had fallen and too many of the halls lay in ruins. If the lord paramount was billeting his men in abandoned steadings, a storm or two would go a long way toward slowing their plans.

"What does that do to the harvest?" Rihaleth asked, and this time Alcis did look annoyed.

"If I had another choice, don't you think I would have taken it?"

"I know you would," Rihaleth answered. "I'm just— thinking ahead."

She relaxed as quickly as she'd flared. "We could have used a decent snowfall, yes. I fear the summer is going to be dry. But we need to hold the Riders where they are for as long as possible."

"Can you see where they are?" Heldyn asked.

She shook her head. "Not precisely. Opposite Callamben, more or less. They're on the far side of the Lammard, which makes it hard to find them, and spread out—in winter quarters, I'd assume."

Rihaleth emptied his cup and set it aside. "They've never wintered here before, and even if they're still south of Esclin's muster ground, that's too far north for comfort. And they'll be able to move before Esclin can."

Heldyn nodded, not liking the picture, but unable to argue with it. "We'll need to engage first, draw them west if we can. Esclin will come." He paused, afraid he'd said too much. "And the rivermaster, too, of course."

Alcis ran a hand through his hair. "Do you miss him?"

Heldyn breathed a laugh and caught her other hand to bring it to his lips. "No more than you do."

"A hit, and fairly!" She was laughing at him, cat-eyed and content in her nest of furs, and Heldyn managed a wry smile. At times like this, waiting for the dance to begin again, it was hard not to feel the pull of old loyalties, old fears and responsibilities. He had known Esclin since he himself had come to Nen Elin to learn arms, second son of the steading-lord at Mag Hestra in the Vale of Aurinand. He had fallen at once under the spell of the most beautiful boy he had ever seen, clever and graceful and gifted with illusion and courage in equal measure. They had all jockeyed to be his friend, and Esclin had answered kindness with kindness and rewarded generosity with equal grace, and bound them in the tangled knot that was the thegen's household. Esmeny was long gone by then, and Aubrin hadn't known what to do with his son, alternating between bewilderment and anger; older voices had whispered that Arra's water horse was born again in him, twisting and unchancy, but his peers had loved him.

He had fought at Esclin's side at Eith Ambrin, gotten him safe to the Westwood, and stayed at his side while he tried to be Alcis's consort; by then he no longer considered himself in love with Esclin, though he loved him still. It was Alcis herself, Esclin's opposite in everything, who drew his heart, and when she had asked him to come back to the Westwood after Talan was born, he had not hesitated to say yes.

He remembered standing with Esclin on the Brow of Nen Elin, the overlook above the main gate, late spring twilight deepening around them while the last of the sun flamed from the slopes of Atha and Arranme on the far side of the valley. The Brow was empty except for them, a safe place to speak without being overheard, and the evening breeze stirred Esclin's gown. It was Westwood silk, a changeable color that went from raven-black to midnight-blue, and the style was from the Westwood, too, a sweeping shape that made Esclin's shoulders look broader than they were. In the fading light, his pale hair shone like silver.

"You're sure you want to go with her?"

Heldyn looked at his feet. "Yes."

"You can always come back. I would welcome you."

"I know."

Esclin said nothing and after a bit Heldyn made himself look up. Esclin's face was tight and angry, and Heldyn winced. *You know I love you*, he wanted to say, but the truth was that he didn't love him enough. Esclin's mouth twitched then, a wry, unhappy smile.

"I want you both. And I can't have her, and I envy you— both of you, having each other. It's...lowering." And this was Esclin, generous to a fault. In the morning he had seen them off with a smile and a parting kiss, and Heldyn had not dared to look back.

"You have that look again," Rihaleth said.

"Look?" Heldyn lifted an eyebrow.

Rihaleth shook his head. "I'm almost sorry I've never

slept with him."

"I imagine he'd be willing," Alcis said, leaning on Heldyn's shoulder, and Heldyn nodded.

"True enough."

"The greatest trickster living," Rihaleth said. "One of us had best keep a clear head." He rested his head on Alcis's thigh. She stroked his hair idly, her smile fading.

"We'll need to hold the Riders as long as possible. Can we do it?"

"We'll find a way," Heldyn said, and saw Rihaleth nod.

Linaren was as good as his word, and proved to have a passable tenor and an excellent memory. So by the time the sun moved from its solstice-stand, Viven had learned a good dozen praise-songs and had begun a set of chants. Those had to be sung under strict rules, without accompaniment and with at least three voices, though those had to sing in unison. For the additional voices, Linaren recruited a sergeant called Juvin and then Aelin, who came first as a chaperone and proved to have a sweet high treble. Viven quickly taught them all to blend voices, so that they kept the rule but no one overpowered the others.

Radoc wanted them to sing at the Rising-fest, Linaren said, and Viven put together a program of songs and dances that followed the forms but would, she hoped, amuse her audience. The thought made her smile when no one could see: it was not in her to give a less than true performance. That was part of what she had sworn when she took up her harp, to give of her best regardless of whether she stood in hall or byre, but she recognized her own pride well enough. Juvin played the reed-pipe that the Exiles called the donkey and Aelin could keep time on a bothy-drum. Viven began to think the dancing might be worthwhile.

The day before the feast she leaned against her window, braving the cold to watch the bonfire being built in the courtyard. She would lead the chant for its lighting, then everyone would troop into the hall to the sound of harp and drum: the sort of thing she had done a hundred times, though the chants' monody was still alien to her tongue. She wanted desperately to add a fifth or a third, a quaver or a full-turned trill against the long-held syllables, but that, she had been warned, was pure sacrilege.

She saw movement beyond the steading's walls and saw Radoc's men snap to attention, only to relax as the blurred shapes resolved to a troop of horsemen under the lord paramount's personal banner. Viven cursed as she recognized Reys himself, swinging down from his horse among the scrambling grooms. If he was here for the feast, there would be little pleasure indeed.

Sure enough, Linaren arrived when Aelin brought her dinner, lips drawn tight with the effort of not saying something he would regret. "There's a change of plan," he said, and Viven breathed a laugh.

"Say you so? I saw the lord paramount arrive."

"He graces us with his presence for the holiday," Linaren said, stone-faced. "Some of our plans must change."

"No dancing, I'll be bound."

"Dancing," Linaren said, "excites the passions. We will have praise-songs between the courses."

"And the chants as planned?"

"For the lighting of the bonfire and for the hall-fire at the end of the feast." Linaren paused. "Can you do that?"

"I can." Viven eyed him thoughtfully. "Would it be wiser of me to say I can't, or that I haven't learned enough? Only I wish to show him that I am cooperative, an honest prisoner who keeps her word, for my sake and my daughter's."

Linaren hesitated, then gave a small shrug. "Better to do it, I think."

Better for him, certainly, Viven thought—proof that he'd done what the lord paramount demanded—but found she didn't grudge him that much cooperation.

The feast-day dawned clear and achingly cold, and the

distant sun did nothing to warm the air. By afternoon it was cold enough that Viven was glad to leave her harp in the hall when they trooped into the courtyard to light the bonfire there. Linaren had found her an extra shoulder-cape of boiled wool, but even with that and two pairs of woolen mittens, the wind cut to the bone. She hunched her shoulders under the cloaks' weight, huddling close to Aelin as they waited, and felt Juvin move up close behind them, snatching what warmth he could. The logs smelled of oil, and Viven saw the lord paramount lift an eyebrow before saying something to Radoc. Radoc bowed in answer and his wheelman emerged from the hall, carrying his burning-glass. One of Radoc's pages, hastily recruited to serve as an acolyte, trailed him with a closed censor on a chain, but the smoke was whipped away in the cutting wind.

The wheelman dipped his head to the lord paramount, but if he said anything, his voice was too soft to carry. He kissed the frame of the burning-glass and lifted it so that it caught the light of the setting sun. A light flared in the crystal depths; the wheelman shifted his stance and a pinpoint of light sprang up amid the logs. He held it, focusing light and will, and slowly a curl of smoke began to rise. The chant was to begin at the first flame and Viven held the note in her mind, steadying her breath. The smoke thickened, the wood beneath it blackening, and at last a thin tongue of fire licked up from the pile, so small that Viven blinked, unsure whether it was really there.

Linaren nudged her and she joined him with the first note, the others chiming in half a heartbeat later. It wasn't perfect but they steadied almost at once, Linaren with her on the same tone, Aelin and Juvin mirroring it at an octave on either side. They settled to the slow measure, a drone like bees in the hive: not at all like fire, Viven thought, in the part of her that stood aside and judged performance. Still, she could feel the power in the syllables—no words she knew, no language she knew, and Linaren had said it was strange even to his kin in Manan—could feel it gathering in the charged air. The wheelman lowered the glass and the flames leapt up in answer. The oil, Viven would have said, except that she felt the fire drag at her, at the song, devouring it now as each tone took shape in the heavy air.

Aelin staggered beside her, and she heard Linaren's breath come as sharply as though they were in battle; the wheelman saw it, too, and spread his hands. The smoke whipped toward him, wreathing him for an instant in its embrace, and the flames steadied. Viven caught her breath as the pressure eased, the music no longer snatched avidly from her lips, and for an instant the chant faltered before Aelin caught it up again, Juvin's bass steadying them all. They finished the chant on the downbeat, and Viven shivered hard in spite of the layers of wool. Aelin swayed again and Juvin caught her, but they managed a ragged bow to the wheelman and the lord paramount. The wheelman returned their bow, his weathered face serene, and they trooped back into the hall, Aelin leaning heavily on Juvin's arm.

"What was that?" she whispered. "That never happened before—"

Viven looked at Linaren. "Must we sing now?"

"That's what's planned." His expression was grim.

Viven flexed her fingers inside her mittens, knowing she couldn't do justice to her harp. "Plans change." She saw his look and shook her head. "Oh, I'll sing—with you, if you can? Let Aelin recover, that took it out of her."

Linaren nodded. "In Praise of Winter-End?"

"Yes, and then Lark's Praise." They had reached the section set aside for the musicians and Viven took her place automatically, stripping off her outer layers and flexing her fingers. Both of those could be sung without instruments, and Lark's Praise could be drawn out with imitations of birdsong between the verses. Beside her, Aelin sank boneless onto her stool, leaning forward as though she were faint. Juvin moved to place himself between her and the high table, and Viven looked at Linaren. "Did you expect that?"

"I didn't think," he answered, shedding his own cloak and hood. "It's not usually like that."

"Will she be all right?"

"I can sing," Aelin said, but her voice was faint and fading. "Just give me time."

That would have to be enough, Viven thought. Already the hall was nearly full, the servers beginning to carry dishes from the kitchen, and Radoc glanced their way as he bowed the lord paramount to his seat in the center of the high table. "Best begin," she said, and gave the count.

By the time they had worked their way through the first two songs, she was steady again, had fallen into that place where she could perform night-long. Aelin recovered enough to add bothy-drum to the second song, and when the second remove came round, she and Juvin joined voices in another praise-song. It was Linaren who dropped out that time, voice cracking; Viven nudged the pitcher of honeyed wine in his direction and watched him drink. She could carry them all if she had to, could carry the entire hall if she must—and that, she realized abruptly, was exactly what she must not do. The last thing she wanted was to add to the Riders' power, and she could not forget that was the intent of the feast. She took a breath between bars, and another, deliberately damping her own energy, began the second verse with less force. Aelin heard it first, gave her a wary glance, and as they finished the Praise of Hawk and Hound, Linaren handed her their shared cup.

"I hope you know what you're doing."

Viven gulped at it, grateful for the reprieve. "There's only so much one professional can do." It wasn't the entire truth, but to her relief he seemed to accept it. No one else seemed to notice.

The servers had cleared the last of the sugar-sweets, grainy paste molded into stylized fruits and flowers, and Viven replaced her harp in its case with a silent apology for her low-key performance. As she straightened, Linaren appeared at her side, once again holding out a cup of the honeyed wine. She took it gratefully and he said, "There's still the hall-fire. They'll notice if you hold back."

For an instant she was tempted to deny it altogether but doubted she would be believed, and in any case the harp was listening, even cased. "Why should I spend myself—" She saw his eyes move and broke off instantly. He bowed and she turned to see the lord paramount approaching their enclosure, Radoc and the wheelman at his side.

"So, it seems you have persuaded our harper to better music," he said, with a smile for Linaren. "I admit, I didn't think it possible."

"The harper is a woman of wisdom." Linaren's voice was deliberately colorless.

"I am very glad to hear you say that of any woman," Nevenel said. "Don't you agree, Radoc?"

"As my lord says." Radoc would not meet Linaren's eyes.

The wheelman looked at Aelin. "Are you recovered enough to sing, Little Sister?"

She dropped a curtsey, her eyes downcast. The wheelman had used the title he'd give an initiate, and she answered in kind. "I am, Uncle."

"I'll tell you the secret," he offered, with an almost wistful smile. "The more you give to it, the more you receive."

"I'll try." Aelin curtsied again, and Viven felt the wheelman's eyes on her as well. She suspected it was true, but she feared that depth of surrender.

They made their way to the center of the hall, where the old-fashioned central hearth had been cleared, the tables taken apart to leave the soot-stained stones exposed. Cold air drifted through the narrow smoke-hole, and when Viven glanced up she could see the early stars. The hall door swung open and half a dozen of Radoc's men appeared, hauling ropes attached to a massive log. It had been cut down to man-height but it was an arms-length thick, and the women had decked it with evergreen boughs and branches of bright orange berries. Behind them came most of the last bonfire-watch, a cauldron slung on a pole between them, trailing smoke and sparks, a few pale flames poking above the rim.

The first group dragged the log to the old hearth and freed their ropes with grunts of relief. In the mix of torchlight and witchlight, the berries seemed to dance, catching the light like tiny gems. The men with the cauldron stopped before the wheelman, the smoke wreathing up between them, and Linaren touched her shoulder. "Now," he said.

Viven straightened her spine, settling her body into a singer's proper stance, and lifted her hand to give the count. They launched perfectly into the first lines of the chant, even Juvin not a heartbeat behind, and she felt the air thicken again. Not bees this time, not the hum and swell of the first chant; this was smoke and coal, the unsleeping fire at the heart of the tallest mountains. The wheelman was chanting, too, she realized, a weird counter-melody that was not harmony but ran alongside their song, as separate as two channels of a stream. She could feel Aelin giving way to the song, felt her voice waver and strengthen again as she was lost to the magic; Juvin's eyes were wide and staring, as though he saw more than smoke and wood.

The wheelman lifted his hands and more smoke billowed from the cauldron. He raised them again and the fire rose with them, lifting in a knot of flame and spark that drowned torches and witchlight alike. The flames rose over the waiting log, the knot stretching, spitting embers and tiny gouts of flame, until it was as long and as wide as the log itself. Viven felt herself falter, but the fire did not change: it hung twisting in the air, serene and beautiful. It tugged at her, the music pulled at her; it was all she could do not to throw herself after Aelin, to give herself over to the song and the twisting light. If only she would reach for it, she could hold fire cupped in her hand, could take that warmth to her heart, to her harp, and send it forth blazing again.

The wheelman bowed his head and the fire fell like rain, a sheet of flame enveloping wood and decorations. They blazed up in answer, so that for an instant the log was covered with wreaths and berries of pure flame; then the chant turned round a final time and the fire settled, was only a blazing log in the center of the steading's hearth. Viven caught herself as the chant ended, clutching at Linaren's sleeve for balance, not caring who saw. She could feel tears on her cheeks, though she had not realized that she wept: that was the true danger, that she might desire what the Blazing One could give.

The forge was busy, as it always was in the long winter. There was the new iron they had smelted at the beginning of the snow to forge into tools and weapons—everything from arrowheads to pothooks—and a summer's worth of mending as well. Kelleiden's main concern was the royal sword, incubating in its wrappings until the stars aligned to draw the right influences into the metal. In those hours he had the smaller forge to himself and all the help he wanted: he had his pick of the youth left unemployed by winter, a chance to let the younger apprentices try their hands at harder things. The blade was slowly taking shape, the ingot drawn to a bar, the bar folded and refolded and the process repeated, each stroke of the hammer driving out impurity. The Cold Moon waned to dark and swelled again before he began the shaping, drawing the bar to the delicate shape that would take a razor's edge.

By the time the moon had waned again, he had done as much as he could. The blade was shaped, a slight smooth curve that would move like an extension of Esclin's arm. It was time to quench it, harden the metal again to take the killing edge, and he set the blade to cool, glancing around the workshop. He couldn't neglect the day-to-day work of the forge, no matter how competent Ilkyn was. At the bench, Kesa was carving a twist of iron and silver—a bracelet shaped into a water horse, front hooves and fish's tail just touching, the elegant head resting sideways on the outstretched forelegs.

"Very nice."

Kesa glanced up, his saw stilled for an instant. "Thank you. It's the arros's commission."

A parting gift, then, for the pretty captain: a nice weight of silver, a suitable memento, and also a thing never worn. Kelleiden nodded and moved on. The sweat was cooling on his back now that he was away from the fires, and he rolled down his sleeves against the wind from the vents, then freed himself from the heavy leather apron. They would manage, as they always did, but he would be glad of the summer's smelting to make things normal again. Unless, of course, the arros wanted him to attend the dance... It was possible, had happened before, though not for some few years, and he couldn't argue that he hadn't been needed. But he was needed here as well—

"Master Smith?" It was one of the newest apprentices, holding out a twisted double-curve of iron: a fancy pothook, and not badly done. Kelleiden closed his mind to worry and took the hook, studying it thoughtfully. "Reimund said I should show you."

Kelleiden glanced past the apprentice to Reimund, bent studiously over his own anvil, and the journeyman looked up to mouth *Trial piece*. Kelleiden nodded, and turned the hook over in his fingers. "Your work?"

"Yes, Master."

"Start to finish?"

"From the bar," the boy admitted, but that was to be expected. He was too small yet to work from raw metal.

"The curves are even," Kelleiden said, "and so is the twist. You've turned the ends under nicely. Any kitchener would take pleasure in its use. You've done well."

The color rose in the boy's face. "Thank you, Master."

"Make me half a dozen more, we've need of them for the kitchen." Kelleiden eyed him thoughtfully, assessing size and strength. "Then have Reimund show you how to dish a ladle."

"Yes, Master." The boy backed away, clutching the pothook.

Kelleiden's eyes strayed again to the waiting blade, set carefully apart from all the rest, and to the chart that hung on the wall above it. The stars were coming into alignment, the moon in his proper house and everything well-aspected, and he beckoned Ilkyn away from his bench. "It's ready for the quench."

They both knew what that meant, another chance for a single false move to destroy everything they'd made so far. "When?" Ilkyn asked quietly.

"Tonight. Once the moon has risen."

"Who do you want?"

"You, of course." Kelleiden looked around the forge. They'd need an experienced apprentice to work the bellows. "Baire. If she's willing."

Ilkyn nodded. "She will be."

"Then I'm off," Kelleiden said. "Leave the main fire banked."

The moon was just rising as they returned to the forge. Baire uncovered the coals and began to build the fire, while Ilkyn lit the lamps and adjusted the shutters to deflect the worst of the drafts away from the working space. Even so it was cold beneath the dome of stone, and Kelleiden was glad of the double hose and boiled wool tunic. He'd be warm enough in time, but not yet. They ate while the fire settled, bread and cheese and spicy sausage washed down with a jug of cider, and finally Ilkyn raked the coals into a narrow bed where the bellows-pipe would do its best work. The color was right, shimmering orange and yellow, and Kelleiden glanced at the moon, just visible through the gap in the shutters. "It's time."

Ilkyn nodded and Baire cleared away the basket, came back rubbing her hands nervously on the skirts of her tunic. Kelleiden touched the forge-wardens that guarded the half-finished blade, feeling their presence fade, then lifted the sword from its shelf, folding back the oilcloth to reveal the metal. It was dark, almost muddy-looking, the lamplight finding no sheen in its surface, but the essential shape was true. He lifted it carefully, checking the gentle curve that drew to what would be a wicked point, turning it to examine the tang and the spurs that would protect the swordsman's hand. There was nothing more that could be done to make it better; only the quenching remained, to harden the metal, and then the temper and the slow work of stone and polish to bring it to a killing edge.

"The fire's ready, Master." Baire sat back on her heels.

Kelleiden glanced at the hearth, coals glowing a solid yellow under the bellows' breath, and turned to Ilkyn. "Get the oil."

"Right."

The quenching tub was already in place, two strides from where Kelleiden would heat the blade. Ilkyn moved to fill it, hauling jugs from the store, and Kelleiden slid the blade into the coals. Baire began to work the bellows again, a steady, even breath that flashed the flame from orange to pink, and Kelleiden drew on his gloves and caught the tang in his heaviest set of tongs. He eased the blade back and forth, stirring the coals in search of even heat, and behind him heard Ilkyn emptying the first jug of sweet oil into the tub. It was virgin, never yet used, and for a moment its cool scent rose over the smell of the fire. Kelleiden heard the second jug opened, and the third, then forced his attention back to the fire.

The trick was to keep the metal moving gently, keep the heat even as the blade began to glow. It was all too easy to ruin a blade at this stage. If the heat wasn't even, or the oil not pure enough, the blade would crack. They'd all heard that sweet, sickening ting that meant the blade would have to be completely re-made, and the second forging was never quite as good as the first. He wrenched his thoughts away from failure, murmuring the smith's prayer under his breath: *Mistress of the Fires, don't let it happen. Consume my fears unregarded.*

The blade was beginning to color, a deep, dull red suffusing the metal. Kelleiden kept it moving, matching the rhythm of the bellows, the snap of the flame in the coal. The red brightened to cherry, crept toward orange. The only sound was the sigh of the bellows, the steady rush of the flames; Kelleiden's back was cold, his face roasting, the leather apron heavy on his shoulders and hips. Still the steel brightened, the last of the red fading away. Close, it was very close... And then it was there, the perfect shade.

"Now." Kelleiden lifted it out of the fire, blade still glowing orange, trailing smoke as it hit the cold air. One step, two, and he plunged it straight down into the cylinder of oil. It hissed and spat, flames dancing on the surface and spilling over the side. He blew out the nearest, and Ilkyn moved to stamp out the other fiery threads before they struck something that would burn.

"Stand clear," Kelleiden said, and Ilkyn skipped backward as he drew the blade out again. It was no longer glowing, but the metal was still hot enough that the oil left on it burst instantly into flame, flaring toward the ceiling and dropping great gouts of fire. Kelleiden blew on it, blowing out the flames, and both Ilkyn and Baire jumped to extinguish the last drops flickering on the stone floor. He had heard nothing, no crack, no sharp high ping, and he allowed himself a sigh of relief. In the flickering light, fire and lamps, it was hard to see the small details, but the line was still true, the form intact.

"Good?" Ilkyn asked after a moment, and Kelleiden nodded. It still needed to cool completely, and he would sleep in the forge himself to keep it company, but for now—

"It's good," he said, and laid the blade carefully in the trough prepared for it. "It's good.

CHAPTER SEVEN

Alcis Mirielos climbed the spiral stair that led to the top of the Carallad's central tower, her calves protesting as she reached the final twist. It had been some months since she'd needed to come here, and she could feel that neglect not just in her muscles but in her secret self. And that was one of many reasons to come now, to make the time in spite of her other responsibilities: she needed to be fully mistress of her power when the dance began. And of course there was the other reason, trailing behind her on the stairs: her second daughter Helevys, who might one day be her heir. She had brought Traher with her, too, when he was the same age, though his talents had drawn him in another direction, his father's blood too strong; Helevys was still unformed, unfound, and there was no knowing whether she or one of her younger siblings would feel the land's pull, and become kore or koros to her kyra.

She came out of the stair onto the circular platform, the chill spring wind plucking at her hair. The sun was dipping toward the west, strong enough to make her squint; she turned her back to it, opening herself up to the currents of power that flowed through the Westwood. The Carallad was its heart, the heart of her realm and her power; she had been given to it at birth, cord and afterbirth buried beneath the stones of the tower's floor. She had done the same for all her children save Talan, and she glanced sideways to see Helevys wide-eyed at the view, her cloak drawn close around her shoulders. It was impossible to say if she felt the power, but Alcis could not resist it. It recognized her, welcomed her, pulled her south and east until she leaned both arms against the sun-warmed stone of the parapet, looking over the roofs of palace and town toward the forest that stretched for nearly fifty leagues before it reached the edges of the Dancing Ground. Callamben lay along that line, no surprise, after the news Heldyn had brought from Willowsford, and Pen Aman and the shores of the Great Bay. Her power did not reach that far, but she could feel the trees at the edges of the forest whispering uneasily to one another—men on horses, men with axes, men with fire—and could guess who that meant. Her own people were not so foolish, nor were her allies.

Helevys had moved to her side, the faint line of a frown between her brows. Alcis closed her eyes, letting herself sink more deeply into the land-trance, the awareness filling her, rock and tree and stone. This was what the Riders feared most about the Westwood, the kyra who could sit at its center like a spider in her web and know what the trees saw and the stones whispered in the dark.

To the north and west along the narrow shore, the land was calm, waking slow and easy from the winter's sleep; she could feel the first shoots thrusting against the thawing ground, roots spreading, the buds taking shape on the limb and the sap rising sweet to the sun's call. South and west the land was newly wakened, and in the village fields she felt the familiar shock of the plow, the cry of gull and crow as the first seeds were sown. To the east, the land was restless, the unease growing the further south it ran, focusing on Callamben and the forests to either side. The harper's curse stung like a sword-cut, the ground where they had buried harp and man reluctant to take them in. She spared a moment to soothe that ache, and felt the grumble of stones shifting as the land sighed and relented.

War was coming. They were called to the dance, to the Dancing Ground, and sooner than usual, by every sign and portent. She turned her face to the sky, the contrast of sun and wind heady on her skin, the first taste of spring in the shifting breeze. She could feel rain gathering out to sea, a long stretch of chill and damp that would slow the spring and make travel harder than it needed to be. She closed her eyes, drawing the land's strength to her, nudged those clouds north. The rain would soak the bogs north of the Ëpasse and fill the lake at Iros, and leave the south dry and mild.

She released her breath and with it the held power, leaned hard on the cooling stones. Nothing came without a price: a dry spring in the south would cost the bread-lands some of their growing seasons, but it was becoming clear that she and hers would have to act first this spring. Esclin could not move until the ground had hardened enough to let his armies travel down the long valleys; and Liulf's men would be even further behind, even if he sent his own horsemen to scout ahead of the main army. But the Riders were already here, already settled into the winter grounds, and it would cost her more men than she wanted to spend to throw them back again, blood and death that made the air around her shiver in unhappy anticipation. They were hers to spend, and the need was there, but she and the land would know their loss.

She put that aside and glanced at her daughter, hunched silent at her side. "Did you feel that?"

Helevys's hands were flat on the stones. "I think so. It was...unhappy? And you—made it better."

Alcis nodded. "You can feel it still, if you try. The sore is still there." She pointed, aligning her finger unerringly with the harp's grave fifty leagues away.

Helevys turned obediently, closing her eyes to concentrate. "Yes," she said, and then with more certainty, "yes, there." She looked up at her mother. "What was it? Is it? I'm not sure what the question is, exactly."

"That's the spot where your father buried the man who killed the harper," Alcis said. She was sure that story had reached most of the Carallad. "And the harp with him. The curse was still working and the land shies from it. It's not a thing that can easily be undone, though in time the land will wear it away."

"And you—dissolved some of it? Washed it away?"

Alcis remembered her own first lessons, standing here with her father groping for the words to name and control the things she felt. "To me it feels as though I've rubbed it away—not the way you'd rub out words in wax so much as rubbing the ache out of a muscle. But everyone finds different words. It's all the same act."

"It felt like water. Like washing a scratch."

"That's your father in you," Alcis said, and for an instant the memory of Nen Elin pressed hard on her, cold water beneath the stones, the nenn itself hollowed out by the rush and press of water, Esclin's illusions dancing like currents in its depths. Heldyn, too, was of Arra's Folk.

Helevys nodded thoughtfully. "But that must be such a small thing. Why do I feel it so strongly?"

"It's not that small," Alcis said. "A harper's curse is a terrible thing—they're sacrosanct, they may not be killed except for the grossest crimes, and even that must be proven before their own harp. Also it was your own father who killed the murderer and had him and the harp buried there. The tie of blood is strong." And Heldyn had felt it strongly, she had heard the horror in his voice even two weeks after. But Helevys was too young yet to have to consider those details. "What else did you feel?"

Helevys considered. "The spring, that it's coming, I feel that, and you—did something with the wind?"

"I did," Alcis said. "Can you tell me what?"

Helevys frowned, turning to the west, and winced at the brilliance of the setting sun. "Pushed it? Moved it north and east."

"Pushed it to achieve what?"

"I don't know. It was there and you moved it. I can't tell why." Helevys gave her a sidelong glance. "What if I can't know? Father isn't—he's from the Hundred Hills, he doesn't have land-right here. What if I don't either?"

Alcis wanted to sweep her into her arms, brush away the fear the way she'd chased every other nightmare, but Helevys was fourteen now, too old to be fobbed off with a child's answer. She rested one hand carefully on her daughter's thin shoulder, feeling the bones sharp as a bird's under her fingers. "You have the land-right. You are my daughter, and I gave you to the land, just as I gave your brothers and sisters. I don't know which of you will step into my shoes when I am dead, but I am sure it will be one of you. And if it is not you, you will have found another purpose."

Helevys gave her a sideways, doubting look, but Alcis pretended she didn't see. Helevys would have to find her own way, difficult though it was for all of them. Traher had done it. She straightened slowly, extricating herself from the web of her realm. The sun was on the horizon now and the air had a touch of frost. "Come along."

The stairwell was nearly dark and she made her way down by touch, Helevys careful not to tread on her heels. In the antechamber, her secretary Ibota stilled her spindle, winding up her thread with neat fingers, and fetched Alcis's cloak to set it around her shoulders.

"Will you change before dinner, Kyra?"

Alcis accepted it, shedding the last threads of the land-trance. "Yes. Yes, we will."

It was late, the fire dying to embers in the brazier. Esclin nodded for the page to pour him a last cup of the cooling wine and leaned back in his chair. A great bearskin softened the carved wood, the skin worn to perfect comfort, and he was glad of its warmth. He had parted with the barge captain— amiably and with a gift, as always—and it seemed certain he would sleep alone tonight, somewhat to his regret.

The royal sword had been quenched and tempered, though for propriety's sake no one had told him so directly; it would be submitting to stone and polish now, and with any luck would be finished by the next new moon. And that was good: the Hundred Hills were safe behind winter's ramparts at the moment, but spring would come, and the Dancing Ground would open. Earlier than usual, too, if the harper's tale was true, and that meant the lower slopes would be even more vulnerable than usual, the small-holders hard-pressed to defend themselves against raids and bandits. If he were the Riders' leader, he would have made sure to attack at least some of the lower steadings, perhaps even a foothill nenn: it would have an effect out of all proportion to the actual damage.

He took a swallow of the wine, tasting spice brought from the coast to Nen Ddaur and then up the Hidden Rivers. All he could do right now was speculate, play guessing games of war like moving counters at tavli—and know that as soon as the roads cleared enough for him to march south in force, the situation would be nothing like he had imagined. Liulf Nestaros was doing the same in Riverholme and Alcis in the Westwood. He closed his eyes, wondering what she had seen and what her plans would be.

There was a soft sound at the door and the page moved quickly to answer, slipping out through the tapestry curtains. A moment later he was back, Kelleiden Smith at his heels. Esclin tensed, but a second look at Kelleiden's face removed the worry. The smith looked uncommonly pleased with himself and Esclin tipped his head to one side.

"I have something to show you," Kelleiden said, and there was a note of excitement in his voice.

"Oh?"

"Will you come with me?"

Esclin nodded. "Where?"

"The smithy."

Esclin nodded again, uncurling himself from the fur and settling his gown more comfortably on his shoulders. "Don't wait for me," he said to the page, and conjured a ball of witchlight to light their way.

They made their way upward through the servants' passages, steeper and less well-lit than the public ways. At this time of night they were nearly deserted, with only the occasional guard on watch at the major junctions. It felt like boyhood, when they had to sneak out of their shared room to steal kisses in unregarded corners, and Esclin smiled at the memory. Kelleiden glanced back at him as they started up the Derwald Stair, its turns full of shadowed angles, and Esclin guessed the same thought was in his mind. He was tempted to pluck at Kelleiden's skirts and pull him back for a stolen kiss, but they were close enough to the upper gallery that he held his hand.

The Derwald Stair opened onto the gallery's western edge. There was a guardpost there, three men half-armed beside a lantern-stove and an alarm-bell, who straightened and then relaxed as they recognized who was approaching. "Sire," one said, his voice barely above a whisper, and touched his brow as they took the Sunward Stair that led to the upper workrooms.

The smithy was empty, the fires deeply banked, but the moonlight poured down from the high window, funneled by the shutters to cast a beam on the workbench. By that light Esclin could see the stubs of candles set out in a familiar pattern, and a narrow bundle wrapped in scarlet lying at their center. Kelleiden glanced over his shoulder, his smile showing bright in the moonlight. "Here."

He moved to the bench, Esclin at his heels, and undid the cords that held the wrapping in place. He folded back the fabric, adjusting it so that the moonlight fell on the object within, and in spite of himself Esclin caught his breath. He had owned swords of Kelleiden's forging since Kelleiden had been named a master, was used to their deadly grace, but even unfinished, this one was subtly better. The curve was more honed, as close to perfect as human hands could make it; the point would be needle-sharp, the spurs placed just so to give extra protection to his hands, and his hands itched to test its balance. Silver lines glinted against the night-black iron, not yet polished to its final sheen, and he frowned.

"What is that—surely not a flaw?"

"Look closer." Kelleiden tipped the blade to catch more of the moonlight, and abruptly the pattern came clear. There was the stretched neck, the arched head reaching down the length of the blade, teeth bared. The mane flowed along the wider back, the front feet with their webbed claws extended reaching toward the point; above the mane as the blade widened, lifted shoulders flowed into the powerful tail, its leafy edges trailing out and into the protecting spurs. An arros, the water horse, symbol and ancestor of his house, flowed along the blade, stylized and sinuous and one with the metal.

Kelleiden said, "I didn't put it there." He tilted the blade again, letting the moonlight pour over it like water. "This was the first full moon since the blade was quenched. I came to see if it had an opinion about its name."

Esclin wanted to touch it, to run his fingers over the silver shape, to pet it as though it were in truth the animal it sketched, but he knew better. "Apparently it has."

"It will be a royal sword," Kelleiden said. "It's shaped and it's named and all the rest is finishing. Your sword."

Esclin reached across bench and sword to cup the smith's cheek. Through exile and return and after, Kelleiden had promised him this, a royal sword to replace the one his father had lost at Eith Ambrin; Esclin had taken it as a pledge of love, not realizing himself that in fact he wanted it until he saw the living blade. "You have earned your mastery. It's beyond beautiful."

Kelleiden leaned briefly into the caress but the moon was moving, the light sliding away from the anvil. He sighed and Esclin released him, watching him return the blade to its wrappings. Kelleiden pulled the last intricate knot tight and set the bundle back in its place—the only object on that shelf, with the humped shapes of forge-wardens at each end to watch over it. Kelleiden touched each one in turn, and Esclin felt their power waken.

"Thank you," he said, wishing he had stronger words, and Kelleiden gave him a wry smile as he reached for his keys.

"I'll do better still."

Esclin put his arm around the smith's waist. "I know."

There was still snow in the shaded spots but Mag Talloc's courtyard was mostly bare, the ground softened enough toward spring that the hall floors were always mud-streaked in spite of the servants' efforts. The first leaf-buds showed on the carefully tended fruit trees that sheltered in the inner courtyard, and where the winds had swept the ground bare beyond the walls, new grass broke through.

Viven watched from her window as the Riders went forth, at first for a day or so, then larger parties on longer journeys. She could not ask outright where they went but there was enough unregarded talk in the hall that she assumed the lord paramount was beginning his muster. She said as much, cautiously, to Aelin as they sat together in Viven's narrow room, the fire in the brazier merely embers and the air that came through the half-open window smelling of spring. Aelin gave her an equally cautious glance and broke what was left of the loaf into two equal pieces.

"So I've heard," she said. "Though no one has said so directly."

Viven spread honey on her share of the bread. "Will you hold Mag Talloc when he's gone?"

Aelin lowered her gaze again. "If I had my way," she said slowly, "I would find a house of sisters to take me in. This winter, when we sang…"

Viven nodded, remembering the touch of power, the heady weight of it. Harpers learned to understand and temper that desire, or they found their own god to serve. She wasn't surprised it had taken Aelin that way, especially not under the circumstances. It might make the lord paramount's life easier, too, let him ease Verwin's widow out of Mag Talloc to be replaced by his own chosen holder. "Will he let you?"

Her mouth tightened. "Not yet. I have spoken to Serrat—" That was the steading's wheelman. "And he spoke to the axial. Neither of them would gainsay me. But the lord paramount has said he wishes to see me wed again."

"To hold Mag Talloc." Viven nodded. "I see his point."

"This is not Nen Poul," Aelin said. "Or any of the other steadings he's taken. I have no child. My only place here is as Verwin's widow—he had no children, not by me or anyone, his nearest kinsman is some cousin in Lakander Vale. And the lord paramount turned off most of our people. He could as easily let me go and give the steading outright."

That was certainly true. A childless widow was more likely to return to her own family than to claim rights from her husband's kin, unless there was some long-established bond. "Difficult," Viven said.

"Not easy, no."

"It does seem to me that the lord paramount might find it more to his advantage to let you go to a sisterhood," Viven said carefully.

For the first time, Aelin met her eyes. "So I thought. So Serrat thought. And yet... He could have married me off this winter. I don't know what he wants of me."

And why are you telling me this? Viven thought. If this were the Hundred Hills, she would suspect one of Esclin's stratagems, but Reys didn't seem capable of anything that complex. "Will he leave someone with you, then, to mind the steading?"

"He plans to take me with him," Aelin said. "And you also. I think I am to bear you company."

"That's—hardly proper," Viven said. She wasn't sure exactly what it would gain her, but no one could argue that it was the place of a steading's holder to wait on a harper.

Aelin shrugged one shoulder. "Or perhaps you're to keep me company, you know he's a stickler for all the proprieties. But I think it's you he wants, so there must be a woman with you. And he discounts my rights." She paused. "They say Esclin Arros gave you a ring."

Viven grimaced. "Yes. In thanks for my playing, though I've paid him poorly for his generosity."

"Hardly your fault," Aelin said. "But I think—I heard the axial say that he might be able to use your tie to it."

That was hardly a surprise at this point but it was painful nonetheless. "My harp will not approve."

"That's the other piece." Aelin lowered her voice. "The axial wants to break the harpers' power—all of it, all of you. And the lord paramount thinks he can use you."

"More fool he," Viven said. "I have given my oaths, on my harp. The harp itself will destroy me if he tries to use me that way."

"He doesn't believe in harpers' law, or anything like it. Only the Blazing One." Aelin shook her head. "And sometimes I think not—" She stopped, closing her mouth tight over unspeakable heresy, and Viven nodded.

"Thank you for the warning."

Spring was creeping toward Riverholme, the latest snow melted in patches to show last season's grass, and snow-stars were blooming against the sunny side of the stable block. The air had changed, tasting of new growth. The horses could smell it, too, and raced each other in the muddy paddocks, belling challenges across the fence lines.

Leicinna had her eye on a couple of yearling colts, currently turned out with their age-mates in the lower western pasture under the watchful eye of an aged gelding. There were better-bred animals among the herd, but these she could afford, and from the look of them, they'd end up sturdy enough to carry an armored rider. Everything else was training, of course, and there were never any guarantees, but at worst they'd make pack horses. The only question was whether to offer for them now or wait for the horse-fair.

She leaned on the fence, watching a wiry little roan take off after a bigger bay, nipping at hip and flank until the gelding rumbled in to break it up. The roan trotted away shaking his head and the bay shook himself, then settled to tug at the winter grass. Beyond the paddock, the ground sloped down toward the Lammard where it curved sharply to the west, and the line of the road was dark against the fields. A rider was moving along it, the horse struggling through the mud just past the ford, and Leicinna eyed them warily. But if it was news, she would hear it soon enough. She turned back toward the stable.

Her page Fisk found her there, deep in conversation with the colts' breeder, and hovered apologetically in the doorway until Leicinna had to take notice.

"Not now, Fisk," she began, and the girl made a hasty bow.

"I'm sorry, Captain, but the rivermaster wants you."

That was not to be argued with. She made her apologies to the breeder, and hurried through the Garth and across the bridge into the city proper. Behind the towers the Falls were wreathed in ice, carved by wind and the currents into fantastic overhangs and cornices that showed blue and green at their heart. Neither the Falls nor the Lammard ever froze completely, the current was too fast for that, and the roar of water against stone was as loud as ever.

It was quieter in the inner halls, the shutters fastened against the draft. Leicinna presented herself at the door to the rivermaster's chamber and was waved through, Fisk determinedly at her heels. The room was crowded, most of her fellow mercenaries there ahead of her, along with the captains of Liulf's scouts and Liulf himself. She sketched a bow to the rivermaster and settled into a shadowed corner as the rivermaster turned his attention back to the room at large. She found herself between familiar figures and nodded a greeting. The taller man elbowed her companionably.

"Did you get those horses—?"

Someone shushed him and Leicinna rested her hip on the edge of a sturdy table. Liulf surveyed the room again. "A messenger arrived this morning with word that Rider companies have been seen in the Dancing Ground east of the Lammard and as far north as Twyford. They've retreated at the first sign of a counterattack, but there's no knowing what's happening to the south. The main army won't be able to leave Riverholme for another month at best, but I want to send out scouts now. And that's your job. I want you to leave in a week—sooner if you can—and strike south along the Lammard to Vassas, then fan out. I don't want you to bring the Riders to a battle—not unless you're certain you can win—just find where they're gathering and report back to me. Is that clear?"

Leicinna saw her own uncertainty mirrored in the others' faces. To leave this early in the season, before the horses were fully recovered from the winter, and while the ground and the grazing were both still poor—no wonder Liulf was telling them not to fight.

"Who's to go where?" one of the older captains asked, his voice carefully neutral.

"Gelern will be taking his scouts with you," Liulf said, "and will be in overall command. I'll let him settle that with each of you."

"If the ground is good enough to let us travel at all," someone said, and Liulf glared in that direction.

"It was good enough for the messenger to get to us, and will be better in a week's time. Though if anyone chooses not to go, they can leave my employ."

There was a little silence at that, and Gelern said, "I've some thoughts about where we should go, if you'd care to hear them." There was a murmur of agreement, the voices sounding happier this time, and Leicinna bent her attention to the task at hand.

They gathered that night in the back room of the Flying Hound, the tavern where Leicinna and most of her officers took their meals. Leicinna had paid for a good fire in the hearth and the better of the day's meals as well as several bottles of wine to soften the news. They ate quickly and in silence, emptying the first bowl of stew and leaving the first loaf only crumbs, and it was only when Finn, the junior of the group, began to carve the second loaf that Gimmell leaned back against the wall.

"So the rumor's true?"

There was no point in playing games. Leicinna nodded. "We're to leave by the end of the week. Gelern Sword-Hand is in overall command, but we'll split up once we're south of Vassas. We're to take the old cart-road east around the bend of the Lammard, then strike southeast toward the steadings by Mag Ausse."

Aylflet paused, pouring another cup of wine, and Nea said, "That's sending us into the thick of things."

"Gelern Sword-Hand thinks well of us," Leicinna said.

"I'm sure he does," Gimmell said, "but it doesn't hurt that we're hirelings, either."

"No," Leicinna agreed. "Though I will say he's taking his men straight south toward Nieve."

Gimmell grunted, not entirely appeased, and Finn said, "Do we know what the ground is like yet?"

"Drying south of us," Aylflet said. "Or so they're saying in the royal stables. I was over talking to a friend of mine who's a saddler, and he heard it from the groom who took care of the messenger's last horse. It's soggy from here to the Rocks of Dee, he doubted you could get even a light cart through, but passable south of the portage there. And better the further south you get, of course. But that all depends on the weather staying decent."

He looked at Finn as he spoke, and Leicinna said, "Well?"

Even in the relative shadow, she could see him blush. Weather sense was a chancy talent, a gift that most of its holders kept secret. "It's spring," he said. "The winds are steady from the west. We shouldn't see storms, but I can't promise no rain at all."

"Fair enough," Leicinna said, and glared at Gimmell when he would have pushed harder. "Aylflet. I know the horses aren't fit yet, but if we take the first week in easy stages, can we work them into shape that way?"

Aylflet wagged his head from side to side. "If we can take it easily. I'd heard the rivermaster was in a hurry."

"Gelern Sword-Hand's a sensible man," Nea said.

"I don't like it," Gimmell said. "Our horses are still

recovering because the rivermaster left us on patrol late last autumn. And now he wants to send us out early. He's using us to spring any traps the Riders have waiting, just like in the fall, and I for one haven't been paid well enough for that."

"Keep your voice down, for the dog's sake," Aylflet said.

Gimmell snorted. "As if every hireling company isn't having the same discussion."

"That may be so," Leicinna said, "but nonetheless discretion is a virtue."

"I've heard," Nea said cautiously, "that the rivermaster was willing for companies who didn't like the job to leave his service."

"That's not how I'd put it," Leicinna said. "Take the job or leave my service, that's what he meant."

"No 'no hard feelings' then," Finn said, with a wincing smile.

Leicinna shook her head. "No. In fact, I'd wager that he won't forget anyone who leaves him now."

Gimmell refilled his cup. "And what if he won't? There are others who'd hire us." And there it was, the thing she had been avoiding laid squarely on the table. She grimaced and heard Nea draw breath sharply, then subside. Aylflet broke a slice of bread in half, then in half again.

"And now is the time of year when we can name our terms." Gimmell passed the pitcher to Aylflet, who gave an ambiguous nod, neither thanks nor agreement.

"We'd have to leave as soon as we've given our notice," Leicinna said. "Or stable our horses—and us—at the regular rates, and we all know how outrageous they are."

"Might be worth it," Gimmell said. "Yes, it'd be a hard slog, but if we follow the Lammard south to Pardessen, we could cut straight across to the foothills, and meet Esclin when he leaves the Hundred Hills. The hill-folk always need horsemen."

"And use them even harder," Nea said.

"Yes, but not to spare their own." Gimmell downed the rest of his wine.

"That would be just as hard on the horses," Leicinna said, "maybe worse."

"The rivermaster does pay better than most," Finn said, his voice doubtful. "Better than Esclin, last I heard."

"And spends us like coin to save his own men," Gimmell said. "We saw that last year, and the year before—how many men did we lose?"

That struck home, Leicinna saw, and she laid her hand flat on the table. "Ten. More than I wanted—more than any of us planned. And the rivermaster lost plenty of his own. It was a hard year, hard fighting, and that's why we're being paid half again as much as last year. And before you say anything, Gimmell, Esclin won't match that."

"I don't like it," Gimmell said.

"You've made that clear." Leicinna reached for the pitcher herself, filled her own cup. "Are you serious, man? Do you want to leave the rivermaster's service?"

There was a sudden silence, broken only by the snapping of the fire in the hearth. "I don't want to leave the company," Gimmell said at last.

Leicinna nodded slowly. "And I don't want to lose you. But I think we should stay with the rivermaster. It's the same work as last year, at the same risk, and better pay—pay that we won't get elsewhere."

"Not even from the kyra?" Nea said timidly.

"They don't hire horsemen," Gimmell said. "Never more than a company, and they favor folk from the edges of the forest. They won't take us." He looked back at Leicinna. "I still think we should try Esclin."

"So you've said." Leicinna looked across the table. "Finn?"

The weather-wyrd shook his head. "Hold me excused."

"Doesn't work that way," Gimmell said, and Finn made a face.

"The money is better here, and we've served alongside these companies before. That counts for something."

Leicinna nodded. "Nea?"

"Gimmell's right about last year, we lost too many men.
I'd like to try the Hundred Hills."

"Even with a cut in pay?"

Nea nodded once. "Even so."

"Aylflet?"

He looked up from a trencher now strewn with crumbs
and bits of broken crust, his fingers still plucking at what was
left of the slice of bread. "I think it's going to be a hard year
whoever we serve, and the rivermaster pays the best. I say we
stay and do the job we're paid for."

Split, of course, Leicinna thought. She'd expected no less.
She heaved a sigh. "I say we stay. We're valued here, even if
we are asked to do more than we might elsewhere. We're paid
for the risks we run—every man killed was paid for, above our
pay."

There was another little silence, but easier this time, and
Gimmell nodded. "That's true enough."

"And she's the captain," Aylflet said softly. "Let's not
forget that."

"I don't," Gimmell said, with just enough of a smile that
Leicinna gave him a sharp look. But Gimmell had always
been loyal.

"That's settled, then," she said, and hoped it was true.

Spring had reached the lowest of the hills, and its breath
could be felt even on the slopes of Nen Elin, a softness in
the air and a new heat to the sun that set the snows melting
and water running in the carved channels. It poured off the
mountain in glittering streams by day, following the paths that
steered it to the Aurinand. The pools froze overnight still, but
the ice was too thin to bear even a bird's weight and cracked
and melted well before noon, while the water whispered in the
channels nightlong.

The stock was cleared from the lower halls though the
weather-wyrds kept an eye to the sun, and Esclin waded

ankle deep in mud with the rest of the men, seeing the horses settled in the summer barns while the horsemasters chose old favorites and new to begin their conditioning. They would be needed soon enough, when the year's dance began.

He should, he knew, consult the speaker. It was time to take the year's omens, with the new year approaching, yet he shied from it like a colt confronted with a blowing leaf. Tomorrow, he told himself, once, twice, five times, and each day found things that were more pressing.

On the last day of the old moon, she was waiting as he came in from the fields at dusk, muddy and sweating and content, one arm thrown across the horsemaster Denior's shoulders as he talked about the mares to be bred. She had put on a wreath of jet and silver flowers, bright against her black gown and hair. It was meant as a concession to the season, Esclin guessed, but made her look even more uncanny.

"Sire."

Her voice tolled like a bell and Esclin lifted his head, feeling the winter's chill strike his spine. "Speaker."

"You have not come to me."

There were a dozen excuses he could make and some of them would even be true, but he would not admit that weakness. "No."

"It is time, and past," she said. "I pray you, Sire, consider this your invitation."

Esclin nodded. "Tomorrow?"

She made a slow curtsey. "Tonight would be better. But as you please, Sire."

"Tonight, then," Esclin said, his voice grim, and moved on into the halls, all too aware of the whispers that trailed behind him.

"And that tale will spread from ground to top before morning," Kelleiden said afterward, while Esclin washed in a basin of lukewarm water because there was no time to visit the baths. "No good will come of it."

"Wait till morning," Maeslin Steward said. "It'll look better."

"I should have gone to her before," Esclin said, scrubbing his chest, and saw Maeslin and Kelleiden exchange nervous glances. "And, no, there was no real reason not to. Best we get it over with."

"The folk will call it an ill omen no matter what we do," Kelleiden said. "They will assume you had a reason not to ask."

"I know." Esclin took the shirt the page held out to him.

"If the omens are good," Maeslin began and fell silent, unable to convince even himself.

Esclin dressed for spring then, in defiance, fine linen and well-cut scarlet wool trimmed with golden braid, with a great river-ruby set in gold to clasp the neck of his gown. He chose gold rings as well, to complement skin already darkening with the sun, and a circlet of golden flowers that made his hair look like bleached bone. He took his place in the hall, watched the wine burnt in offering before him, and leaned back to let the pages serve the tables. He smiled and laughed and tasted nothing of the venison in its sauce or the sugared sweet that ended the meal.

Rota was nowhere in sight when he was finally able to leave the hall—he thought she had left before the meal began—and the fires were burning low in the braziers, the larger lamps already quenched for the night. He turned as though he was going to his own chamber, then sent his page ahead and took a side corridor. A shadow was waiting at the end, and he lifted his head.

"You don't have to come with me."

"I'll at least walk you to the stair," Kelleiden answered. He could not go further, any more than Rota could enter the forge, and Esclin sighed, slipping his arm through the other man's.

"I'm grateful."

They walked in silence: there was nothing to say, in truth, that they had not said in other years, nothing that could make the casting of the year's fortune any less of an ordeal. Esclin leaned against Kelleiden's shoulder, grateful for the warmth and solid muscle beneath the good wool gown. They stopped at the top of the stair that spiraled down into the dark, only a distant flare of witchlight to mark its ending and the passage beyond.

"Wait for me?" Esclin asked, and Kelleiden nodded.

"Of course."

Esclin squeezed his arm, mute thanks, and started down the spiral. This was the deepest point of the nenn, and the corridor that led away from its foot was the most inward-leading shaft, below even the Hidden River. Witchlight flickered in lamps at the entrance to the shrine and he walked toward them, his feet quiet on the stone. The doors were open, waiting, and he straightened his spine as he stepped between them, each one carved with a frieze of dancing skeletons and somber maidens. Rota's servant curtsied and swung them shut one by one behind him.

Esclin looked around the dimly-lit chamber, the beehive roof vanishing into darkness. There were braziers at the cardinal points, flames burning low, and a cluster of witchfire lamps above the offering table. Beyond it the door gaped open to the sanctum, a mirror of polished obsidian hanging on the wall beside it, and the air smelled of salt and grains-of-amber. He took a breath, the sharp-sweet smoke heavy on his tongue, and Rota emerged from the shadows, her skirts rustling softly against the stones like the sound of leaves in autumn. Here in her own place, her hair was uncovered and unbound, falling in midnight waves nearly to her knees, and there were a dozen or more tiny skulls strung in its depths, pale in the witchlight.

"Esclin." She came around the offering table to take his hands in hers, and he bowed his head over their linked fingers.

"Rota."

His hands were cold, he knew, but for once she made no encouraging comment and fear shivered through him. This was why he hadn't come before now, and they both knew it; that she offered no comfort meant that there was none to give.

"Are you ready?"

"As I ever am," Esclin answered, his smile wry.

She released his hands. "Then you know what you must do."

Esclin nodded and lifted the coronet from his head. The girl came forward with a tray and he set it there, added the great brooch and his rings, and finally the small cast-silver ring of Arra's water horse that he wore beneath his shirt. The girl set the tray aside and took his overgown as well, folding it neatly over her arm. Esclin loosed the strip of silk that covered his blind eye and put that aside with the rest, spreading his hands to show them and him unadorned. In the dark mirror the shadows turned his face to a skull: no good omen there.

"Enter," Rota said, and gestured for him to precede her through the gaping door.

Esclin took three steps into the narrow space, the ground rough beneath his feet, and the last of the light vanished as she closed the door behind them both. The darkness was absolute, almost thick enough to feel between his fingers; he heard the whisper of her gown, then the click of flint and steel. The spark struck prepared tinder, blossomed into a flame, leapt at her word to the lamp that stood waiting and from there to the crystals that lined the sanctum's walls. They sparked and shimmered, some as large as his fist that showed a light like a star in their center, a thousand more that carried a pinpoint of flame, set in a bed of crystals small as grains of sand that flickered and winked in the uneven light. He blinked, dazzled, and went to one knee as the rite required. He could feel more crystals even through the fabric of gown and hose.

The air was heavy with light, with unspoken words, and Rota lifted the fire from the lamp and released it into the chamber. It swelled, split, vanished, and abruptly the crystals flared to life, a rainbow fire that filled the sanctum like water. Rota spoke again, and the flecks of light began to move, freeing themselves from the wall to swirl in the air around them. Esclin looked up to see her wreathed in light, shards of fire and sunlight tangling in her hair. The fragments of light began to move, to dance, weaving patterns out of the dark, but there was nothing he could read. Rota's face was still, grave as stone, only her eyes moving as she watched the play of light and shade.

And then it was finished, the light returned to the crystals and the lamp, and Rota drew a long breath that rattled in her lungs. Esclin pushed himself to his feet, wanting to meet this standing.

"Well?"

Rota pushed her hair back with both hands, the skulls clattering. The light wavered, the crystals winking in and out like stars on a windy night. "I can't—sacrifice, I saw. And war, of course, but that's the spring. The rest—I can't tell."

Can't or won't? But that was entirely unfair, when he knew Rota was nothing but honest in her vocation, and he said instead, "Sacrifice. Mine? My death?"

"I can't tell. Yours, yes, I read for you and from you, but it's not death I see." She shook her head. "It's possible, of course—you're the arros. But the word I have is sacrifice."

Esclin drew a long breath as she turned to open the door. He had known this might come—would come someday, one way or another—but he had hoped for more time. As did everyone. Perhaps it wasn't death she saw, but he could not assume less.

He followed her into the outer chamber, let the girl help him back into his gown and resumed his jewelry, though he left two of the rings on the offering table. He was chilled to the bone, though it was no colder here than anywhere else in the nenn, but he managed to make his farewells and climb the long stairs without giving in to the shudders that waited to seize him.

Kelleiden was waiting at the top of the stairs as promised, wrapped in his cloak and solid as the stones around him. He said nothing, merely opened the cloak in mute offer, and in the dim hall with no one watching Esclin stepped into its shelter, letting the smith fold its warmth around them both. He rested his face against the smith's hair, smelling smoke and the amber incense still clinging to his clothes, wrapped his arms tight around Kelleiden's body and let himself be held in turn. He was shivering now and knew Kelleiden felt it, but the smith said nothing, as though only his warm strength could matter.

After a bit, the shivering eased and he straightened, met Kelleiden's eyes with what he hoped was a passable smile. "I want a bath."

"That bad?" But of course Kelleiden knew him too well, and the words were far from joking.

"I'm cold," Esclin said and unwound himself from the cloak. "Come on."

He led the way through the maze of lesser corridors, brought them out at last on the same level but further north, on the nenn's eastern edge. The bath was empty at this hour, the attendants long abed, but it was the work of moments to light the lamps and the brazier and heave back the wooden lid covering the hottest pool. Esclin stripped without ceremony and slid into the steaming water with a hiss of relief. That was better, heat coiling around him from toes to chin, and he looked up to see Kelleiden still clothed.

"Join me, why don't you?"

"I'm not cold." Kelleiden seated himself on the edge of the pool. "Will you tell me what she said?"

Esclin ducked his head under the water, came up spluttering and wiped his hand down his face. "War is coming—"

"That we knew."

"And the word she had for me was 'sacrifice'." Esclin gave a twisted smile. "You may have wasted your star-iron, my heart."

"If she'd seen your death, she would have said so." Kelleiden trailed his fingers in the water.

"Certainly. But she wasn't sure it wasn't."

"Sacrifice doesn't necessarily mean your death."

"I am the arros," Esclin said. It was the oldest bargain: the life of the ruler was the life of the realm, and though no one whispered any longer that his blind eye would maim the Hundred Hills, the fundamental truth remained. If his death could save the Hundred Hills, it was his to pay.

"No one denies that," Kelleiden said. "But I repeat, your death isn't the only possible sacrifice."

Esclin froze. He hadn't thought of that, so certain had he been that his own death was the answer to his own vague unease. "Not Talan. Arra's Horse, I didn't even ask..."

"If she had seen Talan's death, she would have said so," Kelleiden said. "You know that, too."

"I'm not willing to lose my daughter—"

"Ask her tomorrow," Kelleiden said. "The reading was for you—"

"For the realm," Esclin said. "What greater sacrifice than the thegen?"

"I think she would have spoken more clearly if it were true," Kelleiden said.

He was right, of course. Esclin took another breath, the rock-scented steam warm in his chest. Rota had not seen clearly, she had said as much herself. It might be Talan's death she sensed, or something else, but neither one was yet a fixed point in the river that was the future. He tipped his head back, letting his hair float loose around him, water filling his ears until he could hear nothing but his own pulse. He had to take Talan with him in the spring. If he were to die in battle, she would need to be there; he could not change that, though he would do what he could to keep her safe, and would contrive his death before hers if it came to that. There was always something more to be done. He pushed himself up in the water, shaking his head so that Kelleiden leaned back out of range.

"If you're warm enough, then—"

He extended a hand and Esclin took it, levering himself out of the pool. "Let's to bed."

It was generally five days' march from Nen Elin to Nen Salter down the vale of the Aurinand and over the Cattrick Pass into Salter Vale, in high summer and good weather. At this time of year, the river was still swollen from the spring thaws and the ground was soft in places, but the snow had been off the pass for weeks and it only took three days more to bring Nen Elin's levies to the doors of Nen Salter. Esclin had sent messengers ahead, and Huwar Ellemas mustered his own men and the men of Nen Brethil to welcome them to the plain outside Nen Salter's gates. There was plenty of room to make camp, and good water from the Verwynd at the edge of the broad plain; in better years Nen Salter had hosted the midsummer fair, and the ditches and lines of the fairground were still visible beneath the spring grass. Huwar had given his stewards strict orders to keep the men of Nen Elin separated from Nen Brethil's levies, and he was pleased to see them maintaining the division.

The arros's party came on, Esclin's pale hair brilliant in the sun, the banner of his house streaming out even in the gentle breeze. It was made of Westwood silk, a gift from the kyra, and against the scarlet background the white and gold water horse seemed to dance and plunge. He could see Kelleiden Smith among the party—the smith usually came to the muster before returning to Nen Elin as its regent—but he had not expected to see the thegen riding with him. She had her companions with her, half a dozen favorites, and Huwar glanced at his son, waiting quietly at his side. Perrin gave the ghost of a nod: no need, then, to say aloud what they both were thinking. The girl needed to choose a father for her children, and soon, if she was going to ride in her father's train. Even if there was no wedding, both Perrin and Nen Salter would benefit from such a connection.

And that was an old-fashioned thought, these days. More and more people struck a bargain across the anvil, or spoke vows before the Blazing One, rather than mate as they pleased until they found a worthwhile spouse. But Nen Elin was old-fashioned, even more so than Nen Salter; and in any case, he doubted the girl was the sort to marry. She was like her father: she'd do her duty but keep her companions closer than whoever she chose to father her children.

Esclin pulled his horse to a stop and the others copied him, Huwar's pages running to hold the horses for the arros and his party. Esclin swung himself down off a neat dapple-gray gelding that made Huwar momentarily sigh with envy, and came forward with his hands outstretched in greeting. Huwar stepped forward to meet him, hand to heart, and then took both the arros's hands in his. "Welcome, Sire."

"Thank you." The arros was, as always, splendid, despite days on the road. He was only in half-armor, a leather corselet instead of the mail he would wear in battle, but it was covered with a pattern of gilded leaves and vines. Beneath it, Esclin's tunic was a scarlet that matched his banner, and his pale hair was confined by a coronet that also somehow held the scarlet patch that covered his missing eye. "I'm pleased to see you can accommodate us so easily."

That was Nen Brethil's problem and responsibility, and Huwar refused to take that bait. "We had good word of your coming. Will you come within? My people have rooms and the baths prepared."

"I'll take your baths gladly," Esclin answered, "but I'll sleep with my people. Though I'm sure your beds would be more comfortable."

Huwar bowed again. "As my liege pleases."

They did not get down to business until they reached the baths. Huwar was proud of the chamber, built with the nenn and enlarged by his grandmother to expand a natural hot spring. The walls were lined with fluted columns that sparkled in the witchlights—the carvers taking full advantage of the natural stone—and if they had to light a boiler to get all the pools hot at once, no one could fault the drains that kept the water sweet. He claimed the first pool for the arros and lowered himself into the steaming water.

The others joined him, Esclin as elegant naked as he was clothed, only the missing eye to mar his beauty, Kelleiden Smith dark beside him. For a man naturally light of build, the forge had given him heavy muscles; Huwar could see why Esclin kept him as a bodyguard as well as a lover. They were joined by Wellan Prosseros of Nen Brethil and his cousin Reilan Nardenos, both of them looking faintly uncomfortable. Esclin's thegen and her companions had claimed the next-best pool, laughing and splashing, and Perrin and several of his age-mates had joined them. Reilan blushed and looked firmly at the wall.

Huwar waved for the servants to serve the wine, feeling old again. Lately the women had taken to bathing all together in the slack of the afternoon, leaving mornings and evenings for the men of the nenn. He had missed the more boisterous gatherings.

Esclin tipped his head back, submerging himself until only his face was above the water, then straightened, shaking back his hair. "Nen Brethil's levy looks light this year."

And that was straight to the point. Huwar took a gulp of his wine to keep himself from speaking: this was Wellan's problem, not his.

Wellan rested one hand gingerly on the edge of the pool. "It is, Sire. I left a good third of my men behind in Nen Brethil, and gave my kindred nenns leave to do the same."

"And why would you do such a thing?" Esclin's voice was mild enough, but no one was deceived.

"We've been beset all winter," Wellan answered, "raids along the valley and even into the lower nenns. I would not leave my people unprotected."

"And yet you sent no word," Esclin said.

"It was winter, Sire. I didn't want to risk a man's life trying to cross the passes."

Esclin's mouth tightened—messengers had made winter journeys between Nen Brethil and Nen Elin before—but he said only, "Tell me about these raids."

Wellan launched into the story, sketching the details with dripping hands. Huwar had heard it several times already and let the words wash over him, watching Esclin instead. The raids were unusual only in that they had happened outside the common season; otherwise, they were all too familiar. Riders had swept up the valley of Fallas, burning out a few of the smaller steadings, driving people to take refuge within the palisades of their overlord's fortified manors. The raiders had swept like a tide up to the doors of Nen Alta, Nen Faal and Nen Buin, disrupting the winter's work and penning their people within the hills for a month or so. Then they'd vanished again, presumably back to their footholds in Nieve and Reyscant.

Huwar had faced a few raids himself and chosen not to stint the muster: better to meet the Riders on the Dancing Ground than let them come into the valleys where they could do harm to more than the outlying fields. Though admittedly his lands lay further north, and he had not had to meet as many attacks as Wellan's folk. Esclin listened impassively, apparently relaxed in the steaming water, and when Wellan at last ground to a halt, said merely, "And who have you left as regent in your stead?"

For the first time Wellan faltered. "My cousin Aillard."

This time Esclin did raise an eyebrow. And well he might, Huwar thought. Aillard was devoted to the Blazing One, and only just observed the letter of Esclin's prohibitions. Reilan straightened, scowling.

"Aillard is a good man, and a good captain."

Wellan reached under the water to poke the younger man's ribs and Reilan subsided. Esclin's eyebrows rose even higher and Kelleiden stirred uneasily; but when the arros spoke, his tone was still mild. "Aillard Yrdanas is a good fighter, and an honest man. But I needed your levies here."

Wellan dipped his head. "I have an obligation to my people, Sire."

"Besides," Reilan added, oblivious to Wellan's frown, "if the Riders attack south of us, there will be fewer of them here. It shouldn't really matter."

"Unless, of course, the Riders attacked the valley nenns to force you to leave troops behind, and then come on full strength," Esclin said, his tone honey-sweet. The boy walked into that, Huwar thought, and scooped water over his face. Esclin waited a moment longer, letting the lesson sink home, then shrugged one shoulder. "Well. Too late to mend it now. I trust you've brought me your best, Wellan?"

"I have, Sire," Nen Brethil's lord answered, sounding relieved, and Esclin nodded.

"We'll leave you then. I'd like to rest before the night's feast." He heaved himself out of the pool in one graceful movement, Kelleiden following more slowly, and in the next pool Talan moved to copy him.

Esclin waved her back. "No need, enjoy yourselves a little longer." His eye slid sideways. "Perhaps Reilan might care to join them."

Reilan blushed purple, and anger flickered across Wellan's face before he mastered his expression. "My cousin does not aspire to such favors."

"That would be the thegen's business," Esclin answered, "but as you will."

He turned away, not bothering to reach for a shirt until Kelleiden found one for him, and Huwar sank back in the water. It had been a deft rebuke, but not, perhaps, a wise one. He glanced sideways at Wellan, who was wringing water from the ends of his hair.

"You made yourself very plain, my lord."

Wellan scowled, winding his thick hair into a knot that would keep most of it out of the water. "We do not follow the old ways. Should the thegen choose to wed decently, that would be another matter."

From Reilan's momentary look of horror, Huwar doubted Nen Brethil's lord would get much cooperation for a marriage, either. He couldn't let the insult stand, though, intended or not, and lifted his own eyebrows in deliberate imitation of the arros. "We keep both customs here."

Wellan had the grace to look abashed, waving his hands as though he would chase away the words. "I know. And no harm was meant. It's just Esclin—"

"The arros has his reasons," Huwar said, and climbed ponderously out of the pool.

The muster had filled the nenn to bursting, to the point where even Huwar's wife Naïs Merinas had given up her rooms to Wellan and his household, and the least important members of the household were sleeping in the stables and in temporary shelters on the hill above the nenn. It was not ideal but at least the weather was fair, the spring rains past for now, though it made one wish for the days when the stone-smiths had found it easy to carve new sections from the living rock. But the constant wars had ended that, and there was no point repining.

Huwar studied his reflection in the brass mirror Naïs had brought from her rooms. He looked well enough, his chin shaved clean, his graying hair hanging loose in waves, and behind him Naïs held up his best gown. It was green Westwood brocade trimmed in summer-dark fur and the fabric had come as part of Naïs's wedding-gift, a richer thing than he had ever bothered to own before this marriage. He let her lift it onto his shoulders and twitch the long sweep of fabric into shape, and smiled at her pointed face reflected in the mirror. She was his second wife, mother of a sturdy girl ten years younger than Perrin—and just quickened with another, all the gods be kind—and he was still amazed to have been lucky twice.

Naïs smiled back, but turned him briskly to face her. "You must wear your jewels."

"They don't become me," Huwar said. "And anyway, who will notice, with Esclin there?"

"All the more reason to wear them," Naïs answered, and beckoned to the maid who stood ready with the casket. "Beauty is all very well, but gold lasts longer. And speaks louder."

Naïs was one of the sister-daughters of Nen Buin which was noted for its gold streams, and Huwar smiled as she fastened the first of the great brooches that closed the neck of the gown. "I prefer the old ways."

"Oh, do you?" Naïs quirked a smile of her own, looking up under her lashes. She was a brown woman, small and brisk as a sparrow, still in her peach-colored undergown while she bustled about the last preparations. "Perhaps I would, too! He's a pretty man, the arros is."

In generations past, it had been the arros's right to invite the senior consort of his client nenns to his bed, and Huwar snorted. "Much good it would do you."

"There's that." She reached to set the coronet, a broad band of gold studded with pale salt-tears and a single carved onyx at the center. "I expect he'd rather have you."

"True enough." Huwar slanted a glance at her as he stooped to the mirror. "Perhaps I should offer—they're old-fashioned in Nen Elin."

She grinned. "Not that old-fashioned, thank the gods. And I imagine the master smith would have a word to say to that."

"I can't imagine he's a jealous man," Huwar began and saw the door open behind him, admitting his steward. "Well?"

"Your pardon, Lord, but the arros would like a word."

And that was a command, no matter how nicely phrased it was. Huwar allowed himself one quick exchange of glances with Naïs and then she turned to curtsey to the man who appeared behind the steward. Esclin had brought the smith with him as well, dark and silent as a shadow.

"Of course, Sire," Huwar said, with a bow of his own. Naïs motioned for the maid to leave them and turned to go herself, but her expression was faintly wary.

"Stay, please," Esclin said. "I expect this will concern you as well." The maids scurried out, the steward following, and Kelleiden Smith shut the door behind them.

"How may we serve you?" Huwar asked.

Esclin moved his hand, and a sheathed sword seemed to materialize out of thin air—he had been carrying it concealed in illusion the way another man would hide it in the folds of his cloak. Huwar's breath caught in spite of himself and Naïs took one step forward, as though she would put herself between them, before she mastered herself. Esclin gave a wry smile.

"Forgive me. That was ill-done."

He offered it to Huwar, who took it warily. The sheath was plain black leather, though the fittings were of silver, and the hilt was unmistakably of Kelleiden's make. He looked back at Esclin to see the arros smiling.

"Draw it."

For an instant, Huwar held his hand—to draw steel in front of the arros was always a chancy business, and it was not beyond Esclin's imagining to trap a man that way. But he had no designs on the throne nor had ever acted against any ruler, and he slid the blade halfway from the sheath. The steel gleamed in the witchlight and lines of brighter silver traced a shape along the unsharpened edge, as fluid and stylized as Riverholme calligraphy. And then he realized what he was seeing—Arra's horse, a water horse reaching for its prey—and looked up sharply.

"This is the work of Kelleiden's winter," Esclin said.

"A royal sword." Huwar breathed the words with respect. That was the only thing that had ever been lacking from Esclin's reign, since the day he'd come riding east with the Westwood levies at his back and he and his uncle had crushed the Riders between them. Audan had died in the battle— luckily for Esclin, a voice whispered at the back of his mind— and Esclin had claimed his rule without dissent, but he had not had this final symbol of his rule. "Has it a name?"

"Arros," Esclin said, and the silver lines seemed to shimmer at his voice. He held out his hand, and Huwar sheathed the sword, handing it back with the sketch of a bow. Esclin made the sword vanish again, and said, "I intend to display it tonight at the feast and wanted to warn you first— since I would be bringing it into your hall."

"The nenns will be very glad to see it," Huwar said.

"I sincerely hope so," Esclin answered. "And to that end, I want to make this as public and as potent as possible. Will you help me?"

"Of course, Sire," Huwar said, and was not surprised to find he meant it.

He was still shaking his head as he and Naïs made their way to the hall, impressed again by the simple theatrics of it. Nen Salter's Long Hall was built out from the main body of the hill, was more frequently used as a market and a meeting ground rather than a banqueting hall, but the stewards' folk had done their work well. The walls were hung with banners, wood and carved stone alike hiding the seam where the two met, and there were enough tables laid and dressed to seat most of the army. The kitchen promised that everyone would be well fed, though the lower tables would eat brown bread and barley stew, and their meat course would be stretched out with pies rather than the roasted meats served at the high table. But there would be enough, and wine to spare, even if it came close to emptying his cellars, and the people of the lesser nenns would see what Nen Salter could do.

"We've borrowed pages from among the other nenns' people," the chief steward was saying, "and between them and the other lords' stewards that I've pressed to our service, it should all go smoothly enough. They'll wait on their own— except the arros's steward, he's to serve the women's table." That was another new custom and one that Huwar didn't like, seating the wives of the nenn apart from their husbands, but it was becoming the expected thing.

"And there's a question," Naïs said. "Where do we put Talan? She's the thegen, I assume she'll preside at the heirs' table."

"Yes," Huwar said firmly. "And any woman who holds title in her own right will sit with me. You've seen to that?"

"Yes, my lord."

"There's only Nen Arranme," Naïs said, visibly considering, "and Hulda Ingenas. And none too many wives either, for my table. But that should make things easier."

Huwar crossed his fingers in propitiation, hiding his hand in the folds of his gown. No one needed to see him invoke the oldest gods, or notice that he was strung as taut as the youngest page. "As long as this with Esclin goes well," he muttered, and saw Naïs nod.

He met the arros with Naïs on his arm, at the center of the hall where in winter a fire normally burned in the shallow pit, the smoke curling up to exit through the openings to either side of the roof-tree. For the banquet, the ashes had been raked away and the pit covered with boards and a well-worn carpet painted with stars. Esclin had dressed for the occasion, brilliant in scarlet and gold, and Huwar was glad he'd worn all his jewels. He could not match Esclin's looks, but he could flaunt his own wealth with equal pride.

"Sire," he said and dipped his head, Naïs curtseying at his side.

"Nen Salter," Esclin answered, holding out both hands in greeting, rings flashing in the witchlight that hovered along the rooftree. "Consort." Huwar took Esclin's right and Naïs his left, and a smile flickered across Esclin's face before he released them. "I thank you once again for hosting the muster. Your hospitality outdoes itself every year."

"Thank you, Sire." Normally at this point he would turn to escort Esclin to the high table; but this year Kelleiden was at the head of Esclin's train, a long and shapeless bundle in his arms.

"As we go once again to the Dancing Ground," Esclin said, pitching his voice to carry to the edges of the hall, "I bring the fruits of my smith's labors as a pledge of our success."

Kelleiden stepped forward and Esclin took the bundle from him, the illusion falling from it so that the unsheathed blade shone suddenly vivid in the shadowed hall. He lifted it, drawing the witchlight to its tip so that it ran glittering along the blade's edge, the water horse dancing for an instant against the steel and then lifting from it, a shape of pure cold silver sharp against the vaulting, neck arched and teeth bared, half stallion and half serpent. It reared up, balancing on its coiled tail, floating above the arros like a living banner. Below it, the sword shone like silver, gleaming with its own light.

"A royal sword is born," Esclin said, into the crowd's awed murmur. "Arros, patron of my house and kin, born this year to bring us victory."

Huwar went to one knee, the water horse twisting above him, flecks of silver light reflecting across the hall. Naïs knelt with him, though neither obeisance had been in the plan. Out of the corners of his eyes, he could see the rest of the crowd going to its knees, the silver light dancing over them like moonlight on dark water. "We will follow the arros, on our honor!"

He heard the same promise echo from the crowd, a dozen different words and formulations, but all the same intent. Esclin heard it, too, and his face might have relaxed a fraction. He extended a hand to raise Huwar to his feet. "My thanks—my thanks to all of you. Though I had expected nothing less."

Kelleiden handed him the sword's sheath and Esclin slid it home, quenching the silver light. Above him, the water horse wavered and began to fade. "And now," Esclin said, "let us celebrate, both the sword and the dance to come."

CHAPTER EIGHT

When the sweets were reduced to crumbs and the last toasts were drunk, Esclin made his way with Kelleiden back to his own tent, the sword worn openly at his waist. When the flaps closed behind them, he waved a hand to conjure witchlight into the central lamp, then dropped into his traveling chair. It had been a long week's ride from Nen Elin, and he was only just getting back a horseman's muscles after a winter afoot.

"That went reasonably well," Kelleiden said and poured them each a cup of wine.

"They like your sword," Esclin said with a smile, and accepted the cup with a nod of thanks.

"I won't say I told you so."

Esclin lifted an eyebrow but refused the bait. "Nen Brethil may pose a problem."

Kelleiden snorted. "That's one word for it."

"I could certainly have used the men." Esclin leaned back in the chair, stretching legs and spine. "But I can't entirely blame him."

"Then the Riders did cause him trouble?"

Esclin nodded. "I spoke with Nen Alta and Nen Faal, and Nen Buin's marshal. They had raids until the winter set hard and had a lean time of it."

One of the pages emerged from behind the curtains that hid the small bedchamber, carrying a pitcher; Esclin could hear the other boy moving about, opening the clothes chest, and put his wine aside to let Kelleiden take his belt and his gown. He turned back the sleeves of his shirt as the first page filled the standing basin and splashed the cool water on his face. He had not drunk enough to make him tipsy, but between the wine and the day's ride fatigue tugged at him. He would be glad even of the camp-bed tonight.

There was a noise from within, the page's voice raised in pained exclamation, and Esclin lifted his head. The other page looked up sharply as the curtain was flung back, the first boy staggering out, his hand closed tight around his wrist. His little finger and the side of his hand were already swelling, and there was a bright dot of blood at the base of the finger.

Esclin caught him as he staggered, lowered him into the only chair. "Fetch the surgeon," he said to the remaining page, standing open-mouthed with fear, and the boy shook himself and darted away.

"Not snakebite," Kelleiden said, going to one knee beside the chair. "It's too early for snakes." Even so, he pulled off his belt and drew it tight around the page's arm above the elbow.

"Jollan." Esclin turned the boy's hand palm upward. Already his other fingers were swelling, fat as sausages, and the skin at the base of the little finger was purple with blood. Esclin had to look closely to see the tiny cut, barely a pinprick, still oozing blood in the center of the swelling. "Jollan, what happened?"

The boy tried to bend his fingers, and flinched, tears starting from the corners of his eyes. "I'm not—I was laying out your nightshirt, Sire, and I had to move your dagger. When I took it in my hand, something stuck me."

Esclin met Kelleiden's eyes and the smith said, "Not you. I'll fetch it."

"Carefully," Esclin said, and looked back at the boy. "You're sure it was the knife?"

Jollan nodded. "In the hilt—the grip, by the pommel. I was trying to flip it..."

Cat Meirin's trick, that all the pages were trying to learn. Esclin took a breath and wound the belt tighter. "Brandy, Kelleiden."

The smith emerged from the bedchamber carrying both the flask and the dagger, held carefully by the blade. Esclin took the flask and poured a healthy cupful over the wound, then handed the flask to the boy. "Drink."

He could hear running footsteps outside the tent and raised voices in the distance, and a moment later the tent flap was flung back. "Sire, you sent for me?" Avlen Saros, the royal surgeon, blinked once as he took in the scene, then moved to the boy's side.

"Poison," Esclin said.

"Snakebite?" Avlen checked the tourniquet, then turned his attention to the boy's hand. He flexed the swelling fingers, releasing a sudden stream of watery blood, and Jollan whimpered. Esclin rested a hand on his hair, wishing he could do more.

"He said the dagger—"

"Not snakebite," Kelleiden said. He held out the dagger, grasping it by blade and pommel. "See there, where the wire holds the leather to the grip? I'd say that's what stuck him."

More people were crowding into the tent, Ilgae Marshal at their head, but Esclin ignored them for the moment. "Avlen?"

"If I don't know what the poison is," Avlen began, and shook his head. He drew a small knife from his sleeve and slashed the swollen skin. Blood spurted from the new wound and Jollan cried out again.

"Careful, damn you," Ilgae said. "Beware poison, man."

Avlen ignored her, turning Jollan's arm so that the blood ran down into the dirt of the floor. "A poison that can be placed on a pin or the point of a blade—cattepas, maybe? Though it would blacken metal."

"The wire's uncolored," Kelleiden said.

"Nacre," Avlen said, and fumbled one-handed in his bag. Kelleiden took it from him, and came up with a polished disk set in silver. The surgeon pressed it against the bleeding wound, eyes closing as he murmured a healing verse.

Esclin saw Huwar Ellemas shouldering his way into the tent, flushed with wine but still alert. "Ilgae, send someone to warn the thegen." He rested his hand gently on the boy's forehead, feeling the skin already hot and damp with fever-sweat: getting worse, in spite of Avlen's efforts. This was how the girl Meleas had died—except there had been no swelling, no wound. "Kelleiden. Can you do anything?"

The smith shook his head. "I have no art for this."

Avlen squeezed the boy's hand again, wringing another cry from him, and Huwar said, "Sire. The wheelmen have the gift of healing. Let me send for one."

Esclin glared, the automatic refusal trembling on his lips, and Avlen said quietly, "Sire, there's nothing I can do."

He couldn't let the boy die, not for pride and certainly not for politics. Esclin said, "Send." He couldn't bring himself to say he'd welcome it, but that was concession enough. There was movement in the crowd as messengers hurried away, and he looked back at Jollan. The boy's breath was coming short and fast, his eyes closed as though he was slipping out of consciousness. Avlen leaned forward to lift one eyelid, and sat back on his heels, shaking his head.

"More brandy." Esclin handed him the flask, and the surgeon poured another dose of the liquor over the boy's bleeding hand.

"Should we move him?"

Avlen shook his head. "We want to keep the wound below his heart."

He was slipping away, Esclin thought, watching the boy's eyelids flutter as Avlen cut into the wound again. Blood ran over the nacre disk, dimming its polish, but Jollan didn't move. Whatever the poison was, it was quick and deadly.

There was a flurry of movement at the entrance to the tent, and Huwar exclaimed, "Let the man through, damn you."

A slight figure shoved his way past the people at the front, a mouse-haired man in an ankle-length gown thrown hastily over shirt and bare legs. He carried a leather satchel, and as he stooped to touch Jollan's forehead, Esclin realized he was not as young as he looked.

"The poison was on the dagger," Kelleiden said.

"Where?"

"The wire, here." Kelleiden pointed, not touching, and the wheelman grimaced.

"Bynar, then, most likely. Oil of Inheritance, they call it in Manan." He went to one knee beside the chair and Avlen scooted back out of his way, scrubbing bloodied hands on the skirt of his own gown. "Ah, that's ugly."

"Can you help him?" Esclin asked, and because he regretted the admission added, "What's your name?"

"Brelin, my lord." The wheelman was busy with something in his bag. "And I'll do what I can. It was well you tied his arm, that will help."

Esclin brushed sweat-soaked hair off Jollan's forehead, wishing Rota was here. His greatest skill was illusion, light and shadow, nothing that would help here, and neither water nor the smith's fires were of any more use. At his feet, Brelin pressed more blood from the purple flesh and shook his head. "Bleeding was a good thought, but the poison's traveled too far. We need holyfire now."

He reached into his bag again and produced a black stick roughly the size of a man's thumb. It looked like coal, or charcoal, dull in the witchlight. "Is there flame?"

Kelleiden turned to the brazier, ready to stir the coals to life, then stopped, frowning. "Not of your kind."

"Too late to worry about that," Brelin answered, and Kelleiden murmured something that made the flames spring up. Brelin thrust the stick into the fire, whispering a verse, and a blue flame danced for a moment at its end. Brelin blew on it, quenching the flame but waking a cold blue ember, and looked up at Esclin. "Hold him. This will hurt."

Esclin held Jollan's shoulders, pulling him back against the chair, and Avlen pinned the boy's arm. Brelin nodded his thanks, lips moving in another whispered verse, and pressed the glowing stone hard against the wound. Jollan bucked and cried out, the tears that streamed down his cheeks tinged with blood, and Brelin ground the blue ember against his hand. Jollan screamed again, and a thread of blue light worked its way up his arm, following the course of the poison in his veins. Esclin fought to hold him still, watching the light crawl further, until at last it flashed just below the tourniquet and disappeared again. Jollan was still moaning, tossing his head from side to side, but the tears no longer ran pink on his pale skin. Brelin sat back on his heels and cupped his hand over the stick's end, extinguishing its glow.

"He should do now, my lord. But it'll take some days for him to recover. Perhaps a week. He's lost a lot of blood."

"He can go back with you," Esclin said to Kelleiden, and the smith nodded. "Put him in my bed for the night. If you'll stay with him, Brelin?"

The wheelman nodded, rising slowly to his feet, and Avlen and the other page lifted Jollan between them and carried him gently into the other room. Esclin was very aware of the people watching from the doorway, and carefully poured a third cup of wine, holding it out to Brelin. "Thank you. The boy owes you his life."

"Not me, Lord, but the Blazing One." Brelin drained half the cup in one swallow, but shook his head when Esclin offered more.

"Through your hands." Esclin had learned enough of the theology to know that was unobjectionable, and Brelin dipped his head. "I don't know this poison, but you said it's known in Manan?"

"It comes from there." Brelin took a smaller swallow of his wine. "It's distilled to an oil that's as venomous as a snake's bite. It only takes a little in the blood, in a scratch, or in the eye or ear, to kill a man. It's made from a white berry, though I've never seen the plant. I don't believe it grows here."

"Though it could be grown here, I imagine," Kelleiden said.

Brelin shrugged. "Possibly? I'm not really an herbalist, Lord."

"But a healer of skill," Esclin said. By rights, he should give the man a ring off his finger or some other jewel of worth, but his skin crawled at the idea of giving away something so intimately linked. The wheelmen had enough tokens to track him by. He turned instead to his strongbox and took from it one of the pierced gold armlets Kelleiden had made for the purpose, heavy enough to be a worthy reward but nothing that he had worn or cared about. He held it out to the wheelman, saying, "And I am grateful."

Brelin blinked sleepily at it and Esclin saw the moment when he would have refused before he realized he had left it too long. "Thank you, Lord," he said, meekly enough, and drained his cup. "And if you'll excuse me, I'll sit up with the boy—what's his name?"

"Jollan." Esclin saw Brelin repeat the name, then he ducked into the inner room. Esclin looked back at the people still crowding around the door, and lifted an eyebrow. That was warning enough for some of the ones at the back to begin to slip away, but Ilgae Marshal stood her ground, Huwar at her side.

"We should search the camp," Ilgae said, and Huwar bristled.

"And the nenn. I won't have my people suspected."

"To what end?" Esclin didn't bother hiding his impatience. "There are almost a thousand people here, between the army and Nen Salter's folk, and even if whoever did this is among them still, they'll have had hours to lose their supply of the poison. Or place it somewhere where it will cast suspicion. Where's Talan?"

"Here, Father." She stepped around Huwar, still dressed for the feast, Cat Meirin watchful at her side. "I've sent Estor to examine all our weapons, just to be on the safe side."

"Good." Esclin nodded, a weight lifting from his heart.

"We can't just do nothing," Ilgae said.

"See if anyone saw anything," Kelleiden suggested. "Someone who didn't belong in the arros's tent—I'd like to know who came here today, myself."

"I can find that out," Talan said. Her company served as the arros's pages while they were on the march.

"Do that," Esclin said. "Ilgae, question the guards as well."

"Yes, Sire."

There wouldn't be anything to find, Esclin thought, as the others quickly worked out their plans. It would have been the work of a moment to distract a page and slip under the tent's edge, pry loose the wire and poison it. In fact, it could have been done days before, and only now had anyone been unlucky enough to put their hand on the point. He had not worn that dagger since the second day on the road, and had not drawn it then. "Do what you can, and make sure the tent is better watched. Kelleiden, I'll share your tent tonight."

The smith's tent was smaller and much less well appointed: neither of them had expected to sleep there while they were at Nen Salter. The guards disposed themselves outside the tent and Kelleiden drew a flame from the brazier. It was past midnight, and the air was growing cold. Esclin called up a handful of witchlight, letting it drift to the peak of the tent, and settled himself on one of the folding stools. They and the brazier were the only furniture; Kelleiden's bed was a straw mattress on the ground, piled high with blankets. Kelleiden said something to one of the guards, and a few minutes later the man returned with a pitcher and two cups. Kelleiden poured one cup full, sniffing warily, then dipped his own sliver of nacre into the wine. The pearly luster didn't change, but he took a careful sip anyway and waited before pouring a second cup for Esclin.

"I wonder what they really wanted," Esclin said.

"Besides killing you?" Kelleiden looked sideways at him.

"Oh, I don't doubt they'd have been perfectly happy to see me die, but it's a haphazard way to go about it. It was more likely to catch one of the pages—as it did." Esclin took another long swallow of his wine, trying not to think of the boy's body writhing in the chair. Jollan would live; it was time now to look at other things. "It forced me to call on a wheelman—to show that there are crises only the Burning One can answer. And of course I've done it, I wasn't going to let the boy die. But it's a foot inside my door."

"It's possible," Kelleiden said, after a moment. "I hadn't thought of that, but—yes, it's possible."

"And too late now, in any case," Esclin said, and sighed. He was certain there would be a dozen petitioners in the morning, promising him that Brelin was a good man and an excellent healer and begging him to allow the wheelmen to accompany the army south. To refuse outright would look churlish; perhaps if he allowed them to travel with one of the other contingents—Nen Salter, for preference, rather than Nen Brethil... "There were always going to be a few spies among the muster, but putting a wheelman close to me—that's neatly done."

"That's the way you think," Kelleiden said. "The Riders are less...clever."

Esclin grinned, recognizing that as a polite circumlocution—the word most people used was "tricksy"—and drained his cup. "Well, there's no mending it now. Let's see what the morning brings."

Brelin Donderos set his satchel down and closed the door of the shrine with a sigh of relief. The boy Jollan was past the crisis and sleeping soundly in the arros's bed, watched by three of his fellows and overseen by the thegen herself. It had been a near-run thing, and he was grateful he had been summoned in time, but the sleepless night dragged at him. There was work to be done, though, before he could sleep, and he crossed the sanctuary barefoot to open the shutters set into the walls and roof. The morning light entered, bright enough to sting—the sanctuary was outside the nenn, following Esclin's edict—and he swept the remains of the previous day's fire from the altar before laying out wood and tinder for today's blaze. It was a task he should have done the night before, even interrupted, and when he was new-come to his place he had made up the fresh fire in hasty guilt. These days, he had attended too many sickbeds to feel anything more than mild regret: if the Blazing One sent illness for him to heal, the Blazing One would surely understand the occasional consequence.

He raised the burning glass from its niche beside the altar, kissing the frame in quick obeisance, then angled it to catch and focus the sun's rays on the curled tinder. The air was still and cool, and it didn't take long for a thread of smoke to rise amid the shavings. He edged a thin twig into the blossoming flame, and then another, until the fire was well begun. He kissed the burning glass again, this time in thanks, and set it back in its place, then spun the wheel that hung behind the altar. The spokes rattled, clicking off the prayers carved on the spokes and hub and rim; he closed his eyes, managing wordless thanks, then turned to survey the chapel. It was tidy enough, the wooden floor swept bare, and he allowed himself to consider a few hours' sleep. He had not expected to be called last night.

He stepped into the alcove that held his bed, shrugged off his gown with a sigh and stretched out on the rustling mattress. He settled his arm across his eyes, blocking out the light, but the memory of the injured page hung between him and rest. Bad enough that the boy should be poisoned—and such a poison, meant to hurt and maim if it didn't kill—but to be poisoned by mistake, for surely that trap was meant for the arros... He could feel the weight of the gold armlet in his purse, a piece that would pay the shrine's expenses for several months and more. It was a decent price, both for the boy's life and as an acknowledgment of Esclin's—well, one couldn't call it fault, precisely. Responsibility, perhaps. Had no one wished to kill the arros, Jollan would not have been harmed. The light weighed heavy on him, warm as a blanket, soft as a featherbed, and he groaned aloud at the knocking from the outer room.

"A moment!" He snatched up his gown again, wishing he had had time to change his shirt, and slung it around his shoulders, belting it hastily into place before he pushed the curtain aside. The wheel behind the altar clattered and the lord of Nen Salter turned to face him. Brelin made a hasty bow. "Forgive me, my lord—"

"That was well done last night," Huwar said. "I'm sorry to wake you."

His nephew Thedar stood behind him, lips moving in prayer as he reached to turn the wheel again. He had the right, of course, was a priest in all but the final vows, but Brelin suppressed the desire to tell him to mind his own business. "Thank you," he said instead, and knew he sounded wary. "What may I do for you, my lords?"

"The arros wants you to accompany him on campaign," Thedar said. "As part of my uncle's company, but it's a start."

Brelin bowed again. He wasn't at all sure that he wanted to join the campaign, though the small boy who had dreamed of being a swordsman before he proved a better healer woke up and rejoiced. "I am, of course, at Esclin Arros's command, and yours," he said carefully, "but I also have responsibilities here."

"We'll send for another priest from Nen Brethil," Thedar said. "Your acolyte can handle things until he gets here." His tone brooked no argument and Brelin scowled. He was the wheelman here, not Thedar; Thedar might be the lord's nephew, but he had not in fact taken the last vows—

Huwar laid a hand on his nephew's shoulder. "You're too hasty. What I would say is that I think you are needed on this campaign—gods above, someone tried to poison the arros, and in my house! You would travel with me, as part of my household, and I would of course support you and welcome your service in all things. But you would also be at Esclin's command."

Brelin hesitated. That made more sense: of course the arros was worried, after Jollan was poisoned, and would overcome his prejudice against the wheelmen to have a help against any similar attack. It was a wheelman's duty to go where he was most needed, and he couldn't argue that Esclin had need... "I'll come. But I'll need everything."

"Easily gotten," Huwar answered, with a smile. "Can you ride?"

"Well enough." It had been a few years since he'd had to travel any distance on horseback, but he'd learned as a boy, and had not, he thought, forgotten everything.

"A riding horse and a pack pony and a boy to tend them," Huwar said briskly. "A tent. Bedding and necessaries. See to that, Thedar, if you please."

Thedar bowed. "Yes, Uncle."

"You'll leave with us in the morning, and you'll dine with me tonight," Huwar said. "Best pack whatever you want of your own—though I know generally your lot travel light."

"We try," Brelin answered, and bowed them out the shrine's door. He closed it behind them and stood for a moment in the center of the bare room, the fire crackling on the altar, the wheel silent on the wall behind it. A horse and a pony, a tent and bedding and a servant to manage it all: that was more suited to his superiors, to the leaders of the great houses, not to a common wheelman. But it was clearly his duty. Moving without thought, he fed more wood into the fire, and then reached to spin the wheel again, releasing prayers into the sunlit sky.

The levies were supposed to get underway at dawn, but to no one's surprise the sun was two finger's width above the horizon by the time the first company marched south away from the nenn. Talan closed her ears to the curses of the carters struggling to get the baggage train in line, having learned that it was better to leave it to them to sort it out, and dodged the last of Nen Atha's company to join the party milling at the gates. Cat Meirin shoved her way to Talan's side and planted herself, spinning her dagger backward and forward so that the silver blade blurred into the fading fog. Talan frowned, and Meirin lifted her eyes skyward in answer but sheathed it obediently enough. Beside her, Estor hunched himself deeper into his hood, the morning air still too damp for the sun to bring much warmth. The rest of her companions were in the remains of the campsite, readying for the day's march.

Esclin had breakfasted with Huwar that morning—unusually, Talan thought, but perhaps in the wake of the

attempt to poison him, it had been a good idea to reaffirm his
trust in Huwar. Jollan was headed home that afternoon, with
Kelleiden and his party. He was better, certainly, but still weak
and sickly, and she shivered in spite of herself, hoping no one
would think anything of it except that the morning was still
chill. The arros risked his life in battle, yes, but for someone
to have tried to kill Esclin twice since the autumn… She was
more than ever determined to stay at his side.

She glanced quickly around, counting the familiar faces:
Ilgae Marshal already in the light armor she wore for travel,
the lords of Nen Mallar and Nen Buin leaning together like
gossips at a well, Nen Lios's heir with furled banner in hand,
a dozen lesser folk waiting on their masters. Everything was as
it should be, and she let herself relax a little. Whoever had set
the poison might well have done it back in Nen Elin, she had
been unable to track any other time that anyone had handled
that dagger. The poisoner might not be with the army at all.

The nenn's great door opened, and Esclin emerged into
a sudden unexpected shaft of sunlight. The sun caught the
gilded leather of his corselet and glinted from the circlet that
bound his hair, and she saw half the men from the southern
nenns cross their fingers against the uncanny even as they
eyed him with admiration. Huwar Ellemas walked at his side,
followed by Nen Brethil and his heir, and Algrym of Nen
Saal. Ilgae Marshal moved to join them, bowing, her words
too soft to hear, and Esclin nodded, clasping hands with
Huwar and then with Nen Brethil and Nen Saal. Talan took a
few steps forward, making sure she could be seen, and as the
lords turned away Esclin moved to join her, laying his arm
across her shoulder.

"Take Nen Saal's heir with you today."

"Eliadu," Talan said, and couldn't keep the annoyance
from her voice.

"What's wrong with him?"

"Last night at the feast, he pretended to take me for your
son." Or might have done in truth, he was barely fifteen,
hardly old enough for the dance, never mind to pass judgment

on the thegen. But the slight had rankled.

Esclin lifted an eyebrow. "Wear a better gown next time."

There was enough truth in that to sting—she had not chosen to mark the occasion as perhaps she should—and she swallowed any further complaint. "I'll keep an eye on him."

Esclin took her arm, the movement hidden under the sweep of his cloak. "You're a woman grown, sixteen years old. I need you to keep him sweet."

Because Nen Saal's loyalties were not entirely certain. Talan nodded. "I'll do my best."

"Thank you." Esclin smiled but it was for Nen Brethil, who moved past with a bow. "I'm not giving you Reilan."

Talan grinned. "I doubt he'd ride with me—he hardly knew where to look, in the baths, or even last night."

"I'd like it if you could make friends with him," Esclin said, "but I'll grant it doesn't seem likely."

"I'll do what I can."

"Also, the wheelman traveling with us—Brelin, his name is, he serves a shrine outside the nenn here. If he comes under your eye, I'd like to know what he's doing. But don't trouble him."

Talan nodded. She understood the delicate balance there, too, the need to acknowledge the man who saved Jollan and the need to keep the wheelmen as far from their counsels as possible, loyal as they were to the Blazing One.

Esclin's grip tightened for a moment. "And be careful. Keep Cat Meirin by you—I see her there."

"I will," Talan said, caught between impatience and startled affection, and the arros turned away. She caught Estor's sleeve. "You seemed to get on with Eliadu last night. Ask him if he'll ride with us."

Estor nodded. "And then?"

"Show him all respect," Talan answered, and knew the words were sharp because she didn't like the man herself. "Make him feel at home."

"Easy enough," Estor said, shrugging, and Meirin brushed a strand of damp black hair out of her eyes.

"Watch?"

Talan nodded. Meirin showed teeth in a distinctly feral grin, and Talan said, "He's our ally, and the thegen of Nen Saal. Nothing's to happen to him—not a fall, not a ducking, nothing."

"We'll watch over him like he was our born brother," Estor said.

"Better than that." Talan glared at him, and he dipped his head.

"I swear, Thegen." Meirin looked disappointed, and Talan stared her down as well.

The thegen's companions rode in the middle of the column, between the companies from Nen Atha and Nen Mallar. Talan sighed for Sian, left behind at Nen Elin since she was no hand with either sword or bow, and set herself to be agreeable to the other children of the great nenns who had come to Esclin's call. She had met most of them before, and she was gratified to see that the group sorted itself out into an easy company. She was aware, however, that most of the young women came from the nenns to the north of Nen Elin—Nen Atha, Nen Arranme, Nen Gorthen—and that the boys from the southernmost nenns were alternately shy and boisterous with them. She wasn't sure what to do about that except to treat them all as equals, and she was relieved to see that Derein Dalmas of Nen Gorthen seemed to be applying the same tactics. At least Reilan Nardenos rode with the men of Nen Brethil; she was glad to be spared his disapproval.

But there was still Eliadu to deal with, and as they moved out into the flat lands below the nenn, where the valley opened toward the Dancing Ground, she waved Estor aside and edged her horse forward so that she came next to Nen Saal's son.

"A good day for it," she said. "We should make four or five leagues today."

Eliadu gave her an uncertain glance. He was a hand-span taller than she and would be taller still, a lanky brown-eyed boy with wrists that hung too far below the cuffs of shirt and gown. "With a bit of good luck, Thegen."

Talan did her best not to show her annoyance. "Ilgae Marshal says we'll camp at the Ford of Tirthel."

"It's usual." Eliadu seemed to realize that he had chosen his words badly. "I mean, that's where we always meet the levy from Nen Ddaur."

"Yes." Out of the corner of her eye she saw Oriol coming up on her left, and turned her head gratefully to include him.

Oriol obligingly held out a small wineskin. "Drink?"

She took it, letting the reins fall to her horse's neck so that she could drink two-handed. She saw Eliadu stiffen, as though he wanted to reach for them, but then controlled himself. She pretended she hadn't seen and offered the skin. "It's new ale."

"Thank you." Eliadu tipped it awkwardly, the liquid dribbling out the corners of his mouth, and Talan hastily took it back again, suppressing the urge to tell him not to waste it. From his expression, Estor was thinking the same thing, and she frowned as she handed it back.

Eliadu wiped his mouth with the back of his hand. "Will you stand with the sword line, Thegen, or with the archers?"

Talan slanted another glance at him, and decided she had better take the question at face value. "I and my companions are to carry the arros's orders."

"That seems prudent," Eliadu began, then frowned as though just realizing it was not an excuse. "Would you not be safer with the baggage, Thegen?"

"Where bandits will strike first?" Oriol laughed. "And only the old men to watch?"

"I'm not after safety, but service," Talan said. "We'll be the arros's messengers in battle, or stand with the archers if there's need. And you?"

"My father has put me in the sword line, Thegen."

There was a hint of smugness in his voice that made her want to slap him. "Call me Talan. If we're to be comrades in arms, we can name each other."

"Oh." Eliadu flushed to the roots of his hair. "I couldn't—I don't—I mean, it can't be proper, Thegen."

"We all do it," Oriol said. "Better get used to it."

"He's right," Talan said, as brightly as she could manage, and urged her horse ahead.

❦

By evening they had reached the Ford of Tirthel, where the Newborn River turned sharply south, widening and growing more shallow. Once there had been a steading and a town there, tucked into the broad curve of the river, but the silted ford gave little protection now and the steading had been abandoned in her grandmother's day. There was nothing left now but the stump of a tower and a few courses of stones that had been the hall; the villagers had built in wood and turf and sun-dried brick, and their homes had melted into the grass. Talan hung back, Cat Meirin in her shadow, while the body of the army made its sluggish way through the shallows, and surveyed the ruins. That was what the Riders had made of the Dancing Ground, what they would make of the nenns if they broke though into the hills: empty land gone to waste, the people thrown to the seven winds.

Oriol pulled up beside her, scanning the ground. "They were saying it only gets worse the further south we go."

Talan nodded. "Who was saying?"

He shrugged. "People. They were saying Nen Brethil's been putting up with it all winter, and has lost some of the steadings at the valley mouth."

Oriol had no particular talent for politics, though he was an excellent archer. Talan nodded again. "Yes, that's why they only brought a part of their levy."

"And not their best part, either," Oriol said. "Or at least not their best archers. I heard from Falk Garmenas that most of the Nen Brethil company have been out only once before, and some of them never."

"That's useful to know," Talan said. Almost certainly the arros had already heard, but she would make certain.

The crowd at the ford had thinned and the camp-marshals were sounding whistles, the familiar cacophony that herded the army into quarters. Her own servants had already claimed their space near the arros and Talan touched heels to the sides of her horse, urging it through the muddied shallows to join the others. Oriol and Cat Meirin followed and Estor turned away from their tent to take Talan's bridle. Before she could dismount, trumpets sounded on the camp's southern edge and she turned to see an army moving up the valley, banners at the head of the straggling column. Nen Ddaur, surely, she thought, but looked at Oriol. "Well?"

He stood in his stirrups, shading his eyes against the sun. "Nen Ddaur and the southern nenns," he said after a moment, and Talan heard her sigh of relief echoed throughout her party.

"Well, who else were we expecting?" she asked, and grimaced at her own bravado. This was no time to tempt fate. Already the camp-marshals were whistling their folk to order, and she could see the arros mounting his horse to ride out to meet them.

They met that night in the arros's tent, where the pages handed out bowls of stew flavored with spring onion and Talan herself tended to the wine cups. Nen Ddaur's levy was led by its holder's nephew Kellecost Sarrasos, a dark man with quiet good manners. He had never come as far north as Nen Elin, and Talan listened carefully to get his measure. He seemed competent enough, though he admitted freely that he had brought only the minimum number of men.

"They're our best, Sire," he said, "but Nen Ddaur asked that you hold her excused from sending more. We've been plagued by raids all winter long, and she wanted to keep back enough men to hold the upper valley clear for planting."

"You've had that much trouble," Esclin said, leaning back in the chair that the pages assembled every night. "Through the entire winter?"

Kellecost nodded again. "Except when the snow was deep enough to cut the passes, and even then they found a way to cross the lower Birkes after it froze, and came down on a hill steading there. The folk there saved the house but lost their cattle, and counted themselves lucky at that."

"How many Riders?"

"Forty? Maybe more, we were never sure how many different parties there were, but no more than forty in any one group."

Talan swallowed a curse as she refilled their wine cups. That was a good-sized band, about the same size as the groups that had attacked the nenns around Nen Brethil and Nen Salter; by a conservative reckoning, that meant the Riders had spared more than a hundred men for winter raids, along with the men they'd kept to secure their winter quarters. They wouldn't have needed to wait for reinforcements to arrive with the good weather. From Esclin's expression, he had made the same calculation but he shrugged one shoulder.

"With luck, we'll draw them north. Does Nen Ddaur think she can keep the upper valley open?"

It was Kellecost's turn to shrug. "She hopes so, Sire. If not, it'll be a hungry winter."

"We'll see what we can do to prevent that," Esclin said, with a quick smile, and Kellecost turned away.

Talan offered a smile and another serving of wine to Nen Salter. That emptied the pitcher, and she moved back to the sideboard to collect a fuller one. Kellecost was at the sideboard himself, and she handed him a clean cup from among the clutter. He took it with a nod and thanks, then blushed as he recognized her. She smiled to show there were no hard feelings, and said, "I wondered, did the harper arrive safe?"

"Harper?"

Talan frowned. "Viven Harper? She left at the Water Moon, on the last boat going down the Hidden River. She was pledged to someone outside Nen Ddaur, she said, but I'd have thought she would have played a night or two for the folk of the nenn."

"The last boat to reach us came in well before the Water Moon," Kellecost said, frowning himself now. "And you're right, my aunt is fond of harpers."

"The boat was *Cailtie,*" Talan said. Surely this was just ordinary mischance—the river growing too rocky between Nen Saal and Nen Ddaur, perhaps—but something pricked at the back of her neck.

"Our last boat was *Dilanna,*" Kellecost said. "What's wrong?"

"I hope nothing," Talan said, and couldn't bring herself to believe it. She made her way through the crowded tent with more purpose, seeking out the holders whose nenns lay between Nen Salter and Nen Ddaur. None of them had seen *Cailtie* either, and she worked her way back to Kellecost as the crowd began to thin.

"Stay a moment," she said. "I'd like you to share that tale with the arros."

"Tale?" Kellecost blinked. "The harper, you mean?"

"Yes." Talan caught him by the sleeve and pulled him toward Esclin's chair before Esclin could rise to end the night. "Sire."

He turned, eyebrow rising as though he'd caught the scent of her worry somehow. "Well?"

"A word, if I might. I asked Kellecost if Viven Harper had reached them safely, and he says she never came."

Esclin's eyebrows rose even higher. "No?"

"Not to Nen Ddaur," Kellecost said.

"And I've spoken to the rest, everyone between Nen Salter and Nen Ddaur, and they've seen neither the harper nor the boat *Cailtie.* No one's seen the boat since she went upriver. They all thought she was wintering in Nen Elin."

"You cannot be thinking treason," Kellecost said, and Esclin gave him a quick smile.

"No, indeed. Viven Harper is harp-bound and keeps her word. But if the boat were wrecked, and she taken—bandits, perhaps—"

Kellecost relaxed. "No one would dare kill a harper."

"Their harps are better defense than most men's swords," Esclin agreed. "Talan, see what more you can find."

Talan dipped her head. "Yes, Sire."

She started to back away, but Esclin lifted his cup. She dipped her head and fetched the pitcher, dawdling until everyone had left the tent but Nen Salter, Ilgae, the horsemaster Denior, and Garent of Nen Danan. Cat Meirin lurked by the door and no one waved her away. Esclin leaned back in his chair. "What do you know of Viven Harper?"

It was a general question and the others exchanged glances. "Nothing to her disadvantage," Ilgae said.

"She was born in Nen Gorthen," Nen Danan said, "but spends most of her time in the south. She joined a consort there, I heard."

"I've heard her sing—a fine harper." Nen Salter shrugged. "I've nothing more."

"Tell the tale," Esclin said, and Talan set the pitcher aside.

"By chance, I asked Kellecost if Viven Harper had reached them in Nen Ddaur, but she had not, nor was she seen along the Hidden River after she left us. It worries me."

Ilgae grimaced. "No one at all?"

"None. And I asked after the boat as well."

"You think she's taken," Denior said, and Esclin lifted a hand.

"I don't know. I'm...concerned."

Nen Salter looked from one to the other. "Surely it's more likely the boat wrecked? Taking a harper—that's like grabbing a beehive without gloves or smoke."

It was Esclin's turn to make a face. "The harper brought the news of Reyscant. When she left, I gave her a good gold ring in thanks."

Ilgae heaved a sigh. "That would explain a thing or two."

"Not to me," Nen Salter said.

Esclin gave a thin smile. "The claiming of my sword's steel was not uncontested. We wondered how it was done." Nen Salter's eyebrows rose but he asked no more questions.

"There are precautions we can take," Nen Danan said.

"Most of which we're already taking," Ilgae said. "But, yes, knowing the source makes it a little easier."

"Assuming this is the source," Nen Salter said. "Forgive

me, Sire, but you're making a lot of assumptions."

"I am." Esclin nodded, still with that thin smile. "And I hope I'm right, because if I am—we can turn this to our advantage."

There was a moment's silence in the tent. Ilgae shook her head. "If you mean what I think—"

"They can track us," Esclin said. "Very well. Let's lead them somewhere that suits us, not them."

Twister, Talan thought, and hid her smile. Only her father would think of such a thing, clever old fox that he was. Only he would try to turn deadly weakness into the point of the attack.

"It's a risk," Ilgae said, but her tone was considering.

"It is." Esclin nodded. "And we'll have to join up with the Westwood's armies first. But after that..."

"If they'll take the bait," Nen Salter said. "And they'd be fools not to."

"I never count on that," Esclin said, laughing, and pushed himself up out of his chair. "We'll continue our precautions, keep everything well warded, but—we can use this."

The kyra of the Westwood had established herself in Callamben, lingering there while the levies from the western shores crossed the last leagues of forest, and her scouts sought the Riders' army. They had found signs of their passage: a burnt farmhouse here, livestock butchered there, a shepherd despoiled of her flock but alive and unharmed thanks to her dogs. Two of her companies had fought inconclusive skirmishes with Rider scouts, but there was still no sign of the main army. She guessed they were further east, closer to the Hills, and the only question that remained was whether to risk scouts on that more dangerous journey or take the army out in force. Heldyn inclined to the former—he was generally the more cautious man—while Rihaleth argued that they had to leave the Westwood sometime, and better sooner than later.

They were both right, and both wrong; Alcis was reluctant at the moment to leave the forest, where the land itself brought rumor rustling to her ear. And yet they could not remain in its shelter forever, if only because the levies would soon eat up the goods stored for them at Callamben. She had left Helevys and Traher in nominal charge in the Carallad, with competent stewards to back them: she intended to meet the Riders as far from the Westwood as possible, and even the edges of the Westwood were strongly enough defended that the Riders wouldn't dare risk an attack. And she would need her best commanders with her this season, with the first defense falling to her. Everything was ready, and yet she hesitated, feeling a whisper in the earth itself that said *Not yet.*

The most recent party returned with no more news, and she left her consorts arguing over the maps and a pot of tea and descended to the walled garden that lay behind the house where her party always lodged. She dismissed her women at its gate and went on alone, feeling the land wake to her footsteps, kindly and protective. She would be as safe here as anywhere, though she carried both her own magic and a thin dagger just in case. She closed the gate behind her and turned toward the sound of water. It flowed from a cupped shell held in a carved hand, as though someone reached from between the earth and the stones of the wall to pour out cool water into the oval basin. The first evening-star vines were reaching up along almost-invisible trellising, and she caught her breath in sudden memory.

This was where she had first seen Esclin, when he had come fleeing the wreck of Eith Ambrin, he and what was left of his company. She had stood just here: the bell-flower was fuller then, and its drooping branches had been a curtain between her and the couch where the injured man had rested, Kelleiden as always at his side, Heldyn stooping to dip water from the fountain while the other two paced and murmured. Esclin had been startlingly beautiful then, even with a quarter of his face hidden beneath bandages, long and lean and—then—lightly made, not yet come to his full strength. She had decided in the first heartbeat that she would have him, and in the second realized that she could not meet him then and get her way. She had withdrawn as silently as she had come, and met him officially a day later when he was braced and dressed and ready. She had dressed to match his finery, and to everyone's surprise had won him. They were too well matched to last long together, and in any case they both had realms to rule, neither prepared to cede to another, but she did not regret a moment of their pairing. She had gotten a son from him, born in the Westwood while Esclin was still her consort; she still missed the daughter born to the Hundred Hills, when she was consort there.

She smiled at the girl she had been, not able then to put a name to the thing she saw in him, but knowing that it was needful, a gift of rule and meant for her and her line. And indeed, Esclin's blood ran strong in Traher, bid fair to take him down some strange paths, but it was more than the gift of illusion. She had seen and loved the gallantry of it, that a man could be fine and fair and beautiful, and strong and brave and clever as well. She need sacrifice nothing in her consorts, and had taken that lesson to heart when she chose them.

A couch still stood beside the fountain. She seated herself, kicking off her slippers to dig her toes into the cold dirt, and trailed her fingers in the water. The land responded, faint at first but then roused, the Westwood's roots threaded through loam and stone and along the channels that carried the kingdom's streams. She could feel the Carallad, its pulse faint and comforting; closer in, she could feel new-plowed land ready for the seed, sheltered in the clearings beyond the forest's walls. She could feel the town, its roots no less sturdy than the trees', and she could feel the edge where the forest ended, not as sharp as a knife's cut, but fading rapidly from her awareness.

She turned her attention there, banking the Westwood's presence as she would bank a fire, and slowly a few faint strands came clear. They were weak and flickering and not her own but she could still make some sense of them, tease some meaning from their fitful touch. She could feel the Lammard's course, the swift-flowing water a barrier to her power; here and there she could feel an Exile steading, and the slow thrust of the grasses that covered the Dancing Ground. And there was something else, too, a spot, a thread of cold fire, like a jagged edge of ice against the land. Two threads, she thought, feeling with all the delicacy she possessed, two threads that thickened and met…

And then it was gone, the power snatched from her like the flame blown from a lamp, and she gasped and shuddered in the narrow garden, bending to dig fingers into the ground. The familiar touch soothed her, and she straightened slowly. That had been the lord paramount's main army, she was sure of that, and this time as she rose to her feet, she felt the Westwood pushing her forward. It was time now, as it had not been before, and she swept from the garden, collecting her women with a word.

Her consorts were still in the cabinet where they had spread out the maps, the teapot half-emptied and cups and stones laid out in patterns on the parchments. Esten Vargos, the leader of the scouts, was there with them, along with Toldra Meilanos who was this year's captain of the infantry. They all looked up as she entered, and Rihaleth said, "We were just about to send for you, Kyra."

"You've found something." Her voice cracked, and Heldyn put a cup in her hand. The tea was cold but she drank it down anyway, tasting of mint and autumn berries, and nodded her thanks.

"We have," Esten said.

"We think we have," Heldyn said.

"Show me." Alcis set the emptied cup aside and bent over the maps.

"The last of the scouts came in two hours ago," Esten said. "They crossed the Lammard at Baesford, and found signs a league south that an army had passed. They thought from the signs that it was the lord paramount."

Alcis considered, matching the inked lines with the threads

of ice, the traces of sensation she had felt in the garden. Yes, that went well enough, though the Lammard was a barrier—

"Yes," she said. "I think you're right. We need to turn them back against Esclin's men."

"Crossing where?" Heldyn began, and Rihaleth pointed.

"There. It's not strictly a ford but it's never deep, not even in spring, and there's the island to give us a breather."

Heldyn grimaced. "True enough."

"Have the final levies reached us?" This was always the way of it, Alcis thought. You wait and wait and suddenly there's no time.

"Still two days out," Rihaleth said.

"Leave a message that they're to follow with all haste," Alcis said. "We'll try to catch the Riders before they reach Meryenith."

"If we catch them here—" Heldyn traced a line between the Astfora, one of the Lammard's western tributaries, and a village ruined so long ago as to be nameless, only a heap of broken stone. "We'll have shelter for our flanks."

"They won't fight there," Esten said, and Alcis nodded regretfully.

"I agree. But we'll keep it as a fallback position. In the meantime, see that our people are ready to march out in the morning. Now it's time to hurry."

The company had made good time southward, despite taking time at the start to work the horses into shape. At Vassos they split from Gelern Sword-Hand's men, following the old cart road along the bend of the Lammard. The river was in full spate, but at its widest points it ran shallow enough that a careful man could ford it: not a good sign for the coming season, Leicinna thought. It was easier when the Lammard made a better barrier.

Ten leagues beyond Vassos the cart road was in ill repair, almost vanished beneath the tough spring grass. The land was empty, and would stay empty until they came under the shadow of the Exile-built fortress at Mag Ausse. Leicinna herself had no memory of the area as farmland, but Aylflet's grandfather had held a steading there; and if she had doubted him, there were the ruined courses of stones to mark where steadings and whole villages had been wiped away. Something would have to give, she thought, standing beside the ruins of a well while they stopped to graze the horses. Someone would have to win—if not this season, then very soon. Riverholme struggled to feed its people already in the dead of winter; they could not afford to abandon this land forever. The plain stretched empty as they made their way further south, no sign of Riders and only the occasional track or trail-sign to mark the passage of their fellows, and Leicinna was glad to see the low rise of Mag Ausse on the horizon, wearing tower and walls like a crown.

The fort was held from the Hundred Hills, not from Riverholme; brother and sister ruled it together, two brisk, practical people, brown of hair and eye. Faela Custanas was the elder and she welcomed them, willing to share her maps and what little news they had.

"Gelern Sword-Hand was here a week back, though he didn't stay. He said he'd rested his horses at Rassia in the hills and wanted to press on to see if he could find the Rider army. We've seen nothing, and told him so, but Teiram will be back tomorrow and he'll have more to tell." She poured them each a second cup of wine. There was a plump toddler at the other end of the hall that had her look, though there had been no word of a marriage. But then, Leicinna thought, that was common enough among the hill-folk. She wondered idly which of the steading's men Faela had favored, but it was no concern of hers.

"I'd be glad of any word," she said, and Faela set the cup in front of her.

"I wish you'd been sent to reinforce us here—the gods know we could use more horse—but then, I doubt the arros has got our message yet."

"And my commission is from the rivermaster," Leicinna said and briefly wished it wasn't. If they could station fifty horse in Mag Ausse—thirty, even—they could dominate the entrance to the Newborn valley and that would help to block the Riders' advance. Except with the Lammard so low this spring, it would be easy enough to cross and bring troops up the western bank instead.

Teiram returned in the next evening's twilight leading a troop of five on tired horses, to report the holding's home farms still unmolested. "We've heard they've been harrying the lower valleys, but they know we can bring our folk within walls quickly enough to make an attack difficult. And it's too early in the season for there to be much to raid."

"That won't last forever," Leicinna said, and Faela gave a wry smile of agreement.

"Which is another reason I'd be very glad to have your company stationed here."

"We can hold out for months if we have to," Teiram said. "But it would be a starving winter afterward." He shook his head as though to shake the words away. "These tales, though—they're talking Riders in every valley, troops of thirty or forty men, and that's three times the number I'd have believed possible. I'm beginning to wonder how many of their folk actually withdrew last season."

"That's an ugly thought," Leicinna said.

"I'd hire you if I could," Faela said. "And if you weren't hired already, of course. But if you or any company were here…"

Leicinna nodded, glancing at the maps again. Even if they couldn't fully control the valley mouth, they could be a sticking point, a safe haven and a base for scouts. "I'll suggest it when I see Gelern Sword-Hand. Or Esclin Arros."

"Tell him we're more than willing to provide their keep," Teiram said.

"I will," Leicinna said, but doubted that there were horse to spare. Though if they were still looking to change employers at the next season, Esclin and Faela between them might make a match… She put that thought away for later, and turned her attention to the maps.

"We've been called to muster here," Faela said, pointing to the spot where the Tirthel-vale opened onto the plain. The river ran almost due west to join the Lammard, and there was a low rise to the south that would give Esclin's camp the high ground. It was three days' march for a company on foot, burdened with weapons and a baggage train, and she wasn't surprised to see Teiram shrug.

"I called our muster while I was out, and they'll gather within the week. We'll be late, probably, but that's how it is, this year."

"And short," Faela said, her voice grim. "But I won't strip my house when we don't know what's happening. Give Esclin that word, if you will."

"As you wish," Leicinna said, and hoped the other holders were able to be more generous with their men.

They rode out the next morning with filled saddlebags and more supplies on the remounts, heading east toward the Lammard. If the Riders were bypassing the fortress, it seemed more likely they'd do it on the western side rather than risk being caught between Mag Ausse and the valley nenns. Once they were onto the river plain the ground was harder going, the wind-tangled grass obscuring the paths that game and strayed livestock had cut. Most of them led toward the river, seeking water; she took the time to trace one of the larger tracks to within sight of the banks, but saw no sign of anything larger than a hare. The Lammard ran deep here, its spring-brown surface deceptively smooth; she doubted anyone could cross, but it was still a relief to see the western bank bare and empty. The Westwood's army would probably cross by Baesford: time to track south and see what she could find.

They made their way south for two days, keeping in the lee of a scrubby line of trees that had sprung up along a slight rise. It gave cover to the east, and to the west the plain stretched empty to the Lammard's edge. In the middle of the third afternoon the land flattened again, the trees dying out, and the plain opened southward before them, the Hundred Hills a shadow to the east. This was the true Dancing Ground, where the Riders and the hill-folk had fought for generations; there were no settlements left here, save one or two strong points far enough south and east to be supplied from the coastal towns or the nenns in the lower vales. The sun was hot on her right side, the shadows falling to her left as the sun waned; ahead, a few clouds rose darker against the hazy sky. There was no cover, no tree to be seen, just the long grass bending toward the distant sea.

"Finn."

There was a stir and snorting as the weather-wyrd edged up beside her. "Captain?"

"What's your guess?" She watched his eyes flicker from sky to ground and west to east, reading traces no one else could see.

"About the same for the next few days," he said at last. "Warm and dry. Rain after that, maybe, but I can't be sure."

The weather would be with them, but nothing else. She gnawed her lip, considering, and Gimmell pulled up on her other side.

"Turn back? Try to find Esclin?"

"We've seen no signs of the Riders," she said, working the thoughts out as she spoke. "Maybe they've gone east of us, but I think we'd have heard something. Seen something. Smelled a fire. But they have to be coming north if they want to make battle." Gimmell nodded. "Another day south," she said. "Then we'll cut back west, see if we can pick up a trail."

In the end they went south for two more days, crisscrossing the plain in hopes of picking up some sign of passage. They found nothing, and when they sat round the fire the second night, Leicinna could read the same thoughts on every face. "We'll turn west in the morning," she said, and pretended she didn't see the relief.

At dawn they buried the embers of their fire and turned due west, their shadows stretching for ells ahead of them, making the younger horses snort and shy. After they'd gone a league or so, Leicinna turned north as well, their shadows swinging away from under the horses' hooves. There was still no sign of any other presence, though a little past noon they reached a low-lying seep, where a spring had spread into a shallow pond. The depression around it was full of flowers, drifts of cream and pale pink star-like shapes, and Leicinna had them water the horses one by one, to leave as few traces as possible. They filled all the water skins as well, though that left the seep nearly dry, and headed out, the sun on their flanks, sinking toward the shadow on the horizon that was the Lammard.

The sun was a hand's-breadth above the distant riverbank, its light gold and thick as honey, when they saw it: grass trampled and broken, bent to the north. Leicinna rose in her stirrups but there was no movement anywhere in sight. At her nod, Jemme dismounted, handing his reins to his brother Alnoth, and followed the track a few ells further, stooping to get a better look at the marks. Even from horseback, it was obvious that this had been good-sized group, at least a company, and Gimmell nudged his mount to her side.

"It'll be dark soon. Do we follow?"

Leicinna shrugged, her eyes on Jemme. As if he'd felt her look, he straightened and came trotting back to stand at her stirrup.

"I'd say they're a couple of days ahead of us, Captain. Maybe twenty, thirty men—about our own number would be my thought."

"Pressing hard?" Gimmell asked.

Jemme shook his head. "They look like a patrol to me."

Leicinna looked south, squinting in the heavy light. Nothing moved there, but if the Riders' main army was behind her she didn't want to be caught unaware. And yet—that didn't feel right. The Riders had to know as well as she where Esclin would hold his muster. And if the Riders had not retreated to Manan over the winter but had stayed in the Dancing Ground, they would surely need and want to bring Esclin to battle as quickly as possible. And if she guessed wrong, she would be between the main army and its patrols, in no position to save herself, never mind bring a timely warning to anyone.

"North," she said aloud. "We'll follow them as long as we have light and then we'll see."

They camped that night in the ruins of a steading, where two walls still stood to hide the fire and offer a point of defense if they were surprised. The other company had camped there, too, Leicinna was unsurprised to see, and she hoped that if she had guessed wrong, anyone still behind them would have trouble telling their leavings from the people who had been before. At first light they pushed on, following a trail that became increasingly easy to see. They were gaining ground, Leicinna thought, and she was glad the ground was not yet summer-dry, to leave betraying clouds of dust. They rode in scattered order but still they would be too visible if anyone cared to look for them.

By the end of the second day they were only hours behind, and Leicinna halted the company in the shelter of a line of scrawny trees—planted as a windbreak, perhaps; the row was unnaturally straight, but if there had been buildings they had melted into the ground. There was water, though, another shallow seep that the Riders had ignored; and grazing for the horses, if they could win time to make use of it.

"You're going to scout ahead," Gimmell said, before they had even gotten a fire lit under the shelter of leaning rocks, and Leicinna gave a wry smile.

"If you have a better idea, I'll hear it."

"Not I."

Nea joined them, pushing off her leather cap so that it hung by its ties, making her look hunch-backed in the shadows. "Jemme and I walked on a bit. If they stop for the night, I'd guess we're half a league behind them."

"They'll have sentries out," Gimmell said.

Leicinna nodded. "If it's just a company—"

"We could take them," Gimmell said, in the same moment, and she grinned.

"That's explicitly against our orders, remember."

"That was months ago."

"We're here to find the main army, if we can," Leicinna said. "Either they'll lead us to it, or, yes, we can try taking prisoners and beating it out of them."

Her tone must have betrayed her dislike of that idea, because Gimmell shrugged. "It's a good deal safer than finding the army."

And that was true, too, no question. Leicinna scratched her scalp, waiting for the rest of her officers to join them. They came straggling up out of the twilight, smelling of sweat and horses, the same knowledge written on all their faces. "We need to find their camp."

"Assuming they stop the night," Gimmell muttered, but the complaint was habit. The Riders had camped every other night; there was no reason to assume this was different.

"I'm scouting," Leicinna said. "Finn, I want you—and Jemme, and Aylflet."

There were nods around the circle, and Nea said, "Signals?"

"If we're spotted, you'll know it," Leicinna said. "Get out of here and get word to Esclin or Gelern Sword-Hand."

Gimmell nodded, though she suspected he would at least try to rescue them. But if they were caught she intended to see that she was dead, so it wouldn't matter either way.

They went on foot so as not to rouse the Riders' horses, following the line of broken grass and horse droppings. The moon was a fat sickle overhead, enough light that they only needed to unshutter the dark lantern twice to check their way. She sniffed hard, then cocked her head to listen. Yes, she had certainly smelled smoke, the clean smoke of a campfire, and there was a distant whisper that might be voices. She hadn't thought they were that close to the camp, and went to one knee, motioning for the others to do the same. Aylflet wormed closer, the grass barely rustling.

"That sounds—there's more of them than we thought."

Leicinna nodded. In the distance, she thought she could make out the pinprick brilliance of a fire, and perhaps movement, though they were still too far out to spot any sentries. She looked at Finn. "Fog?"

The weather-wyrd grimaced. "There's not much to work with. I'll give you what I can."

"That's all I want," Leicinna said. "All right. A little closer."

They wormed their way through the grass as quietly as possible, moving in fits and starts so that if they were heard, they might be mistaken for some small animal. As they came closer, Leicinna was sure she smelled more than one fire, and the voices were louder, the Riders calling back and forth as though they were at ease in their own lands. Then Aylflet's hand closed over her wrist and she froze, hunching her shoulders to hide her shape.

"Sentry."

The word was a bare breath, and Leicinna saw the movement an instant later, a tall man armed with spear and shield, pacing through the grass only a dozen ells from where they crouched. She waited until he turned away and shifted to her left, looking for the next one. Yes, there he was, another spearman. The Riders' scout companies generally didn't carry shields, any more than her own people did.

There was only one way to be sure. She waited until she was sure she understood the rhythm of the sentries' patrol, then gestured for the others to stay still and eased forward toward the camp. She crossed the sentry line without drawing attention, went down to her belly to work her way closer still. This was no mere scout camp, she could see that already; the nearest fire was too large, and from the sounds and smells there was a full picket-line of horses not far to her right. The only question now was whether this was the main army, or only a large part of it.

She was close enough now to make out figures moving about the camp, a dozen men or more—perhaps as many as thirty—and beyond this outer ring of fires, she could see the tall shapes of proper tents. The Riders had been here a while, then: maybe this was their muster point? It was a reasonable spot to collect the men who'd been raiding the valley nenns all winter, and she drew herself another body-length closer hoping to overhear something of use. Something moved in the darkness to her left and she flattened herself to the ground, pressing her face into the dirt. She could hear footsteps and the steady rattle of iron, and when she risked a glance saw only a servant carrying two buckets on a yoke. Of course there would be water nearby, one of the many rivers that came out of the Hundred Hills, and she kicked herself for not having scouted that first. If she was too close to the path that led to water—and yes, there was another one, a page by the size of him, hauling a wooden bucket—she wasn't going to get a better look at the camp.

And maybe that didn't matter. She made herself take a steadying breath, considering her options. Whether or not this was the main army, it was a large enough piece of it to warrant taking that news back to Gelern Sword-Hand—or, more likely, to Esclin and the kyra of the Westwood, who'd be easier to find at their muster point. Better to send away a fast rider of her own, then shadow this group for a day or two until she was sure where they planned to go. That was the sensible choice—the only choice, thirty against some hundreds. And that was another reason to lurk a little longer, to get an accurate count...

She crawled backward away from the camp, got carefully to her knees to time the sentry-go. The watch had changed, or they'd been set to a different pattern; she had to study the rhythm again until she could slip through. For an instant she feared she'd lost her people, but then her eyes adjusted to the deeper dark and she picked out their shadows in the grass. She slid in among them, put her face close to Aylflet's ear.

"Back."

Once back in their own camp, Leicinna ordered the fire doused for the night—there was no point risking more notice— and drew her officers close to tell them what she'd found.

"No good news," Gimmell said when she'd finished, and Aylflet shrugged.

"We knew they were somewhere."

"I want a rider," Leicinna said, as though they hadn't spoken. "Two riders. They'll take our fastest horses and go separately, carry word to the muster site. Gelern Sword-Hand should be there by now. The rest of us will stay here a day or two, see if we can tell which way they're going." Leicinna closed her eyes, trying to remember the maps. She didn't think there were any fords nearby, and in any case the Riders had no reason to avoid battle. "Then we'll ride for the muster, too."

The others nodded, and Nea said, "I'll go. And the other should be Alnoth, he's light and quick."

And old and tough enough to have a chance to get away if he was attacked. Leicinna nodded. "See to it, then." She glanced over her shoulder, even though it was too far to see any sign of the Riders' camp. A day or three, no more—surely that would be time enough to answer some of their questions.

CHAPTER NINE

The low rise of the muster hill made a strong point for the camp and Esclin watched the last contingents straggle in. The folk of the southern nenns all reported a winter spent beating back Rider raids, and there was still no sign of their main army. At least the rising ground was some protection against horsemen, particularly with the bowmen set along the ridge behind the line of the main camp and smaller companies on the flanks. The ground to the north hummed like an anthill, banners flaring to mark each camping spot. There was water and good grazing for the few horse they had so far, and they were not yet low on supplies: Esclin touched Arros's hilt to ward off ill-luck and climbed to stand beside the muster stone, its carvings so blurred by wind and weather that it was hard to make out the shapes of the water horses that coiled around its sides. Legend said it had been set up by Arra herself, to mark the spot where the folk of the plains and the hill-folk met to settle their differences; now it marked a different meeting.

From there, the highest point on the ridge, he could see perhaps two leagues, the grasslands blurring into a distant haze that blended with the horizon. To his right, the Lammard shone like a ribbon, curving toward the ridge and then back west; to the east, the Hundred Hills rose purple beneath a crown of clouds.

He rested one hand on the muster stone, idly tracing the shape of a horse's head, and someone cleared their throat behind him. He turned, lifting an eyebrow in question, and Denior touched his forehead. "Your pardon, Sire, but how far out do you want our patrols to go?"

Esclin looked back at the plain, regretting his missing eye. He was no judge of distance now, when once he'd prided himself on being the best archer among his peers. But that was an old loss; he looked back at Denior and the pair of captains hovering at his shoulder. "I've worried that we've seen no sign of Riders. How far can you go before sunset and still find your way back in the dark?"

"The moon's half full," Denior said with a shrug, "and there are the fires to guide us. We could go some leagues."

The Riders would expect them to be here, Esclin thought. It was the usual muster-point, and if they were using the harper's ring they could be sure of his presence without need of scouts. But there was still no good way to come up on the ridge without being seen. "Send patrols on a broad front," he said. "Have them turn back at sunset."

"Sire!" One of the captains pointed south. "Look, there."

Esclin squinted into the haze, following the man's extended arm. Was it—yes, something moved on the plain, some leagues distant still. Too far for him to distinguish more than its existence, and he looked at Denior. "Well?"

"Kolle!"

At Denior's shout, a man came jogging up the last slope, scratching his beard. "Captain?"

"See there?" Denior pointed. "Can you make out a banner, anything?"

Kolle was one of the archers' long-sighted men, their best shot at extreme distance, and he shaded his eyes with both hands. "Horsemen," he said, after a moment. "Not Riders, I don't think. They're carrying a banner, but I can't quite—no, wait, I see it. It's Gelern Sword-Hand. With maybe fifty men? It's hard to tell."

"Well, that's a relief," the other captain said, but Denior frowned.

"Riding hard?"

"Coming at a good clip," Kolle said. "I don't see anything else."

Esclin shaded his own eye, for all the good it would do him. He could barely make out the movement, never mind the details, but something felt wrong, a chill touch of warning at the base of his spine. "Fetch Ilgae Marshal. Nen Salter and Nen Ddaur, too. My thumbs prick."

The hovering pages darted away, and Denior said, "Let me take a troop out to meet them, Sire. If they're pursued, we'll be fresh."

"We've time yet," Esclin said, and hoped it was true.

Ilgae arrived in a hurry, Huwar and Kellecost not far behind her, and they peered into the distance with the rest.

"Gelern's men for certain," Huwar said at last, and Ilgae nodded.

"And in haste. But why—"

"Sire." Kolle had moved a little apart from the rest, still shading his eyes with both hands. "I think—there might be something behind them." Esclin swore under his breath, but couldn't make out movement in the distant haze.

"I don't see anything," Ilgae said, doubtfully, and Kellecost shook his head.

"If what you said was true, that they could follow us..."

"We can't take the chance," Huwar said grimly.

"No," Esclin said. "There I do agree." He turned his back deliberately on the plain and the distant company, their banner a tiny point of gold where it caught sunlight. "Denior, take out both your companies to meet him, bring him in safe."

"If they're pursued?" Denior tucked his thumbs in his belt.

"If we can take them, we'll do it," Esclin answered. "Ilgae, get the men into battle order on that side of the hill. If we're facing the main army, I want to pick our ground."

"Yes, Sire." Ilgae touched her forehead.

Esclin looked at Denior. "I'll ride with you."

"Sire," Ilgae began, and stopped at Esclin's look.

"Hold the line for us," Esclin said, and turned toward his tent.

He begrudged every minute it took to trade his gown for a short tunic and for the pages to help him into the mail shirt and greaves. They were as quick as possible, though, neat-handed and well-practiced by now, and his horse was waiting when he emerged from the tent helmet in hand. He was unsurprised to see that Talan held its reins, and gave her a nod of approval. "You'll have the rearguard, with the archers."

She stopped, her mouth open, and then gave a wry smile of her own. "I had thought to go with you."

Which is precisely why I'm giving you the rear. He said aloud, "I need you with the archers—someone who can rally the line if it falters."

"Do you think this is the main body?" She held his stirrup and Esclin swung himself up into the saddle, settling the sword ready for use before he took the reins.

"There's enough of a chance that I want us ready," he answered. "I want a messenger."

"Estor," she said instantly, and beyond her Esclin saw the boy already armed and mounted.

"Good." He wheeled his horse away, Estor falling in at his heels, and trotted toward Denior's company.

They rode out forty strong, plus a bannerman and a pair of messengers, a party large enough to raise a plume of dust from the drying land. Below the brow of the hill it was impossible to see Gelern's party, though by the time they'd gone an eighth of a league they could see a corresponding plume on the horizon, little more than a thickening of the haze. They were making good time across the flat land, and Esclin glanced sideways to see the sun still perhaps three fingers' height above the distant Hills. They would make it back to camp in daylight, he thought, but not by much. Barring unforeseen encounters.

The breeze had been fitful all day but now it was rising, backing toward the southwest, carrying a touch of the river's damp. Esclin wiped his face beneath his helm and heard on the wind the ghost of a shout. Blais, Denior's second, heard it, too, and kicked his horse to a canter, half a dozen men spurring after him on instinct, and Denior shouted, "Hold! Hold, damn you! We're too far yet."

Esclin controlled his own instinctive reaction, holding his horse to a trot, and Blais and his men stopped and wheeled.

"They're under attack—"

"We're too far," Denior said again, lifting his voice to carry to the entire company. "All of you, if we charge now, the horses will be blown before we get there. Ride on, and keep my pace."

He nudged his horse forward, a faster trot this time, and Esclin matched him, the company forming up around them, the bannerman at his side and Estor keeping close behind him. For a moment Esclin considered sending him back, but decided against it. Better to let him go once they knew what they were facing.

And then there it was, a knot of men and horses half a league ahead, Gelern's sun-and-moon banner still flying above the central group. Riders darted in and out, trying to cut individuals out of the pack, and Gelern's company turned, ponderously. The Riders scattered before the charge, but a horse went down, screaming, and another kicked free of the melee, fleeing riderless across the grass. Esclin flinched, knowing the tactics of old, and Denior said, "Now."

The bannerman lifted his pennon in answer, and Esclin drew sword with the rest, cold settling over him like mountain mist. "Arros!" he shouted, and the blade flamed silver, bright even against the sun.

The company surged forward, a compact knot, and for a moment Esclin thought they might take the Riders unaware. But before they had covered a third of the distance, someone shouted and a group of the Riders wheeled to face them. Esclin gathered his horse, matching the others' pace, his sword lifted and ready. Gelern's company saw them and raised a cheer.

And then they were in and among the Riders, the two groups tangling briefly and drawing apart. Esclin slashed wildly at the nearest men but felt the blade slide against leather-backed mail. And then he was past, pulling his horse up and around to strike again, ducking as a Rider swept in, blade swinging for his face. He struck low instead, under the guard, and felt the blade strike home. The Rider tumbled backward out of his saddle, hung for a moment in the stirrups before the horse kicked itself free. Esclin's horse dodged the rolling body and he spurred toward another knot of men, swinging at the nearest man's shoulder. The Rider ducked, but the blade caught him anyway and Esclin parried the return stroke, the impact knocking him back against the high cantle. Kelleiden's sword sang in his hand, the blade trailing light like water, and abruptly the Riders were fleeing, a dozen or more men still mounted and whole outdistancing another handful of wounded.

"Blais!" Denior yelled, and the captain whistled to his men, half the troop setting off in pursuit.

Esclin reined in instead, surveying the trampled and bloodied ground. There were horses down, and more men, Riders and the folk of Riverholme together, though the bulk of Gelern's troop clung together around the banner. As he turned toward them, the knot loosened, a few people swinging down from their horses to search the wounded, man and beast, while ten or fifteen formed themselves into a line between the banner and the fleeing Riders. Esclin searched the group, but Gelern himself was nowhere in sight.

"The sword-hand?" he said, to the nearest rider, and the woman pushed back her helm, her chin and neck spattered with blood that was not her own.

"There." She jerked her head toward the banner, and Esclin saw the bannerman had a second horse under tight control, a body slumped forward on its neck. A man dismounted, and another, one soothing the horse, the other reaching for the man.

"Not dead—" Esclin began, and saw him stir, one hand flailing, as his people drew him from the saddle and laid him in the grass, one man going to his knees to search the wound.

"No, but grievous hurt." The woman slanted a glance southward. "And the main army's not a day behind us."

Esclin swore. "How many men?"

She shook her head. "I don't know, I was with Gelern. But they said it was the main army."

"Who said?"

"Diran." She pointed to one of the horsemen, now circling back to join the main group. Blais's men had broken off as well, and Esclin looked over his shoulder. Estor was waiting, pale but steady and mercifully unwounded, and Esclin beckoned to him.

"Take the horses." Estor did as he was told, and Esclin swung out of the saddle, went to join the group around Gelern. "How is he?"

He winced as he spoke, seeing the mail shirt broken, the padding beneath torn and blood-soaked. A blow had taken Gelern in the ribs on his left side, someone cutting in under the guard; he lay sprawled and unconscious, his skin sweaty beneath a tan that looked like dirt. A young man knelt beside him, bloody hands busy with bandages, and an Exile woman looked up at Esclin's approach.

"As you see. He's hurt bad."

He wouldn't be riding on his own, that much was obvious. "What's this about the main army?"

The Exile woman shook her head. "Diran would know."

Before Esclin could say more, another horseman reined in beside them, sliding from the saddle of his tall bay. It fought him, not liking the smell of blood, foam spattering its neck and the ground as it shook its head, and Esclin took a step toward them. "Diran?"

"Esclin Arros." The man managed a bob of the head. "We were coming to tell you, the Rider army is on our heels. A day back, maybe less. They sent a troop to slow us down but we fought free."

A day behind, and a third of the horse still missing, and none of the Westwood's levies yet arrived. "How many?"

"Two thousand? Maybe a third of that mounted?" Diran grimaced. "We weren't able to get close enough to make a good count."

Esclin glanced south, wondering if it was worth the risk of another scouting party to get a solid number. No, better to get Gelern to safety and the army ready to meet the Rider attack.

"Can he be moved?"

The young man tending him shrugged and the Exile woman said roughly, "Put him up before me, I'll see he doesn't fall."

"Moving him—" the young man began, then closed his mouth tight over whatever he would have said.

"We've no choice," the Exile woman said, straightening, and Diran nodded.

It took four men to get Gelern secured, and even then he hung limp in the woman's arms, head lolling. "He'll not make it," Denior said, under his breath, and Esclin couldn't argue.

"There's no choice. We ride."

Gelern was still alive when they reached the ridge and the Exile woman followed him into the healers' tent, her sunburned face bleak and empty. Esclin gave his own horse into the care of his groom and ordered the rest of his captains to join him in the royal tent. They crowded in, filling the space until the canvas strained outward to contain them, and Diran and Blais and another of Gelern's men told what they had seen. It was not good news, with more than a third of the army still missing, but if it was handled right it need not be a disaster. Esclin sprawled in his chair listening to the captains argue, while Talan and her companions carried watered wine to the speakers. The choices were obvious, for all that everyone wanted to have a say in the matter, and Esclin let them talk themselves out. Only when they had begun to repeat themselves did he look up at Ilgae.

"Marshal. Can we hold the southern side of the ridge?"

Ilgae gave a slight shrug. "The odds are good. With the horse to keep our flanks, and archers on the slope above—yes, I think we can. Even if they outnumber us somewhat."

The question, of course, was by how much, but there was no point in saying it. "Then so be it," Esclin said. "Denior, I'll want scouts out, a company now and another at dawn."

The horsemaster nodded and Gelern's lieutenant Diran cleared his throat. "I'd guess they won't be on us before noon, maybe not even then. They weren't expecting you to back us."

"And that gives our people a good night's sleep," Esclin said, rising, "and a good breakfast before we come to a fight."

His signal was clear and the bulk of the officers made their bows, heading off to complete their preparations. Esclin poured himself another glass of wine, unwatered this time, and glanced around the tent. The ones who were left were his most trusted people, and he could see the same calculations in their eyes that he had made himself: they could hold the Riders here, but without the Westwood's army it would be hard to do more than hold.

"No sign of them yet?"

Ilgae shook her head, and Huwar said, "Nen Ddaur sent a party almost to the Lammard, but they didn't see anything."

The Lammard was just passable there, as the spring flood subsided. Alcis knew where they would be, and would surely be coming on—unless they had met with some disaster of their own. Esclin closed his mind to that fear and said, "Is there any news of Gelern?"

"The healers are with him," Diran said, "but he's mortal bad."

It would do them no good if the rivermaster's heir died in their camp. Esclin said carefully, "There is a wheelman in our train who's a proven healer. I could send him to you if you'd like."

Diran gave a reluctant nod. "If he's willing—yes, I'd be grateful."

"Talan," Esclin said, and the thegen turned gracefully from the sideboard where she had been lighting the lamps.

"This way, Captain."

"That's that, then," Ilgae said, and Esclin straightened.

"You all know what you need to do. But there's one thing more I have in mind. If you'll stay, Huwar."

Nen Salter bowed, though his eyes were wary. "Of course."

"I want a witness." Esclin beckoned to the waiting page. "Fetch my silver gown."

It was the best he'd brought, though certainly not the best he owned, a long sweep of cloud-gray silk thickly embroidered at neck and hem with silver suns and roses. The page adjusted it so that it hung properly on his shoulders, not quite long enough to drag behind him, and brought a heavier coronet and an ice-clear crystal set in silver to lie at his breastbone. The finery was wrong for the field, yet impressive. Huwar's eyebrows lifted and Esclin laid a hand on his wrist.

"Walk with me."

He led them through the camp, past the fires, each with their knot of soldiers. It was slow going, stopping to speak with the ones he knew, but at last they climbed the rise to stand beside the muster stone. To the south, the plain stretched away into the night, an early-summer haze veiling the stars, and the moon was just past the zenith, a little more than half full. At the base of the hill a few shielded fires were briefly visible, the advance watch waiting for the scouts to return, but beyond them nothing moved. The Riders would be taking the night to rest men and horses, tend their wounded; they'd come on more cautiously once they moved.

And that was the best he could hope for, delay to give time to the kyra to bring her men, and caution to keep the Riders from striking with all their strength. Whether it would be enough was another matter, and he laid one hand on the muster stone, feeling the sun's heat still warming the stone. There was a deeper power, too, a hundred years and more of armies gathered on this rise, this plain, a hundred years of blood, of death and bravery and promises fulfilled. There were broken promises, too, but those he would not draw on. He felt that power stir as he touched the worn stone, sparks snapping at his fingertips.

He heard Huwar gasp as the lines that shaped the coiling water horses filled with silver light. Arra's horses writhed beneath the stone, its base reaching deep into the earth where still waters pooled; he reached for it, drew it shimmering to the surface until the entire stone shone with a light more brilliant than a full moon. Behind and below, he could hear voices calling in the camp, startled and amazed and not yet frightened, and he drew the first of the water horses free of the column, set it dancing above the blur of light. He pulled out another, and another, the deep waters fueling them, the blood of the dead, so that the three turned, playing, sparring like colts in a field. He heard amazement turn to delight, to cheers, and stood listening, the light shivering from the surface of the silver gown. At his side, Huwar drew a shaken breath.

"So beautiful…" Esclin gave him a crooked smile and saw his expression sharpen. "And…should the kyra be within ten leagues of here—"

"She should see it, and come on faster," Esclin agreed.

Huwar took a breath as though he would speak, then let it out again, shaking his head. *Esclin Twister*: the epithet hung between them, but Esclin made no complaint. The display would hearten his own men and warn the Westwood's levies— he hoped—and certainly it would worry the lord paramount. That was enough for an evening's work.

Brelin had fallen easily into the rhythm of the army, especially with the boy Astin to help with routine tasks. It was not so very different from his first years under vows: wake before the sun, in time to pray at its rising, then bustle his goods together and join the flow of people moving south and west. In Manan, that had been the crowds moving along the great Trade Road that ran from the port of Samas to the great hall in Mal-Manan; later when he'd crossed the Narrow Sea it had been merchants and travelers on the coast roads from Nen Ddaur to the Westwood.

Still, he was older now and used to a settled life, and he wasn't sorry to retreat each evening to his tiny tent, Astin jealously watching to be sure that he got a decent site and more than his share of the food. Brelin would have protested, but realized in time that it was a matter of the boy's position among the other servants. It was hard enough for him to serve a wheelman; let him seize status where he might.

And it would behoove him to check his chest of simples:

there had been no great call for his skills, but most evenings a handful of stragglers crept up to his tent, asking for his help. They were mostly small injuries, bruises and swellings, the occasional cut that had been allowed to fester, but each one took herbs to mend, as well as time. He had gathered feverbane along the way, it grew thick as a weed along the little streams, and yesterday there had been stands of calamint just in bud that he had gathered in haste. He unbuckled the chest's lid, working methodically through the bottles and boxes. More linen for bandages, and soft string to hold them, more of the cleavis salve, for all that he had brought his two largest jars... The light changed, and he looked up, expecting to see Astin with his dinner, but instead it was the thegen, the silent Cat Meirin at her side.

"Your pardon," Talan said, "but there's one in need of your healing."

Brelin blinked, his hands automatically repacking the chest, reading the tension in the girl's shoulders. "Is it Gelern Sword-Hand, then? I hadn't heard he was so bad."

"Bad enough," Talan said. "Will you come?"

"Of course," Brelin answered, and swallowed the *child* that rose instinctively to his lips. She was Esclin's heir even if she was not yet a woman grown. He stooped to lift his box and Cat Meirin moved faster than he would have believed, hoisted it in one fluid movement. "Thank you."

"This way," Talan said, and Brelin trailed after her, squinting in the gathering dusk.

They had taken Gelern to Nen Gorthen's tent—their mothers were some sort of cousin, Brelin remembered—and Nen Gorthen's heir had been displaced to her cousin Nen Mallar, their people milling like disturbed bees outside Nen Mallar's tent, the smoke of their bonfires drifting across the camp. Cat Meirin shouldered past Nen Gorthen's banner to sweep back the tent flap and Talan ducked inside, saying, "I've brought the wheelman."

"Let him come," a man said, and Brelin took the chest from Cat Meirin, stooping under the drooping canvas.

"My lords."

There were seven of them in the room, counting the wounded man: an auspicious number. An Exile woman, her sun-bleached hair fraying from a long braid, sat at the head of the camp-bed sponging Gelern's forehead. Her face was filthy with battle and there were suspicious streaks in the dirt, more likely tears than sweat. Another woman, still half-armored, stood at the back of the tent, knotting her hands together as though that would keep her silent, while a young man tended the brazier and Esclin's own physician looked up from beside the bed. Three more men murmured unhappily together and fell silent as he spoke.

"I'm glad to see you," Avlen said, rising. "I've done what I can, but—" He shook his head. "He's lost a lot of blood."

Brelin went to one knee beside the bed. Gelern had been stripped and hastily washed, though flecks of blood still clung to his skin. The wound was in his left chest, below the collarbone, and Brelin winced in sympathy, tilting his head to listen to the man's breath. Not deadly, that blow, at least not immediately, but from the sound of it, the lung was touched, the air whistling in his throat.

"I washed the wound with spirits of wine," Avlen said, "and pulled out several chips of bone. A sword thrust, I'd say, four fingers wide and nearly as deep. I took some stitches, and we got the bleeding stopped. But—you can hear."

Brelin nodded. "May I?" He spoke as much to the Exile woman as to Avlen, and she managed a shaky nod.

"Yes," Avlen said, and helped part the bindings until Brelin could get a look at the wound. It was as ugly as he had feared, the edges red and swollen, the silk blood-black against the sweating skin. Brelin laid a careful finger on the edge of the cut, grimacing as he felt the heat. He could feel Gelern's heart, a weak pulse beneath the skin, could feel, too, the blood that still seeped sluggishly deep beneath the surface, weakening him further and poisoning bone and muscle.

"He bleeds still."

Avlen breathed a curse. "Within?"

Brelin nodded. "Not as much as before, but...I fear it will enter his lung."

"More pressure?" Avlen sounded doubtful, and Brelin shrugged.

"Maybe. Though if you tried it before—"

"And we did," the Exile woman said, fierce and tearful.

"I don't know if more would help."

"What, then?" Avlen said.

"Cautery is the best answer," Brelin said, and ducked his head apologetically at the Exile woman's glare. "Not hot iron, we'd have to open the wound again, and that would do more harm than good. The inward fire..." He sat back on his heels, considering his options. If he could wait until sunrise, it would be easier, the Blazing One's strength visible to draw upon, but it would do Gelern no good. He probably wouldn't die overnight, but he would be weaker; it made more sense to act now, while the man's own fires still smoldered.

Of course, he had no proper fire to draw on, only the stick of holyfire, and its power was lessened by being kindled from an unsanctified flame. If he were back in Nen Salter, he could draw on other wheelmen's strength to help, but there was no one here who was trained. Perhaps there were lay servants, acolytes and near-priests, but if he was not going to wait until morning, there was no point in taking the time to find them and asking them to betray themselves to their ruler. "Fetch my chest, please."

Avlen drew it within reach, and Brelin found the bag that held the sticks of holyfire. He chose the newest, not yet used, and rose to hold it in the brazier's flame. "If you will permit me, I will try to stop that inward bleeding."

"He'll drown in his blood if you don't," the Exile woman said.

"He may not," Brelin said, with scrupulous honesty. "He's young and healthy, I can feel the strength in him. He could recover on his own, though the way will be long. But I believe this will shorten it."

One of the men at the foot of the bed bit at his thumbnail,

his brows drawn together in unhappy calculation. "Can he do it?"

He was looking at the thegen and she shrugged one shoulder. "He saved my father's page. I'd chance it."

He gave a jerky nod and the Exile woman said, "We have to."

"Thank you." The holyfire was well alight now. Brelin lifted it from the brazier and blew out the feeble flame, leaving the hot blue coal. He knelt beside the bed again, focusing his will, and held the holyfire just above the wound. The Exile woman made a soft sound that might have been protest, then closed her mouth tight, blinking hard. With his free hand, Brelin reached out to lay a careful finger against the swollen skin. He could feel the angry heat beating in Gelern's blood, the severed strands of muscle and the cracked bone, blood and air and water mingling as the lungs labored for breath. He found the worst of it, the point that drew and drained the sword-hand's life, and closed his eyes, concentrating to draw a thin blue spark from the holyfire. He felt it slide beneath Gelern's skin, running along bone and sinew as he urged it toward that deepest wound. Yes, there it was, a mess of air and blood too thinned to clot. He laid the spark against it, feeling the ooze hiss to steam, called a second spark to join it, and then a third. There was no more bleeding then, and the rush of air had eased: he left it to heal on its own, and drew another spark into the wound, letting its fire trace the path of the sword that had done the injury.

He was dimly aware that he was breathing as hard as a man running, his own pulse pounding in his head as he coaxed the fire to take the willed shape, to do no more than would help, searing only the blood that still leaked between the fibers of the muscle. He felt his hand waver, the holyfire dipping toward Gelern's skin, and sat back on his heels, the holyfire quenched in his hand, steadying himself against the bed frame. He struggled to catch his breath, groping for the prayer that needed to be said. He formed the words, his eyes closing of their own volition, and dragged himself awake again. "I've done what I can." His voice was a crow's rasp, and Talan pressed a cup against his shoulder.

"Drink."

Brelin let the holyfire fall into his lap and took the cup in shaking hands. The cold infusion soothed his tongue, as dry as though he'd been shouting the words that he spoke merely in his mind, and the thegen poured him a second cup without comment. He drank that more slowly, then collected the holyfire, stretching to put it back in his chest. "He should be watched. He'll be fevered still, but the bleeding's staunched. That should give him a better chance." He was babbling, and he closed his mouth, shaking his head.

"I'll stay the night," Avlen said, and the Exile woman looked up quickly.

"And I."

"Yes, of course."

Brelin tightened the straps on his chest and pushed himself slowly to his feet. The night breeze was bracing and he straightened more fully, his mouth falling open as he looked toward the ridge. The muster stone ran with light like water, as though it had become a fountain made of moonlight, shapes forming and reforming above its peak. They were water horses, of course, dizzyingly beautiful, flaunting Esclin's power against the night.

At his side, Talan said, "Will he live?"

"I think he has a good chance," Brelin answered. "It'll take time, though. The arros might want to consider sending him north toward Riverholme."

"Mag Ausse might take him," the boy who was carrying the chest said, and Talan nodded.

"I'll take that word to my father," she said.

They had reached his tent, and Brelin couldn't repress a sigh of relief. The flap was open and he could see the brazier lit, a lantern hanging at the peak, while Astin stirred a pot at the edge of the fire. It smelled of lamb and onions, and Brelin swallowed sudden hunger.

"Rest," Talan said, her eyes on Astin as though she were

passing some private message. "You've earned it. And my father's thanks, as well as mine."

"My duty," Brelin said, but his knees wobbled, and he was glad to sit heavily on the edge of his own pallet.

"It'll be a while before your dinner's ready," Astin said hastily. "Rest a bit, like the thegen says, there's time."

Brelin was sure he should protest, but his muscles were limp from the effort. In a moment, he told himself, in just a moment he would move, and drifted into sleep thinking of twisting silver horses.

❦

The Westwood's army had reached the Lammard the day before and turned north along the bank, heading for the ford below the Muster Hill. They were camped now in the grasslands west of the river, a steady stream of grooms and pages ferrying horses and men to the swift-running water and back again, while captains-of-ten organized fires and the army settled for the night. Heldyn stood in the door of the kyra's tent, the sweat dried to salt on his skin. The evening breeze was from the north, carrying the river's cool scent, and he was glad to let it sweep over him.

"Lord Winter?"

Heldyn turned at the page's apologetic voice and let the tent flap fall closed behind him. He accepted the glass of wine the girl offered, and joined the others at the table where maps had displaced the night's meal.

Alcis looked up with a smile and a nod. "How are the horses?"

"Fit and ready." Heldyn took a swallow of the wine, cool and tart. "We've been able to cut fodder as we go."

"We'll reach the Muster Hill tomorrow," Rihaleth said, studying the topmost map. "By late afternoon even if we don't press too hard."

Toldra Meilanos, the infantry's captain, nodded in agreement. "And I'd rather not push them. I can't feed my men on grass, Lord Winter."

Heldyn grinned at that, though Alcis's expression was more thoughtful. They had been pushing the men steadily since they left Callamben, and he would be glad to have a day or two to rest them once they joined Esclin's army. "Ostin and I took a troop up to the ford itself. We could see smoke from the Hill, so I'd say Esclin was there ahead of us. The ford's clear."

Alcis nodded again, plucking at the neck of her short gown. She was dressed for the campaign, kirtle and gown that fell to mid-calf with sturdy boots beneath, her hair piled up in a crown of braids studded with silver pins. Her armor stood on its stand at the back of the tent beside her camp bed, browned mail and leather, entirely practical and startlingly plain. She made war only of necessity, not to make a show of it.

"No sign of the Riders?" Toldra asked, and Ostin shook his head.

"Of course we were on the west bank, and we didn't cross. But, no, we saw nothing."

Alcis lifted her head and Heldyn said, "It was too late to risk the crossing by the time we got there. But I don't think the Riders would camp on Muster Hill. Before it, but not on it."

Alcis relaxed at that, nodding, and beckoned to the page. "Open the tent flap, please, it's stuffy here."

Rihaleth moved to lay weights on the map, and the girl drew aside the heavy canvas, looping it up and back to admit the breeze. Heldyn turned toward it, licking at the sweat-salt at the corner of his lips, and blinked as something flickered on the distant horizon. It came again, a tiny spot of silver like a star, but far too low, and he saw Rihaleth frown.

"What—"

Alcis stiffened without a word, pushed past them and out of the tent. Heldyn followed, glad he still wore his sword, the others shouldering up behind him. The silver light still flickered in the distance, the wrong color for flame, too steady for lightning, and he heard Alcis draw a harsh breath.

"Muster Hill."

It could be, it was in line with the ford, and if it was... "A signal?"

Alcis nodded grimly. "It's a warning, at best. How fast can you get a troop there, Heldyn?"

"Mounted?"

"Yes."

"We could be at the Hill by dawn, but we'd be in no shape to fight."

She nodded again, her eyes on the distant light. "And if you rested on the way?"

Heldyn considered. "If we stopped at the ford, crossed at dawn—we'd be there midday." Ostin nodded his agreement.

"And if you took a company of archers, took them up behind you at least part of the way?" Alcis asked.

Heldyn looked at Ostin, who gave a fractional shrug. "It would work out about the same, I'd think. We take the horse first, have the archers follow to the ford, and then go on together."

"Do that," Alcis said. "We'll rest the men here, and come on hard at dawn. We'll be a few hours behind you at the end."

"Are you sure?" Rihaleth asked. "To get them there— they'll be hard-pressed to make it in that time."

"If I'm wrong, they can rest at the Hill," Alcis answered. "But I'm not wrong." She caught Heldyn's wrist, fingers closing painfully tight. "Go now."

Her unease was palpable, as chilling as her cool touch against bare skin. "Yes, Kyra," he said and turned away, Ostin behind him shouting for his captains.

The new orders threw the camp into chaos, as men doused fires and collected the most rested remounts. The captain of archers sorted out a company about half the size of Heldyn's troop and sent them trotting toward the ford. They would be useful cover, Heldyn thought, but if it came to a fight on the open plain they were terribly vulnerable, and he made a silent resolution to get them to the Hill as quickly as possible. The moon was past the zenith before his own men were ready and he led them out into the moonlit plain, the silver light still dancing on the horizon. By the time it was halfway down the sky they had passed the archers, half of them toting short pikes, the ribbons tied beneath their heads all one pale flicker in the dark. The moon was setting when they reached the Lammard, its waters black and loud, and Heldyn ordered his men to dismount and rest and let the horses graze. They built no fires, though here and there someone called a speck of witchlight and as quickly dismissed it; instead, Heldyn sat at the base of his standard, half-drowsing between questions from his officers. The light still flared from the Muster Hill, a moving shape now, twisting against a sky that slowly filled with clouds.

Ostin dropped to the ground beside him, holding out a half-filled wineskin. Heldyn took it with a nod of thanks, drank, and handed it back again. The year was still new enough that the nights were cold, and he was glad of the weight of his cloak on his shoulders. The archers, though, would be sweating, and would need a rest.

"Do you think the Riders are there?" Ostin asked quietly. "Or is this some trick of Esclin Arros's?"

Heldyn ran a hand over his face, swallowing his instinctive defense. "If it's a trick, there will be a reason for it."

Talan rose with the sun, tense and wide-eyed, though she wasn't entirely sure she had slept the night before. Oh, she had settled into her tent, curled into the nest of blankets with Cat Meirin while Estor lay across the tent's door; but she had lain wakeful for what seemed like hours, and then drifted into a state that if it was a dream was hard to tell from waking. There were no cocks to crow here on the empty plain but the waxing light was enough, and she eased from under her blankets to find Cat Meirin open-eyed.

"Well, get up, then," Talan said—softly, she thought, but her words were loud enough to wake the others. Oriol fetched water for washing while Celein and Cat Meirin stirred up the fire and Estor set porridge to cook in the coals. Talan wasn't hungry but she made herself finish her share, scraping the bottom of the bowl. Estor was usually a clever cook, but today she tasted only salt.

She could hear the army rousing around them as she ate, and when she had finished ventured out half-armored, Cat Meirin at her heels. There was no need to ask where Esclin had gone. She could see him for herself, standing beneath the Muster Stone, the water horses still twisting overhead, fading to nothing in the rising light. She knew, more or less, what her duty was: she was to stand with the archers, in nominal command of the reserve, though she was well aware that she was expected to follow Aredan Gammelos's advice. But that meant that she should hear Esclin's plans, and she started up the low rise, her breath smoking in the chill air. If she also wanted the comfort of her father's presence, that was no one's business but her own.

At the top of the rise the morning's breeze struck cold and she hunched further into her cloak. Most of the other captains were there already, Nen Salter, Nen Brethil, Nen Gorthen, Ilgae Marshal and the horsemaster Denior and Kellecost of Nen Ddaur, huddled in their own cloaks to peer into the southern distance. For a moment she faltered, unsure how to insert herself into the group, but then Nen Salter saw her and edged aside, letting her slide into the spot at Esclin's blind side. He turned his head sharply, then relaxed, seeing her, and turned his attention back to the horsemaster.

"Go on."

Denior nodded in her direction. "The first scouts are back and they say the army's coming on, though they didn't stay to number them. A large force, nearly half horse, or so they made it."

That was hardly good news, but Esclin merely nodded. "How many men are still out?"

"Ten or so," Denior said. "We should have better news soon."

Clearer news, anyway, Talan thought. She doubted they

would get much good news before the Riders broke on them like a wave.

Esclin nodded again. "Send to me as soon as you have word."

"I will, Sire." Denior backed away and Esclin shaded his eye, staring south across the plain. Nothing moved that Talan could see, though the horizon was still blurred with haze. They had thrashed out the line of battle the night before; the captains studied the ground muttering low-voiced commentary but no one proposed any actual changes.

The sun was fully up now, riding high over the Hundred Hills, a blinding disk in a cloud-hazed sky. Esclin glanced at it and reached out to the Muster Stone, quelling the fires that danced above and along its surface. The horses became waves and water, spilling back into the rock, and then the light that ran along its surface ran down into the dirt and vanished. The Westwood levies had either seen it or not, she guessed, would be hurrying on or not, would be here in time—or not. And besides, sunlight faded the delicate silver, and Esclin was not about to let his symbols show to disadvantage.

"How is Gelern Sword-Hand?" he asked, and she shrugged one shoulder.

"I haven't seen him since last night. Shall I check on him for you?"

"Later." Esclin stared off into the distance. "Your thought was a good one, to send him to Mag Ausse."

"That was Estor," Talan said.

"A good thought," Esclin said again. "If he's well enough to move, it might be wise to do it now." Talan stiffened, afraid for a moment that he might send her with it, and Esclin laid an arm across her shoulders. "Before you complain, yes, I'd thought of it, but I need you here. Who would you send, among your companions?"

"Celein," Talan said. He was the worst shot of all of them, but a strong swordsman. "And the Exile woman who's been with him—she's not mine to send, but I don't think she'd be much use, as worried as she is."

"See if he's fit to move—maybe the wheelman can do something to help with that—and if he is, talk to Diran." Esclin's arm tightened, pulling her close against his side. Talan leaned hard against him for just a moment, grateful for the touch, for his presence, for the wordless comfort, then straightened with a sigh.

"I'll do that. And then—join the archers?"

"If the Riders are in sight," Esclin said. "Otherwise, come back here."

And that was all there really was to say, for all that she wanted to find something more. She managed a brisk nod and turned away, heading for Nen Gorthen's tent.

Brelin had made his morning prayers with circumspection, hoarding his strength. Everyone said there would be a battle and he would be needed later. He made his way to Nen Gorthen's tent and found the physician Avlen still there, red-eyed from lack of sleep. A bowl simmered on the brazier, scenting the air with the cool tang of feverbane, and the Exile woman was fast asleep at the back of the tent. A boy sat beside the brazier, ready to leap to any needed service.

"How is he?" Brelin asked, but his eyes were searching the injured man. He looked better than he had the night before, face eased of pain and body relaxed against the pallet. It was early days, though, and he was not surprised when Avlen shrugged.

"He was fevered overnight. It broke a bit before dawn and he's been resting comfortably since then."

"Has he awakened?"

"Not yet."

"Probably just as well," Brelin said, and the other man nodded.

"I've made up a simple of feverbane and honey and just a touch of poppy-syrup for later."

He would certainly need it; a wound that deep did not

heal in an instant. Brelin said, "I agree, that's wise."

Avlen touched his sleeve, drew him closer to the door, lowering his voice even further. "Is it true that we'll face the Riders today?"

"So I've been told—" Brelin broke off as the tent flap swept back, admitting the thegen and her shadow.

"Oh, good," she said. "I wanted a word with you."

Avlen waved at her to be quiet, and Brelin said, "Outside. If you please, Thegen."

She grimaced, stepped back, and they all followed her, letting the tent flap close again behind them. "How is he?" she asked, lowering her voice.

"Better than yesterday," Brelin answered.

"We mentioned sending him to Mag Ausse to recover," Talan said. "And certainly he'd be safer away from here. Can he be moved?"

Brelin looked at Avlen. "You've examined him more recently."

The physician pursed his lips. "I don't think it would kill him, but it would set him back. It might well set him bleeding again, and unless the wheelman accompanies him—"

"I'm bound to the army, unless the arros excuses me," Brelin said.

"Then I'd prefer not to risk it, unless we absolutely must." Avlen spread his hands. "And there's the chance he might be overtaken on the road."

Talan looked from one to the other. "If he can't be moved, he can't be moved. I'll tell the arros. Where's Diran, do you know?"

"He went to the horse lines, Thegen," Avlen said.

"Tell him from me that he should leave a man or two with Gelern—the Exile woman should be one—just in case of trouble. Though I expect he's already thought of it."

"I'll pass the word," Avlen said with a bow, and Talan gave him a thoughtful look.

"And you should rest, yourself. We'll have need of you today."

"I intend to, Thegen."

Talan nodded and turned away, Cat Meirin trailing half a pace behind. "Have them send for me if the sword-hand needs me," Brelin said, and turned away.

Back at his own tent, he pulled his chest of supplies out into the sunlight and began again to sort through its contents. They would always be short of bandages, and he set Astin to cutting more strips from the length of linen he'd begged from the sutlers. He had never been so close to a battle before, nor had wished to be since he outgrew childish games; he thought his robe and wheelman's badge would keep him safe enough as long as the fighters had time to see it. There was little anything could do against fear or error. For a moment, he considered telling Astin to hide beneath the baggage wagons if the Riders broke the line, but on second thought guessed that the boy knew hiding places he would never think of. This was his second summer on the Dancing Ground, or so he'd said.

"Uncle?"

It had been days since anyone had addressed him by his proper title, and he looked up in mild surprise to see a trio of soldiers looking down at him. They wore Nen Brethil's badge, an older man and two young ones, and he pushed himself to his feet.

"How may I help you?" He could guess the answer, of course, could read it in their worried eyes, but the rite demanded that they speak aloud.

"A blessing for the day," one of the younger ones said. "If it please you."

Brelin reached for the wheel that hung on its staff before the tent's door, glad that he had chosen to keep the custom in spite of Esclin's disapproval. Though, to be fair, no one had said anything on the march to the Muster Hill. He stilled his mind and spun the wheel on its glittering axis. "The light of the Blazing One be on you, the flames of the Blazing One guide you, the strength of the Blazing One guard you."

The wheel clattered to a stop and the three bowed, backing nervously away. Brelin could see others hovering, alone and in little groups, and drew himself up to his full height. This was his duty and his place, for all that he knew that too many of his prayers would serve only to send them into death. The words were the same for the living and the dead: the Blazing One alone would choose between them.

The sun was well up by the time the main body of Alcis's army reached the Lammard. It ran shallow enough here that the men could cross waist-deep and she urged them on, using what horse she had to break the current and sending the strongest men across first, carrying lengths of rope to help the rest. Even so, more than a dozen men were swept away and had to be plucked from the deeper water by others who could swim. No one drowned, but at the end a handful lay sprawled in exhaustion or knelt to vomit up the Lammard's murky water.

She slid down from her own horse to let it rest and graze a while, though her eyes strayed to the eastern horizon. The Muster Hill wasn't yet in sight, not even the slightest rise to break the sun's dazzle. One of the household grooms came to take her horse, leading it to better grass, and a page brought a skin of honey water, sharply cool and sweet in the rising warmth. It would be a hot day later, she feared: one more factor to consider. This was not the Westwood, and for a moment she felt its absence like an ache behind her breastbone. The land here was wild, unclaimed, uninterested in the doings of men, not like the wood she tended. The grass hungered, roots thrusting deep into spring-damp soil; in the distance she could just feel a confusion of movement, stalks bending every way without a wind to push them, but there was nothing more.

She came back to herself to see Rihaleth waiting, a sideways smile twisting his lips. She shook her head in answer to his unspoken question and saw him sigh. "Everyone's across and resting," he said. "Kendrith thinks we're perhaps four hours behind Heldyn."

Alcis nodded, closing her eyes for an instant to recall the maps. They were perhaps six leagues from the Muster Hill; if Kendrith was right, Heldyn would be there in a bit more than an hour, though there was no telling what he would find there. Men and beasts would be tired, too, and they still didn't know the size of the Rider army. And wouldn't know until they came in sight, yet another unknowable piece to add to her calculations. She looked over her shoulder, her army still strung out along the Lammard's bank, some with wit enough to eat or drink, some even quick enough to refill waterskins, but already they looked tired. Best to rest now, while they could—though no matter what she did, they would be coming to the Hill at the end of a day's exertions.

"We'll stay a little longer, let them dry off and get their breath back." Her own hose were uncomfortably damp beneath her greaves, but there was no time to disarm. "Make sure they eat."

"I'll tell the captains," Rihaleth said.

Alcis stretched, the morning's ride tugging at her muscles, too. Another page brought journey-cake and she chewed at the heavy square without really tasting it. The sun was almost overhead, hot on her armor, and she was grateful for the first curl of the westerly breeze to stir her hair and tickle her sweaty skin. Behind her the army gathered its strength, men and horses calling as they reformed their order. Rihaleth came toward her, helm left behind somewhere, the sun striking red highlights from his brown hair, every inch of him her summer king. And then she heard it, carried on the wind, faint but impossible to mistake: the sound of horns from the Muster Hill. Rihaleth's head jerked up, his mouth tightening, and Alcis took a deep breath.

"My horse," she said to the waiting groom, and held out her hand to Rihaleth. "You heard?"

He nodded. "We don't know—"

And of course they didn't, there was no telling whether it signaled the enemy's approach or urged the lines together, or even called retreat. And she could not hurry them too hard, or she would do no good once she got there. "Get the men together. We move out now."

The scouts straggled in throughout the long morning, reporting several hundred horse and nearly twice as many infantry behind them. None of that was any surprise; and by the time the Rider banners were legible in the distance, Esclin's army had taken up its position at the base of the Muster Hill. They numbered about as many as the Riders, though they had more foot and archers; Huwar's levies anchored the right wing—steady men, Esclin had said, with his wry smile, and hardened. The ground there had little natural defense against the Riders and Huwar had had his men setting stakes for much of the morning, but they would do no good if they were driven out of that protection. He had Nen Brethil on his left, wedged between him and Esclin's own levies and the folk of Nen Gorthen, and he hoped Wellan had more sense than to take offense. Kellecost held the left wing for Nen Ddaur, the smaller nenns filling in between him and Esclin. He had not commanded a wing before, and Huwar hoped he was up to the task.

If only the Westwood's troops were here, they might stand a chance; but as it was, this was going to be a hard fight. The archers were waiting on the hill above, commanded by the thegen and Aredan Gammelos, and for a moment he wished he'd sent Perrin to join her. But Perrin was too old to be fobbed off that way, kept out of danger as though he was a child. Huwar glanced sideways, looking for his son beneath the banner. That was honor and risk enough for any day, but at least it kept him out of the front line at the start.

He could see the first troop of Riders now, under a swallowtail pennant half blue and half saffron, saw Denior's troop spur forward to meet them. Even at this distance, he could tell that Denior's mounts were tired. They met the Riders and the two troops tangled, wheeling in a confused knot as a second Rider company spurred forward, avoiding that battle and heading straight for the army's flank. All along the line, his troops braced themselves to spear and shield. Huwar drew his own sword, looking left and right along the line. "Steady, now!"

Behind him he could hear the lines shift, the less experienced men drawing back from the edges of their square, and heard his sergeants curse them back into place. The Riders saw the movement and their leader shouted in answer, lifting the banner. His troop rushed forward, shouting together, and Huwar braced himself behind his shield.

"Hold the line!"

The cry was picked up and repeated, his people closing ranks behind the hedge of stakes. It looked flimsy against the oncoming horsemen, but at the last minute the Riders swerved away. A handful flung light javelins, but they struck shield and mail and did no harm. His own troops raised a cheer and Huwar raised his sword.

"Steady, they'll come again."

Sure enough, the Riders regrouped and came on with another shout, banner snapping in the wind. The line held firm, but this time several of the Riders swung swords at the protecting stakes. One snapped short, another tilted, and the Riders swerved away again.

"Archers!" someone shouted. "Where are the archers?"

"Saving their shafts," another voice answered, and for all that it was the literal truth, there was more bitterness behind the words than Huwar liked to hear. He looked over his shoulder, searching for the man who'd spoken, and the Riders swung in again. This time, the shower of javelins found their mark: a man fell backward, silent and surprised, the shaft clean through his neck between mail and helm. Another cried out, going to his knees in the front line, and the Riders charged the gap that opened as someone dragged him to safety. Huwar cursed, but the line closed cleanly behind the stakes and the horses turned away.

He couldn't see where Denior's men had gone—driven off, presumably—but the main body of the Rider army was only just in sight, a smudge and a flicker of banners against the horizon to the south. Still an hour or more away, Huwar judged, and shouldered his way along the line, heading for the group that anchored the flank. They were his best men, but even so they'd need all the help they could get.

"Father?" Perrin called, lifting their own banner, but Huwar waved for him to stay put. He tapped his senior sergeant on the shoulder, and when the man turned, slid into the second line beside him.

"They're coming," someone called, and Huwar lifted his shield with the others as the Rider company swept close again. The front line gave way, swaying back, and Huwar set his shield against the spine of the man ahead of him, grunting with effort. The Riders gave a shout, high and harsh and wordless as a hawk's, but the horses fought shy of the stakes. One slipped as it tried to turn away, fighting the bridle, and a boy leaped from the front line to slash at its hind legs. He missed, and the Rider swung in his saddle to cut him down. Another boy started forward but the sergeant caught his arm.

"He's dead, son." He raised his voice. "And that, my lads, is why you keep the line."

Huwar licked his lips and reached for the water bottle slung at his waist, then stopped himself. Better to save it for later and, besides, no amount of drink would cure his trouble. On the plain a second company trotted up to join the Riders, a second pennon joining the first and then the two groups together wheeled and charged.

"Hold!" he shouted, and the cry was picked up along the line, each man bracing shield against shoulder.

The Riders shouted in answer, the high, hawk cry as merciless as the sun, the horses' hooves a thunder against the earth. In spite of himself, Huwar leaned back and the men ahead of him pressed back as well, a single step, and then another.

"Hold, damn you!"

The sergeant shoved hard against the man ahead of him, nearly knocking him forward out of the line. The man stumbled and recovered and then the horses were on them, Riders leaning far out of the saddle to try for even a glancing blow. There was a clash of metal on wood, and a confused shouting, then the Riders wheeled away again.

"Straighten the line!" Huwar called, but they had lost a solid ell, had been pushed back so that the stakes were barely a defense. "Sergeants—"

The Riders had seen it, too, and half of the newcomers wheeled with a shout of triumph, driving for the break. Huwar felt his men give, two more steps and then a third. The line was still unbroken, shield pressed to shield, but the first of the Riders shoved his way between the stakes and the front rank. One of Huwar's men stabbed at the horse from behind the shields, and it reared, screaming, and fell. Its rider went sprawling, too, falling hard on the stakes, but they were angled away from the falling man, and his weight just flattened them beneath him. Something flashed in the air—a thrown dagger? a hand-axe?—and the man went down and didn't rise.

"Forward," Huwar shouted. "Forward, Nen Salter—" But the Riders had already turned for another charge, and there was nothing to do but hold the line. He felt the first of the horsemen shock into the men to his right—trying to turn the flank, a part of his mind noted, even as he thrust hard at the whirling mass of men and horses in front of him, and this time they left dead men as they retreated. Dead Riders, too, three of them that he could see; but his own ranks were thinned, and it was too late to try to get back into the shelter of the stakes. Perrin was at his side, banner held high, and Huwar couldn't spare a moment to see whether the boy had come to him or if his own line had been that drastically shortened. It was turned, though, curving back as the men sought the slight shelter of the Muster Hill: not ideal, but not disastrous, not as long as they could hold...

There was a definite note of triumph in the Riders' call now, and Huwar braced himself against the men to either side. The shouts, the drumming of hooves was deafening; he called orders but could barely hear his own voice in the sudden clamor. The horsemen came on, bulling their way past what was left of the stakes, but at least the wreckage slowed them a little. Huwar turned slightly, putting his shield forward, and a man on a tall bay came in hard, sword raised. Huwar thrust hard at the horse, felt his blade sink into its shoulder and saw it falter, then the sword came down against his helm. It was enough to stagger him, and the man to his left caught him under the shield, holding him up for a vital instant. A weight battered his sword arm, then fell against his knee, and he looked down to see the sergeant crumpled in a bloody knot. The horseman tried to crowd in over him and Huwar struck again, aiming for the horse. On its other side, Rouden did the same and the animal went down, thrashing, pinning his rider beneath him. Huwar stabbed awkwardly, point slipping on mail, then struck again more carefully and felt the blade drive home.

He wrenched his sword free to see the Riders pulling back but his own line was shrinking, forced to turn back on itself. "Form up," he shouted, and grabbed the nearest man, dragging him into line. The man cried out and Huwar's hand came away slick with blood. "Form up!"

His men were doing their best to obey but there were bodies in the way, men and horses, Riders and his own men, and still no good ground. At least Perrin was still there, still clutching the banner, face white and set beneath his helm. If they broke, if the flank crumbled—he would not think of it, would not admit the possibility, and turned to shove another man forward. "Hold the line!"

They could hear the fighting before they could see it clearly, faint shouts, the clash of metal, a distant trumpet and the shrill blast of a whistle. That changed things: Heldyn left the archers to make their own way—*Cautiously*, he ordered, *and wait for the kyra if you need to*—and urged the horsemen forward. They were always short of horse, and on the open plain of the Dancing Ground the disadvantage was deadly.

Heldyn could see the battle now, Esclin's men drawn up at the base of the Muster Hill, letting its slope guard back and flanks, while the first companies of Riders wheeled and charged, trying to turn the flanking companies. The fighting had been hot already, he could see the bodies of men and horses humped in the grass; the infantry was hard-pressed, Nen Salter's banner wavering, the company forced back on itself. The main body of the army was still three quarters of an hour back, though it would be in bowshot sooner: time enough, room enough, and he drew his sword. His ensign spun their banner, unwinding the ribbons that had been wound close to its shaft, and the white and silver streamers lifted as he urged his horse to a faster trot. There was no subtlety here, everyone could see the obvious action, and he lifted his sword, pointing them on toward the Rider companies harassing Nen Salter's line.

They surged forward, picking up speed in spite of themselves, in spite of common sense, and Heldyn didn't try to hold them back. They were tired enough; if there was a chance of driving the Riders back in a single charge, it was worth taking. He saw the first Rider turn, mouth opening to shout a warning, and shouted himself in the same moment.

"On, on!"

His troop held their loose formation, a wedge with the standard at its center, while ahead of them the Riders struggled to disengage and turn to meet them. Perhaps a third had managed it before they were on them, the point of the Westwood's wedge ramming between two Riders like a ship driving ashore. Heldyn swung his own sword, got one good blow with his and the horse's weight behind it. He saw the Rider go down and ducked away from an awkward swing. It slowed him, just as all around him the troop was slowing, hacking at the Riders and their mounts.

Nen Salter's men raised a cheer and surged forward, just far enough to push the rear-rank Riders and send them skittering against their fellows. Heldyn shortened his grip and thrust, thrust again, the blade skidding along leather and mail, finally managed an awkward, backward slice that drove his enemy back in his saddle. He braced for the killing blow, but another of his men was there before him; the Rider went down without a cry and Heldyn wrenched his protesting horse around for another attack. The Rider barely parried him, his horse forced back on its haunches, and another cheer rose from Nen Salter's line.

Another company of horse swept in, these troopers wearing Riverholme's barbed crescent. There weren't many of them, but they were enough; Heldyn thrust again at a fleeing Rider, and then what was left of the company was gone, trailing back toward their own main army. A couple of his own men started to give chase and he shouted them back to their line. On the hill above, the archers loosed a single volley, dropping three more Riders, and Heldyn swung his own horse in a wide circle, trying to take stock.

Four horses were down, and another riderless; he couldn't find all the bodies at a first look, but already both his own and Nen Salter's men were hurrying to tend the wounded. He spun again, fixing his eyes on the Rider army, but for the moment there was no movement there.

"Lord Winter!" That was the commander of Riverholme's men, a dark-haired man with pale eyes, his armor hastily patched where a pauldron had been ripped away. "Is the kyra with you?"

"Behind me," Heldyn answered. "But coming."

Some of the others heard that and raised a cheer. Heldyn made no effort to stop them, though inwardly he flinched. There was no knowing just how far behind him Alcis was, or what shape the men would be in when she got here. But he had come in good time, and that was enough for now.

"The arros wanted us to screen Nen Salter," Riverholme's man said. "Will you join us?"

Heldyn nodded, looking again at the oncoming army. Still an hour out, at least, he thought, and in the same moment, a new horseman reined to a stop beside Riverholme's man.

"Lord Winter!" The boy's voice cracked painfully, and Heldyn saw the wave of color wash up his beardless face, but he carried on in spite of his embarrassment. "Lord Winter, the arros would like a word."

"And I with him." Heldyn looked around, found his nearest sergeant. "Syket! Round up the men, get our wounded to safety, and form up with Riverholme. I need to speak to Esclin. Serlo, Henna, with me."

Syket tossed him a salute, his hand so bloodied he seemed to be wearing a scarlet glove. Heldyn gestured for the page to lead the way and the troopers he'd named fell in at their heels, Henna with the ribboned banner still securely planted in her stirrup. Nen Salter's men raised a cheer, seeing the ribbons flare and flash, and the call was picked up as they cantered along the army's front. *Earned, too*, Heldyn thought. *If we hadn't come just then, Nan Salter would have been hard pressed to hold.*

The page pulled to a halt near the line's center where Esclin's banner hung limp from its staff, folds barely stirring in the heated air. Heldyn lifted a hand in greeting, raising another cheer, and the front line shifted allowing Esclin to step free. He was in full armor, mail shirt and a thin tabard marked with his water horse to provide some protection from the sun. He had shed his helm and pushed back the mail coif, and his pale hair was matted with sweat. He held out his hand, and Heldyn hastily switched his reins to his off hand to take it, bending low into an awkward embrace.

"Your timing proves excellent once again," Esclin said.

"I do my best," Heldyn answered. "The kyra's some hours behind me, with the rest of our army."

"How long?"

Heldyn suppressed a shrug. "As fast as they can come. We saw your beacon last night. I came on at once with the horse, and Alcis will have left at dawn."

"I knew you'd know what it meant," Esclin said with a quick smile, "and I guessed you'd be within sight. And now you've saved Nen Salter. I'm in your debt."

Typical, Heldyn thought, but that had always been Esclin's gift, to see a chance where no one else did. "In the kyra's debt," he said aloud, and Esclin dipped his head in acknowledgment.

"I'm sure she'll think of something." The brief amusement vanished from his eyes. "How are your men? Can they join with Diran—that's Gelern's second, Gelern was wounded yesterday and won't be in any shape to fight for some weeks. Nen Salter's flank is badly exposed."

"I don't think we have a choice," Heldyn answered. "We're tired, man and beast, but—we'll do what we can."

Esclin reached up again to clasp his wrist, the touch reminding Heldyn of more intimate caresses. "I know you will."

Heldyn returned the grip with sudden fervor, words crowding his tongue, but swallowed them unsaid. Esclin didn't need them, any more than he himself needed to say them, not after all these years. He gathered his horse instead and turned away, cantering back along the length of the line, Serlo and Henna at his back. The winter king's ribbons floated above them, and as they rejoined his men, he allowed himself one brief glance as they settled against the shaft. *Let me be worthy*, he thought. That was prayer enough for the day.

CHAPTER TEN

Esclin watched Lord Winter's banner move away along the front ranks, followed by more shouts and cheers, and stepped back into the ranks. His men shifted to make way, formed up again behind him, a fragile wall of shield and sword. As long as Heldyn's men—and Diran's—could screen the flank, they stood a chance. As long as Alcis arrived in good time. The archers would get one, maybe two good volleys; then it would be line to line and he'd have to trust the horse to take care of themselves. Kellecost's men were better screened, the ground rougher on their end of the line, and the horsemen protecting them were better rested; it was up to Huwar to hold his ground no matter what.

Ilgae Marshal touched his arm, offering a waterskin. Esclin took it, drank carefully—watered wine, warm from the sun but soothing to a dry mouth—and handed it back. "Well?"

"Nothing yet." Ilgae slanted a smile that didn't touch her eyes. "Well, except the Riders, and that we can see for ourselves."

Esclin nodded. The Rider foot soldiers were coming on steadily, perhaps half a league away, their banners displayed above each company. The Blazing One's golden circle was the largest, marking the center; he recognized most of the others from previous years: twin hawks, a star, a spur, and half a dozen horses, rearing, running, standing.

There were flashes of light above the marching heads, as though the sun struck sparks from the banners, and he swore under his breath. Wheelmen were marching among the Rider foot, their burning glasses lifted high. They could do no real harm but the flashes were distracting, could blind a man at a crucial moment, and the wheelmen seemed able to direct them where they pleased.

He glanced up at the sky. The sun was just past the zenith, a white-hot disk barely obscured by the haze of cloud that turned the sky almost to milk. To the east the clouds were thicker, gathering over the Hundred Hills; he closed his eye, feeling their distant promise, rain and darkness, but his strength was not enough to draw it near. The Lammard was closer, and the still-damp ground beneath his feet. He reached for them both, drawing the fog that lurked along the river's edge and under the hill, teasing it out to thicken the clouds overhead.

For a long moment there was nothing, but he held his hand. This was not a moment for force—and even if it had been, he didn't have the strength to spare, not before a battle. The fog was there, was always there, waiting to rise; all he could do was call it forth and let its kinship to the clouds draw it up. For long minutes nothing happened, and then the light changed. He opened his eye to see a thicker band of cloud veiling the sun, and his men raised a ragged cheer.

"That'll help some," Ilgae said.

"It should hold a while," Esclin said.

"Yes." Ilgae nodded. "They'll try to blind the archers as they charge."

"Yes." They'd been over the tactics a dozen times already, the night before and then again this morning over a snatched meal: the archers were primed to loose their first volley when the wheelmen made their move. Esclin shaded his eye, peering over the heads of his men toward the advancing line. He could hear the rattle of drums, the sharp rolling cadence that meant these were the Riders' best foot: they held the center, just as his own men did, and had proved themselves a match before this. If they could just hold—Alcis's men would sweep down on their flank and roll them away like a stone in the Hidden River. If they held. If she came in time.

"Not long now," Ilgae said after a bit. Esclin shaded his eye again, aware that the Riders were closer but not how much so. A whistle sounded to his left, was picked up all along the line, *Attention* and then *Make ready.* He heard Ilgae murmur something, a curse or a prayer, and settle her gorget more comfortably against her neck. Esclin drew up his own coif and tucked the end of his long braid back into the hood. He settled his helm, heavy and hot, then drew on his gloves, working his fingers to ease the sweat-stiff leather. He collected his shield and worked his shoulders under the heavy mail, loosening muscles, and the lines of men rippled as they took up their places. He had not spent too much of himself to raise the fog; it would be enough.

Light flashed along the Rider line, sparks that seemed to snap into space, and Esclin heard Aredan shout something on the hill above. The whistles echoed him and the archers gave a great *Hah*, their first volley keening overhead.

"Oh, too soon," Ilgae said, and Esclin grimaced. Sure enough, nearly half the flights fell short, and the ones that reached the Rider line were nearly spent, doing little damage. The wheelmen's lights flashed again, snapping sparks that caught and echoed the changing rhythm of the drums, and the line surged forward. Whistles answered all along his own line, sounding *Ready*, and overhead the archers shouted again, releasing another volley. This one was better timed: Esclin saw men stumble and fall, the line ragged for a long moment before men filled the gaps. They came on shouting, the wheelmen's lights flashing above their heads. The archers managed a final volley, less coherent, a third or more falling long, and Esclin braced himself.

The lines collided, shield shoving against shield as the front ranks fought for openings for their swords, men shouting without words as they heaved back and forth. In the third rank, Esclin moved forward, bringing himself into line with Ilgae and a stocky gray-beard on his right, lifting shields to brace the men ahead of them. Someone screamed; the line wavered and then pushed back, heaved forward a few paces, fell back again. Esclin stepped on an out-flung arm and nearly fell, managed to catch himself against Ilgae's shoulder.

The whistles shrilled, calling the men to form up, to hold, but their notes were blurred by the rattle of the Riders' drums. Ahead of Esclin a man went down and he stepped up over the body to take his place, bracing himself against the people to either side. They heaved forward, and stalled. The Riders pressed in, shouting, steel thrusting in the gaps between soldiers. Esclin parried but there was no room to counterattack, and he ducked behind his shield. The front line was tiring, giving back step by step. Esclin gave way with them, trying to keep step with the people to either side, but the ground was churned up by their struggle and there were bodies underfoot, the wounded struggling to save themselves from being trampled.

To his left, Ilgae stumbled and fell, rolling as she tried to protect herself. Another man gave way, and another, and suddenly there were Riders among them, slashing and shoving as they tried to open a break. Esclin stabbed at the nearest, felt Arros slice through leather and mail, drew the blade back bloodied and bright with silver flame. He slashed again, knocked another man back, and heard the banner-guard running forward to contain the break.

"Form up!" he shouted, and the call was taken up along the line, ragged against the drums.

Another man came at him, slashing blindly. He ducked, taking the blow on his shield, and it rattled him back on his heels. He thrust anyway, felt the point catch and tear, drew back his arm to strike again, his shoulders burning. Were there fewer Riders? Had the line held? A Rider swung at him from his blind side and he staggered sideways, the edge of his shield cracking. One of his own men stabbed the Rider, took up position at his left, and Esclin crouched for an instant, gasping for breath.

And then he heard it, high and clear, cutting through the shouts and chaos, first one horn and then another, echoing up from the west. Alcis had come. He straightened, pushed himself back toward the line, heedless of what he trampled in his path.

"Hold the line! Hold the line, the Westwood has come!"

He could hear a cheer spreading from his own right wing, Nen Salter's men already relieved, felt the moment the Riders faltered. "The Westwood!" he called again, and leaned forward with the others.

❧

She sat her horse in the gap between the twin companies of her army, surrounded by her captains and her personal guard, the great green-and-gold banner of the Westwood floating above her, the light silk and ribbons lifted high by their forward movement. Ahead, she could see the battle laid out before her like counters on a map, a breathless instant of clarity that she knew to seize before it dissolved into chaos. There was Esclin's line, the water horse banner tilted but standing; Heldyn's banner flashed on the near flank, a tangle of horse shielding Nen Salter's men. There were the Riders, the wheelmen's glasses flashing above the men's heads as the foot pressed hard into a yielding place between Esclin and Nen Salter. That same success had thinned the Rider line, opened gaps that Nen Salter was too harried to exploit, but she…

She lifted a hand, beckoning the captain of the remaining horse. They were not quite half the force, but at this stage of the battle, and relatively fresh themselves, they should be more than enough. "Anstys. Take your people—all of them— and support Lord Winter."

"Let me leave ten with you," Anstys said.

Alcis grimaced. "The banner-guard, then. But take the rest. Now."

Anstys touched her forehead and wheeled her handsome bay, gathering her troop with a shout. The banner-guard, six troopers plus the one who carried the royal standard, shifted uneasily but kept their places at her side, pacing between the two great companies of foot. Horns sounded for the charge, high and sweet, and one of the banner-guard's horses broke stride, trying to join its fellows. Its rider hauled it back, cursing, and Alcis lifted her hand.

"Walk on. Keep the pace." Out of the corner of her eye she saw Rihaleth stir, and glanced down to see him frowning where he walked with his sergeant and the left wing's commander. "Well?"

He tilted his head to one side, familiar half-smile beneath the heavy helm. "We've still a bit of ground to cover."

"Let Anstys clear our way," she said, with more confidence than she entirely felt, "and we'll have them. Hit them between Nen Salter and the arros's men—Nen Brethil's banner."

Rihaleth's smile widened. "Very well, Kyra."

She reached down to clasp his hand, all the farewells they could not in honor make when no one else could. "Time you joined your men. And you, too, Josse."

She clasped hands with Josse Iros, too, and they turned away, each to their own wing. Alcis shaded her eyes, straining to see into the dust-hazed distance. The Riders had heard the horns, had fought to turn to meet Anstys's charge but they were fully engaged, Heldyn's people and Esclin's holding them locked. She thought the gap was still there, perhaps even widening, but could no longer be sure. And then Anstys and her troops were among them, the dust and the confusion of men and horses clouding her sight.

"Sound the advance, Kyra?" the ensign asked, and shook the standard to make the ribbons flare against the sky. To her right the summer king's ribbon-banner rippled, scarlet and gold and new-leaf green; to her left, the blues of Iros and the purple of Ëpasse flicked like snakes' tongues in the freshening breeze.

"Not yet. Keep the pace."

They moved forward, the air filled with the creak of harness and the clatter of metal, the drumming of feet on the hard ground, but without a word spoken. Ahead there was noise, shouts and crashes, the shrilling of whistles and the sudden, urgent batter of a drum, but they were caught in the moment before, poised to choose. And then she saw it, the sudden shift as the remains of the Rider horsemen fought free of Heldyn's and Anstys's men, breaking away south across the plain. Someone raised a breathless cheer and a horn sounded, Anstys charging after them, and Alcis lifted her hand.

"Now!"

The horns sounded all along the line and the footmen picked up their pace, going from a walk to their practiced trot, the banners flaring above their heads. The banner-guard closed up around her and they matched the pace, the horns now sounding a hunting call. She saw the moment the Rider foot tried to turn to meet them and was swept away, driven back into their own center. A horseman came at her guard; she drew her sword, but her page Griseld flung himself between them to block the blow and Sergeant Radamy took the man's head off, blood fountaining across her knee as the horse and falling corpse raced past. Another horseman charged, and a handful of foot, dodging the hooves and striking at horses' legs and bellies. She swung her horse in circles, sword cocked and ready, but the guard surrounded her, holding them off.

And then there were no more, only horsemen with her own badge or Riverholme's, streaming past in pursuit of an army suddenly fleeing southward. She caught her breath, standing in her stirrups, and sagged again to see blocks of Riders withdrawing in good order, while what was left of their horse struggled to regroup and cover the retreat. Not a complete victory—it was never the rout she dreamed of—but it was a victory, and more than she had feared they might achieve.

They met in the flattened grass at the foot of the hill, the Muster Stone thrusting up into the sky above them. The remains of the battle spread before them, the twists of the fighting mapped in bodies dark against the new green. They had held the ground, Alcis thought, and that counted as victory, but at a cost. People were moving slowly across the field seeking those wounded who could still be saved, men and beasts alike. A knife blade caught the sun, mercy given, and Alcis turned her head to focus on the living.

"Esclin."

He looked up at her with a smile. He had shed helm and mail coif somewhere, and his hair fell in a fraying braid that exposed his scarred face and missing eye, the shadow of his skull strong beneath his skin. He was marked with dirt and blood, though she didn't think that much of the latter was his own.

"Alcis. You're here betimes."

"I do my poor best." She leaned down from the saddle to take his hand, feeling the tendons jumping under her fingers. "And your message was hard to miss."

"I did hope so." His smile flickered again, then faded. "We don't have the strength to pursue them."

"I know." She could see all too clearly: his people were spent, foot and horse alike, and her own were in only slightly better shape. And that meant this would all be for nothing, just one more skirmish and a mound to mark the dead. But that was still better than a defeat, better than being the army spread out over a league or more, unable even to bury their dead. She had done that and had resolved not to do it again. "What now?"

"Hold the hill another night," Esclin said, though his tone was less certain than his words. "Rest the men, treat the wounded, bury the dead... Follow on? It depends on what the horse say, when they return." Alcis nodded, having no better advice to give. Perhaps once the pursuit ended and scouts could be sent, she could think of something more. "I've lost Ilgae."

Alcis drew breath sharply at that. She had known Ilgae Illaros when she was one of Esclin's companions, all of them refugees in the Westwood, had liked her then and liked her just as well as Esclin's marshal. "Not—is she dead?"

"Not yet." Esclin's voice was grim. "But she may be before the night's over. I saw her go down, but there wasn't anything—the wound wasn't so bad, but she was trampled, too."

Alcis hissed in sympathy, wishing for the thousandth time that her own powers lay in healing. But that was not her gift, so she tightened her hold on his hand again, wishing there were words.

"There's a wheelman in the camp who's proved himself good with such things," Esclin went on. "I've sent for him, but—it'll be a near-run thing."

"A wheelman?" Alcis heard her own voice sharp and startled.

"It's a long tale... Someone tried to poison me at Nen Salter, poisoned one of the pages instead. The wheelman—Brelin, he's called—Brelin saved him, and there was pleading enough from the southern nenns that I had to bring him with me."

Alcis eyed him warily. "I'm sure that's what the lord paramount wanted."

"Well, of course it is," Esclin said. "But I'm betting he's a pawn, not a spy."

"That's a bet with high stakes."

"Less so than it might be. The lord paramount has a ring I gave a harper, last winter."

"What folly—" Alcis closed her mouth tight over the rest of what she might have said, knowing it to be pointless. The rules were different in the Hundred Hills.

"It's a long tale," Esclin said again. "Another long tale. But to balance it—" He drew his sword, the elegant curve dimmed with use. "My royal sword. Arros."

Alcis gave it a respectful nod. Kelleiden's work, unmistakably, and as unmistakably his choice of name; she only hoped it served them better than Deep-Biter had served his father. "I thought you said last year that the auguries were ambiguous."

"They were and are." Esclin sheathed the sword. "But I needed something to draw the hill folk."

Before she could answer, a tall boy—no, a girl—came trotting up to make a brisk and general bow.

"Father—Sire. Nen Brethil wants a word. Seems they've collected some number of those burning glasses."

Alcis sat frozen, her hands folded on the pommel of her saddle, her eyes widening as though that would let her take in more of this unexpected person. She was dark-haired and dark-eyed, her cheeks and chin still childish, though her bones would be as sharp as her father's once she reached her full growth. She wore a leather corselet like the archers—and indeed she carried a short mountain bow and a quiver as well as a practical-looking sword—and Alcis guessed she had been stationed with them. Which was the safer place, behind the shield line, but even so her heart skipped a beat. She had not seen Talan since she was three, a stolen visit to Nen Elin that she had never been able to repeat. If anything had happened, if she had not had this moment at all—this was the same fear she felt for Traher, for Helevys, and for their fathers, and she swallowed it down.

Esclin was speaking, had been speaking for a moment, and she made herself smile as she understood the words. "—make yourself known to your mother. This is Alcis Mirielos, the kyra of the Westwood."

Talan's eyes widened, shock giving way to suspicion, but she made a proper obeisance. "Kyra. I am honored."

"I am very glad to see you again." There were a thousand things Alcis wanted to say, a thousand questions, and this was the time for none of them, and the thing that fell from her lips was not perhaps what she would have chosen. "Is Lysse well?"

That was the dear friend who had been Talan's nurse and foster mother, and Alcis saw her daughter's face soften. "She is, Kyra, and Cat Meirin, too."

"I'd best deal with Nen Brethil," Esclin said, and Alcis shook herself.

"Would my presence help or hinder?"

"Hinder," Esclin said, with the honesty she always admired, and she nodded.

"I'll see to my people, then, and we'll finish this later."

The wounded had been coming since noon, carried by their fellows or limping in on their own, to drop down at the corners of the pavilions that had been set up to receive them, like birds broken by a storm. Brelin moved from cot to cot and then from man to man, Astin at his heels carrying the box of simples, but there was little use for it. Mostly the wounds wanted the quick, sure cautery of holyfire, and those who needed more were mostly so far gone that the effort would be wasted. Once, twice, the pain was so great he could not bear it, and with a whispered prayer, apology and blessing, he crushed out the fluttering spark of life that remained. The second time, the man who had brought the gutted body—his son?—collapsed wailing over the corpse, and Brelin tasted blood where he had bitten his own lips to keep from speaking.

At one point he heard that the Westwood's troops had come, and then that they had not and all was lost; but he put it all aside, focusing on the work at hand. At another moment he found himself curled in a corner, Astin crouched protectively beside him, fanning the stick of holyfire back and forth to keep the coal alive. Brelin knew what this was, the empty exhaustion that came from spending all his strength in the outward gift of healing; he was not yet recovered, but he could hear the need all around him. He closed his eyes, whispered a prayer though he could not feel the Blazing One's fires, and dragged himself back to work.

He was forced to rest again around sunset, curled this time in the corner of a tent where most of the troops had been at least bandaged, woke to witchlight and Avlen's apologetic voice.

"—if you could see her."

"He's dead on his feet," Astin protested, and that was enough to make Brelin sit up again, working his shoulders.

"I'm sorry. What did you need?"

"It's the marshal," Avlen said. "I know you looked at her once already, but if you could look at her again."

The marshal had taken a sword cut into the ribs, bad enough on its own, but she'd been ground beneath the feet of the soldiers of both lines, lay with bones shattered and bloody bubbles on her lips. Brelin had done what he could to stem the bleeding, but there was little he could do to make the bones knit faster. "Of course," he said, and let Avlen haul him to his feet.

They had taken the marshal to her own tent, lit now by witchlight and a brazier, and a young woman was carefully dripping a thick liquid onto her lips. Ilgae stirred and sighed and licked at it, and Brelin glanced at the arros's physician.

"Poppy syrup," Avlen said. "The longer she sleeps, the better."

Brelin nodded, though privately he thought there was little chance Ilgae would wake unless she took a turn toward life. Lying there on the cot, her broken bones lightly splinted, bruises blackening on bloodless skin, she looked more like a corpse than a woman, with only the wincing movement of her lips to betray that she lived. He came close anyway, and the woman wiped Ilgae's lips before stepping quietly aside. Brelin folded back the coverlet—the lightest linen, to ease the weight on the broken bones—and surveyed the bandages. They were at the moment unbloodied, but he didn't like the liquid sound of the marshal's breathing, and glanced over his shoulder.

"Astin."

The boy brought the holyfire, and Brelin breathed on it until the coal glowed brilliant blue, considering his choices. If there were not so many injuries—but the worst, he thought, was to the lungs, and he called up the last spark of his strength to send the holyfire deep into the mangled tissue. Heat to staunch the last bleeding, to drive off the cold that sapped a woman's life. He gave what he had, but felt no response. That meant nothing; the body did not need to answer to be healed, but it was not a good sign. He stepped back, cupping his hand over the holyfire to quench the ember, and only then saw Esclin standing quiet at the foot of the cot.

"Will she live?"

Brelin heaved a sigh. "I can't tell. I've done all I can, but it can still go either way."

The young woman glared at him for that but Esclin merely nodded. He had shed his armor and loosed his hair, though he didn't seem to have found time to bathe. "Come with me, then. I want a word with you. If you'll stay with the marshal, Avlen?"

"Of course," Avlen answered, and Brelin followed the arros from the tent. Twilight was almost past, the first stars just visible, and the moon was rising over the Hundred Hills, half veiled by clouds. The noise of the camp was muted and he could feel the night's damp through his worn shoes.

The arros's tent was chilly in spite of the brazier and in spite of the numbers gathered within. Esclin was immediately drawn aside by the Westwood's summer king and Brelin stood blinking in the entrance, wondering if he wouldn't be wiser just to slip away. Before he could move someone nudged his elbow, and he accepted a spoon and a bowl filled with thick stew. It smelled of wine and spring onions and had visible chunks of mutton, and he wolfed several bites before registering who had handed him the dish.

It was not the thegen's place to wait on him, and he felt the color rising in his cheeks. The thegen herself didn't seem to mind, though, went on scooping stew from the pot and handing it to the group gathered around the brazier. That done, she took a bowl herself and leaned cautiously against a tent pole to begin eating. Food was the best thing for him, Brelin knew, and he concentrated on it, the rich broth and barley beneath the meat, lending only half an ear to the conversation. He was still light-headed; the food drew him back to his body, to the earth beneath his feet and the fire in its basin, to smoke-bleared eyes and cold toes and an ache like overstretched muscles in his soul.

Witchlight glowed at the peak of the tent, casting soft shadows. The arros and the Westwood's kyra shared the single couch, she curled compactly against the support, he leaning companionably against her shoulder, his bowl set aside and a wine cup in his hand. Nen Salter hunched exhausted on a stool, elbows on knees, half-emptied bowl forgotten for the moment. The winter king and Nen Brethil stood by the brazier, talking quietly as they ate; Kellecost watched them both without joining in. The summer king had slipped out some time ago, Brelin realized, along with Esclin's horsemaster.

"I'm in your debt again," Esclin said. "You did good work this afternoon. There are any number who'll live because of you who would have died."

Brelin glanced up, and only then realized that the arros was talking to him. He felt himself blush again but managed to keep his voice steady. "It's my duty, Sire."

"Nevertheless." Esclin still leaned on Alcis's shoulder as though by right, heedless of her consort—who seemed, indeed, oblivious. Brelin lowered his eyes, but not before he had registered the tired shadows in the arros's face. "You have a right to ask a favor, and I acknowledge it here and now."

And before witnesses. Nen Salter, at least, will hold him to it. Brelin's breath caught, and he had to make an effort to set his bowl aside without an unseemly squeak of surprise. He knew what he should ask, certainly, as surely as everyone in the room—including the arros, the slightest of wry smiles hovering on his lips: let the wheelmen enter Nen Elin. It was certainly what his superiors wanted, what Thedar wanted, and all the southern nenns that leaned toward the Blazing One. But was it what the Blazing One wanted? He glanced toward the flame that flickered in the brazier, not his own but close enough kin to serve, seeking the familiar touch of the divine. The power was there, of course, even in this poor reflection, but there was no push, none of the pleasure he had expected at a battle won by the right weapons, nor even any sense of urgency. There was only the presence and the silence, undemanding and calm.

"I think," he said slowly, "I think that this is not the time to speak of favors. It's too soon, there's too much yet to do, and I would not distract you from it. When this dance is ended, may I ask you then?"

Esclin's smile widened. "I may have less to give."

"Or more."

Esclin dipped his head. "Very well. Ask me when this dance is ended."

"I will do so, Sire," Brelin said, and bowed in answer.

They had heard from the last of the captains now, the count of dead and wounded higher than Alcis had hoped, but not so bad as she had feared. If they had pursued the Riders... But Esclin's troops weren't up to it, and her force alone was not enough to inflict a substantial defeat. She shivered, the brazier not enough to warm the tent, and Heldyn draped a fur about her shoulders. She gave him a smile of thanks and Esclin offered her his wine cup. She shook her head, her eyes lingering for a moment on Talan as she bent over the maps spread out on the narrow table. By all accounts she had acquitted herself well, and Alcis admitted to an unreasonable surge of pride. She had had nothing to do with this daughter's raising, though she had not expected any less from Esclin, but—her heart swelled nonetheless.

And perhaps there would be time to say that later, but there were more important matters at hand. "In the morning, we should follow them."

Esclin took another drink of the wine and waved his free hand at Gelern's captain, Diran. "Tell us again what you found."

Diran heaved a sigh, and Talan turned away from the table to offer him another cup of wine. He ducked his head in thanks and said, "Not so very much, Sire. We followed their foot back along the plain and harried as we went. Three leagues, maybe four? Then their horse regrouped to screen the retreat, there where there's a line of scrub and trees, so we disengaged and came away. They were still moving south then and showed no signs of stopping."

"They'll stop for the night, surely," Heldyn said. "If only for the horses' sake."

"They lost more men than we did," Nen Salter said, "but they still outnumber us in horse."

"They always do," Esclin said.

"We barely held them," Nen Brethil said, his voice tight. "We can't afford to chase them. The muster hill is defensible, we proved that today. Let them come to us if they want to continue the fight."

"We didn't beat them that badly," Kellecost said. "And I don't like the idea of them running wild in the south so that you don't have to keep your doorstep clear."

Esclin lifted a hand. "Peace. It's been a long day, no need for hard words among us. In any case, we can't stay here, there's no food for the men. Either we push on, or we fall back on Mag Ausse, and I'm not inclined to retreat just yet."

"The quicker we follow them, the more likely it is we can catch them off guard," Kellecost pointed out, and Alcis shook her head.

"For that, we would have had to maintain the pursuit. And we couldn't, so that's that." She closed her eyes, calling up the lines traced on her well-used maps. "What's the most defensible point south of here? We'll be ceding that to them."

"There are a dozen steadings in the Dassends," Kellecost said, and Talan lifted her head.

"They'd have to cross the Darbuin first. They could make a stand there."

Alcis looked at Heldyn, who shrugged. "It's not much of a river. But I'd hate to cross it opposed."

"It would keep them from using their horse to effect, though," Esclin said, straightening. "If they choose to stand there."

"The winter king's right, it's not much of a river," Kellecost said. "If we took our own horse upstream, they'd have no trouble crossing. We could surprise them that way."

"No reason they couldn't do the same to us," Nen Brethil said, and Nen Salter nodded.

"Only if they know the land," Kellecost said.

"Only if they're fool enough to try to hold us there," Nen Brethil said.

"They might regroup and try to come back west of us," Nen Salter said. "See if they can pin us against the Lammard."

"Also possible." Esclin straightened, setting his cup aside. "And whatever they do, we need to follow on as quickly as we can. How soon can your people march?"

"Midmorning if we must," Nen Salter said, grimacing.

Nen Brethil shook his head. "My folk are spent, Sire. They need another day."

Alcis saw Kellecost's mouth close tight and could guess his thought: Nen Brethil's men had been less heavily engaged than many. "At least half the army must move by mid morning. Our folk can do it."

"Agreed," Esclin said. "Wellan, if your people can't march, I'll leave you here and you can follow on as soon as you're able. The kyra's right, we're already giving them too much time to regroup."

Alcis leaned back against the arm of the couch, listening as Esclin's commanders made their last comments and protests and bowed themselves out, like candles snuffed one by one at the end of a feast. Talan had disappeared, too, though one of her companions yawned by the door, and Heldyn had vanished long since, leaving just herself and the arros with the sleepy page. The night air breathed frost across the ground and she tucked her feet under the heavy fur, glad of its warmth. Esclin still paced, poking at the maps on the table, before he felt her eyes on him and turned to face her. She freed a hand to beckon him to her side, and he smiled and obeyed, settling himself beside her on the couch.

"I should return to my people," she said, and his smile widened.

"If you must."

"I must." She returned the smile, though, and saw behind the lines and the weathered skin the flawless beauty he had once been. Not that he was not still compelling, and she shook her head. "He won't sleep with you, you know."

Esclin blinked. "Brelin?"

"Yes."

"Oh, yes, he'll keep his vows."

"Then why?" It wasn't like him to exert himself to seduce a man who was neither available nor interested; she might have called it habit, except that he was always well aware of his effects.

He made a soft sound that she realized was meant for laughter. "I don't want to sleep with him. I want him to love me."

It was her turn to blink at that. "Why? What need?"

Esclin closed his eye, dropping his voice so that his words wouldn't carry to the page now frankly asleep beside the door. "We are not winning this fight. Oh, yes, today, but not this month and not this year, not when they keep coming back every spring. We're holding our own and that won't be enough. I need all the possibilities, all the options I can muster. I will let him into Nen Elin if I must."

They both knew what the prophesied price for that would be, and she laid one hand on his wrist, feeling the pulse beneath his skin. "If he loves you…"

"If he loves me, he will not be just a wheelman," Esclin said. "I can admit him, and no other. And not bring down our doom."

Twister, Alcis thought with admiration, though she swallowed the word unspoken, knowing he would hear only the insult. But that was his gift, to see—to make—another path through the tangle of prophecy and possibility. Whether it would actually work was another matter, but he would bend his considerable will to make it so.

He reached for his wine again. "There has to be a way out of this."

Alcis sighed and leaned hard against his shoulder. "Short of granting them the Dancing Ground."

"Which would give them the Hundred Hills in a generation," Esclin answered. "The Blazing One drives them on—no matter how many times we beat them, how many of them we kill, the Blazing One sends them back again." He gave her a sidelong glance. "I begin to think their god doesn't love them."

"If it's truly the Blazing One who speaks." Alcis shook her head. "And it's a thought, to turn their god or turn their preachings, though I don't see—ah."

"It was in my mind that Brelin might have something to contribute to that," Esclin said carefully.

Twister indeed, she thought. The idea had merit, too. If the mass of wheelmen could be persuaded even to stand neutral against the lords protector and the lord paramount— at the very least, it would be an opening they had never had before.

There was a sudden commotion outside the tent, raised voices and heavy footsteps, and Esclin was on his feet, sword in hand, before the tent flap opened. The page was on his feet, too, sword drawn, but fell back, seeing Diran. With him came a tall woman in battered armor, her face gray with exhaustion.

"Your pardon, Sire," Diran said, "but Leicinna has word that won't wait."

Esclin poured a cup of wine and held it out. "Drink, then tell me."

The woman shook her head. "I'll be drunk if I—I'm dead on my feet, Sire."

"Tell me, then," Esclin said. "And then rest. Leicinna—I knew you last summer?"

"Yes, Sire. Leicinna Elloras. I'm in the rivermaster's service, like Diran here." She stopped, shaking her head. "I, my company, was sent to scout south along the Lammard, and we went some leagues beyond the Darbuin. We found the Rider army there, and turned back to warn you, only—Sire, there are two armies, and the one you've fought is the smaller of them. The larger was at the Lammard—they'll be across by now—and heading for the Westwood."

Alcis's breath caught in her throat and she heard Esclin swear. She had stripped the Westwood, confident that the fighting would be on the Dancing Ground—she had needed all her troops and both her consorts. There had never before been a Rider army large enough to risk attacking both the gathered armies and any of their strongholds.

"How do you know that's their plan?" Esclin demanded.

"We caught a messenger," Leicinna said, and reached under her cloak to product a ragged scroll. Esclin took it, unrolled and read it in a glance, then handed it to Alcis. She took it, aware of the stains that marred the jagged writing: a note ordering all recipients to rejoin the main army and march on Callamben.

"Callamben's well defended," she said, "but the garrison—I took at least half of it with me. The Riders can bottle them up and cut through the wood."

"The Carallad's never been taken," Esclin said.

"It's never been truly besieged," Alcis answered. "But I'd say that's their intent." And they couldn't have picked a better time, with most of their men here with her, leagues away in the Dancing Ground. The Westwood itself would fight for Helevys, of course, but she was young, untried—Alcis had barely begun to teach her to use the land's strength, and there was no one else to guide her—

"Summon the captains," Esclin said, to the page. "We need new plans."

Esclin's tent was crowded again, filled with his commanders, but the night was waning and they seemed no closer to any decision. Leicinna had told everything she knew and had apparently fallen asleep where she sat, her head against one of the tent poles. Alcis bent over the maps as though she could find some escape written there, while Nen Salter tried to keep the peace between Nen Brethil and Kellecost. Esclin rubbed his forehead above his missing eye, a familiar ache growing behind the bone, and pitched his voice to cut through the other conversations.

"One thing's certain, we can't stay here. The question is, do we go after them, or do we try to make them come to us?"

There was a little silence and Alcis looked up from the maps. "The Westwood can't hold. Not as I left it."

"We can't spare those men," Nen Brethil protested, and Esclin lifted a hand.

"Two armies, Leicinna said, and the one heading for the Westwood is larger—slightly larger—than the one we fought. The kyra has every reason, and every right, to be concerned."

"And yet we—" Nen Salter shook his head. "We barely held off this attack, and only with the Westwood's levies. I doubt we could take even their lesser force without that help."

And that was the conundrum, the knot they'd been worrying at for hours without any better answer. Esclin shook his head. "We don't have that choice. My question is, do we chase them, or do we try to pull them away north? There's decent ground in both places."

Alcis gave him a long stare. "It's better to the north. If you mean Eith Ambrin."

There was a little murmur, a shiver of voices protesting that ill-omened spot. Esclin said, "It had occurred to me."

"We cannot stand there," Nen Brethil said. "That's proven."

"The ground's not as bad as that," Esclin said. It was as close as he would let himself come to saying the truth of it: Aubrin had thrown away the advantage in response to Rider provocation, need not have died there if he had kept his temper.

Heldyn grunted agreement, swallowing the same bad memories by the look of him, and Alcis said, "There is also Mag Ausse."

"I don't know if they'll follow me that far," Esclin answered. "And it's too easy to bottle us up within the walls."

"But it would be safety," Nen Brethil said.

"And leave the southern nenns in the lurch," Kellecost said. "Again."

Nen Brethil put his hand to the knife he still wore at his belt and Nen Salter said, "Not to mention that we don't know how long Mag Ausse could feed our folk. We'd have to come out sometime."

Esclin rubbed his forehead again. "Can they take the Westwood?"

Alcis looked at him with hooded eyes. "As I left it? An army like that? Yes."

"If you'd left the summer king to hold it," Nen Brethil began, and quailed under Alcis's glare.

"If she'd brought any fewer troops, we wouldn't have won," Nen Salter said, and Esclin nodded.

"These are new tactics," Alcis said. "They haven't tried to take the Westwood in two generations. And if the two armies join..."

She didn't need to finish the sentence: if the entire Rider force took the Carallad, it would take all the rest of the season to dig them out again—if they could be beaten at all, tucked safely inside those walls. And in the meantime the Riders would be free to bring still more troops from Manan, with no one to stop them or to protect the hills. "If we go south," Esclin said. "All of us together—that's what they'll expect, and if I were their commander, I'd keep falling back, draw this out as long as possible. But if the kyra breaks off at the ford at Owlstead, takes her forces back across the Lammard, she'll have a chance to either intercept the Riders or to break their siege." He managed a smile for Alcis. "That I leave to you."

She nodded gravely, though the corners of her mouth twitched in response. "You can."

"So. We march in the morning." Esclin looked around the tent. "And that means as many of your men as are fit, Wellan."

"Sire." Nen Brethil spread his hands. "I cannot—this new danger doesn't make my men any less spent."

Esclin eyed him for a long moment. If at dawn he went to Nen Brethil's camp and called for volunteers—drew the royal sword and asked for them in its name—they would come, he was sure of that. But that would shame Wellan before his peers and he couldn't afford that, at least not yet. "Any man who's fit, I said. You'll have to follow on as quickly as you can, I've no desire to bring our folk to battle until we have all our companies present."

There was nothing more to be said, though both Kellecost and Nen Brethil did their best. Esclin heard them out and with Nen Salter's help got them moving toward their own companies. One of the other captains shook Leicinna awake and led her away to someplace more suitable for her to sleep. Alcis uncoiled herself from the couch, drawing her cloak more tightly around her shoulders. It was late, the moon almost set, and Esclin could see the day's exhaustion in her eyes.

"Can your men make it tomorrow?" he asked, keeping his voice low enough that they would not be heard beyond the walls of the tent, and she gave him a wry smile.

"They'll have to. No, they can, especially if we're not intending to fight. But I worry that I'll have to rest them before we catch up with the Riders."

And that would let the Riders reach the borders of the Westwood. Esclin chose his words carefully. "Is there anyone at the Carallad who can rouse the wood against them?"

Alcis grimaced. "That's the question. Traher is old enough and then some, but he's never shown the gift. The wood might work with him, if it were desperate, but... Helevys is fourteen. I know she feels the land, but she's never had to use that talent. And then there's Rocelyn, but he's not even twelve." She shook her head. "That's why I have to go back. You see that."

"I do." Esclin took her hands, their fingers cold together. He wanted to ask her for horsemen, but knew what her answer had to be and bowed his head with a sigh. "We can't risk losing the Westwood. I know that."

"And we can't lose the Dancing Ground, either," Alcis said. "Can you hold them?"

"Not at the price we paid today." Esclin looked past her, out into the dark, the fires burning low. "Not for long. If we can retreat to Eith Ambrin, maybe..." At least one more battle, more likely two or three, without the Westwood's horse to reinforce their own: he didn't much like those odds. Maybe it would be better to fall back to Mag Ausse, though then the Riders would either sweep past them to attack the eastern nenns or, worse and more likely, turn to join their fellows in attacking the Westwood. Reys en Nevenel was more foresighted than most of the lords paramount.

"If I can reach the wood," Alcis began, then shook her head. "There's no point planning now. We've said all there is to say."

"And morning will come early." He pressed her hands against his chest, his mouth sour with all the things he wanted to say and could not, and she nodded as though she heard them anyway. "What can you see?"

"This is not the Westwood."

"That's not what I asked."

"No more is it." She dipped her head, sighing. "Everything has come to this knot, and I can't see past it. I've done everything I can to change it, and still everything leads here."

Esclin took a long breath, not sure whether that was cause for relief or despair. "Then I suppose we're where we're meant to be."

"No." Alcis shook her head. "I don't accept that. I've never known you not to have a bolthole, never known you without some twisting plan. If you don't see it yet, you will, and that's as sure as any prophecy."

Esclin rested his forehead against her hair, comforted in spite of himself. She was indomitable; he might twist and turn, crossing his own trail like a hunted fox, but she was iron and adamant, as unyielding as the towers of the Carallad. He could not, would not say farewell, but embraced her without words, feeling her pull him fiercely close.

Viven Harper hunched her shoulders, the straps of the harp-case pulling, trying to ease her muscles in the uncomfortable

Rider saddle. The army had divided and this part was traveling more or less due west, toward the Lammard itself. They would need to find a ford, the river would be in full spate, but she had been kept under close enough watch that she had no real sense of where they were along the Dancing Ground. They had to be heading toward the Westwood, though she couldn't make sense of that, and she lifted her hands to wipe sweat from her eyes. They had kept her shackled while she traveled with the baggage train, but at least they had left a decent slack between the cuffs.

Her escort glanced back at her movement, saw what she was doing and looked away again. He was one of the decent ones, part of the company Radoc had had in Mag Talloc over the winter, an older man with three crooked fingers on his shield hand and a son somewhere among the scouts. Aelin traveled with them, too, with a few of her own people to tend to her, but she was no less well-watched, that chore divided between Radoc's troops and various wheelmen. They had the real power here: the axial commanded this half of the army. Viven had shared her tent most nights, for propriety's sake, and still didn't know why the axial had brought her, unless he was that deeply concerned about their morals. More likely she had kin in the Westwood, and he hoped to use her against them.

The baggage column slowed, the horses slacking off joint by joint until her mount could drop its head to tug at the new-grown grass. Her escort reined in as well, standing up in his stirrups as though that would help him see the cause of the delay, and then slumped back into his seat, letting his own horse lower its head to the grazing. Ahead and behind the wagons rumbled to a stop, drivers calling commands to oxen and stolen draft horses, and Viven risked a look at her escort.

"What's happening, can you see?"

The man spat into the dust, not in comment, she thought, but just to clear his mouth. "They missed the ford."

"Oh." Burdened by the harp and the chain on her wrists, she couldn't comfortably stand but instead turned slowly, looking for any landmarks she recognized. She thought the stand of trees looked familiar—it had certainly once been the windbreak for a steading, though it hadn't been tended in a generation—and if it was the one by the ruined town of Eventide, then they were indeed a league or so north of the nearest ford. If she was right, of course: she had been traveling without reference to anything she knew for so long that they might well be halfway to Riverholme by now.

They waited for a while, the horses drifting slowly sideways, seeking the new grass. After a bit, her escort freed a waterskin from his saddle, drank, and then nudged his horse closer so that she could take it from him. She accepted it gratefully, and managed to drink without spilling it down her chin. "Thank you," she said, and remembered his name. "Graland."

"It's no good going thirsty." Graland reslung the skin, his eyes on the river ahead. "Oh, by the—" He bit off whatever he had been going to say—not an epithet of the Blazing One, she guessed.

"What is it?" In spite of her best efforts, fear sharpened her voice. If there was a fight, she was in no position even to run.

Graland shook his head. "Looks like they're going to try to force the crossing here. Why we can't just go a league south—" He swallowed that complaint as well, still shaking his head, and gathered up his reins and the leading rein as the baggage train shuffled slowly into movement around them.

"My harp," Viven began, and shook her head in turn. There was no one here who was going to help her protect it.

They shuffled toward the river, the shouts of the camp-marshals growing louder the closer they came. She could see the river now, down a slight incline and then a short drop to the water, and there were men on horseback strung out in the stream, clearly there to catch anyone swept off their feet. The first of the big wagons was stopped at the edge of the drop, and then it began to back and turn, heading for a spot where the bank had broken down. The other wagons followed, Aelin's small cart backing and filling to make room. Aelin clung to the edge of the bench beside the driver, the wheelman at her side. The water was high and fast, and toward the middle of the stream, the water lapped at the riders' thighs.

"We'll have to swim it in the middle," Graland said grimly. "Shouldn't be too far. She'll make it."

And that was unexpected kindness. Viven managed a smile in thanks, though it was the harp she was worried for. She plucked at the straps, but there was no time to shorten then further as one of the camp marshals waved them on.

"Go on, get moving!"

Graland lifted a hand in acknowledgment and looked over his shoulder. "Ready?"

"Not particularly," Viven muttered, and tightened her grip on the low pommel.

Graland chirped to his mare and she picked her way down the bank. Viven's horse followed, sliding the last ell. It came upright, though, and Graland looked back, twitching the lead rope. Viven leaned forward, urging it on. It obeyed, the brown water swirling past its fetlocks and rising toward its knees.

Men were crossing on foot as well, wading chest deep in the water, clinging to each other as though that would help them against the current. As Viven watched, one stumbled and went down dragging his fellows with him; they reappeared a dozen ells downstream, heads popping out of the water like otters, goods abandoned in order to swim. One of the watching horsemen started toward them, then visibly decided they were safe enough and turned back to watch the main part of the baggage train.

The water crept rapidly up her legs, her horse wallowing after Graland's mare. She heard Graland call something, and felt her own horse's feet leave the riverbed. She lay forward on his neck, praying the harp along her spine didn't overbalance, felt his legs thrash and churn before he found his rhythm. She was soaked from chin to toes, only the harp on her back fully clear of the water, the horse straining forward beneath her, eyes and nostrils wide.

And then at last a flailing foot struck ground and the horse hauled himself out of the river, water running down his body. Graland's mare was just ahead of them, shaking head and mane so that Graland cursed and shielded himself. Viven sat up cautiously, shivering as the cool air struck her wet clothes, and Graland turned back to look at her. "All right?"

"Wet. And cold."

"Looks like we're making camp."

She shivered again but Graland proved to be right. Less than half a league from the river's edge, the camp marshals were whistling the companies to quarters, and they pulled up beside the tent Radoc had reserved for the women just as the last rope was staked into place. Viven accepted Graland's help to slide out of the saddle, still damp and chilled. She could just see a thicker line on the horizon, dark between the tents: the first edge of the Westwood. She glanced over her shoulder to see Graland looking in the same direction, and said, "Surely we're not going there?"

His expression froze. "I wouldn't know."

"Attacking the Westwood? Are you mad?"

"I wouldn't know," he said again, but his eyes showed white like a nervous horse: he'd heard the same stories everyone had, and Viven allowed her own voice to drop, so that she barely breathed the words.

"Into the trees... The kyra's trees..."

A hand fell on her shoulder and she jerked away, her heart racing, to find Radoc frowning at her, Linaren and a strange wheelman behind him. "You'd do well not to repeat those tales."

She dipped her head. "Very well. But..."

"Are you trying to cause trouble?" That was the wheelman. He was one of the young ones, his hair shaved close to his scalp, his robe cut knee-length for riding.

"Never. Not I..." She faltered under his cold stare, suddenly afraid she'd gone too far, and Linaren cleared his throat.

"You should get within, get some dry clothes."

"Not without a woman to help her, surely," the wheelman said, and Linaren blushed.

"The holder Aelin is within with her maid," Radoc said, wearily. "She can help."

"It isn't wise to leave a harper unwatched," the wheelman began, and a second wheelman loomed behind him. He was an older man, his robes draggled from the road, and there was something oddly familiar about his face.

"There you are, Nicaron," he said. "The axial was looking for you."

The younger wheelman hesitated, obviously wanting to pursue the question, but turned away. The older wheelman watched him out of earshot, and Linaren touched Viven's shoulder.

"Best you go within."

Best to be out of sight, you mean, Viven thought, shivering now from fear as well as cold. She had not meant to challenge the wheelmen so directly. She straightened, angry now at herself, and fixed Linaren with a cold stare. "And is there word of my child?"

He barely flinched, the movement so small it would have been invisible had she not been watching for it. "No. How could there be?"

"Because I was promised." Viven was aware that the older wheelman was listening now, along with Radoc, but she wanted to see Linaren hurt. Unfair as it was, that he cared to keep his word was one of the few weapons she had.

"To the best of my knowledge, your daughter is still in Nen Poul," Linaren said, tight-lipped. "And that is all I know. It was all I knew when we left Mag Talloc."

"I was promised," Viven began, and the wheelman lifted his head.

"Enough," Radoc said. "Go within."

She had pushed this far enough—perhaps too far, with the wheelman listening. She took a breath and nodded, letting Linaren hold the tent's flap for her.

It was a little warmer inside, a fire-bowl already lit and a pair of lanterns hanging from the center post. Her saddlebag lay on the ground beside a makeshift screen that would hide her pallet, and she shivered again. Aelin was sitting on a low stool, her stockinged feet stretched to the fire, and her maid Eliseve looked up from the chest that held Aelin's goods.

Linaren reached into his purse. "Give me your word to cause no trouble, and I'll free you to change." He held up the keys to the cuffs and Viven hesitated, for once deeply tempted.

"Please you, Harper, there's bread toasting," Eliseve said. "And cheese to come."

That was enough to decide her. She held out her wrists to Linaren, saying, "You have my word. I'll give you no trouble while I find dry clothes."

Linaren's expression was wry but he unlocked the leather cuffs, and Viven shed the cased harp to set it carefully behind the screen. She pulled off her wet cloak and overgown, aware that Linaren had turned away, and that the wheelman had come all the way into the tent, was standing now with his back to her so that Radoc was forced to do the same.

The screen was low enough that she had to change on her knees, wrestling with the fabric, but years of traveling had made her quick. Eliseve took the wet clothes and hung them from a tent pole, as close to the brazier as she could. Viven stood, settling her skirts, and waited for the men to notice. Her wrists were sore, though they had used leather cuffs; she stood silently, her hands inside her sleeves to soothe the chafed places, and the wheelman glanced sideways at her.

"I see I can report her cooperative."

"I think so," Radoc said. The lamps threw shadows that emphasized the bones of their faces: he and the wheelman were kin, Viven realized.

"The axial will be pleased. He has hopes of her cooperation." The wheelman gave no particular emphasis to the words, but Linaren cut a quick glance at his lord, as though he would have protested.

Radoc sighed. "And you know as well as I that it's a bad plan."

"I am only telling you what I have heard." The wheelman turned toward the door. "I'm doing what I think best." He let the tent flap fall behind him, and there was a long silence until Radoc swore under his breath.

"He means well," Linaren said after a moment, and stooped for a wineskin. "Holder. I trust you have everything you need?"

"For the moment," Aelin answered.

Linaren nodded. "Harper. I'll leave you unchained tonight if you'll swear on your harp to make no attempt at escape."

Viven hesitated, but it would be good to be free of the cuffs and chains. "And where would I go? Very well, I swear it. On my harp."

"Thank you," Linaren said.

Eliseve had found cups and a tray, served wine all around. Aelin took her cup absently and set it down untasted, but Viven took a long swallow and edged closer to the fire again, the flames leaping in the metal bowl. "What is it the axial wants from me?"

Linaren shook his head. "It's nothing—"

"You are here," Radoc said precisely, "because the lord paramount and the axial believe you are tamed enough to answer questions about the Westwood. And because they believe that Linaren desires you and that shames him and me."

Viven caught her breath. So this was what it felt like to hear your death pronounced, casually, as though it were of no more account than their embarrassment. And she still didn't know if Gemme lived, or Nichita, or if she had found any way to save them even by her own death. She had worked on Linaren, fed his guilt, perhaps he would do something for the child... Did they even know what they had said? "I'm a harper. I can't do what they want."

"They don't believe or understand." Radoc dropped onto an empty stool, not quite spilling his wine. "What you do is your choice, Harper, I don't care. I was told to bring you with us, and I obey."

He knew, she thought. He knew and didn't like it. Perhaps she could use that, that and everything else she had learned, to save her daughter. She had no other weapon, no other choice, only her death waiting a day or three or five ahead. She saw Aelin straighten, the same knowledge stark on her pale face, but the other woman did not speak. "I'm a harper," she said again, and felt the resonance of the instrument in her words.

"We know," Linaren said, and there was sorrow in his words. Radoc grunted something that might have been agreement or might have been simple annoyance.

"She is a harper," Aelin said. "Will you permit her to play, my lord?"

Linaren looked wary but Radoc gave a sour smile. "Why not? No harm in it."

"No, indeed," Aelin said, and looked at Viven. "Play for us, then."

It was the last thing Viven had expected, but any excuse to play was too good to pass up. She would not have many chances left. She brought the case into the circle of firelight, took out the harp and began to tune it, stiff fingers loosening as she worked up and down the scales. She found herself surprisingly content: her own fate hardly mattered if she could save Gemme. She chose a song of the Westwood, wordless, light as summer, a scrap of tune she had watched the folk of Callamben dance to two years past, women circling men under a moon so bright it drowned the stars. Let them think it surrender—let them take what they would from the music. She would not betray her harp.

CHAPTER ELEVEN

Helevys woke to silence and the memory of sound, a crash in her dreams like a great fall of stones. There was nothing now, not even the faint scrape of the guards' feet on the slates on the walls below, and she unwound herself cautiously from her blankets before she remembered that she no longer shared bed nor room with her nurse. She sat up then, frowning. The room was lighter than it should be, moonlight pouring over the boards of the floor: a shutter must have blown open, she thought, and cocked her head to listen for the wind. She heard nothing, but as her eyes adjusted, she could see that indeed one of the narrow shutters had blown back.

She muttered a word she had learned in the stables and climbed out of the bed, shivering a little as the night air bit. It was not yet truly spring; the nights still threatened frost. She crossed quickly to the window, but rather than closing the shutter at once, she leaned out, looking past the roofs and courtyards of the Carallad to the edge of the forest, where the sickle moon was sinking through a haze of cloud. She had the odd feeling that the sound had come from behind her, not from the window at all, and she leaned further still, heedless of the cold stone, as though she might see something if she just pressed hard enough.

Something scraped against her door. "Helevys! Wake up."

That voice she knew—Rocelyn, her next-youngest brother—and she unlatched the door. "What's wrong?"

"Did you hear it?"

"What?" Helevys shivered. "Where's Ennie?"

Ennie was the younger children's night-nurse, the one who was supposed to wake if any of them were troubled or wandered in their sleep. Rocelyn scowled. "Asleep. I don't think she could hear."

"What did you hear?" Helevys backed away, beckoning him into her room. They were both shivering, and she jerked her head toward her bed.

"Like a drum." Rocelyn climbed onto the bed, dragging one of the blankets around his shoulders. "Like a stone."

"You were dreaming," Helevys said. She pulled another blanket around herself.

"Was not." He paused. "I think we should tell someone."

"Tell them what?" Helevys drew the blanket more tightly around her shoulders, affected in spite of herself by her brother's unease. Rocelyn was sensible and plain-thinking; he never made a fuss about anything that wasn't important. "Tell who?"

"I don't know." Rocelyn bounced impatiently. "That's why I came to you."

A strange noise in the night that awakened them both: it was not so very much, easy to dismiss as nightmare, the ordinary result of the kyra and her consorts all being away. Helevys closed her eyes, summoning the memory of that moment before she woke, the heavy, hollow sound reverberating in the dark. It reminded her of the afternoon she had stood with her mother at the height of the Carallad, to watch and feel her work her magic over the land. Was this the land speaking to her, to Rocelyn? There was only one way to be sure.

"All right," she said. "Get dressed. I know what we can do."

"I can't, I'll wake Ennie."

Helevys was already rummaging in her chest, found an old straight-cut tunic small enough not to smother him. "Here, put this on. I don't want you to freeze. Why didn't you put your boots on?"

"Because they were under Ennie's bed." Rocelyn pulled the tunic over his head, emerged scowling.

"See if these fit." Helevys tossed him a pair of her old slippers, the soles worn but the fur lining mostly intact.

"I'm fine," he said again, but stuffed his feet into them anyway. She found her second-best cloak and handed it to him as well, and he shrugged it around him. "Where are we going?"

"Mother's tower."

"But—" He stopped, eyes widening. "Oh."

"We need to know," Helevys said, and pulled on her warmest gown and gloves.

The heart of the Carallad was deadly quiet, so quiet that Helevys could hear the rustle of a mouse in the wood of the stair and the faint voices of the guard on the middle walls as they exchanged the password. There were fewer guards within, and none on the floors where the kyra's children lived: their nurses and tutors were trained to arms, if it came to that, but no one truly believed that the fortress could be threatened.

There was just one patrol to cross to reach the kyra's tower, and Helevys waited in the shadows until the guards had met and spoken and turned back along their patrol. As soon as they were out of sight, she dragged Rocelyn with her across the exposed stone, flattening them both against the sides of the doorway. She had a key, trusted to her by her mother before she left, and the lock turned smoothly.

Helevys dragged her brother into the narrow antechamber and pulled the door closed behind them, then leaned against the wood, waiting for her eyes to adjust to the deeper dark. She should have brought a candle, but it was too late to worry about that. She pressed her back against the cold stone, felt her way along the wall, past the bench where Alcis's attendants sat to wait, and swallowed a yelp when she stubbed her toe on the first stair. Behind her Rocelyn bumped against the bench, wood grating over the stone floor, and she hissed him to silence. There was nothing from outside and she drew him to her at the bottom of the stair. It was a closed spiral, straight to the top; they should be able to feel their way even in the blind dark. "Come on."

She began the long climb, one hand on the wall, the other groping ahead of her on the stairs. She could hear Rocelyn panting behind her, but the further she climbed, the softer it seemed, until she stopped, worried, only to choke back a cry as his hand fell on her heel.

"You're going to make me fall!" His voice was barely above a whisper and the tower deadened it further, closing around them like a storm cloud.

"Be more careful," she retorted and started climbing again, trying to push away her growing sense of dread.

At the top, the door swung open at her touch. The moon was not quite set, the lower point of its crescent just touching the horizon, a hazy veil of cloud smudging its edges. There was no wind but the air was bitter, and Rocelyn burrowed against her, shivering. She opened her cloak, wrapped him in it, and they stood together for a moment, neither of them sure what to do next. Overhead the stars were fading, blurred by the rising clouds. Helevys took a deep breath, trying to find that inward point, the precarious balance she had felt when Alcis stood beside her. For an instant, she thought she had it, and with it came a clamor of silence, as though the stones and roots beat one on another in a sound so deep she could only feel it in her bones. Then it was gone again, and Rocelyn looked up with a worried face.

"Are you all right?"

"Around here." It had come from the east, whatever it was. Helevys tugged him with her around the narrow top of the stairwell, until she was looking into the dark where the sun would eventually rise. It was too early yet for even a hint of dawn; instead, the Hunter was about to rise above the horizon, its stars jewel-bright against the night. There were no clouds there, nothing to hide the Hunter's Bow or to blur the Great River as it arched overhead, and she spread her feet wide, bracing herself again to find that center.

She heard a sweep of wind, though the air was still, a rush of wind and water and tumbling stones, and she clutched wordlessly at them, trying to force some sense from the cacophony. For an instant she had it, the tolling of stones like a bell as a thousand hooves beat the ground and sparks leapt from torches. She swallowed a scream and lost the vision, felt Rocelyn wrap himself tight around her as though he'd been a much smaller child. For an instant she thought she smelled smoke, and with that came a sudden rush of anger. How dare anyone threaten the Wood? She reached behind her, feeling for the rain she knew was in the west. It came, slowly at first, then faster and faster, until a whirl of cloud crossed the sky like a migration of birds, and a curtain of rain passed over them. The noise and the cold water broke her concentration, and she tugged her hood up too late to spare herself.

"The Riders are coming," Rocelyn whispered, still clinging tight to her waist.

"The Riders are here." They had to tell someone, Helevys knew—the guard, she supposed, but all that would do was cause a tumult without real need. The riders were at the edge of the Wood, nowhere near the Carallad itself. And anyway, what would she say? *I heard the trees and stones*: all well and good, she was the kyra's daughter; but she was not the kyra, nor even yet the kore, and the roads from the east had been quiet since the army left. And of course she would have to tell Roue Arnos, who had been her mother's steward since before Helevys was born, but the thought of waking him in the predawn cold was almost as alarming as the Riders. And yet they could not wait—she could not wait till morning, not carrying this knowledge alone. "Come on," she said again, and turned them both back toward the stairs.

They made their way back to her room and she paused in the doorway, letting her eyes adjust as she tried to decide what to do. Lord Roue would have to know—maybe if she woke one of her mother's women, told her what she had seen—

"We have to tell somebody," Rocelyn said.

"Yes, I know that—" Helevys broke off, abruptly aware of candlelight visible beneath one of the hall doors: Traher's room. A wave of relief washed over her. "We'll talk to Traher."

She tapped softly on the door and a moment later Traher

pulled it open, the candle's light hovering at his shoulder. He waved it back to the candle and beckoned them in, saying, "What's wrong? Did the rain wake you?"

"The Riders are at the Westwood's eastern edge," Helevys said. She saw Traher take a breath and hurried on. "We both heard it, Rocelyn and I, and then I went to Mother's tower, and I could feel them—"

"I believe you." Traher went to one knee beside his fireplace, began coaxing the banked embers to light. "Why are you wet?"

"She did it," Rocelyn said.

"They were burning part of the forest, I was trying to stop them." Helevys shed her cloak, letting it drop with a damp splat. "Don't you feel it?"

Traher shook his head, the long braid slithering across his back. "I don't have the land-gift. The rain woke me and then I heard you two."

"We have to tell someone," Helevys said. "You do believe me?"

Traher pushed himself to his feet, nodding. "Sit by the fire for now. Here." He found a napkin-wrapped bundle, opened it to pull out half a loaf of bread, which he broke in half. Helevys waved it away, but Rocelyn took both pieces and settled himself on a stool by the fire.

"I don't want to wake Lord Roue," Helevys said, and to her surprise Traher grinned.

"No more do I. And I think we can wait until dawn— unless you think otherwise?"

Helevys blinked, startled to be asked, and shook her head. "I think it'll be all right."

"I'll talk to the night captain," Traher said. "See if he thinks we need to wake the lord steward. In the meantime—"

"Please can we stay here?" Rocelyn asked, his mouth full.

"I suppose." Traher shot Helevys a quick glance and she fought to hide a yawn. "Get some rest if you can, I don't know how long I'll be."

"I'm fine," Helevys said, but sat down heavily on the end

of Traher's bed. She was suddenly painfully tired, as though she'd danced all day at the summer festival. She watched Traher light a candle-lantern for himself and slip out the door. Rocelyn started to say something but Helevys waved him to silence. "In a minute," she said and lay back on the mattress, sleep overwhelming her.

Despite the camp marshals' best efforts, the army did not begin to move until nearly noon, and even then Nen Brethil's men remained behind, Wellan promising to follow as soon as they could. At least that had given him time to see the worst of the wounded off, Esclin thought, though he grudged the men he sent as escort. It was a sad and shabby caravan, litters slung between unhappy pack horses, and he hoped they would reach Mag Ausse in safety. Faela would shelter them, he had no doubt of that, and it would take more than horsemen to breach her walls. Ilgae had not yet regained consciousness, though she moaned and mumbled as they lifted her into the litter, and her daughter had dribbled more poppy syrup onto her cracked lips before she had let the bearers take her away. At least they had both seen Ilgae swallow—surely a good sign— but Esclin had also seen the worry in Ida's face before she had mastered herself and turned to join her company. Ilgae's second, Reinall Parinas, would take her place as marshal: a good man, but not Ilgae.

They skirted the battlefield and the still-smoking pyres, glad of the wind that blew the smell away to the east, then made their way south along the line of the Lammard. It gleamed bright in the distance, less than a league away, and Esclin edged his horse forward so that he could join Alcis.

"Where do you plan to cross?"

"I haven't decided." She was plainly dressed, leather corselet over a padded tunic, her hair caught back in a twist of silk the only finery about her. Esclin's gown and armor both were more elaborate, and he was aware of amusement from the nearest men. "I've sent Rihaleth to scout ahead. There are at least two spots where we should be able to make our way across, and if that fails, there's always Owlstead. But I think that brings me too far south."

"Are you going to try to take them before they reach the wood?"

Alcis shrugged. "I won't know that until we're across and I've had a chance to send out scouts. It might make more sense to head straight for the wood and meet them there."

The wood itself would fight for her. Esclin nodded. "We'll keep this lot occupied as long as we can."

"But not—" She stopped, shaking her head, and he lowered his voice.

"It will cost what it costs. It's a delicate thing we're attempting."

"Be careful nonetheless."

"Talan will command the archers." He wasn't sure if that was what she had been asking, but it earned a smile.

"You should be proud of her."

"I am." He broke off, seeing one of the scouts returning, pushing his horse to a trot. "Let me know what you decide."

"Of course," Alcis said, and he turned his own horse away.

It was easy to follow the Riders' retreat, still marked with discarded gear and the occasional body. Now and then a horse was running free; most were lame, but Heldyn and the Riverholme companies made an effort to retrieve any that looked sound.

In the middle of the afternoon, one of Alcis's pages carried word that Rihaleth had found a suitable crossing and the army divided again, the people of the Westwood turning back toward the Lammard and their home. Esclin paused to watch them go, the streamers and ribbons bright against the pale sky, and Nen Salter drew rein at his side.

"We shouldn't let them go, Sire."

"I'm not the Westwood's master," Esclin answered. "Besides, she's right, we can't risk losing the wood."

"Surely if we'd brought the Riders to battle here, they'd

have had to turn back." Nen Salter shook his head. "No, I see we can't risk it. But they outnumber us, and without Nen Brethil—"

"Wellan swore he'd follow on tomorrow," Esclin said. "If you doubt him, I want to know it."

"I think he'll come. But I don't like it."

"No more do I." Esclin made himself smile, slow and easy. "I want to harry them, not bring them to battle. Unless we can find a place where we can have the advantage."

"As if there's such a place on the Dancing Ground," Nen Salter muttered.

"If we pull them further east," Esclin said, though he was well aware it was far from an ideal solution.

"It could work," Nen Salter said—more loyalty than tactics, Esclin thought, but he was grateful for the support.

They camped that night well short of the Darbuin. By their trail, the Riders were still a day or so ahead and there was no point in coming up on them in the dark. Diran's scouts had probed south along the Lammard's banks and had caught sight of the Riders' main body. There had been no sign that they were turning west, and the scouts had come away without pressing further.

Esclin listened to their reports without comment, sitting in his tent with the rest of the commanders, and dismissed them with thanks; listened, too, to a sweating man from Nen Brethil's camp who begged the arros's pardon for the delay and promised that Nen Brethil would catch up with them mid-morning. Esclin dismissed him as well and waved for the nearest page to refill his cup.

"They should have been here tonight," Kellecost burst out. "If my men made the march, as hard-pressed as they were— Sire, there's no reason he can't be here." Nen Salter grunted something that might have been agreement and Esclin sat up straighter.

"But he's not here, and nothing we can do will bring him here faster." He studied Kellecost's face, tight with anger, and said, "I am keeping count. But now is not the time."

Kellecost subsided, still scowling. Nen Salter said, "Wellan can be too cautious. But he'll be here."

He had better. Esclin paused just long enough to let everyone imagine the words, then set his cup aside. "What we need is a place to draw the Riders in. Someplace that we can defend without the Westwood's horse, someplace that we can hold and slip away from once the battle's over. I want to keep the Riders busy, make sure they can't reinforce the troop they've sent to the Westwood."

Reinall Parinas—Reinall Marshal now—lifted one of the maps, and Talan and the pages hastily made space for it on the table. "There's nothing on the Dancing Ground, we all know that. But you were right, Sire, there's broken ground upstream along the Darbuin, and scrub forest east of that."

"So if we anchored the line here," Kellecost said, and Esclin rose to look over his shoulder.

"And if we had the archers in the trees," Talan pointed out, then blushed sharply.

"It's not a bad thought," Nen Salter said, and Reinall nodded in agreement.

"Archers there, then, to cover the flank. We could hold them."

"How would we lure them on?" Denior asked. "The horse will chase us but we won't bring their foot."

"If we show ourselves and then retreat," Reinall said, "they might follow us, try to catch us while we're still outnumbered. Particularly if they think we're joining up with levies from the Dassends."

"We'll have to give them a fight," Nen Salter said.

And whoever was in that advance party was likely to be mauled. Esclin said, "If we have to, then we will. But let's see what the scouts find tomorrow before we make any further plans."

There was still too much to go over, too many complaints and questions, but at last Esclin had emptied the tent of all but the duty page. The boy brought water; Esclin washed, shivering—the sun was long down and the fire had died—and rolled himself into his blankets, the royal sword in easy reach beside him. So far it had done its job, but at the moment he would rather have its maker at his side. With more forethought, he might not have been left alone, but it was too late now. The choice of a campaign lover required a certain tact and caution on both sides, and there was no time left for that now.

He dealt ruthlessly with desire, trusting the page to hear nothing once the witchlight was quenched, and then lay spent and sleepless. Nen Brethil was a question not yet asked, for which he as yet had no answer. The army was too small, the Riders too many; to lure them east was clever but dangerous, required everything to go just so... Perhaps the scouts would bring better news in the morning, he told himself, and tried again to sleep.

◌

Helevys sat in her father's chair in the kyra's council room, her fingers closed tight on the arms to keep herself from fidgeting. Roue Steward had the kyra's seat, of course, and Traher sat at his left hand, in the place that properly belonged to the summer king. Rocelyn was wedged in next to him, looking even smaller than his years in the tall chair. She frowned as he started to chew a thumbnail; he scowled back but hid his hands in his lap. There were more familiar faces around the table—the kyra's secretary Ibota, Halcin Lanelos who commanded the Carallad's guard, Savadie the chief observer, Isabar Maras whose scouts were the only horsemen left within the walls, Alisand Ferentas the storekeeper—and a handful of steading-lord's men whom she knew only by their badges. The Council seemed very small in the absence of the kyra, and Helevys wished with all her might that her mother had never left the Carallad.

She scowled at her own weakness and sat up even straighter against the carved wood. She and Rocelyn had spoken their piece, told everyone what they had felt at the top of the kyra's tower, and the last hour had been spent letting them all argue themselves to a standstill. She had watched Roue out of the corner of her eye, doubtfully at first, and finally decided that he was doing it on purpose. Now he leaned forward to take up his glass—honey water, Helevys thought, probably because of the children's presence—and everyone quieted as he took a careful sip.

"It seems to me that Isabar has made a worthwhile point," he said at last, and favored Helevys with a small sharp smile. "While no one doubts that the kyra's children have seen something, we need to know more. Isabar has volunteered to take a scouting party toward Callamben, and I believe that to be a wise first step."

"I would like to go with him," Traher said. Someone gasped softly—clearly Roue was not to be interrupted—and both Traher and the steward struggled for a moment to seem unruffled.

"Your courage does you credit," Roue said, "but we cannot risk losing you to the Riders."

"I have gifts of illusion that are of use in the field," Traher said. "More use there than here. And we all know that I'm not the land's heir."

"But you are the kyra's son," Roue said softly, implacably reasonable. "I cannot risk you."

"I risk myself," Traher said.

"You would make too good a hostage," Roue said, and looked deliberately down the table. "In the meantime, Alisand, you tell us that we still have stores enough to hold the Carallad for three weeks?"

"Between two and three," the storekeeper answered, "depending on how much food the folk from the surrounding steadings can bring. We won't eat well or lavishly, but we'll eat."

"To that end, the steadings will report their supplies," Roue said, and there was a murmur of agreement from the men at the end of the table.

"And the seed in hand as well," Alisand interposed, and there was more agreement. Three weeks didn't sound like nearly enough time, Helevys thought, but Roue left no time for questions.

"Then we are decided. I declare the meeting ended."

Helevys rose to her feet obediently and Rocelyn scurried to join her. "We should go up the tower," he said, and Ibota paused at their side.

"Do you think it needful?"

It was a question for an adult, and Helevys exchanged glances with Rocelyn before she answered. "I think we should try."

"Then I'll escort you," Ibota said, and motioned for a maidservant to bring her spinning.

The climb to the top of the kyra's tower was easier in daylight, though Helevys felt her mother's absence like toothache as she looked toward where the harp was buried. Overhead the sky was white with clouds, though they were thin enough that the sun was a patch of light too brilliant to look at directly, and the stones had warmed underfoot. Below them the Carallad sloped away, slate roofs and stone towers and walls joining the steep ground where the cattle grazed in safer times. A long league beyond that rose the trees of the wood, the sharp new-leaf green mingling with the near-black of the wood and the narrow leaves that never fell, a parti-colored carpet stretching into the distance.

They were looking toward Callamben, and Helevys rested her hands on the stones of the parapet, turning her face to the sun and closing her eyes. For a long moment, she felt nothing and cringed, wondering if she and Rocelyn had started all of this for nothing. But then at last she heard it, a grumble of stones so deep that it was almost as much sensation as sound: the land groaning under the strangers' tread. They were not in the wood itself, she thought, at least not now, and she no longer felt the pinch of fire—but the wood's unease was palpable. Rocelyn edged up beside her and she took his hand, wishing she had better comfort to offer.

"We ought to do something," he said.

And so we should, she thought, *but what?* The rain had been a good thought, had stopped the attempt to burn some part of the wood, but there was no such moisture left to wring from the thinning clouds. The Riders were closing on Callamben, she knew suddenly, and did not know what to do.

She groped for more but the image was gone; she felt only the wood's anger and the people's fear. *Tangle them*, she thought, *root and vine and branch obscure the path.* She could feel work already laid to that end and tightened her grip on Rocelyn's hand. "Feel that?"

"Yes..."

"We want more of it." She closed her eyes again, concentrating, and thought she felt ground shift, foliage thicken. And then the wood slipped through her fingers and she was back in the kyra's tower, blinking at the sun.

"Do you think it worked?" Rocelyn sounded doubtful.

"I think so," Helevys said, and willed herself to sound certain.

Whether it had worked or not, the exertion left her exhausted, so that she fell asleep in the afternoon and found herself alone and wakeful after dark. Dinner was long over; she had finished the sweet she had wheedled from the kitchen, less out of hunger than boredom, and still she paced open-eyed.

She pulled open her door, peering out into the corridor. Light showed under Traher's door, and she collected her candle-lantern and stepped out into the dark. He opened to her knock, surprise turning to annoyance, and behind him she saw saddlebags on his bed, half packed.

"You can't go with Isabar." She hadn't meant to speak, the words startled out of her, and his frown deepened.

"Neither you nor Roue can stop me."

"It's—" She stopped just in time, swallowing both *stupid* and *dangerous*. "I don't like him, either, but he's right, you'd make a dangerous hostage."

"I won't get caught." His shape blurred and shifted, became a plain-faced, older man in the dun tunic of the scouts, blurred again and became a stunted pine, a twist of fog, before he became himself again.

Helevys caught her breath. "I didn't know you could do that."

"That's the one thing I can do," Traher answered. "Isa and I have talked about it, he knows what I can do. Imagine how close the scouts could get with me to protect them."

"But that's exactly what's likely to get you caught," Helevys said. "Or—does it work for touch, too?"

"Not as well," Traher admitted.

"You can't just leave me." Helevys felt her face heat at the words and Traher turned back, his frown easing.

"Oh, Helevys. If I could help you here, I would, but—"

"You're not helping me there."

"At least I'd be doing something useful."

"Can't you do it from here?"

"Do what, exactly?" Traher tilted his head to one side.

"What it is you do." Helevys gestured vaguely, not sure herself what she was asking, but determined not to let him leave. "Illusion. Lead the Riders astray. Show them monsters. Anything."

"Not from a distance," Traher began, but his frown was thoughtful now. "At least I've never tried."

"Well, then. You should try."

"It's leagues and leagues to Callamben," Traher said. "I don't think it's possible."

"You said you hadn't done it," Helevys said. "Traher, if you try to sneak away, I'll tell Roue Steward."

"You wouldn't know." Traher's face was set again.

"If you were captured and made hostage and he didn't rescue you somehow, Mother would have his head. I don't like him either, but that's not fair to any of us." Helevys saw Traher flinch at that. "Besides, I really need you."

"I don't have the land-gift," Traher said. "All I can do is illusion."

"Rocelyn and I have the land-gift," Helevys said. "We can tell you where to put your illusions, how to drive them— maybe we can scare them so badly they won't dare come any further."

"We won't be that lucky," Traher said but dropped onto the end of his bed, pushing the saddlebag to the floor. "All right. Maybe we can make it work." He heaved a sigh. "Isa said he wouldn't take me."

"That doesn't mean he doesn't love you," Helevys said, and to her surprise Traher gave a crooked smile and flung his arm across her shoulder, drawing her down beside him.

"Maybe not. Let's plan what we can do."

They were camped at the edge of the Westwood, the bulk of the army a scrupulous half-league from the first trees. Viven Harper waited just inside the shade of the open tent flap, ear cocked for the sound of returning scouts. Rumor said they'd been sent to probe toward Callamben, looking for some way either around that stronghold or for some weak point by which it could be taken. She doubted they would find either: there were few roads into the Westwood that did not pass through Callamben, and the city had been well-fortified generations ago for just this reason. It was the cork in the bottle; the Riders would have to go through the wood or take the city, and neither would be easy.

In the distance she could see a cart rumbling slowly up the gentle slope that led to the camp, the horse uneasy in its traces, tossing its head and fighting the reins. Woodcutters, she guessed, and did not hide her smile. That was the least-coveted job in the entire army just now, venturing in among those trees to gather deadfall and cut live wood: everyone knew that the trees fought back, branches slamming into men when there was no wind, venomous insects swarming when there had been no sign of a hive, even a honey-dragon that had burned two men and escaped hissing into the shadows. She'd had no need to stretch her word, much less break it; when Radoc's guards spoke of such things, she merely looked worried and shook her head.

In the tent behind her, Aelin and her maid were busy at

their spinning: proper women's work by the Riders' lights, though Viven couldn't help wondering what use either Aelin or Eliseve thought they could make of the unfinished thread. Most likely it served only to keep them from thinking or uttering unwise words, just as her own harp kept her quiet. At least she was allowed to play most evenings, quiet accompaniment for the slow talk that came between dinner's end and the dousing of the fires. It was also, she suspected, the only time Radoc and Linaren could meet in relative privacy, for all that they were scrupulously proper with each other. They were as worried about the Westwood as their men were, though they tried to hide it.

"Harper." That was Graland, moving toward the opening. "Come inside."

Viven did as she was told, blinking a little in the relative darkness, and Aelin looked as she wound the thread onto her spindle. "Will you play for us, Harper? If that's permitted, of course."

"As the holder wishes," Graland answered, and moved to stand in the doorway. Viven fetched her harp and settled herself on one of the little stools, letting her fingers wander through the tuning scales. She had played more in the last few days than she had in weeks and the music woke at her touch, her fingers loose and easy on the strings, though she kept the notes as quiet as she could. There was no need to draw attention to it, or her. She felt sorry for Aelin, as trapped as she herself was, unwilling guest and potential hostage, and so she chose a simple dance, a tune she'd heard in houses up and down the coast.

Aelin smiled and set her spindle back in the basket. Eliseve's hands never faltered, setting the spindle turning and the drawing out the thread, only to wind it up and repeat the movement, and when the dance was done, Viven slid through a set of transitions until she found a tune that captured that slow rhythm. Eliseve gave her a surprised smile, her hands still busy with the forming thread, and Aelin laughed softly. Viven let herself spin variations, drawing out the tune, and out of the corner of her eye she saw Graland stiffen.

"Ware," he said, and Viven instantly stilled the strings.

"Here," Aelin said, sweeping her skirt to one side, and Viven set the harp between them, arranging her own skirts to hide it as much as possible.

"My lord," Graland said, and stepped aside. Radoc entered, half in armor, his helm tucked under his arm. Linaren followed, but at a greater distance than usual, and behind him came a pair of wheelmen. One was tall, his graying hair clipped close to his scalp, a silver torc bound in gold circling his neck: the axial himself. Across the brazier, Eliseve hastily scrabbled her workbasket out of the way and drew over the great chair Radoc used in the evenings. Aelin rose to her feet as well, curtseying respectfully, and the wheelmen both sketched a blessing. The second wheelman was the one who had called Radoc "cousin," his face carefully expressionless.

"The axial has some questions for you, harper," Radoc said. Viven managed a gracious nod and the axial seated himself in the great chair. His ivory robe was spotless, in spite of the rigors of the campaign, and she wondered irrelevantly if the wheelmen had brought a team of laundresses.

"Her harp should be present," the axial said.

Aelin stirred as though she might have said something, but Viven drew her skirt aside and brought the instrument into view. "It's here." Neither her hands nor her voice trembled, though she would not have wanted to try to play.

"Very good." The axial nodded gravely.

Viven let her hand rest on the harp's curved top, the wood silken under her fingers. She had known since she had been taken from Nen Elin that this moment was coming, when she could keep neither her oaths nor her life, but now that it was here she felt slow and stupid.

"You have visited the Westwood many times, I think," the axial said.

Viven hesitated, but she could see no harm in that. "Yes. I have."

"Callamben? And the Carallad?"

"Yes." She braced herself for the questions she could not answer, about the walls and the gates and the numbers of men, but instead the axial leaned back in his chair.

"When were you there last?"

"A bit more than a year ago. I stayed a night in Callamben then, on my way north to Riverholme."

"You've traveled through the Westwood," the axial said.

"Not that time. But, yes, before I did."

"Under what protection?"

Viven blinked. The question was too easy, had to be a trap... She said carefully, "I am a harper, my lord, and my harp protects me. I was also known, and traveling with permission. The wood had no reason to dislike me."

"You speak as though the wood itself has feelings."

"It does." Viven hesitated. "That's well known, my lord. No one disputes it."

"It is generally agreed," Radoc said.

Aelin looked up once, pale eyes flashing, then bent her head respectfully. "I beg your pardon, my lord, but that is so. The Westwood has its own kind of life."

"But whence comes that power?" the axial asked, voice deceptively mild. "This is clearly not the light of the Blazing One."

It's the Westwood. Viven closed her lips over that pointless statement and Aelin bent her head again. "Indeed not, my lord."

"Fire has been tried." The axial kept his eyes on Viven. "A storm whipped up out of nowhere and drowned the torches. Whose magic was that?"

The harp bound her to tell the truth. She had been braced to refuse all questions, to neither lie nor answer and to accept her inevitable death, but this—what harm could there be in answering? She had heard the storm wash over the camp, a fading rush of wind and thunder and rain as heavy as if thrown from buckets: surely there was no harm in naming the kyra as its creator. "I assume it was the kyra of the Westwood who sent it."

"The kyra is with the main army," the axial said. "We know that to be true. And that puts her beyond reaching the wood. Who else can wield that power?"

Viven shook her head, honestly baffled. Radoc said, "She has children. The kyra, I mean."

"Ah." The axial steepled his fingers. "Could they use that power?" Viven hesitated and the axial frowned. "Come, harper, I require an answer."

"I don't know," Viven said. "I'm not of the Westwood. I don't know their magic."

"Your best guess, then."

"I—" There was no safe answer, nor any one truer than another. Viven said, "I would guess so? But I don't know. There might be others—" She stopped there, edging up to falsehood: the Westwood's power lay in the royal line.

"She has some number of children," the other wheelman said, looking at Radoc who gave a small shrug.

"I don't know."

"There are six or seven, my lord," Aelin said, without raising her head. "The oldest would be grown by now."

"Did you meet these children in your visits, harper?" the axial asked.

Viven chose her words carefully. "I believe I met the eldest? Or the eldest boy, at any rate. The others were too young to attend the feast."

"Tell me about the boy."

"There's not much to tell." View could see him clearly, slender and graceful in what was surely his first silk gown, a deep, true rose-red that flattered his dark hair and aged-ivory skin. He'd sat quietly in his place, halfway down the table from his mother and the summer king, roused from his best behavior only when she played. "He likes music, though whether he has any talent for it I couldn't say—"

"That is unhelpful," the axial said. "His age?"

"I don't know." Viven saw his frown and added hastily, "He was accounted of age two years ago, that's all I can say."

"Has he his family's talents?"

"I don't know."

The axial was silent for a moment, then shrugged. "Even if he's come of age, he's still a child. His magic won't stand against the Blazing One. What's the best way to pass through the wood?"

"I went by the road," Viven said. There was a certain fierce satisfaction in telling the exact truth. "Through Callamben."

"Protected by your harp."

"I was an invited guest," Viven parried.

"Can your harp win passage for us?"

Viven took a breath. That was the question she had feared, the one she couldn't answer. "I don't know if I can," she said. "I may not."

"Certainly you can try," the axial said.

"My lord. I'm sworn to take no side in any war. I may not do it."

"My lord." Aelin went to her knees in a billow of skirts. "My lord, I pray you, let me speak with her. I believe her to be misguided but of good heart—you heard her at the winter feast, how she led us in the praise songs. Let me persuade her."

There was a moment of silence, the decision balanced on the knife's edge, and then the other wheelman said thoughtfully, as though he spoke to himself, "We've time still..."

The axial glanced at him. "Perhaps so." He rose to his feet, the white robes gleaming in the shadowed tent. "Think well, Harper. You know the price of refusal."

Viven bent her head, murmured, "Yes, my lord."

She felt the axial's eyes on her, though she had more sense than to look up. "Very well," he said and ducked out through the doorway, the other wheelman at his heels. Radoc followed, more slowly, but Viven caught at Linaren's sleeve.

"Will you find me word of my daughter? You know what's at stake."

"I'll do what I can," Linaren said, and followed the others out.

Viven sat back on her stool, took a breath that was more shaken than she would have liked. To cover it she glared at Aelin, who met her eyes calmly.

"Would you rather he cut you down now? Or burned you, that's more his method. I've bought you time, Harper. Use it."

Viven closed her mouth over her first shocked answer, said more carefully, "I'm grateful, truly. But I'm not sure what you want—"

"You not to die for his folly," Aelin said, her voice too low to be heard beyond their little circle. "And I know what a harper's oaths mean."

"I don't see a way out," Viven said.

Aelin made an angry noise that was almost a laugh. "No more do I, Harper. But at least—"

She broke off as Graland stepped back into the tent, but Viven knew what she would have said—*At least you have some time.* And maybe it would be enough, maybe she would see some chance to slip away, to use stealth or bribery to free herself from the tent. Maybe the harp could win her some unregarded chance. After all, there had been nothing that she could not in honor answer, no answer that the harp would forbid. That Alcis's eldest son was young was hardly a secret, and the Riders might undervalue him to their detriment.

For an instant she thought of her own daughter, thin and brown and smiling. They had played at kites the last time she had been in Nen Poul, in the windy days of autumn, the bright scraps of silk stretched taut against the vivid sky. She had given up a year of harping to have her, had thought it would be enough to know she was there, to steal a day or three out of every season; and now that it was all ending, she wanted more. She tasted tears, her chest burning, and forced those memories back into their place, but Eliseve had seen and held out a cup of wine.

"Drink now," she said. "You and the holder can talk later."

Leicinna's company had drawn a long straw this time and had been given the westernmost track, following the Lammard itself south toward the confluence of the Darbuin. It was easy ground, grassland untrammeled by the armies' passage, and she let them ride in open order, the breeze from the river barely lifting her banner. The river was still in spate: no one would be making a crossing except at the fords.

They caught a glimpse of smoke on the eastern horizon as they made their way along the river: the Rider army, unmistakably, but that was not their mission. They were to scout the ground along the Darbuin, still ten leagues to the south, and she waved the company on.

They had not ridden half a league when the lead rider lifted his lance. The grass thrashed ahead of him and Leicinna spurred forward, lowering her own lance, only to rein to a halt as a woman rose from the grass, raising empty hands in surrender. Leicinna swung left, getting between her and the open land, and more of the company filled in around her, surrounding the stranger. She lifted her hands higher in answer, turning on her heel as though searching for the captain.

Leicinna shortened her grip on her lance. "Who are you, and where are you going?"

"I'd ask the same of you." The woman's voice was sharp with fear. She was dressed for hard travel, gown and cloak all of the same grass-colored homespun, a short sword at her waist and a faded pack fallen at her feet. Her accent was of the southern nenns, and Leicinna relaxed a little.

"Leicinna Elloras, in service to the rivermaster. And you?"

She saw the woman's chest heave in what might have been sigh or sob. "Celica Loisas, captain of Nen Poul. Is the rivermaster here? Or the arros? I bring news."

"What news?" Leicinna saw the other woman hesitate and clarified, "How urgent? We've still some way to go."

"Urgent enough." Celica's smile was wry. "Nen Poul was taken last winter, along with three more of the smaller nenns in the vales of Hern and Kalle. But this spring we've fought free, Nen Poul and Nen Mar and Nen Rassa, and there are risings all through the vales. I'm sent to ask for aid."

Leicinna kicked one foot free of its stirrup. "Finn. Take her pack. And you step up behind me. I'll take you to the arros."

They chewed over the news that night at council, the lamps and the brazier burning ever lower as the captains argued. Leicinna leaned against an outer tentpole nursing her cup of wine: she was there by courtesy and by virtue of having brought the messenger; she had no other claim to speak in council and no particular desire to do so. As far as she could see, there was only one real choice and the arros had already made it: carry on as they had planned, and try to keep the lord paramount from turning back to help his people.

And still they had to argue, particularly Nen Brethil whose troops had only just that night caught up with the main army, and who their lord claimed were still worn out from the fight at the Muster Hill. Esclin merely lifted an eyebrow at that, but neither Nen Salter nor Kellecost of Nen Ddaur were as restrained and Nen Brethil gave way, swearing they would do their best or die trying. At her side, Celica swayed toward sleep and jerked herself awake.

"We've said all there is to say," Esclin said. "Celica." She straightened, trying valiantly to look alert, and he gave her a sympathetic smile. "I'm grateful for your good news, and to your lords for their bravery. But I need one more thing, if you can do it. Can you take my message back to Nen Poul?"

Celica took a deep breath, visibly considering, then gave a jerky nod. "Yes, Sire. I can."

"Then tell them that we will draw the main army off to the north. That will give them time and space to rescue their own people."

Kellecost stirred beside the map table. "Sire. Can't we send even a token company? I know these nenns, they don't keep a great muster."

"A company would be seen," Esclin said. "And met and overwhelmed. And the nenns have already done the hardest part. Now we need to support them."

"If she's taken," Nen Brethil said, "she knows all our plans."

"So does anyone here," Esclin said mildly.

"I won't be taken," Celica said. "I'll ride the Lammard south if I have to." She spoke as if in jest and there was a ripple of laughter in answer, but Leicinna thought she might well be serious. It was not so bad a plan if she was.

"So." Esclin rose to his feet, loose overgown flowing around him like water. Even on campaign, he drew the eye without even trying. "In the morning we'll engage and pull the Riders north."

Leicinna saw her company saddle up a little before dawn and they rode east under a lightening sky, all but the brightest stars faded to nothing. They were meant to be following the distant line of the Darbuin, and as the sun crept above the hills, she was relieved to see that they weren't far off. They were further south than she had meant, far enough that she could see the smoke of the Riders' camp, and that meant they were in range of Rider scouts as well. She drew off to the north again, traveling more quickly, but by the time the sun was fully up they were clear and there was no sign of the Riders. She could see now where the grass had been trampled by Talan's archers, who had made a night march to take the wood where the ambush was to be laid; they followed to the north of it, and by the time the sun was halfway to the zenith, she could see the line of scrub on the horizon.

At noon they reached the wood, and stopped among the trees to rest and water the horses. The thegen and the archers' master Aredan Gammelos were in position, well-protected by barricades of brush and rough-cut stakes, and Leicinna was glad to share their skin of watered wine while the horses grazed.

"Where will you place your folk?" Talan asked. She was young still, it showed in her face, but she carried herself like a seasoned campaigner.

"We'd agreed on the southern edge of the wood, unless there was something wrong with the ground there." Leicinna wiped the sweat from her forehead. The sky was clearing after the morning's thin cloud; it would be hot later on in more ways than one. "I haven't had a chance to look at it yet."

"Not much different than what you see here," Aredan said. "Does Esclin Arros still intend to lead the attack himself?"

"That was the plan," Leicinna answered, keeping her voice scrupulously neutral. There were as many reasons for Esclin to send one of his commanders as there were for him to go himself; the deciding factor, as he himself had pointed out, was that he was the better bait. That was the part that none of them liked, though there was no point in saying so. "Diran's horse will be with him."

"That'll help," Talan said. The dark girl at her side scowled ferociously but said nothing. Leicinna could not remember ever having heard her speak.

When the horses had rested, they refilled their waterskins and made their way through the fringes of the wood to its southern edge. By now, Leicinna thought, chewing on a piece of dried beef, Esclin's men should have made contact with the Riders, were probably even now locked in combat; but she could hear nothing to the south and west, no shouts or faint calls of drum and trumpet, and she could see nothing but the endless grass. She counted the company into thirds, let two at a time rest dismounted, and turned a blind eye to dice and counters. She shaded her eyes to peer into the distance; the sun, slanting toward the west, left her dazzled and she looked away.

"Fisk!"

Her page hurried over, leaving their horses loosely staked where they could reach the better grass. "Captain?"

"Can you get up into one of those trees?" The branches were thin, the trunk twisted by the winter winds; they wouldn't bear a grown man, but Fisk was light for her age.

"I can try." Fisk hauled herself up, feeling her way into the middle of the tree, the branches thrashing. Leicinna glanced from her to the horses, still grazing quietly, and back to the tree.

"Anything?"

"Maybe some dust? Nothing clear."

"Keep looking." She should have borrowed one of the archers' far-sighted men.

The watch changed again. She thought she heard, faintly, the sound of a trumpet, and stood frozen, head tilted, until she was sure it wouldn't come again. The wind had faded and there was nothing to carry the sounds of battle. Gimmel strolled toward her, thumbs hooked in his sword belt, and she lifted an eyebrow. "Did you hear it, then?"

"I heard something," Gimmel said. The tree rustled above them and they both looked up sharply.

"There they are!" Fisk called. "Coming toward us —"

Leicinna swung herself up into her saddle—any elevation at all helped—and shaded her eyes. Sure enough, there was the thicker haze, dust raised by hundreds of marching feet, and the movement beneath that had to be fighting men.

"Mount up?" Gimmel asked and she hesitated, trying to judge their speed.

"Not yet." She didn't dismount herself but joined the troop on watch, staring out into the grass and dazzling sun until her eyes swam with color. The fight was on, and it was coming closer.

The breath caught in her throat as she realized what she was seeing. This was not the orderly, fighting retreat that had been planned; the footmen were coming on at a run, the horse skirmishing behind them, and she heard whistles shrieking as the Riders broke through and bore down on the fleeing men. Somehow they got the line formed before the Riders were on them, but they were too far away for the archers to cover them. The Rider horse wheeled and reformed, putting themselves between Diran's men and Esclin's foot, and Leicinna swore under her breath. It was too early, far too early, a long charge that would wear down the horses even if she didn't take it at top speed, but there was no other choice. She lifted her lance, the sun catching the tip as Fisk raised her scarlet banner.

"Leicinnas! Mount up!"

The company officers echoed her and the troop settled into loose formation. They came on at a trot, covering the ground without yet exhausting the horses, and for an instant she thought they were going to get away with it. Then one of the Riders saw them and pointed, and a group sorted itself out of the melee to throw itself between her and the main battle.

"Now! Leicinnas, now!" She set spurs to her horse in the same moment and the company lurched from a trot to a canter and then a gallop, a spearpoint with herself at the tip bearing down on the Riders. They spurred to meet her, but her company was rested, and they drove through the shielding company and into the flank of the company attacking Esclin's foot.

Leicinna's lance struck hard and stuck; she flung it away and drew her sword, shouting for her company to form on her. Their charge was blunted, stopped by sheer numbers; they were caught in a tangle of men and horses and flailing swords. It was everyone for themselves and Leicinna struck out wildly, without time or space to plan her blows. "Cut through! Cut through!"

She heard Aylflet take up the shout and spurred her horse again, only to check as a Rider swung in on her flank. She ducked under his stroke and caught him in the ribs, muscled past him without trying for a killing blow. More Riders drove in, pushing her back toward the infantry, still holding a ragged line, and she fought her way free again. Diran's horse came back on the Riders, and in the momentary respite, she realized Fisk was still beside her, the scarlet banner flaring.

"To me, Leicinnas!" A dozen horse formed up on her and she pointed them at the knot of Riders, but before she could speak, the air was full of a hum like a thousand angry beehives. "Cover!"

Most of the arrows overshot them—overshot the Riders, too, but the intent and the danger was clear. The Rider captain shouted something, an order to break off, and she ducked again as a second flight shocked home. She saw Diran across a sudden gap, his face bloody and his horse streaked with pink-tinged foam. "Cover the archers!"

For a moment she wasn't sure he understood, but then he wheeled away, the remnant of his company trailing behind him. Leicinna swung her own horse, afraid the Riders might try a final charge, but they were already a quarter league away. Behind them, banners vivid between the bright points of the burning glasses, the main body of the Rider army was on the move.

"Oh, that's not good," Finn said, and she swallowed a laugh that might have become hysterical. There was a plan for this, she reminded herself, and turned back toward the line of footmen, searching for Esclin.

She rode along the line of men, Fisk still trailing her with the banner. Behind them, she could see the archers coming toward them, Diran's horse now deployed to cover them, but she wrenched her eyes away. "Esclin Arros?"

"Here."

That was not Esclin's voice. It came from a knot of men just behind the front line, two of them on their knees, three or four more pressed close, and she saw with a shock that Esclin was one of the men on the ground. He heaved himself to his feet as she watched, swaying slightly, and one of the captains caught his sword arm to steady him. On his shield arm, the pauldron was crushed and he gestured at it vaguely. "Get that off me, someone." A red-haired woman leaped to obey, her fingers deft on the buckles, and she saw him heave a sigh of relief as she freed his shoulder.

"I'm not wounded, all's well," he said, and looked up at Leicinna. "Well-timed, Captain."

"Thank you, Sire, but we're not done yet. The main army's in sight."

"How far off?"

"Not quite a league. But I doubt they'll send the horse again, they'll be blown."

"They'll have fresh companies with them," one of the captains said, and Esclin straightened.

"We planned for this," he said, and looked past Leicinna as one of Diran's man rode up, Talan mounted behind him.

"Back into the scrub?" she asked, and Esclin gave a smile.

"Just as we planned. Diran. You and Talan will lead the foot. Skirt the forest, but keep moving. Once we're out of clear sight, we'll split and make for the rendezvous as planned."

"Won't you come with us, Sire?" Talan asked.

Esclin shook his head, lifting his hand to his shoulder, and then seemed to think better of it. "They'll follow me. So I'll go with the horse, and we'll lead them a dance."

Leicinna suppressed a groan at the thought of more fighting, tired as her horses were—but Diran's were worse off, she reminded herself, and her own were not impossibly pressed. Talan gave a jerky nod.

"Let me see to your shoulder first," an older man said.

"It's just bruised," Esclin said. "There's no time. Leicinna. Will your horse carry two?"

"She will for now, and we'll find you a mount as we go." Leicinna started to kick a foot free of the stirrup, then realized he was coming around to her other side. She made the adjustment, and he hauled himself up behind her with a gasp. She felt him sway, leaning hard against her back, and a bolt of fear shot through her. But then he straightened again, resting his good hand on her waist, and she motioned for Fisk to raise her banner.

"We ride."

They pressed on into the night, passing through the muster point where they joined the remainder of the army, and headed north, making camp finally when the Wain was overhead. The moon was dark and Esclin knew the army straggled, but at last the rearguard reported no sign of the Riders following and he thought it was safe enough to rest. He needed it as much as any of the men, though he did his best to hide it: his shoulder throbbed in time to his heartbeat, his left hand tingling as if he'd stuck it in a beehive. It seemed unfair that he could feel both at once.

He tucked his hand into his belt, trying to immobilize his shoulder unobtrusively, and downed the cup of wine Estor held out to him. His was one of the few tents that had been erected—most of the army would sleep rough—and the pages hadn't had time to set up the furniture, were still spreading pallet and blankets in the inner chamber in lieu of the campaign bed still with the baggage train. Instead, he braced his good shoulder against the central pole, and tried to focus on the discussion around him. Estor brought a second cup of wine; he drank half of it in a gulp, feeling the sweat break out again as he moved incautiously.

"Enough!" He had meant to lift his voice only enough to cut through the noise, but it came out a shout that silenced his commanders. "We've been through this three times, and the answer remains the same. We fall back toward Eith Ambrin, and we march at sunrise."

"All our men need rest," Nen Brethil said.

"Yours are better off than most, Wellan," Esclin answered, "and if I thought there were enough of them, I'd set them to ambush the Riders. But I don't think they can do any better than we did today. And that means we need to choose our ground very carefully. Eith Ambrin is still our best chance."

Nen Salter nodded. "And we can reach it before the Riders do, all the gods willing. Do we stay on the eastward track, or steer for the Lammard?"

"If we stay east, we bypass Mag Ausse," Kellecost said, and Denior nodded.

"I agree."

"And I," Esclin said. "So. We march at sunrise, on the eastward track."

He hoped that would be enough to clear the tent, but as always there were stragglers—Talan this time, hovering with the pitcher of wine, and Nen Salter, turning back just as Esclin thought they were all gone.

"Has Avlen seen to that, Sire?"

"I've sent for him," Talan said, and Esclin frowned.

"I didn't give you leave."

Talan ducked her head and Nen Salter said, "My man said you took a hard hit—he thought it would take your arm off, but you were lucky."

Esclin leaned back against the tent pole. "I still have two arms."

"And you move like a man with a broken shoulder," Nen Salter said bluntly. "They've found your chair. Sit and be tended."

Esclin turned his head, saw the chair within reach, and drew himself up carefully. He managed to seat himself without making a sound, but as he started to lean back a bolt of fire shot through him, and he hissed in spite of himself. He rested his weight on his good shoulder and took another gulp of the wine. His stomach rebelled and he fought it back, swallowed metallic saliva.

"Here," Nen Salter said, beckoning to Estor, and Esclin braced himself to let them ease off his gown. Beneath it, the padded gambeson was scuffed and scored, and Esclin plucked unhappily at the laces. Nen Salter moved to help, and there was a dreadful few minutes as he and Estor worked Esclin out of it. When they were finished, Esclin leaned against the side of the chair, eyes closed, unable to do more than breathe through the sickening pain. It eased a little, and he opened his eyes to find Avlen kneeling beside him, long hands deft on the strings of his shirt.

"Lean forward, Sire."

Esclin did so, unable to suppress a groan, and felt Avlen's fingers cold on his arm. "Must you?" He managed a smile and Avlen matched it, but his hands were merciless.

"Can you lift your arm?

"No."

"Try."

"No." Esclin made an effort, and managed to lift his arm a hand's-span away from his body before falling back, wincing.

"That's good." Avlen ran his fingers along Esclin's collarbone, lightly at first, and then, when that produced no sign of pain, more firmly. Following the movements, Esclin could see that the skin at the top of his shoulder was bruised black, the angry color traveling down his arm and staining the edge of his chest. "Take a deep breath." Esclin tried and froze, a pain like fire stabbing through him. "That hurts?" Avlen urged him to lean forward and Esclin managed to obey.

"Yes."

"And this?" He pressed gently along the line of Esclin's shoulder blade.

"Not as bad."

Avlen hissed softly to himself, then drew Esclin's shirt back up onto his shoulder. "Everything is badly bruised, but I'm not sure anything is actually broken. Except possibly your shoulder blade, and there's not much I can do for that."

"I have to be able to fight," Esclin said.

"You need to let it heal." Avlen rummaged in his satchel, came up with a bottle and a long strip of linen. Estor handed him a cup; Avlen poured a dose from the bottle and nodded for Estor to add wine. "Syrup of poppies. Drink up."

I'll be sick. Esclin closed his lips firmly over that admission and took the cup, forcing himself to swallow. He gagged, tasting the dregs of poppies, but managed to get it down. Avlen nodded, helped him lean back in the chair, and Esclin closed his eye, at last finding a moment of respite.

"Now," Avlen said and caught his wrist, folding the injured arm across his chest. Esclin drew breath at the fresh jolt of pain, and then Avlen was looping the linen strip around wrist and neck. It felt somewhat better held that way, and Esclin felt taut-held muscles ease. He let his eyes close and heard, as if from a great distance, Nen Salter speak.

"Get him to bed. Gods willing, he'll be better in the morning."

"Yes." That was Avlen, and Esclin opened his eye. "Drink."

Esclin accepted the second cup of wine and poppy syrup, sipped cautiously at it, and then, when his stomach did not rebel, took a larger swallow. He finished the cup, and let Avlen help him to his feet and steer him toward the tent's inner room, Huwar on his other side. The pain flared again as they got him down onto the mattress, bracing him with bolsters and saddlebags so that he couldn't fall back on his injured side, and he lay for a moment gasping and sick and furious while they talked over him.

"Can you stay with him?" Talan asked, and Avlen hesitated.

"I've other men to tend to. And I've done all I can. I'll leave you the syrup of poppies, you can give him more if he wakes in pain. Or...there's Brelin. The wheelman." Esclin saw her hesitate and tried to speak, to tell them he'd be well enough, but the words wouldn't come.

"It's not a bad idea," Nen Salter said, and Talan nodded.

"Yes. Send for him, if you would."

"No." Esclin's voice was little more than a croak, but they all turned to look at him. He squinted up at them, his vision blurring, and said again, "No. No need."

"But, Father—" Talan stopped, the bright color washing up her face. "Sire. If he could help."

"I don't know how much more he could do," Nen Salter said carefully. "But surely it's worth the asking."

"Not now," Esclin whispered, and sought an excuse they could believe. "Tired..."

"I've given him enough to stun a horse," Avlen said. "He should rest."

Nen Salter nodded sharply and turned away, the healer following him, but Talan hung back, looking worriedly over her shoulder.

Esclin tried to shape a smile for her, perhaps even an explanation—he could not let any wheelman see him this weak, had to be fully the arros even for Brelin, if he was going to win this long game—but Avlen's syrup had pushed the pain far enough away that exhaustion conquered it, and he slipped into something like sleep.

CHAPTER TWELVE

Flares rose over Callamben that night, distant pops of light and color spelling out a double warning: the Riders were here, the Riders were coming. Helevys was awake when the page came to fetch her, half-dressed already and staring out the east-facing window as though that would help. She came to the council chamber in the first light of dawn, shivering a little at the touch of rain pushing in from the sea, and took her place at the steward's right hand. Traher was there as well, his face pinched and intent, and even Rocelyn, perched awkwardly on a cushion to bring him closer to the table.

"This is hardly unexpected," Roue Steward pointed out, silencing the quiet murmur of conversation. "But now we need to act."

"The first of my scouts left when we saw the flares," Isabar said. "Another flight will follow once this council ends, and a third will follow this afternoon. That will give us a relay of fresh men and horses to carry news as we need it."

"Do we know where they are?" Alisand the storekeeper asked.

"If they have any sense, they'll try to go around Callamben while keeping to the roads," Roue answered. "Whether or not they'll leave a company or two to besiege Callamben is an open question."

"Yes," Helevys said. That was what she had felt last night, waking to distant confusion and alarm. "They have done that, but most of the army is coming on."

The steward hesitated a heartbeat, as though he wanted to question her, but then bowed his head. "Very well. So Callamben will have to hold."

"Tamman's a good commander," Isabar said. "And the walls are new-mended."

"So what does that leave us?" Alisand asked. "It's four days from Callamben to here—"

"They should make it in three," Isabar interjected.

Alisand spread her hands. "Three days, then. That's not much time to bring everyone within the walls."

"Do the best you can," Roue said.

Traher said, "The wood itself will fight them. That should buy more time."

Roue hesitated again. "If the kyra were here, she would direct it..."

"And so shall we," Helevys said firmly. Roue opened his mouth to say something, but she pushed herself to her feet before he could speak. "I think we all know what must be done. Let's be about it while we can."

She turned and swept out of the room, praying that they would follow and that she wouldn't have to go crawling back. She heard chairs scrape on stone and a moment later Rocelyn was at her side, the rest of the council milling behind him. She kept walking, not daring to look back, and Traher called after her, "Wait!" She did not look back but slowed her step a fraction, and he slid to a stop beside her. "You'll want my help."

She scowled, stung, but he was in fact right. "Yes."

"Kore." Ibota had caught up with them, but it took a moment for Helevys to realize that she was talking to her. "Will you dine first, or shall I have food brought?"

"We'll eat later," Helevys began, but Rocelyn gave her a pleading look. "All right, maybe bread and cheese?"

"And honey?" Rocelyn added hopefully, and Helevys saw Ibota suppress a smile.

"And perhaps some tea," she said. "And I'll send someone to fetch warmer cloaks."

"I have mine," Traher said, "but thank you." Ibota made a small curtsey and turned away.

A page was waiting with the cloaks by the time they reached the tower and they climbed to the top in silence, saving their breath for the endless twisting stair. They emerged under a clearing sky and Helevys looked up at the shredding clouds. She could feel the Riders now, an unwanted presence like stinging nettles, east and a little north along the edges of the wood. "I was hoping I could make it rain…" She turned toward the sea as she spoke, trying to feel what lay over the water, beyond the Westwood's borders, but could feel nothing.

"Will they burn the wood?" Rocelyn asked.

"They may try," Traher answered.

Helevys turned back to the east, walking around the curve of the tower until she stood where the sense of unease was strongest. She could almost see it, if she closed her eyes, as though the colors were dimmed, the roots and branches frayed away from her mother's rule. Rider magic, she guessed, trying to force a road through the wood, and she reached out cautiously, trying to feel what they were doing. It snapped at her, like a spark from a fire, and she fell back with a squeak, instantly annoyed at her failure.

She reached out again, not for the dimmed spots but for the wood around them, feeling it bend, groaning, under invisible pressure. She could feel, too, places where her mother had knotted land and trees and scrub into a complex barrier; she could feel her own attempts at tangles as well, and boggy spots made more treacherous by the rains she had sent. The Rider magic hovered just out of reach, shapeless as fire and as dangerous, strength she dared not meddle with. She contented herself with finding the road and weaving more tangles across it, spreading vine and leaf to cover the path.

She felt Rocelyn beside her then, groping clumsily after the same power, and showed him what she'd done. He fumbled for the growing things, unable to quite get his mind alongside them, but the heavy loam rolled and shifted for him, and he gleefully strewed pits and sinkholes along the path. They emerged together into new sunlight, breathing as hard as if they'd been running, to find Traher sitting cross-legged on the stones, a covered basket at his side. He had been playing with a shard of polished steel, making shapes of light flash and flutter against the wall, but looked up as they moved.

"Well?"

"We found them," Rocelyn announced.

"At Callamben, and coming on around it," Helevys said. "Nothing we didn't know. I put down more tangles, hopefully that will slow them down."

"And I put holes in the road." Rocelyn dropped to his knees beside the basket. "And I'm starving."

"You're always starving," Traher said.

Helevys snatched one of the thick wedges of pie, suddenly aware that she was starving herself, and seated herself beside her brothers. She wolfed the pie, secured a second piece before Rocelyn could take it all, and leaned back against the tower's stones. "Can you feel their magic?" she asked Traher. "The Riders, I mean?"

Traher grimaced. "A little. I can tell it's there, that they're using it, but not much more."

"You should make them some dragons," Rocelyn said. "Like the ones you made to scare us."

Traher flushed and Helevys controlled her own grin. Four years ago, Traher had gotten tired of his siblings' aggressive interest in his business, and fenced his room with the illusion of creatures that had not been seen in the Westwood in living memory—stone-dragons, poison bats, crawling shadows that had sent Rocelyn into a screaming panic and given the twins, the next-youngest among them, nightmares for a year. Alcis had not been pleased with any of them. "I wonder if that isn't a good idea."

"They're illusions, Hel. It might give them a scare, but they won't do any real harm."

"But that's something." Helevys leaned forward, wrapping her arms around her up-drawn knees. "We want them scared. We want them thinking anything might jump out at them, that the wood itself hates them and is fighting against them, it and all its creatures. That'll make the real things even more scary."

Traher nodded slowly. "All right. So how to get them to the Riders? I can't see them, not the way you can."

"Make them and I'll place them," Helevys said. She wasn't entirely sure how she would do it, but it was better to keep moving. "Rocelyn can do it, too."

"All right." Traher reached for his mirror again, caught a fleck of sunlight and drew it down onto the stone as his feet, turning it from formless light to the mottled green-black hide and yellow eyes of a honey-dragon. It flicked a scarlet tongue at her, and Helevys couldn't help but hesitate.

She reached for it then, folding it into her awareness of the wood, winding her own power around it until she could lift it and send it soaring, rising above the wood like a wind-blown seed until she could tuck it into a tree beside a stream where a Rider might stop to drink. Traher then shaped a poison-bat, and she found a spot for it; the next, a stone-dragon, she set beside the road, ready to leap and terrify the advance guard. Rocelyn sent a knot of serpents writhing through the soft ground along the trader's path, and she filled the swamp with nameless things that spat venom and disappeared. A congress of salamanders followed, burying themselves in the leaves and loam at Rocelyn's command, ready to spring and fright an unwary horse, and she hung the trees with hives and stinging bees and yet more bats. She lost count of how many she had placed, lost all sense of time and place except for the pull of the wood itself. It seemed to understand what she was trying to do and new places opened to her, ready for her to conceal something beneath their leaves and branches.

She was tiring now, each illusion seeming to weigh more heavily, but she struggled forward, striving for one more spot, one more creature. Then the last poison bat slipped from her grasp, diving out of the tower before Traher dissolved it into a shiver of sunlight, and they sat back, gasping. Rocelyn reached for a final illusion, checked, seeing the stones empty, and burst into tears. Helevys pulled him close, stroking his hair, and felt him slowly calm beneath her touch. Traher tipped his head back against the stones, new shadows under his eyes.

Do you think it will work? Helevys let the words lie unspoken: none of them knew any better than she whether or not this would have any useful effect, not until the Riders came into contact with the illusions. And not all of them would be illusions: they had already roused the wood's creatures and set them on the Riders, and if they had done it right the Riders would never be sure if they faced a real threat or not. Rocelyn burrowed closer against her shoulder, already three-quarters asleep, and Traher slanted a look at them.

"We probably shouldn't have let him do so much."

Helevys nodded and reached for the flask of tea. Traher opened it and handed it to her so that she could drink without waking her brother. She took a long swallow, aware that she was hungry again, and set the flask between them. "Now we wait."

The Westwood's army camped at sunset, and even so it was full dark before the last companies came stumbling into the camp. Alcis received their commanders' reports with outward calm, but in the privacy of her tent she slammed her hand against the nearest tent pole.

"We have to make better time."

Rihaleth didn't look up from the little stove where he was brewing the night's tea. "And arrive with our men too tired to fight?"

Alcis narrowed her eyes at him, but he was right. The army was worn down by the hard traveling and the battle at the muster hill; she needed to let them recover. And yet the Riders were at the Westwood—probably into the Westwood by now, and if she was lucky they'd have taken the time to besiege Callamben before moving on toward the Carallad. She didn't really think they'd be that foolish, and every wasted moment grated on her.

"We're not wasting time." Heldyn set a platter on the table, the stewed chicken neatly disjointed beside a stack of flat campaign loaves. He spread one of the loaves with butter and began to eat, his eyes shadowed with the same fears. "We rebuilt the walls at Callamben two years ago, and Tamman's a canny man. He'll be a thorn in their path."

"If they have any sense, they'll just go around him," Alcis said. She was not particularly hungry, but knew she had to eat and pulled loose a sliver of the breast meat. It was chewy and savorless, but she made herself keep eating.

"Straight through the wood?" Rihaleth shifted the pot to the cooler edge of the fire and came to join them. "I'd like to see them try."

"They have power," Alcis said. "Never forget that." It had been years since they'd made a direct attack on the Westwood, and they'd barely gotten beyond the forest's edge, but her father had been alive then, too old to ride with the army but still master of his powers. He had damped their fires, then raised the very stones against them, tangled them in vines and tree-roots, opened swamps and streams beneath their feet. They had stumbled back out of the wood in confusion, and Alcis herself had led the army down on them. It had been her first victory and still her most complete, but circumstances were very different now. The Riders were stronger, their magic shaped by the growing familiarity of the wheelmen with the land along the coast, honed by a winter in the coastal towns and the Dancing Ground. If she were in the Westwood she had no doubt that she could defeat them, but she was still too far away.

She closed her eyes, reaching out as she had done over and over these last days, feeling for the roots of the grass that ran entangled the length and breadth of the Dancing Ground. She could find that, could find the knots and breaks that were trees and streams and seeps, the remains of old steadings and ground barren by nature or old loss, she could even feel the fringe of the wood, like the breath of cool air on a midsummer day, but she could reach no further. She sighed and made herself eat more of the tasteless chicken, took the cup of tea

Rihaleth brought her. The steam was rich with spice, but she tasted only ash.

"Tamman can hold Callamben until we get there," Heldyn said. "And they'll have to leave a force behind to watch him, even if they try to press on..."

"Traher lacks the land-gift, and Helevys is fourteen," Alcis said. Once her fears were given voice, she found she couldn't stop. "Rocelyn might have it, but he's not even twelve, and the twins turned nine at midwinter. There is no one to rouse the wood, and I stripped the Carallad to bring this army to the Dancing Ground."

"Don't underestimate Traher," Heldyn said. "He acquitted himself well this winter."

"But he lacks the land-gift," Alcis said again.

"He has other skills," Heldyn said, and Rihaleth dropped to the ground at her feet.

"And Helevys is clever, and Roue Steward and Ibota are old and canny, and between them Isabar and Roue can hold the Carallad even against the Riders. And we are coming."

"Not fast enough." Alcis shook her head. "I should not have stripped the wood. They're children. I should be there—" She stopped there, not knowing if her next words would have been *I am their mother* or *I am the kyra*. Both gnawed at her.

"We guessed wrong," Heldyn said. "But we can still make it right." Alcis turned her head away, fear and anger clogging her tongue.

Rihaleth looked up at her, the easy mask of summer's king for once discarded. "Esclin's given us this chance. We need to make the best of it."

Alcis leaned back in her chair. If Esclin was not distracting half the Rider army she would have a far greater fight on her hands, might be managing a running battle instead of a calculated march that should see her reach the Westwood with an army capable of fighting. She touched his hair, agreement and apology. They were right—they were all right, all three of them, and she would hold the balance and bring them home in time.

C

At midafternoon the army reached another of the little unnamed streams that ran from the hills to feed into the Lammard, and Esclin called a halt to let horses and men drink and breathe a while. His shoulder still hurt and he eased it cautiously in the linen binding, grimacing as he woke to a new round of stabbing pain from fingertips to elbow. It was better, he told himself, and turned as he saw Denior trotting toward him.

"A scout just came in, from the rearguard. No sign of the Riders."

"Good." Esclin glanced up at the darkening sky. They had not made a proper camp the last three nights, but the rain that he could feel gathering made that an unpleasant choice for the day. Maybe he could hold it off, nudge it south to drench the Riders instead; he put that thought to one side as Nen Salter came to join them, followed by Kellecost and Reinall Marshal. "Well?"

"We've let the men rest," Reinall said. Esclin could see that, the army scattering in threes and fours and fives to sit sprawling on the new grass and share the contents of their packs. There was no time to order them properly fed, though Reinall would do that tonight, and Esclin nodded.

"But?"

"We're losing men," Nen Salter said quietly. "Stragglers... they're falling back and not rejoining."

"Most of them are Nen Brethil's men," Kellecost said. "But I say to my shame some of mine are among them."

It was expected. The folk of the Hundred Hills were not truly soldiers in spite of years of war, and they'd been mauled twice now. He couldn't entirely blame anyone for thinking it was better to slip away to defend their home rather than stay on this uncertain course. "Who are Wellan's captains? The nephew I know, but the others?"

Kellecost shrugged, but Nen Salter said, "Two others, Coppin Lennas and Gryffet Sinaros. Coppin's a cousin of some sort, through Wellan's wife, and Gryffet holds Nen Geyl. They're due for the rear guard."

Esclin nodded. Gryffet was more likely to be loyal to the arros than to his immediate lord; it would be worth having a word with him before they moved on. "Reinall. See that Nen Brethil camps toward the center, let's not make it easy for them."

"Yes, Sire."

"How are your men holding?" Esclin looked from Kellecost to Nen Salter, reading the answer in the tired slump of shoulders, the battered tack and frayed clothes.

"They'll hold," Kellecost said, his voice grim, and Nen Salter sighed.

"So will mine, Sire, but—it's a bad business. They'd almost rather stand and fight, even knowing how we've come off the last two times."

Esclin gave a wry smile at that. "I can't say I haven't felt the same. But at Eith Ambrin we'll at least have the advantage of the ground. And before you say it, we won't go charging into the ford."

Nen Salter had been there for that disaster, standing at his own father's right hand, and he gave a snort of not-quite laughter. "I'll hold you to that, Sire."

"And well you may." Esclin beckoned to the nearest of the pages, who pulled himself back into the saddle. "Huwar, I'd like you with me. Kellecost—"

"If you're planning to talk to Nen Brethil's man, you're better off without me."

"Just so." Esclin tempered his words with a smile, and Kellecost returned it. "You've done well, you and your men. I need you sharp."

"We'll be ready," Kellecost promised, and turned away.

Esclin collected his reins and nudged his horse forward, searching the untidy crowd for Nen Geyl's banner. He found it after a moment, three yellow bands on a field of deep blue, promisingly far from Nen Brethil's red and white checkerboard, and made his way toward the banner.

He spotted Gryffet Sinaros quickly enough, standing by the banner listening to an older man in good armor: younger than Esclin, and with the hill folk's long-limbed build. He looked up at Esclin's approach and waved the older man away, coming forward to meet the arros with a jerky bow.

"Sire."

"Nen Geyl." Esclin touched his own shoulder lightly. "You'll forgive my not coming down to you. I wanted a word with you before you take your turn at the rear. You'll have heard that the scouts say we've outdistanced them."

Nen Geyl nodded. "Though by the time we get moving..."

He didn't finish the sentence. Esclin looked down at him, groping for the right words, the promise, the gesture that would shift him from Nen Brethil's camp to Esclin's. None came to mind; Nen Geyl looked back at him without expression, willing enough, Esclin thought, but not involved. He could feel the air thickening, the rain closer now; the first horns sounded to get them all moving again, their notes deadened in the heavy air. "Huwar. Tell the marshal I'll be with the rear guard for a bit."

"Sire—" Nen Salter bit off a question that Esclin suspected would have been a disastrous *Is that wise?* and said, "I'd like to come with you."

"I need you with your men," Esclin said. "I want to set a small trap."

Nen Salter lifted an eyebrow at that, but nodded. "Very well, Sire."

Esclin waited, letting his horse crop idly at the grass, while Nen Geyl brought his men into order and then mounted himself, sending an occasional nervous glance to the south. Esclin squinted, thought he could see a horseman coming toward them, and bit back a curse of his own. If the Riders were too close, his idea wouldn't work, or at least not as well.

It was one of his own people, trotting back with the welcome news that the scouts had gone as far as they dared and seen only the most distant signs of the Riders. "Dust on the horizon, Sire," the man reported, "nothing more. The captain says she'll cover the rear guard in case they come on, but she doesn't see much likelihood that they will."

"Good news indeed," Nen Geyl said, and Esclin nodded and sent the man on to Reinall with the message. It was time they'd had some good fortune.

"Form your men up north of the stream—not too close, we'll not have to defend it. A dozen ells back at least."

Nen Geyl looked as though he wanted to ask questions and Esclin waited, hoping he would, but then simply nodded. "Yes, Sire."

It didn't take him long, proof that his men were well-trained and still willing, leaving Esclin and his page on the southern side of the stream. Nen Geyl rode back to join him, curiosity finally getting the better of him. "My men are in place, as you ordered. Can I—"

He stuck there, but Esclin nodded as though he'd finished the question. "I want to lay a—trap of sorts, though I fear it won't do more than slow them down. It's all illusion, but they won't know that."

He settled himself as he spoke, letting the rain weigh down on him. The stream was full, snow-melt still running from the distant hills; a quarter league beyond, the ground was dry, the grass straining to drink. He reached for the lowering clouds, tugged them south and down, so that the sky seemed to shift and shiver, like wind rippling across the surface of a pond. The land craved water and he gave it water, urging the clouds to come down, a mist billowing, not up from the land but tumbling from the sky. A spatter of rain passed over them; he pulled more and more mist into the waiting ground. Another swirl of rain swept through, drops as hard as stones, and he released the clouds, let them rise again perceptibly lightened.

The ground was waiting, full and primed. He closed his eyes, shaping the mist that would rise with the Riders' approach, with the first touch of the wheelmen's magic. Fire would draw water, a thickening wall of fog to confuse them, an uneasy drift of mist and shadow that might contain anything. He could feel it waiting now, coiled among the grasses, a few tendrils already rising like wisps of smoke. It was tempting to do more, to fill the illusion with yet more illusion, shapes out of nightmare, but he knew the limits of his strength and the temptation of the illusion. Instead, he worked himself free, left the illusion standing, and turned to the stream.

It was strong and full; he would need to add so very little to shape it, and he reached for it almost before he had made the decision. The water leaped, flashed to spray, leaped up again to form a horse's head, then a head and forelegs, a water horse rising from a sudden wave that was not truly there. He shaped another, and a third, tumbling and nipping at each other as they plunged down invisible rapids. As if from a great distance, he heard Nen Geyl's men cheer, and heard Nen Geyl mutter something he could not take time to hear. He sank the water horses into the spate, raised them again, bound them to the fog, so that when it vanished, they would appear.

He took a deep breath then, his body suddenly present and aching, his shoulder throbbing and a new tight ache crawling down the small of his back. He stretched, wincing, and saw Nen Geyl's eyes wide. "If you can do that, Sire…"

"It's illusion," Esclin said. "It can do them no harm."

"It looks real enough," Nen Geyl said. "I'd not like to face it."

On the far side of the steam, Nen Geyl's men raised another cheer and Esclin lifted his hand in answer. The water horses were an indulgence, a defiance, unnecessary, except that Nen Geyl's men had seen and loved them. That was reason enough, and he urged the horse forward. "Let's hope the Riders feel the same way."

The Riders were on the move again after two days milling about at the edges of the wood. A company remained to pen Callamben's defenders behind their walls, and the rest of army moved warily onto the roads new-cut through the thick forest. Rumor said the roads had cost as much as a small skirmish, between deadfall trees and a stream that proved unexpectedly deep and a rash of common accidents. As the train passed under the canopy, Viven could see the men staring nervously around them, hands on weapons as though the very trees themselves might launch an attack. Aelin rode in one of the wagons with Eliseve huddled beside her, the canvas top drawn close as though that would protect them. Viven herself rode shackled and Graland led her horse on a short rein, his sword loose in its scabbard. She was all too aware of Aelin's worried stare, silently urging her to make her escape, to find some way to use the time she'd been given, but Radoc's men kept too close a watch.

She had traveled the Westwood before, and found it pleasant enough—dark, always, and cool in the spring, the loam settled deep enough to dampen the sound of travelers even on the main road. Now, though, the shadows took on peculiar shapes, and things seemed to writhe through the underbrush beside the road, only to vanish before any eye could find them. The broken tree trunks showed white splinters that threatened to catch at men and beasts, and the path had a tendency to pitch abruptly sideways, or open into soggy puddles that did their best to swallow the wagons' wheels. Each time a cart bogged down, it took longer to free it, and the men were too cowed to curse aloud. It took them most of the day to rejoin the main road where it passed west from Callamben, and they camped that night in a straggling array, huddled uneasily in rough clearings to either side. The wheelmen ordered bonfires, the flames leaping up into the night, but the woods beyond the fires' light seemed even darker by comparison.

There was no harping that night, nor even a tent. Aelin and Eliseve took shelter beneath their wagon, huddled in their cloaks as well as blankets, but did not come nearer to the fire. Viven sat closer, grateful for the warmth and sure she could get nowhere with her hands still bound. When the rations were passed round, Radoc freed one of her wrists but fastened the other shackle to the wagon's wheel, and set his own bedroll between it and the shadows. Viven gave it one sharp tug, saw him turn, and resigned herself to waiting. If she could free herself she might use the harp's power to lose herself in the wood, but at the moment she was too closely watched. She finished her meager bowl of barley pottage and hunched closer to the wagon.

"Harper." Aelin's voice was barely a whisper, not enough to carry to Radoc's bedroll. His attention was on his people, anyway, on a sergeant offering some complaint and Linaren crouching by the fire. "I have a pin, if you can reach the lock."

"I don't know how," Viven answered. "If you had the key…"

Aelin breathed a laugh. "On Lord Radoc's belt. I never thought I'd regret not knowing how to pick a lock."

"No more did I," Viven answered. Harpers were protected by their harp and its magic and generations of respect. Possibly it would have been more useful to learn more dubious talents.

"You have to get away," Aelin said.

I would if I could. Viven swallowed the words, said instead, "I have been trying. But you see how well watched I am."

"I know." Aelin closed her eyes. "But the axial…" She couldn't finish the sentence.

"You bought me time," Viven said. "Never think you didn't."

"I would like to see you live."

"So would I," Viven answered.

Aelin paused. "We'll do what we can for you, Eliseve and I."

"Thank you." Viven hesitated. "You've heard me ask. I have a daughter, Gemme, she's a prisoner in Nen Poul. If they let her live…"

"I'll do what I can," Aelin said.

That might not be very much at all and they both knew it, but it was more of a promise than Viven had had before. She clasped Aelin's cold fingers, wordless thanks, and drew herself back against the wagon wheel as Radoc glanced their way. His gaze passed over them and did not linger. She wound herself in her cloak and settled into a cold hollow, her free arm clutching her cased harp.

She didn't sleep well, waking over and over to the call of the watch and the shuffle of feet, but as she pulled herself together in the cold light of dawn, she realized that she had done better than most. *Eyes*, someone whispered, *Eyes in the dark*, and Radoc lost his temper and shouted for them all to hold their tongues until they had something useful to say. The company ate in silence then, savorless porridge cooked in the remains of their bonfire, and she allowed herself to be put back onto her horse. The lead companies were already on the march and the baggage train's carters were prodding their animals into motion, too afraid to be left behind. Someone shouted, a horse screamed and reared, and Viven whirled to catch a glimpse of color that might have been a honey-dragon diving into the cover of the brush. The horseman got his animal under control while a couple of Radoc's men beat at the undergrowth, trying to drive the creature out, but nothing appeared.

They rode on into the sullen morning, only the barest glimpse of a clouded sky visible in the rare breaks in the trees. The ground was soggy, spotted here and there with the dead-white mushrooms that grew on rotting trees; the water in the sluggish streams ran brown with peat and bitter iron, barely drinkable even before the passage of the army churned it to muddy slush. Along the line of march the wheelmen lit torches, but they did little to drive back the gloom or to frighten off the creatures that lurked in the shadows.

Something scuttled through the leaves to the left of the path. Viven's horse did not shy, but the man riding to her left half-drew his sword, standing in his stirrups as though that would help him see better. A bird called harshly from the trees on the opposite side of the path—a crow or some other carrion bird, Vivian thought, or perhaps a king frog. They weren't deadly, but they spat a yellow slime that could send a grown man into waking nightmares. Usually their bright green stripes made them easy to spot against the dark ground, but in the gloom nothing was simple and Viven's toes curled inside her boots.

Abruptly there were shouts ahead, and the sound of metal on metal. All around her the guards of the baggage train drew their swords and Graland drew her horse close alongside his own, both animals rolling their eyes and tossing their heads, not liking the enforced proximity or the rising tension. Someone shouted for orders and got no answer; another Rider spurred forward, disappearing around the road's gentle curve. And then, as abruptly, men were shaking their heads and sheathing their swords, and Viven heard someone mutter something about snakes and a stream's bank that had given way under one of the horses.

Through it all she could feel the Westwood's magic gathering, soundlessly tightening the strings of her harp until she feared they would snap under the unanticipated pressure. She didn't dare play; she handled the case with aching caution, at every stop fearing to loose some sympathetic echo from the harp itself. But she was not summoned, and that night she curled herself beside the case, throwing her cloak over them both as though it were a living being.

Her luck ran out the middle of the next morning, as the baggage train dragged itself along in the army's wake, too afraid to straggle and yet unwilling to get too close to the main body. A page in Radoc's livery rode back along the line, said something to Graland that she couldn't hear. She couldn't read his expression, either, as he looked back, shortening the lead rope, but his words were a death knell.

"Lord Radoc says the axial wants a word with you."

That was the end, though she might prolong things a little further. She made no protest as Graland led her out of the plodding line, their horses picking their way along the road's soft shoulder. It was hard going, ducking in and out of trees and dodging low-slung branches; Viven kept her eyes open for any chance to bolt and run, but Graland kept the lead rope snubbed too tightly. If she had had a knife—might as well wish for sword and armor, or her harp itself in hand.

The marching men slowed as they moved further up the column until their horses were stumbling along the road's rutted edge, trying to keep from slipping into the ditch while the soldiers stood motionless, swearing under their breath, or called after them to find out what the trouble was. At the head of the column, men and horses milled aimlessly at the edge of a shallow stream, ceding as much space as possible to the axial and a single wheelman in white, who stood together at the edge of the ford staring at the wall of thorns that filled the opposite bank. Another pair of wheelmen sat their horses a little behind them, the burning glass they carried like a banner unable to catch sunlight to conjure with. Viven suppressed a bubble of laughter, and Graland pulled them both to a stop beside Lord Radoc.

"The harper, my lord."

He had spoken quietly enough, but the axial looked over his shoulder, some of the anger fading from his face. "Good. Bring her."

Radoc took the lead rope from Graland, who looked happy to fade back into the mass of men. Radoc clucked to the horses and nudged his forward; Viven's mount followed, blowing unhappily, to stop beside the wheelmen.

"Dismount," the axial said impatiently, and a page hurried to take their horses' bridles. Radoc swung himself down, then loosed the rope that attached Viven's manacles to the pommel of her saddle.

"Can you—?" he began, but she was already swinging herself free, her harp settling against her back. Radoc looked back at the axial. "My lord."

"You've traveled these woods before," the axial said without preamble. "Under the protection of your harp."

"I've traveled here, yes," Viven said. "And true it is that my harp is some protection; but also I was a known guest, welcome in the Westwood's halls."

"Do you remember this barrier?" the other wheelman asked, and Viven shook her head.

"No, my lord."

"Snakethorn," Radoc said, not quite under his breath, and the wheelman's frown deepened.

"We had determined that, yes."

"But the harp is a key," the axial said. "Very well, harper. Take up your instrument and give us passage."

Viven took a deep breath, wishing this had come to a better end than a sword-thrust beside a muddy stream. "My lord, I cannot."

The axial eyed her for a long moment, and she braced herself not to cry out, not to beg, when he gave the order. Her bowels griped, and she swallowed the taste of fear. "This is not reasoning magic. Unbind her hands and put them on her harp."

"No," Viven began, and took a step backward. One of the soldiers caught her by the shoulders and she stopped, knowing that further struggle was pointless. "It won't work." The axial ignored her, gestured for Radoc to hurry. Radoc dug in his belt pouch for the key to the manacles, then unlocked them. "It won't work," she said again.

"Take up your harp," the axial said.

"My lord—"

"Take up the harp," he said again.

Viven hesitated, but there was no reason not to win a few more moments of life. And, who knows, harp in hand she might at least be able to take some of them with her, or at least set the harp on her murderer. She swung the case off her shoulder and opened it, the polished wood warm and silken under her touch. The strings rang gently as she lifted it, a soft, testing note in the heavy air, and she stilled them with a touch.

There was a moment in which the entire army seemed to hold its breath, but then, as nothing happened, the axial frowned more deeply again. "Walk into the water."

"I will not." Viven didn't bother to add an honorific or to apologize for its lack, digging her heels into the muddy ground like a balky mule. On the far side of the ford, the snakethorn seemed to writhe and darken.

"How did you cross here?" Radoc asked.

"On foot," Viven answered. "The way was open, I had no army with me—"

"Play." That was the other wheelman, his voice as hoarse as if he had been shouting.

"Play what?" Viven asked. "I have no key for this—"

"Enough." The axial lifted his right hand, something bright glinting between his fingers. It brightened from a spark to a sphere bright as the sun, and leaped to the nearest burning glass. Its bearer lifted it and fire shot from its heart, crossing the stream and boring into the wall of thorn. The thorn thrashed as though in a high wind, but a thin coil of smoke began to rise from among the knotted branches.

Viven clutched her harp, feeling the Westwood's magic trembling in its strings: the wall of thorn, fighting to throw off the burning light; the ground uneasy underfoot; the distant rippling of something that wasn't wind in the trees.

"Play!" the other wheelman demanded. "Radoc, walk her into the water."

She saw Radoc hesitate, then felt his hands on her shoulders. Still avoiding the harp, she realized, and let him turn her toward the ford. If this was to be her end, she might as well make it count: she shifted her hold, feeling for the strings and the power they contained. The air trembled around her, the wheelmen's fire seeking a point of attack, the wood shifting and writhing to damp it out, and she took a breath and set fingers to the strings, striking a single ringing chord. She felt the stream answer, the water lifting into the already-damp air, beads of fog forming on her skin, on the harp's polished body.

"Stop that," the axial said, and she ducked away from Radoc's grasp, stepping deeper into the stream and putting her back to the snakethorn that filled the far bank. The harp's power filled her, cold and dangerous as a summer storm; her fingers found the chords without thought, calling the rain out of clouds that suddenly thickened overhead. The downpour rushed over them, hissing into the stream, and there were cries of alarm from further down the column as the trees to either side of the road thrashed in a sudden wind. Another great gust struck the snakethorn, rattling its branches and sending more rain and bits of twig and leaf swirling across the stream to strike at the Riders.

Any minute now they would strike her down, but until then, she reached for the next chord and the next, calling the storm out of the cloud, out of the angry wood. Behind her, she could feel another hand at work, inexpert and not entirely certain but stronger than she had expected in the kyra's absence, a hand that groped for wood and stone and earth to feed the storm that was already starting to fail. There were shouts from the Rider army, from further off, from the baggage train, but she couldn't spare the time to sort them out, could only concentrate on the strings singing to her touch.

The axial seized the burning glass from the other wheelman, lifted it with a shout that lit a spark of sunlight in its core. The storm faded further, the clouds raveling overhead to reveal streaks of open sky. Viven struck chords again, and then a ripple of song that mimicked the hasty spill of a stream. The water strengthened around her ankles, rising toward her calves, and she felt that other hand reach for it, too, drawing it up to feed the storm.

"Stop her!" the axial shouted, and she ducked at the sound of a bowstring too close at hand. She felt the arrow pass her—perhaps it plucked at her cloak—but kept playing, the music rising with the water. Nowhere else could she have done this, only in the Westwood, eager for any guidance against its enemy; she called rains from the distant sea, snow from the mountains above Riverholme, the deep waters beneath the earth, rising to fill the stream and send her staggering, while the rain lashed harder, the clouds darkening overhead. Thunder rolled, louder than the Rider drums, and a flash of lightning split the sky.

Another bowman fired, and another, vague shapes through the curtaining rain. One creased her hip, the other her shoulder, and then a third shot slammed home above her left breast. It knocked her backward, knocked the breath from her. Her left hand fell nerveless from the strings and the water surged against her knees, driving her stumbling sideways. She lost the thread of the tune, tried to recover it, blood and rain dripping from her useless fingers. Another bowstring sang, and a stone turned under her foot, sending her sprawling in the cold stream. It was deeper, suddenly, than she had thought; her feet found no purchase, and the rushing water rolled her away, still clinging to her harp as she fell into the dark.

Her scouts reported that the Riders had left a single company at the walls of Callamben. Alcis allowed herself a quiet smile and dispatched Rihaleth to deal with them, turning the rest of the army into the wood. Here at last she was on her own ground, at home—if not at the heart of her power then close enough to touch it—and she rode with her attention turned inward, tasting wind and root and branch, every trickle of a stream that lay between her and the Carallad. She could feel the scar of the Riders' passage, could feel, too, the twists and traps that lay between them and the fortress: Helevys's hand, certainly, and Rocelyn's, and even Traher's, his illusions woven not unskillfully into the web of the wood. *Well done*, she breathed, and felt the land acknowledge her, gather itself anew at her touch.

"The Riders are staying to the road," Heldyn said, two days in. With the wood on their side, they were making good time, the ground drying underfoot, the boggy spots and thorny tangles melting away at Alcis's approach. "If we carry on, we'll plow into their baggage train."

Alcis pulled back from the Wood enough to consider the situation. She had been so busy smoothing their passage that she had not yet taken time to consider the strategic situation, but now... They needed to take out the column as quickly as possible, the leaders before the stragglers if at all possible, and she pursed her lips. "Take a company through the woods, parallel the road. Try not to be seen until you can take out the head of the column—" She stopped abruptly, a new image coming clear. Helevys had set a barrier of thorn on the far side of the Mairell ford, seemed to be planning to make a stand there, though she had no troops to back up her power. "Wait. They'll be stopped at the ford, Helevys has set a trap there. If you can come up—"

"The Mairell?" Heldyn asked, and whistled for the nearest page.

Alcis nodded. "It should hold them long enough, I'll make sure of it—"

"We'll be there," Heldyn said, with the simple certainty that she had always loved in him.

"Go," she said, and he spurred away, his officers falling in behind him as he went.

Alcis took a deep breath, steadying herself as she gave hasty orders to her captains and watched them gather for a moment around Josse Iros before turning back to their own companies. Her sergeant Radamy took charge of her personal guard, and she let the reins lie slack as she felt her way carefully into the structure Helevys had built. Here the wheelmen had broken its threads but illusion and a few real traps were as yet unsprung, waiting to ambush the oncoming army. Alcis found those points and eased them away, easing the land back to its natural state. It went willingly, recognizing her touch; paths opened, paralleling the road, and she felt Heldyn's men pick up speed, moving through land that welcomed their passage.

She stretched further, reaching toward the Carallad, and recoiled, swaying in her saddle, as she struck the roiling knot where the wheelmen struggled with Helevys's work. There was more power there than she had expected, dragged awkwardly from stone and root, but skill as well, illusion deployed to dismay and delude, laid together with real traps of bog and branch to throw the Riders into confusion: they'd done well, her children, and she allowed herself a moment's pride before disciplining herself to the work. She could not reach Helevys, not through that mess and not without distracting her when she needed all her wits about her; Alcis would have to trust that her daughter would recognize her father's men, would at least recognize the opening of the wood and let them through.

She worked her shoulders under the stiff pauldrons, aware that they had come some distance while she felt her way through the wood. The knot of power was closer now, and overhead the sky darkened, a chill unseasonable wind whipping through the tops of the trees bringing with it a drumroll of thunder. At the same time she could feel the wheelmen's fire, a spark growing in strength and substance, a light ready to become flame. The wood shrank from it even as Helevys tried to push it on, tried to bring down the storm at the same moment. Too soon, Alcis thought, too soon, first the wind to lay them flat while you pull the rain from every quarter, first the wind and then the rain—

She felt the wheelmen act, will focused to flame, focused through the burning glass, a spark that grew, eager to leap to wood and leaf. The light leaped from glass to branch, a spot of white-hot pain, branches writhing to avoid it. And then, out of nowhere, the sudden angry clamor of music that called to the Mairell, to all the streams that fed it; she felt the clouds thicken, drinking the stream, and the rain lashed across the Rider column, momentarily blinding. That was harp-magic, unmistakable, the wood answering because it was the best and strongest guidance. Alcis fitted herself to that tune and added to it, calling the rain to damp the fires, the wind to batter the wheelmen to their knees, the Mairell to rise and sweep away everything in its path. She felt Helevys's hand then, felt her daughter recognize the touch and felt the sheer ferocious delight leap between them, brighter than the wheelmen's fire. They reached together into air and earth, driving the storm before them.

In its wake came Heldyn and his men, riding out of the thrashing woods, the rain sweeping away ahead of them so that they came on dry-shod and unblinded, smashing into the Riders' flank. She felt the collision, felt them turn the Rider army back against itself, the sound of thunder drowning the signal drums until the column shattered and there was only a milling pack of prisoners begging to surrender, and a handful of stragglers fleeing, snuffed out by ones and twos by the vengeful wood.

Alcis reached through the rags of the storm, already blowing away on its own winds, winds that would carry it to the seacoast towns to rattle masts and batter sails, stretching her senses until she found the Carallad. There was Helevys at the top of the tower, Rocelyn clinging to her skirts while Traher embraced them both, all of them weeping from sheer exhaustion. Alcis reached for them, caressing them as though they could feel her touch, her pride and gratitude and plain relief that they were there and well and had done well. She could not spare the time now to offer more, only that wordless momentary overwelling of her feelings, but she knew they felt it, knew they knew their victory. And then she slumped back in her saddle, gasping as though she had ridden to the Carallad and back again, working arms and legs as she drew herself back into her body, back to the business at hand.

Esclin felt the first Riders reach his illusion, felt them slow at the rising fog, then start into it and turn back, horses fighting against bit and spur rather than enter that cloud. He felt their fear, felt the outriders falter, the army slow. All that was expected; he kept half his mind on that and half on the northward road and his own straggling army, working their way through scrub and grass and stone toward the rendezvous point at Eith Ambrin. They had split the companies to spare the land but even so the men were hungry, stores running low and little time to forage. Supply parties had gone out, but there was no knowing how many of them would return.

He felt the illusion stretch and thin and reform as the lord paramount's men pushed warily forward, felt the mist rise with every step, then flinched as the first of the wheelmen turned their burning glass on the drifting shapes. They writhed and clung, but he could feel the heat like sun on his own skin, felt each layer burn slowly away, loosed into nothing. He felt the water horses leap and tumble, pure mockery, and vanish before the wheelmen could destroy them, disappearing back into the water that was now only a mountain-fed stream. He hoped he had bought enough time.

They reached Eith Ambrin in the slanting light of sunset, their shadows stretching the length of the ford. The river was in full spate still, running white over broken stones, and beyond it the land rose slightly: not as high as the muster hill, but enough to offer some protection. There was a scrap of wood beyond, fair cover for the archers, and behind that the ground ran uneven up into the lowest hills. He knew every step of this ground, could feel that first battle echoing in the earth, blood still unquiet beneath and beside the rolling river: an ill-omened choice, but he had none better.

Across the ford, the camp marshals were laying out the pickets: there would be time, at least, to set up a proper camp, get the men fed and under shelter for the night, even if the meals were meager. He touched Arros at his side and urged his horse into the ford, trying not to think about the other royal sword trodden to destruction somewhere among the stones.

Talan's archers were next to arrive, then the companies from Nen Atha and Nen Arranme. They had been sent to hunt and had done better than Esclin had expected, some brace of hare and ducks and even an old unwary buck to add to the pots. Kellecost's men straggled in after, and Denior's horse, and finally the rearguard and the last of the scouts. Nen Brethil was conspicuously absent. It was twilight now, the sun well down and the light faded. Esclin stood for a long moment in the doorway of his tent, feeling the weight of the dead clinging to his feet. Without Nen Brethil they had no chance at all of holding the Riders, no matter what advantage the ground could give them.

He turned at last and went into the tent, accepting the scant cup of watered wine that one of Talan's companions offered him. The waiting captains exchanged glances, and Reinall Marshal heaved a sigh.

"The scouts say there's no sign of him." He did not have to say a name; there was no one else who mattered just at this moment.

"He won't come," Kellecost said furiously. "He's gone back to his hill to protect his own, and I hope the Riders burn him out."

Talan made a noise of agreement, and Nen Salter shook his head. "I can't believe Wellan's made any bargain with them—"

"Enough." Esclin didn't raise his voice. "Is Nen Geyl here?"

"He is," Reinall answered.

"Fetch him."

Esclin turned his back on the council, trying to order his thoughts. They couldn't hold Eith Ambrin with so few men; and if they couldn't hold Eith Ambrin, there was nowhere short of the northern nenns themselves that could withstand an attack. If he'd gone to Mag Ausse instead—but the time for that was past. He had chosen Eith Ambrin and its omens, and he was paying the price. And there was every chance that the Riders would turn south again, to retake the nenns that had rebelled, or head west to join their fellows in the Westwood. He had to prevent that, whatever the cost, but he had seen slaughter here before and could not bring it on his people.

"Nen Geyl, Sire," Reinall said.

Esclin turned and Nen Geyl went to one knee at his feet.

"Sire. I swear, I didn't know—"

"Enough," Esclin said again. He didn't entirely believe him, the odds that Nen Brethil wouldn't have at least hinted at his plan were far too high, but he found he didn't particularly care. "Be that as it may, I can't stake my men's lives on it. I must dismiss you from my service."

"Sire!" Nen Geyl sounded genuinely wounded, and out of the corner of his eye, Esclin could see Nen Salter swallow a protest.

"But. Because I do believe you, I will ask one favor. Carry a message for me to Nen Brethil."

"I will."

"Hear it first." Esclin smiled. "Tell him I will give him one chance only to redeem himself. I will call for his men, and he will come, or else I will break him as I will break the Riders. I will name him outlaw and traitor and everyone's hand will be against him. Are you still willing to take that message?"

Nen Geyl took a breath, but nodded. "Sire, I am. If you won't let us stay—I am willing."

"Then go," Esclin said. "Be on the road tonight, I want you well clear before the Riders come."

"I—" Nen Geyl visibly thought better of whatever he had been going to say. "Sire, I will."

He backed away. Reinall hastily motioned for one of the camp-marshals to accompany him, and said, "Sire. We can't spare those men."

"There aren't enough of them to make a difference," Esclin said. "And we can't hold Eith Ambrin without Nen Brethil." For just an instant he hoped Nen Brethil defied him—it would be a pleasure to break Wellan for this, him and his smug nephew—but put that thought away. "We need another plan."

He saw the others exchange looks, and finally Nen Salter said, "If we don't hold them here, we can't hold them at all. Let me go after Nen Brethil—at least let me bring back Nen Geyl."

"It's too late," Esclin said. "Huwar, you are going to take your men back to Salter Vale and hold the nenns. Kellecost, you'll take your men west to the Lammard—cross it if you can—and turn back south to help Nen Poul and the other rebels. With your men, they can finish casting off the Riders. Denior, I want you to send half the horse with him—the people from the south for preference. The rest of you—" It was a poor rest, but he didn't betray that by any look or shift of tone. "The rest of you will follow Talan and Reinall Marshal to Nen Elin."

"If you split the army, they'll destroy us piecemeal," Nen Salter said.

Talan said, as though Nen Salter hadn't spoken, "Where will you be, Sire?"

Esclin gave her a nod of approval. Of course she had guessed. "The lord paramount wants to take the realm—and its ruler. I'm going to give him Nen Elin."

There was a murmur of disbelief, but Talan said, "And the prophecy says that when a wheelman enters Nen Elin, Nen Elin will fall."

"Just so."

"And also you're going to give him the arros." Her voice was flat.

"If he thinks he has me, he'll ignore everything else until he has secured the Hundred Hills." Esclin kept his eye on his daughter, though he could feel the rest of the council listening just as closely, with just as much doubt. "And that's where we can stop him."

"He'll kill you if he takes you," Reinall said.

"If he kills me, Talan rules," Esclin answered. "That doesn't serve his purpose." He shrugged his uninjured shoulder. "But if he does, Talan will carry on. It's the best we can do for our folk."

"It's a gamble." Nen Salter shook his head. "By all the fires, such a gamble! But if you can pull it off..."

Esclin smiled again, though his lips felt stiff as though with cold. "It's the best way."

"Mistress help us," Nen Salter said, half under his breath. "Very well, Sire, I'm with you."

"And I," Kellecost said, and the others echoed him as well.

"Then get your men a good night's rest," Esclin said. "You'll march in the morning."

He watched them file out of the tent, unsurprised to see Talan hanging back, and managed a smile as she let the tent flap fall closed behind the others. "Pour me more wine, will you?"

She did as he asked, filling his cup from the pitcher. "That's the last. Unless you have more somewhere?" Esclin shook his head. "When I take our people to Nen Elin—what then?"

"Warn Kelleiden." The was the most important thing, Esclin thought; he could trust Kelleiden to see the shape of his plans, and to respond. "Rota, too. Tell them to be sure the cisterns are full and the larders stocked, in case this goes badly. Then—clear the nenn, there should be room for our people in Nen Atha and Nen Arranme, but I trust your judgment. If I die, no matter what is said, you are the thegen. You will be arros after me."

"You make it sound simple."

"But it is." Esclin set his cup aside, rested his hand on her shoulder. After a moment, she leaned against him. "It is simple. The details may be complicated, but the truth, the mystery—that is simple. The arros serves the people, in life and in death."

"We haven't sacrificed an arros in a thousand years."

"I'm not planning to start."

She snorted at that. "I will hold you to it."

"Go," Esclin said, and pushed her lightly toward the door. "You have work to do."

He drained his cup, barely tasting the watered wine. Nen Salter was right, it was a gamble, but like all gambles it offered the chance of outright victory when every other road only barely held off defeat.

CHAPTER THIRTEEN

It was a full day before the Rider army came into view, the lord paramount wary of even harmless illusion. It was satisfying in some sense, Esclin thought, standing in the doorway of his tent just below the minimal height of Eith Ambrin. At least the lord paramount was still concerned enough to be cautious: Esclin would use every advantage he could find, no matter how scant. He could see dust on the southern horizon, gilded by the setting sun, and guessed he would have one more night. Reys en Nevenel was not one to miss the symbolism of arriving with the rising sun.

Esclin knew he would lose more men overnight and could hardly blame them; he had ordered his remaining captains to turn a blind eye where they could, but now as the sun melted into the distant shimmer of the Lammard and the fires were lit, he found himself wondering if it would have been better to fight. It was too late for that now. He was committed to this plan, would need to see it through to the end.

In the fading light he could see horsemen moving on the plain beyond the river, little knots of three and four that stayed well clear of each other: the scouts of both sides, surveying the terrain before the morning's meeting. He moved his shoulder injudiciously, grimacing at the pain, and retreated into his tent. A page brought a bowl of porridge and a jug of what proved to be weak mint tea. The porridge was dull and savorless despite the bacon rind and a visible handful of sharp spring onions, but he made himself finish it, knowing there would be fewer chances later.

At moonrise, the scouts and the remaining captains gathered to discuss the next day's plan. There was nothing new to say—not even the scouts' news was unexpected—but he could feel them listening, waiting for him to reveal some final twist that would save them all. He had none to give, not yet, and his shoulder ached, so that it was hard to keep an edge from his voice as he dismissed them all. "Except you, Leicinna," he added, and knew he had spurred hope where there should be none.

The scout captain turned back from the tent's doorway, letting it fall behind her. "Sire?"

"How tired are your people?"

She blinked once, schooling her face to hide a sudden blaze of hope. "We had the inner circuit. We're better than some."

Esclin winced, grimaced again as her shoulders slumped. "I want you to watch what happens tomorrow and take word of it to the thegen. She—" He stopped himself, knowing that explanations would only destroy what hope she had. "She'll know what to do."

"Yes, Sire." Leicinna straightened her shoulders. "Can we leave tonight, or do you need some of us to stay?"

"Leave," Esclin said, and made an effort to put no great emphasis on the word. "Just be sure you can see what happens."

Leicinna ducked her head. "We'll see to it, Sire."

"I know you will." Esclin gave her his warmest smile. "Go now, before anyone thinks to question."

"Yes, Sire," she said again, and slipped from the tent.

Left at last to himself, Esclin sprawled in the single chair, wincing as he tried to find a comfortable position for his shoulder. After a moment's hesitation, he sent the page for the flask of poppy syrup and poured himself a generous dose. Under other circumstances he would have saved it for the morning and the inevitable wounded, but the whole point of his plan was to forestall further losses. He would need all the rest he could get, to be sharp for the meeting.

He woke in the predawn light, chilled and stiff. The shivering page brought him hot water and he shaved with care, then combed out his hair, leaving it unbound. He chose the most austere of his gowns—this was not a day for more than the bare minimal of armor—and covered his missing eye with a patch of silver brocade stiffened and shaped to fit the hollowed socket. The sun was up by then, low and ruddy gold, drawing up the dew in thin curls of fog, and he could hear the distant sound of the Rider drums: not much time left, and he wondered if he dared take another dose of the syrup. No, he would need all his wits about him, though his shoulder still ached distractingly as he let the page finish arming him. Nen Saal arrived then, Nen Lios and Nen Mallaer on his heels, the last of the commanders who remained, and Esclin braced himself to play the arros.

"I don't like this," Nen Lios said. He was older than Esclin by a decade, old for the field and old enough, by his own proclaiming, to speak his mind.

"I don't love it, either," Esclin answered, with a smile that he knew didn't touch his eye. "But it's the only way. Back me on this and I'll pull us through."

"You can't surrender," Nen Mallaer said. "There's still time. Take a small party, we can hold them."

Esclin rested a hand on his shoulder, acknowledging the loyalty behind the words. "No. I don't intend to lose any more men today."

"Nor do we want to lose our arros," Nen Saal said. "You are not our sacrifice."

"I am not," Esclin agreed. "Trust me, Algrym—all of you. Keep silent and trust me." None of them looked happy but they all bent their heads in agreement. Esclin smiled, though his face felt stiff and strange, and led them from the tent.

Their horses were waiting, the men already formed up in rough companies on their side of the river. The Rider army was closer now, less than an eighth of a league from the river's southern bank, the wheelmen's burning glasses catching the swelling light. Reys en Nevenel rode in the vanguard, a wheelman on horseback holding another burning glass among a cluster of banners, and Esclin swung himself up into the saddle. The air was very still, all the banners hanging limp from their staves; the last of the dew had burned away, and the sun was hot on his blind side as he led the commanders down to the river's edge. The water ran shallow here, two deeper channels split around a central bar, and the midpoint of that bar was dry even in the spring.

"Wait here," Esclin said, and nudged his horse forward into the stream. He stopped on the bar, waiting, trying not to remember the battle. His place had been with the reserve, on the high ground to the army's right; for a moment, the water was full of thrashing ghosts.

The lord paramount's party stopped at the edge of the ford, and Esclin could see heads turning as they conferred. Then Reys laughed, the sound carrying in the quiet morning, and spurred forward into the stream, his horse heaving itself out of the water onto the bar in a fine splashing spray. Esclin sat very still, his own horse too tired to do more than shift its weight once unhappily at the other man's approach.

"Esclin Aubrinos." Reys was young and well-made, broad-shouldered and strong-jawed with high cheekbones and long eyelashes and red-brown hair cropped short, though it still curled on his forehead beneath the plain gold circlet. A beautiful creature, Esclin admitted, young and strong and flawless. Against that perfection, he himself looked scarred and old, a lightning-struck leafless tree.

"Reys en Nevenel." Names held no particular power over either of them; it was well to get that out of the way. Esclin was silent then, waiting, and Reys smiled, showing perfect teeth.

"So, Esclin Arros, Lord of the Hundred Hills. Are we to have a battle this fine morning?"

"I would prefer not," Esclin admitted. "Lord Paramount."

"There's only one way to avoid it," Reys said. "Own yourself beaten—surrender your kingdom, and there'll be no need for fighting."

I don't fear the battle. Esclin swallowed the words, said mildly, "I cannot win a fight this day, no. Let us talk terms."

"There are no terms," Reys said. "Surrender or fight: that's all there is."

"Surrender what?" Esclin asked. "My person, my people, my lands—that's not simply done."

"Begin with your person," Reys answered. "The rest will follow."

Esclin felt his eyebrows twitch—surely Reys did not in fact believe that—but said, "Very well. I will surrender my person, and you will let my people go their way."

"That's ridiculous," Reys said. "To let them come back, nip at our heels? They'll follow under guard."

"So there are terms to be decided," Esclin said, and Reys scowled.

"There are none. You will surrender yourself to me, and you and what's left of your army will ride north with me and surrender Nen Elin itself into my hands. The Blazing One has decreed it."

And that was what he wanted: there was only danger in prolonging the discussion. Esclin bent his head. "Very well."

Reys grinned in honest delight. "So be it! The Blazing One has led you to this."

"The Blazing One is no part of the bargain," Esclin said.

"The Blazing One is all things," Reys answered. "As you'll learn. But—first, I'll have your sword."

"Surely you don't fear that I'd attack you," Esclin said.

"We have all heard that you gained a royal sword over the winter." Reys held out his hand. "It's mine now."

"Very well." Esclin drew his sword slowly, but even so he heard the creak of bows from the Riders on the bank, and Reys raised a hand to warn them off. Esclin laid the sword across his knees, feeling the power in it, and handed it over before he could change his mind. Reys took it, lifting it so that it caught the sunlight, and a cheer rose from the Rider ranks. The rest of the vanguard started through the shallows to join them, the Rider drums sounding behind them, and Esclin drew a slow breath. He'd made his play; now he would have to see it to its end.

Leicinna held the reins of Jemme's horse, keeping it and her own well back among the trees and bushes. Above her, the leaves rustled as Jemme climbed higher; she spared him a quick glance, then peered down at the river. It was a long way off, the figures blurred by distance, but she could see the gleam of metal as Esclin handed his sword to the lord paramount, and then the sudden flash of spray as the Rider vanguard made its way across the river. She waited long enough to be sure that it was indeed surrender and not execution, then looked up into the tree.

"Jemme. Time to go." There was more rustling and Jemme dropped out of the branches, his horse stamping backward and snorting. Jemme steadied it, checking his saddle, and Leicinna said, "Anything I should know?"

"He surrendered." Jemme swung himself up into the saddle, gave her a sidelong glance. "There's not so many of them—they wouldn't be expecting it. We could take him back."

The army was outnumbered nearly two to one, and the company numbered barely twenty-five. Leicinna shook her head. "We have our orders. Let's go."

They rejoined the company an hour or so up the wooded track that paralleled the rising ground. The Riders had scouts out ahead of the main body, but Gimmell led them unerringly through the foothills until they reached the narrow pass that would allow them to catch up with the thegen's forces. It was evening then, the sun low over the distant Lammard, but Leicinna pushed on until it was too dark to follow the crooked path. They made a sort of camp at one of the flattened turnings, setting out a picket line to keep the horses from straying, and huddled around a small and sheltered fire to bolt a cheerless meal and snatch a few hours' sleep.

They rose at first light and again Gimmell took the lead,
finding his way in the fading dark with a certainty Leicinna
envied. The pitch at the top was steep and they had to lead
the horses; but once they were through the descent into the
next valley was easier, and they were able to find the track
where the thegen's army had passed. They were moving at
speed, heading for Nen Elin by the most direct route, and it
was not until moonrise that Leicinna's troop overtook the
rearguard's watch. Leicinna left most of her people there,
with orders to rest the horses—they'd go on foot tomorrow
if they had to—and pressed on another quarter-league to the
main encampment.

It was nothing like the arros's, just a huddle of tents and
a wider scattering of fires; but as Leicinna was escorted into
the thegen's tent, she was relieved to see Reinall Marshal and
Denior Horsemaster among the officers waiting there. Talan
had claimed her father's great chair, was sitting in it with a
fair assumption of ease, though her head rose sharply when
she saw Leicinna.

"Is there news?"

"The arros is taken," Leicinna answered. "As he planned. We
didn't stay to see further, but they will be heading to Nen Elin."

"Also as planned," Talan said, with a wry twist of her lips.
She was not much older than Leicinna's own page, Fisk, but
she carried herself with her father's assurance. Almost literally
so, Leicinna guessed; Talan was borrowing stance and gesture
as much as her father's gear.

"Have they split their forces?" Reinall asked. "Are they all
coming on?"

"We didn't stay to see," Leicinna answered. "Our orders
were to be sure it went as planned, then join you."

Reinall grimaced, but Talan nodded. "There's no reason
for them to divide their forces. Half their army is already in
the Westwood, their next move has to be to take Nen Elin.
But we'll be there before them."

"Can we get there in time?" That was one of the younger
captains—Nen Arranme's man, Leicinna thought.

"We'd better," Talan said with a sudden grin, and the young man smiled reluctantly.

"Well, yes, Thegen. And we can. But if we're to evacuate—"

"We need time to do it in," Talan answered. "Nen Salter will hold Salter Vale. If we have a bit of luck, the Riders will see if they can't talk him out and that will buy us another few days—"

"We can't count on it," Reinall said, not quite under his breath.

"No more do I," Talan said, suddenly sharp. "But they'll have to do something about Nen Salter, and talk is cheap. Even if they pass him by, we'll be two, maybe three days ahead. If we send our folk down the Hidden River to Nen Salter, and north-abouts along the summer road to Nen Atha, they'll be clear and hidden by the time the Riders come into the vale of the Aurinand. And we won't need so many men to make that happen, which is why I intend to send the bulk of this force on to Nen Arranme. If we can get into shelter there, we'll be ready to act at the arros's command."

Or to try to take Nen Elin if Reys killed the arros. That would be no easy task, even knowing all the hidden ways in and out of the nenn, but Leicinna saw the same grim determination on all their faces. They would save Esclin if they could; and if not, they would avenge him.

The Rider army made its way north and east by easy stages, banners and burning glasses held high to catch the spring sun. Reys sent messengers ahead to announce his victory, and made little attempt to keep the remains of Esclin's army from slipping away. Wisely so, Esclin thought: they would carry the bad news as they fled and would be more easily believed than the official messengers. He himself was not ill-treated; he rode unbound, though Reys kept him close within the vanguard, and there were always half a dozen guards in sight. At night he had a small tent of his own, attended by one of Reys's own servants and supervised by whoever of the wheelmen was free. Esclin noted their arrangements, but made no complaint nor any attempt to escape. He was fed at the lord paramount's table, under Reys's eye, and maintained his silence in the face of the Riders' pleasure.

The third night he had been returned to his tent so that the lord paramount could talk strategy—they were coming within reach of Nen Brethil, and he gathered that Reys intended to send for Wellan—when he heard an oddly familiar voice at the tent's door. He frowned, unable for the moment to place it, and then his wheelman guard rose to join the conversation. A moment later, the door opened again and Brelin ducked through carrying his box, the boy Astin at his heels. Esclin lifted his eyebrows but didn't move from his seat on the cot.

"My lord," Brelin said. He pitched his voice low enough that it wouldn't carry through the walls of the tent. "I thought you might like someone to look at your shoulder."

Esclin's breath caught. Yes, he would, very much; it ached worse than ever from riding and from the effort of pretending that there was nothing wrong. *But not from you*, he thought, and swallowed the words as ungracious and unhelpful. "I doubt there's anything you can do," he said, "and I don't want to trouble the lord paramount."

"You did not trouble him," Brelin answered. "Nor have I." He opened his box, rummaging among the bags and bottles, and Esclin sighed. There was nothing to be gained by suffering needlessly; if there was anything Brelin could do— even just another dose of poppy, and a decent night's sleep— he'd be a fool not to take it.

"Very well." He shrugged out of his gown, then loosened the strings of his shirt, easing his arm carefully out of the sleeve. The healing bruises throbbed and he didn't bother to hide his grimace.

Brelin nodded as though he'd spoken and set the jar he'd chosen aside, exchanging it for a thin slice of crystal. There were signs carved into its surface, but Esclin couldn't read them, wasn't even sure if they were from the Hundred Hills or from Manan. Brelin cupped it in both hands, closing his eyes, and murmured something too softly for Esclin to hear. He laid the stone against Esclin's back. It was warm, and Esclin, who had been braced for chill, relaxed in spite of himself. The bruising that had crept around the cap of his shoulder had faded; he hoped that meant that any cracks and tears were mending.

Brelin held the stone in place for a long moment, his fingertips cooler than the stone, then exhaled sharply and set it aside. Esclin worked his shoulder cautiously, feeling the muscles looser. Perhaps he'd been foolish not to let the wheelman treat him before this—and that was one more thing he could not afford to regret. "That's better. Thank you."

"I'm glad." Brelin was searching for something else in his box, an abstracted frown on his face that cleared as he found the vial he wanted. "Ah. Here." He poured a dose into a horn cup the size of his thumb and held it out. "It'll help you sleep."

"Poppies?" Esclin sniffed the liquid, his nose wrinkling at the bitter scent.

"And other things. Less of the syrup than your man uses, but a dose of other herbs that ease pain and swelling and promote healing. Drink it fast, it tastes terrible."

Esclin hesitated at that—was there a better way to poison an unwanted prisoner?—but dismissed the thought almost in the same moment. For the moment Reys wanted him alive, needed him alive to gain Nen Elin. He tossed it back, unable to stop himself from grimacing at the bitterness, and Astin was quick to hand him a cup of watered wine. He rinsed his mouth with it, shaking his head.

"You don't lie."

"Honey would weaken it," Brelin said. He wiped the mouth of the bottle, restoppered it, and set it back in its place. "I'm to be your watcher tonight."

"Ah." That was an unexpected grace, and Esclin worked himself free of his gown, then pulled his shirt back over his shoulder. "I fear I won't give you much to do."

Brelin gave a small smile. "Indeed, I hope not, Sire."

Esclin hid a smile of his own and stretched out cautiously on the cot, drawing blanket and gown over him against the rising chill. He had not lost yet, not when he could still draw that title from a man who had never given him allegiance.

◐

The arros was not what Angeiles had expected. Everyone always spoke of Esclin's beauty: he had been expecting something ethereal, androgynous, even knowing that the arros was old enough to have sired grown children. Instead, he was lean and honey-skinned, with the bone-white hair of his northern mother. He had northern eyes, too, the one that remained the color of winter sky and ringed in black. Even under a silken patch the empty eye socket was starkly apparent, and it was clear he was no longer young—not a beauty by any ordinary reckoning. Probably he had been once, Angeiles thought, but no more. Next to him, the lord paramount looked twice as alive, Esclin a silent wraith on a led horse, no threat to anyone.

Except of course that had never been true. It was dangerous to underestimate the old twister, even if it seemed his fangs were drawn. Angeiles urged his own mount forward, making sure he stayed within a short sword's-blow of the arros, and saw the good eye flick toward him though Esclin's expression did not change. He had retreated within himself, Angeiles thought, forced inward by his own surrender. Far better to have died fighting than to give up his rule so tamely, and perhaps Esclin was suffering those regrets. He had no name as a coward, and Angeiles could not understand the choice.

As they made their way deeper into the Salter Vale, the lord paramount ordered a stronger watch kept and the army marched in arms. It was unlikely that anyone would mount an attack or even attempt a rescue after Esclin's surrender, but there was no point in taking chances. The glittering disks of the burning glasses made a bright brave show that drew the eye and warded off any threat. They came into a streamside meadow that evening still in perfect order, the hills that held Nen Elin rising in the distance. Soon, Angeiles thought, and felt the thrill of it wash over him. Soon the lord paramount would have it all.

One of the small tents had been erected for the prisoner, placed so that the guards on duty could easily see any attempts to escape. Angeiles escorted him to the narrow space, noting as he swept the flap aside that the servants had laid out a camp bed and provided stools and a brazier. There was also a length of chain fastened to the tent's center pole, ending in an empty shackle. He felt Esclin check for an instant, seeing it, and was meanly glad.

"Do you seriously mean to chain me?" Esclin's tone was merely amused, but Angeiles had not missed that moment of hesitation. He kept his own expression blank.

"The lord paramount commands it."

"Then at least let me get my boots off," Esclin said. "Or do you insist I sleep shod?"

Angeiles hesitated, but it was not, all things considered, an unreasonable request. He waved toward the cot, but instead Esclin seated himself in the tent's single chair, extending one foot as though waiting for a page. Angeiles lifted an eyebrow but nodded to the nearest soldier. "Give Aubrinos a hand, then."

"My thanks." Esclin smiled briefly at the man as he knelt to help haul off the long boots, then rose to his feet as the man reached for the shackle. The soldier hesitated, and Esclin shifted his stance to make it easier even as Angeiles scowled.

"Get on with it."

The soldier hastily fastened the shackle, tugging at the cold-iron lock to make sure it had caught, then backed away. Esclin gave Angeiles a sidelong look. "Excessive, surely."

"Your reputation precedes you—Twister." Angeiles made his voice poisonously sweet, and to his surprise Esclin laughed.

"It would take more than I have to twist out of this." He scuffed his foot so that the chain rang softly. "There must be ten pounds of iron here."

"Enough to hold you," Angeiles said.

"Did I not say so?" Esclin was still laughing and Angeiles took a step closer. He was no taller than the arros, but he was broader in the shoulder and fifteen years younger, and he expected the other man to give way. Esclin didn't move, eyebrows lifting in languid question. "I assure you, the lord paramount overestimates me."

It was too much, mockery from a man who had not merely been defeated but who had surrendered, and Angeiles shoved him backward. "Mind your tongue."

They stood for a moment, eyes locked, Esclin still with the ghost of a smile on his lips, Angeiles sure that he was red-faced with fury and shamed by it. But a man who had surrendered had no business speaking out, no business laughing at the victors, shameless and cowardly and twister to the bone. *Say one more word*, he thought, *only one*...but the lord paramount would be displeased if Aubrinos was injured now. He took a deep breath, dragging his dignity around him, the strength of his office and the lord paramount's faith in him, and stalked from the tent, the soldiers scurrying in his wake. Esclin would pay later, and in full.

Esclin scuffed his foot on the worn grass, testing the weight of the chain. The shackle already chafed his ankle; perhaps it would have been wiser to leave his boots on after all.

"Was that wise?"

He looked up, startled, to see Brelin ducking through the opening. "Were you there for that? I didn't see you."

The wheelman let the flap fall closed again behind him. "You had other things to occupy you, clearly. Most of us heard."

Esclin lowered himself to the cot, grimacing as his healing shoulder throbbed. The shove had awakened pain that had receded to a dull bruised ache, and he seized on Brelin's presence, grateful for someone to perform for, something to take his mind off pain and fear and exhaustion. "He is very fond of the lord paramount—"

"He is the lord paramount's man," Brelin interrupted, sitting beside him. The tone was a warning. "His knife hand, the men say."

"And what says the Blazing One to that?" Esclin smiled.

"The Blazing One chose him," Brelin said. "Don't forget that."

Or discount it. Esclin sighed, and Brelin produced his stump of holyfire. He rested his free hand gently on Esclin's back, directly above the healing shoulderblade, and hummed thoughtfully to himself before bringing the holyfire into play. Esclin grimaced as he felt the heat against his skin, transferred almost instantly to the bone beneath. The pain eased, dwindling to a more bearable ache, and then retreated further, as though he'd swallowed poppy-syrup. Brelin made a pleased sound and quenched the holyfire. He returned it to his basket, turning back with a covered bowl. Esclin took it, aware that he was hungry, sniffed cautiously at what seemed to be an ordinary stew.

"Perhaps things aren't so bad for me." It wasn't precisely good, but it was food, and he finished it methodically.

Brelin took bowl and spoon, packed them both away. "I think you believe you have a plan," he said seriously, his voice too low to be heard beyond the walls of the tent, "but the Blazing One rules all." He ducked out of the tent before Esclin could decide how to answer that.

Left to himself in the growing dark, Esclin lay back on the cot, the chain clanking with every move, dragging at his foot. For a moment he thought about calling for a light, one more bit of trouble for his guards, but his earlier provocations had not gone as well as he'd hoped. He could always summon witchlight if he needed it. He drew blanket and cloak over himself, moving cautiously to avoid waking the pain in his back, but to his relief it stayed quiescent. They were still some

days from Nen Elin; he would be nearly healed by then—
thanks in good part to Brelin, he admitted, and wondered if
that had been Reys's intent. The surrender of an uninjured
man was worth more.

He curled into the blankets, huddling into the hollow his
body made in the cot, waiting for it to warm around him. In
the dark, alone, it was easy to regret his choice—but if there
had been an alternative, he would have taken it. This last
throw was desperate enough, but it had the chance of true
victory at the end of it. Or so he believed.

He wished Rota were there, to throw the bones and share a
cup of cider, to tell him bluntly that he was risking everything
on the flip of a coin. He wished Kelleiden were there, comfort
and company and distraction and so sharply desired that his
breath caught in his throat. He had not been this alone since
the first Eith Ambrin and exile—not even then. Then he had
had his companions, and Alcis, and he had come through.
And he still had them, they were still waiting, acting—surely
Alcis had reached the Westwood by now. Talan would carry
his message to Nen Elin, and Kelleiden and Rota would know
what to do. He was the fox at bay, the old fox in the trap,
snapping at his enemies where he could and waiting for the
chance that would set him free.

Heldyn urged his horse south and east along the edge of the
Mairell, skirting the fringe of debris still caught in the bushes
along the stream's edge. Alcis's storm had sent the stream into
unseasonable flood, sweeping away the first rank of wheelmen
as they tried to force the crossing; Heldyn's people had found
most of their bodies, but not all. They had also not found
the harper, quick or dead—and certainly from everything he
had heard from Alcis, proffered in fragments between other
business, they owed her for her stand against the wheelmen.
She was probably dead, Heldyn thought, but at least they
could bury her and her harp with honor.

"Lord Winter!" Elian's voice came sharply from beyond a copse of young willows, their dragging branches trailing scraps of cloth and a long length of golden cord. Heldyn urged his horse forward to find her knee-deep in the stream, tugging at a broken spear shaft. No, he amended, the haft of one of the wheelmen's burning glasses, and in that moment she hauled it free of the mud. Even muddied, the flattened orb caught what light there was under the trees, a spark waking in its heart.

"Cover it," Heldyn called, and dismounted to help. The thing was surprisingly heavy, even taking into account the gilded frame, twisted and broken from its passage downstream. Together they wrestled it into one of Elian's saddlebags and she fastened it to her saddle, the horse snorting and sidling in protest.

Heldyn took another few steps, careful of his footing, to see around the curve of the stream. It widened out around that bend, the trees parting, and a stream itself divided around a shallow sandbar. Something was caught on the bar, a scrap of blue bright as a jay's wing, and he realized abruptly that he was looking at another crumpled body.

"Elian!" He waded back to shore, swung himself back up onto his horse. "Around the bend. Another—"

"I see it," she said, pulling herself into the saddle, and another voice called from ahead.

"Lord Winter! We've found the harper."

By the time Heldyn reached the bank opposite the little island, one of the men was kneeling beside the body, and two more were hacking at saplings—for a litter, presumably, and Heldyn said, "Leave that, she won't care how she's carried now."

"No, she's alive," one of them answered, and went on chopping.

Heldyn lifted an eyebrow at that and dismounted, tossing the reins to Elian. He waded across the stream and frowned down at the body stretched on the sand. The harper was unconscious and limp, one arm still hooked around the wood of her harp, but he could hear the rasp of her breathing, and he looked at the kneeling man instead. "Well, Gemund?"

"She's alive," Gemund answered, his hands feeling delicately along her legs, and then reaching carefully under her head to test the back of her skull. Heldyn could see a bruise on her temple, swelling around a cut washed clean by the river, but it didn't seem to be bleeding any more. Whether that was a good sign or a bad he didn't know, and waited for Gemund to elaborate. "She has an arrow wound and broken bones—her shin, some ribs, very likely more I haven't found yet—but she hasn't drowned and her head isn't broken and she doesn't seem to be bleeding badly. Whether she'll go on living is another matter, but if we get her back to Callamben, she might stand a chance."

They made a litter for her, and took turns carrying it back to the camp where Alcis was still sorting through the wreckage of the Rider army. She had accepted the surrender of the senior surviving officer, a man called Radoc, and was talking with him, her guards watchful at his back, when the party finally returned. Heldyn turned his horse over to one of the grooms and moved to join her. Alcis turned unerringly at his approach, her face lightening. "Any news?"

"We found the harper," he said, "and she's alive still. Gemund is taking her to the physicians' tents."

"That is good news," she said, with a quick smile. "And Lord Radoc and I have agreed to terms. We will hold them in the wood outside Callamben until either their king—their lord paramount—makes some bargain for them, or we have men free to escort them to their ships. The wood will hold them, I think."

"I should think so," Heldyn agreed.

"Helevys can manage it," she said, and stopped as though she realized she was saying too much in front of a stranger. "See to him, Josse, if you would."

Josse Iros nodded, plucking at Radoc's sleeve, but the man resisted. "Did I hear you say the harper was alive?"

For now. Heldyn said, "She is."

"Tell her this, then. She has a child, a daughter, we had her hostage in Nen Poul. But Nen Poul rose in revolt, drove our men out. As far as I know the child's well and free."

"And you kept that from her," Alcis said. There was an edge to her voice, and Radoc lowered his head.

"I was so commanded, yes. But there's no point in keeping it secret now."

And the knowledge might give her a reason to live. Heldyn nodded. "I'll see that she's told," he said, and Alcis released the breath she had been holding.

"A wise choice. Take him away."

This time Radoc went willingly, and Heldyn sighed. "Let's hope it helps."

"Surely so," Alcis answered, but her thoughts were already visibly turning elsewhere.

"What did you mean, Helevys can hold them?"

"With Rihaleth's men at her back." Alcis didn't pretend to misunderstand. "She understands the wood well enough now, she can keep this lot prisoned."

She's fourteen. She's a child. Heldyn swallowed the words, knowing that what he really meant was *She's my child*, and rubbed his forehead, feeling dirt gritty under his fingers. "You're sure?"

"I don't have a choice." Heldyn tipped his head to one side, not understanding, and she sighed. "We have to rejoin Esclin. His army can't take on the lord paramount, and a good third of it's not reliable."

"Quarter," Heldyn corrected. "But you're right. Send me. Your strength is in the wood."

"Esclin gave me the chance to save the Westwood," Alcis said. "Now it's my turn."

She was right, and in any case there was a note in her voice that foreclosed argument. Heldyn nodded, his mind already busy with the details of turning the army in its tracks, gathering people and supplies for the long march back toward the Hundred Hills. It could be done—anything could be done, with effort and enough time, but that was the problem. Could they rejoin Esclin in time to prevent a disastrous defeat? Esclin was a twister, knew every trick, but even he was running out of clever ploys.

In the end, it was Wellan's cousin Reilan Nardenos who arrived from Nen Brethil under a flag of truce, his escort bunched close at his heels. Esclin, summoned under guard to join them at sunset, gave the younger man a single look, then nodded to the lord paramount. "My lord."

Reys gestured for him to take one of the empty stools, and Esclin obeyed. "As you see," Reys said, with a smile for Reilan, "Aubrinos is my prisoner and no longer claims your allegiance."

Arros lay unsheathed on a side table, the blade sullen in the lamplight. Esclin could just pick out the lines that sketched the water horse, but doubted anyone who didn't know they were there could decipher the design. Reilan's eyes slid to it, wary and momentarily disbelieving, and then he dipped his head. "My uncle has sent me to seek terms."

Which would not be necessary without your treachery. Esclin damped that flare of anger. He would have come to this in the end without Alcis's troops; he'd lost the moment they'd been forced to split their armies. He allowed himself a raised eyebrow, however, and was pleased to see Reilan blush.

"And terms you shall have," Reys answered. "Your folk are near kin to us, and I know Nen Brethil serves the Blazing One."

"We do our poor best." Reilan would not meet Esclin's eye.

"Then say this to your uncle. We will meet as kin and I will accept his service and confirm him and his in his holdings. Say—two nights from now? At the mouth of the vale?"

Reilan bowed deeply. "We will be there, Lord."

Nen Brethil's men arrived as promised, Wellan himself and half a dozen lesser lords riding in a tight bunch. They were greeted with meticulous honor but separated from their escort, and Esclin watched from the door of his tent as they were brought into Reys's presence. He was chained again but contrived to ignore it, watching as the sun slid slowly down behind the hills.

The Riders had set out the banquet tables in two lines, with a fire in a long trench between them and torches behind each of the places. The flames streamed upward in the still night, sparks rising brighter than the distant stars. Angeiles, as dark as Reys was golden, loosed the shackle around his ankle and escorted him to the table. He was given the place opposite Reys and Nen Brethil, the bonfire between them casting strange shadows, and Angeiles seated himself at Esclin's right, clearly as ready to act as the archer who waited at their backs. Esclin ignored them both, fixing Wellan with a single long stare, then turned his attention to the ritual of the meal. The order of service was different from that of the Hundred Hills, but the manners were close enough that he could follow without disgrace. Beyond the leaping fire he saw Nen Brethil struggling to match Reys's example, and he made sure that Wellan saw him smile.

Conversation was loud and boisterous, the Riders savoring the greatest victory in a generation. Much of it questioned his manhood and his generalship, and Esclin turned a blank face to it, daring anyone to address him directly. None of them did, though he was sure Reys was merely biding his time, and he made himself eat, filling his stomach before Reys could question him. The courses came and went, the wine made the rounds, and the jibes grew louder; Esclin ignored them still but kept a close eye on Reys, flushed now in the firelight. Nen Brethil was sweating visibly though the night was growing colder, a thin veil of clouds creeping across the stars.

Then Reys lifted his voice, raising his cup as well. "A toast to Nen Brethil, our newest ally."

Wellan stammered something in answer and Esclin deliberately left his own cup untouched. The flames in the central bonfire had sunk far enough that Reys could not miss the gesture, and his face darkened. "Come, Aubrinos, you cannot grudge me his service."

"Hold me excused," Esclin said. He pitched his voice to carry, felt the silence follow, like ripples spreading from a flung pebble. "He and I are not yet quit."

"I am master here," Reys said. "Lord Paramount under the Blazing One and by your defeat—your surrender—I hold the rule here in these Hundred Hills."

"You have not yet entered Nen Elin." Esclin could feel the night pressing in on them, the air heavy with dew, the clouds thickening overhead. He reached for it, careful not to let his expression change, not moving a finger from their places on cup and cloth. The damp swept over them, a sudden breath from under the earth, and the torches and even the great bonfire guttered at its passage. Reys swore and Esclin instantly relaxed his own hold, letting the wind pass by as though it were entirely natural. Reys was trembling on the edge of fury and Esclin was quick to speak first. "That is a part of the rule, as Wellan himself will tell you—no doubt has told you. You cannot be acclaimed arros if you do not hold Nen Elin."

"And you will give it to me." Reys opened his hand and before him the bonfire blazed up, twice as tall as a man, driving back the night's breath.

"I am your prisoner," Esclin said. Out of the corner of his eye he saw a flash of light on metal, and realized that Angeiles had drawn his dagger. "I cannot stop you."

He saw Angeiles relax, sliding the dagger back out of sight, and fought to control his own expression. That had been closer than he'd realized, Angeiles all too ready to strike in the service of his master, but he had timed it right after all. Reys threw back his head and laughed, the sound echoed all along the tables, but Nen Brethil barely managed a smile and Reilan, sitting two seats down, looked frankly afraid. That was all Esclin could hope for, an inch regained in this long game, and he reached for his cup with a hand that he would not allow to tremble.

C

The outrider reached Nen Elin a little after noon, catching Kelleiden at the forge. The master smith listened, closing his lips over angry questions that he knew the girl could not answer, and climbed to the observatory terrace to peer out into the clouded afternoon. He could just see movement at the forest break by the Aurinand's first ford: four leagues off, about an hour away. He swore under his breath, heading down the Dereward Stair to don clothes more suitable for facing disaster.

Washed and dressed, he made it to the great hall in time to take his place at the head of the notables, the speaker Rota sliding into place at his side. He gave her a sidelong smile and she matched it, shaking her head. "It won't be good news."

"Is that sight or logic?"

"Both." She sighed. "The doom I saw—it's hanging over us like a wave."

There was nothing Kelleiden could say to that, or at least nothing that would be of any use. His heart rose seeing Talan's banner, but then he saw her grim expression and the exhaustion of the men who marched behind her. He went forward to meet her, one hand automatically reaching for the bridle as he had done when she was a child. But she was not a child, and he let his hand fall, bowing as she swung down stiffly from the saddle.

"I bring ill tidings," she said. She had not pitched her voice to carry, but nor had she lowered it unduly. "The arros is a prisoner. Reys en Nevenel and his army are a scant six days behind me." She paused, something like a wry smile crossing her dirty face. "The arros surrendered. He has a plan."

Of course he does. Kelleiden swallowed the words, though he could see the same thought cross the steward's face. His guts knotted: Esclin in the hands of the lord paramount and always too clever for his own good. "Ill news indeed. What does he want of us?"

"We must clear the nenn," Talan answered. "Get the elderly and the children and those who can't fight into shelter, and the rest to come with me to Nen Arranme."

"That can be done," Maeslin Steward said. "Not easily, but—it's possible."

Reinall Parinas had come to join them, moving as though his joints ached, and Talan looked over her shoulder. "More ill news, I'm afraid. Ilgae Marshal was hurt fighting at the muster hill; Reinall is marshal now."

"Not dead?" Kelleiden asked, sharply.

"She was living when we sent her to Mag Ausse," Talan answered. "But she was badly hurt."

Kelleiden wanted to demand more but that was clearly all she knew. He put that dread aside, one more worry to nag at him, and said, "Come within. You and your men can bathe and rest and eat while we make our plans. The arros wants the nenn emptied?"

"That's his plan." Talan nodded.

"Then we'll do it." *Somehow.*

What was left of the day was spent tending to the new arrivals, and making plans to follow Esclin's orders. That night, Talan sat for the first time in the royal seat, presiding over a feast that no one really wanted but that Maeslin Steward had decreed necessary. Kelleiden played his part, sitting at the thegen's right hand while Cat Meirin hovered at her left, and when the last dish was carried off, escorting her back to the royal chambers. She balked at that, her Companions milling at her back, and Maeslin said, "You stand as regent. It's your right."

"My father is alive and arros," Talan answered. "And I want my own bed." She paused. "Was there more you wanted to talk about?"

"There are some questions we should answer tonight," Kelleiden answered, and saw her sigh.

"There's room. Oriol, go ahead and make sure there are seats enough."

The boy darted away, and Kelleiden followed her through

the winding corridors to the quarters she had claimed. The space had been tidied since she'd left but it still felt somehow in disarray, caught between a child's room and a woman's. Oriol had found servants to light the brazier in the outer room and to bring wine, and there were—barely—enough stools and benches to seat everyone. Talan took the best chair with only the slightest of hesitations, and Cat Meirin poured the wine. "So," Talan said. "What needed to be decided tonight?"

Kelleiden accepted his cup with a nod of thanks, took a token sip without tasting what was probably a decent vintage. "We need to hear again what the arros wanted. Clearing the nenn is—it won't be easy."

"Do you think I don't know it?" Talan's voice scaled up, but she controlled it instantly. "But that's what the arros wanted. The nenn cleared, the cisterns and the larders filled."

Kelleiden glanced at Maeslin Steward, who shrugged one shoulder. "I've had the sluices opened, though there should be plenty of water already after the spring floods. The larder—how many soldiers do you plan to have stay?"

"As few as plausible." Talan spread her hands. "He told me he intends to surrender Nen Elin, and he wanted it empty, or as near as possible, when he did that."

Kelleiden couldn't help looking at Rota, her head bowed beneath her heavy headdress. Talan saw his look and scowled. "He promised me he wasn't planning to get himself killed. Though I'm damned if I know exactly what he's planning."

Something chancy and deadly dangerous, Kelleiden thought, if he wasn't sharing the details with the thegen. And Esclin could say all he liked that he intended to come out of this alive, but he'd spend his life if he had to, and his summoned shade would swear that he had never intended to die... He realized that Talan was watching him, the same bleak knowledge aging her face in the firelight, and clamped down hard on his own fear. "We could hold the nenn with twenty-five or thirty men. Assuming they don't bring siege machines, of course—"

"The scouts didn't see any," Estor put in.

"And that would give us time to cross from Nen Arranme and catch the Riders in a vise," Talan said. She sounded happier at the idea. "We should be ready to do that anyway, I don't see what good it does to let them into the nenn."

"I don't, either," Maeslin Steward said. "We should be ready to take them."

"We haven't the men," Estor said. "Once the arros springs his trap, then, yes, we'll be ready. But we can't attack until they've been defeated."

"Estor's right," Talan said, and Kelleiden nodded in agreement. "The whole problem is that we're outnumbered, and have been ever since he sent the kyra back to the Westwood."

But how would letting the Riders into Nen Elin prove a trap? Kelleiden thought, and Rota lifted her head, the skulls in her hair clattering softly.

"He's trying to twist the prophecies. Letting the wheelmen in brings down destruction." That would be like Esclin. Kelleiden sighed, knowing just how thin a thread prophecy was to hang a realm on.

"Will it work?" Talan asked, looking at Rota. "And, yes, I'll pay the price of the question."

Rota shook her head. "Ask me tomorrow. The stars will be better."

"I will, then," Talan said, chin jutting. "And also tomorrow, we'll find volunteers to stay and start getting people to move. We can send some of their goods by river; Nen Salter or Nen Ddaur will take them in, no need for people to leave everything behind to be stolen."

"You'll go with the army to Nen Arranme?" Kelleiden asked, and she nodded.

"I'd rather stay! But that would defeat the purpose. If the arros is here, I have to be somewhere else."

That was solid sense, and he should have expected it from Esclin's daughter. "I'll stay as regent." That was the least he could do, be here to give whatever help he could and to stand witness if all else failed.

"I'm not going anywhere, either," Rota said, and Talan nodded.

"Very well."

"I'll stay, too," Maeslin said, with some reluctance. "Though who I'll send in my place—"

"We'll settle that later," Talan said. "I may need you."

Maeslin dipped his head and Kelleiden caught the look of relief in his eyes. Better to send him away, then, he thought, and realized that Talan was thinking the same thing. Only the truly willing should stay behind. And that would mean servants and kitcheners and grooms, at least a handful to tend the soldiers, all volunteers… He put the thought aside along with its implications, too tired and afraid to face them tonight. Tomorrow would be time enough.

CHAPTER FOURTEEN

Huwar's contingent returned to Nen Salter in good time though he grudged every plowman pulled from the fields and into shelter within the nenn. Already a handful of steading-folk had made their way up the vale in his wake reporting that the Riders were on their heels, burning the steadings as they came.

"We must submit," Thedar said. "They have the arros, they will take Nen Elin—we have no choice."

Howard looked out from the platform above the nenn's great door, squinting west into the setting sun. There was no sign yet of movement on the distant horizon, but he could not believe the lord paramount would not come to Nen Salter. It was the second-greatest of the nenns after Nen Elin, and it overlooked the best route into the deeper hills. Reys would want it secured before he went much further. From what he'd seen of the Rider army, he could hold Nen Salter against them: the walls would hold, short of siege engines, and even at this start of the year it would take months to starve them out. But the Riders had Esclin and Esclin had a plan, and even if it involved surrendering Nen Elin, Huwar had known the old twister long enough to believe it had some chance of working. "We can hold the nenn for some time," he said aloud, as much to see what Thedar would say as because he believed it, and the younger man grimaced.

"We can, yes, but at what cost? We can't bring all our folk within the walls, and we'll lose the spring planting entirely. If we don't surrender, it will be a hard winter indeed."

That was not the argument Huwar had expected, and he nodded agreement. "True enough. But I've no reason to think the lord paramount will treat us well."

"We have long served the Blazing One, even if we've had to be discreet," Thedar said. "Our wheelmen will speak for us."

"But will the lord paramount listen?" Huwar shook his head.

They dined in state that night, everyone pretending that the portions were not carefully watched and that the conversation was only ordinary. Huwar did his best to listen to the daily gossip of the household but he was profoundly grateful when Naïs rose from her place beside him, one hand on her swelling belly as she apologized for cutting short her attendance. Huwar watched her go and brought the feast to an end not long after. The younger folk lingered at the back of the hall but he found a chance to lay a hand on Perrin's shoulder. Perrin nodded once, and by the time Huwar made his way back to his own rooms he was unsurprised to find his heir there before him. Naïs was there, too, formal gown discarded for a more comfortable overcoat, and the nenn's steward was heating wine over the fire.

"I've taken stock of our provisions, lord," he said, never hesitating as he stirred the wine. "We can hold two months in comfort, double that and perhaps a week or two more if we go to short commons."

"Thank you," Huwar said.

"Have you decided, then?" Naïs settled herself in one of the two great chairs, stretching her feet in their brocade shoes toward the fire.

"I have not." Huwar sat heavily and accepted a cup from the steward. "We can hold, yes, but to what end? We don't have the men to defeat the Riders."

"Talan will have her own army," Perrin said. "And the arros—he has a plan, doesn't he?"

"So he says." Huwar took a swallow of the spiced wine, grateful for its heat.

"That plan involves him giving up Nen Elin," Naïs said. "And the omens for that were very bad."

"I've seen him pull off stranger."

"It's a terrible risk, my lord," the steward said. He leaned against the mantelpiece, resting his lame foot, and Huwar waved for him to be seated. "The senior wheelman has asked your permission to try to make terms with the lord paramount."

"Not yet," Huwar said. "It may come to that, but—we're not there yet."

"If we resist, they'll have to stay and take the nenn." Perrin frowned, working through the problem. "And that spoils whatever the arros is planning. But I can't see any good that would come from letting them into Nen Salter."

"We're all agreed on that, I think," Naïs said, with a quick smile. "But what other choice do we have?"

What would Esclin do? The thought made him smile in spite of everything, because the answer was simple: twist events and threats until they made some new and better shape. And if he himself could do that—and perhaps he could. Perhaps, just perhaps, there was a way to protect Nen Salter and give the arros what he wanted. "There's a possibility," he said, "but you, my son, must be ill—at death's door. We'll raise the fever-flag as well."

The nenns were prone to sickness at the end of winter, when the air changed and everyone was still on the winter's meager diet. This would be late for such an illness, but not outlandishly so. The others gave him frankly doubtful looks and he forced a smile. "This will work, but we've not much time."

The Riders came on at a steady pace, not hurrying, but driving anyone who would not submit to the lord paramount and the Blazing One ahead of them. *Like wood deer*, one woman said, despoiled of house and land in favor of her sister's son, *and we have about as much to defend us.* Huwar promised to hold all titles in abeyance until the matter was settled, welcomed any who'd brave the fever-flag, and braced himself to meet the lord paramount.

The Riders arrived with the rising sun, riding into the light as it spilled over the tops of the Hundred Hills and flooded the plain before Nen Salter's doors. Huwar's troops stood ready behind the outer defenses, but Huwar himself raised a parley-flag and waited while the messengers went back and forth settling the terms. He rode out at last on his best gelding, the gold he had worn for the muster feast glittering in his hair and at his throat. Naïs's fingers had been cold as she fastened the great brooch, and he felt that chill again as he reined in opposite the lord paramount. Reys en Nevenel was young, with flashing good looks, and he wore only a great gold torc as a badge of office: nothing at all like Esclin, Huwar thought, and made his best bow. "Lord Paramount."

"The lord of Nen Salter," Reys answered. "Huwar— Ellemas? You took the rule from your mother?"

"My mother ruled here before me," Huwar confirmed. "I inherit from her." *As my son will inherit from me, all gods willing.* He had more sense than to say that out loud.

"Esclin Aubrinos has surrendered to me, himself and his rule both. I require your allegiance."

"Lord Paramount—Sire." The word was bitter on his tongue. "I am caught between two oaths."

"One, I would think, has been entirely superseded," Reys said.

"I swore my oath to the arros in Nen Elin," Huwar said. "And—forgive me, Sire, but you are not yet that."

Reys shook his head. "I cannot accept that. I will have your oath, Huwar, if I have to dig you out of your hill like a badger. You know you can't defeat me."

Huwar bent his head. He hadn't expected that first gambit to work, but at least Reys seemed willing to bargain. "I do know that, Sire, and I have no desire to meet you in the field again."

"Then surrender and swear." Reys crossed his hands on the pommel of his saddle.

"My lord—Sire." Huwar bent his head again, aware that there were a dozen men in earshot, Reys' and his own, and chose his words with care. "There is another matter. As you can see, we have fever within—my son among them, and we fear he has offended the Blazing One. Will you lend me healers—wheelmen—to tend to him?"

He saw the white-robed wheelman—the order's second-in-command, by his badges—raise an eyebrow, and saw men behind him exchange glances. Spring was a chancy time for fevers in the nenns, when so many folk had been crowded together for so long. Reys frowned. "Your son's illness—"

"Is of course concerning," the wheelman interjected. Reys looked over his shoulder, his eyebrows rising, and the wheelman bowed low in his saddle. "As is any such spring fever. But, Sire, we have no men to spare for this."

For an instant Huwar thought Reys was going to argue, but then he shrugged one shoulder, putting on a passable look of unconcern. "Nen Salter must swear."

"Indeed so," the wheelman said. "We will absolve Lord Huwar of his previous oath."

Huwar said, "I have sworn to the arros in Nen Elin. I will swear to him again, Lord Paramount. And I will pledge to you now if you will aid us."

"Swear to serve me," Reys said. "Swear that your people will stand aside from all battles against me, swear to send word of any rebellion or treachery planned against me. I'll send more aid when I've taken Nen Elin."

Huwar took a deep breath. "So do I swear."

Esclin had expected the halt at Nen Salter—Reys was not going to leave that powerful nenn unpacified—but the fever-flag worried him, left him hoping Huwar wasn't trying to be clever. He needed to reach Nen Elin, and to do as little damage in the process as he possibly could; he didn't need Nen Salter trying to be clever. When the news came of Nen Salter's submission, he received it blank-faced, hiding his relief, and hoped the Riders would move on. Instead, the lord

paramount ordered his army to camp an extra day at Nen
Salter's gates, just out of bowshot but still close enough to
demand attendance. He was not winning the hearts of the
folk of the lower vales, even though they had long served
the Blazing One, and he had not won Nen Salter, no matter
what Huwar had sworn. Esclin guessed he was planning some
demonstration of his power, and braced himself to meet it.

He heard the sound of armed men outside the tent, and
was on his feet before the guard swept back the flap. Angeiles
said, "The lord paramount requires your presence."

Esclin didn't try to keep the irony from his voice. "I am
entirely at his disposal."

"Loose him," Angeiles said to the nearest soldier, and the
man knelt to unfasten the chain at Esclin's ankle.

Esclin shrugged off the next grasping hand and went
quietly, following Angeiles and letting the soldiers fall into
place around him like an escort. They brought him through
the camp and out into the space that the wheelmen had
cleared for their devotions, the piled wood burning steadily,
the flames pale in the sunlight. There was nothing between it
and Nen Salter's walls, and Esclin guessed that whatever was
to happen was meant to send some message to the nenn. The
fever-flag still hung above the gate, drooping in the still air;
he could see a few people moving about the overlooks, and
guessed Huwar would be among them. A crowd had gathered
on the Riders' side as well, Nen Brethil among them, along
with Huwar's nephew Thedar.

"Aubrinos."

"Lord Paramount." Esclin glanced from Reys to the
senior wheelman. There was a tension in the air that he didn't
like, a tightness to Reys' shoulders that spoke of anger and
frustration.

"You see the banner." Reys gestured toward Nen Salter's
gates.

"The fever-flag? I see it."

"Reigar has read the embers, and says the fault is yours."

"My fault that there is fever in the spring?" Esclin shook

his head. "As well blame the wind and rain."

"The embers say that it is resistance to the Blazing One and to the lord paramount," Reigar said.

"And that your proper penitence can restore good health to the nenn," Reys said.

Esclin looked from one to the other, choosing his words with care. "You have said they are no longer my people—you claim their rule now. And I do not serve the Blazing One."

The color rose in Reys' face. "The sin is yours. And also the penance. Angeiles!"

Angeiles moved more quickly than Esclin anticipated, stepping from his blind side to kick him sharply behind the knee. The joint buckled and Esclin fell, pain blinding him. Before he could push himself back to his feet, Angeiles had caught him by the hair, wrapping the braid quickly around one hand. Fresh pain flared from his shoulder, and he froze until it subsided enough for him to breathe.

"Be still," Angeiles said through gritted teeth.

"Cut his hair," Reys said. "All of it. Cut it off. That's the price, is it not, Reigar?"

Esclin controlled the urge to pull away, knowing he couldn't free himself. "I do not consent," he said to Reigar, but it was Reys who answered.

"The Blazing One doesn't care." He nodded to Angeiles, who wound his hand more tightly in Esclin's hair. Angeiles slashed once, cutting halfway through the twist of hair on the first stroke. Esclin tried to jerk away, and Angeiles hacked the rest of it free. One of the junior wheelmen came running to take the ragged braid.

"All of it," Reys said. "A shaven head is the visible sign of repentance."

Esclin fought then, in spite of himself, in spite of knowing better, but Angeiles put a knee into his injured shoulder. Esclin collapsed, gasping, unable to move as Angeiles cut away the rest of his hair. He knelt on the muddy ground while Reigar lifted his hands in supplication and the younger wheelman cast the hair into the flames. The mass caught instantly; a few strands lifted flaming above the fire before they winked out, and there was a cheer from the watching crowd. There was only silence from Nen Salter.

"What's that?" Reys said, pointing.

Esclin realized that Arra's ring had fallen free of his torn shirt, the silver catching the sun. Angeiles grabbed it, jerking hard to break the chain, and it came free, leaving a burning welt on Esclin's neck. He held it up. "A ring. A water horse."

"Arra's ring," Nen Brethil said. "A mark of the arros."

Reys held out his hand. "And therefore mine." Angeiles laid the circle of silver in his palm, bowing, and Reys looked at Esclin. "You thought to hold this back. The Blazing One thwarts you at every turn."

Esclin swallowed bile. He could not defeat Reys until Nen Elin, he had to hold to that. He made himself nod. The lord paramount grinned and turned away. Esclin dragged himself to his feet, knee throbbing, new sharp pain running down his back. There was nothing he could say or do to twist this to advantage.

It was after sundown before Brelin ventured toward the prisoner's tent, and then only after he was sure Reigar was elsewhere. But the wheelman was dining with the lord paramount, at a great table laid out between the tents and the Blazing One's fire where they could be seen to celebrate the day's victory. The guards were used to Brelin and passed him through without question. He let the tent flap close behind him and lit the nearest lamp.

The arros was sitting on the cot, his arms folded on his drawn-up knees, the shackle and chain heavy on his ankle. He looked up but said nothing, watching in silence as Brelin lit the rest of the lamps and brought a stool to sit beside the cot. It was the first time Brelin had seen him without the patch, and shadow filled the hollow of the empty socket as though it was the eye of a skull.

"I've brought food," Brelin said, and set his basket on the cot at Esclin's side.

Esclin stared at him, expressionless, and Brelin grimaced. Angeiles had done a crude job with his hair, tufts and ragged hanks remaining between bloodied scratches, and Brelin reached into the basket for the other bag he had brought. He brought out a cloth and a flask of triple-distilled liquor, and began to dab at the worse of the cuts. Esclin endured the touch unmoving, his gaze elsewhere while Brelin washed away the blood, careful not to disturb the scabs. Esclin's skin was cold to the touch, all his fires banked and inward.

"I've brought scissors, too, if you'll permit."

Still no answer. It was past time for words, Brelin thought, and cupped one hand to Esclin's cheek. Esclin's head jerked, eye widening; then he drew breath and leaned into the touch, closing his eye as though he drew strength from that minimal contact. Brelin froze, stubble rough again his palm. He yearned to do more but didn't dare move. Esclin drew breath twice beneath his hand.

"I could trim your hair."

He felt Esclin's mouth curve into a smile. "What's left of it. The lord paramount will not be pleased."

"I answer to the Blazing One."

"Who, I am told, required this."

Brelin dropped his gaze. "I—believe Reigar to be in error."

"It's probably unwise of you to say so," Esclin said.

"You won't tell them," Brelin answered.

"You're very trusting."

Brelin shrugged. He was sure enough that Esclin would not betray him; he would pay the price if he was wrong, but he had no desire to play games. "You need not be treated so. And I don't like to see it." He felt in the basket for the shears he had taken from his own medical kit. "Hold still."

Esclin managed something like a smile but did as he was told. Brelin frowned and snipped, trying to make the ragged strands at least somewhat more even. It could not be considered a good job and certainly wasn't intended to be becoming, but with the strands even and the blood washed away, the arros looked almost human again. Perhaps more so, Brelin thought, with the missing eye and the stark white scar at the edge of the socket. The old wound drew the eye more than the fine-boned grace of the rest of his features. The scar looked like a burn, and he couldn't help frowning curiously. "How—?"

"I was in a burning building," Esclin said. "Lead from the roof melted and fell on me. The wound was infected, and the kyros had to take the eye."

Brelin nodded. That would have been in Esclin's youth, before he took back the Hundred Hills. "Does it still pain you?"

"Rarely."

"And your shoulder?"

"That—" Esclin paused. "That hurts."

Brelin nodded again. "I have a draught for that." He reached into the basket again and found the bottle, worked the stopper out and handed it across. Esclin took it, grimacing, and Brelin said, "All of it."

Once again Esclin obeyed, with a lack of complaint that made Brelin look hard at him again. "There's food, too." Esclin shook his head. "You must eat." Brelin paused, considering the other's reluctance. "We will ride tomorrow. If—you chose to surrender. I don't know why, but if you live, you have to eat something."

"Very well." Esclin accepted the covered dish and spoon and began methodically to eat. It was clear he tasted none of it. He finished it, though, and Brelin tucked the emptied bowl back into his basket. Esclin drew a deep breath. "If you continue this—" He waved one hand, encompassing the basket and the wisps of hair scattered on the grass. "I will be your death."

It was not a threat, nor even a promise, just a statement as dispassionate as the royal accounts. Brelin considered it, testing the truth of it against the Blazing One's inner fire, but could not call it false, either. "As the Blazing One wills," he said, and ducked out into the night.

❡

They could hear the drums long before they saw the army, the first bright banners and the glitter of burning glasses emerging at last from the forest at the end of the valley, a great column of men and horses easily a thousand strong, crossing the Aurinand at the lowest ford and moving up through the empty grassland of the Vale. Kelleiden watched them from the Observatory and thought of the empty halls behind him. Talan had cleared the nenn, its people scattered south along the Hidden River, north and west into Nen Arranme and Nen Atha; thirty men could hold the gates against a thousand, but not forever. And not if their enemy had the arros.

He dressed in his finest, mail of his own making under Westwood silk, and came out onto the platform above the main gate as the Rider vanguard drew to a halt beneath the walls. A flourish of drums announced the lord paramount, the lines of Riders parting to let him through. He was followed by half a dozen men on horseback: two of them wheelmen with burning glasses, the rest nobles richly dressed. They, too, had dressed for the occasion, and Kelleiden's lip curled as he recognized Nen Brethil among them. Esclin rode with them, his hair cut close to his scalp and his bound hands resting on the saddlebow. Kelleiden swallowed fury—there was nothing to be gained by treating him as a felon—and heard the rustle of stiff silk as Rota came up beside him.

"That is ill done," she said, and he nodded.

A dark man spurred his horse forward, the Blazing One's banner hanging limp from his staff. "Who speaks for Nen Elin?"

Kelleiden drew a deep breath, pitching his voice to carry. "I am Kelleiden Smith, master smith of this nenn."

"And you speak for it?"

"Until Esclin Arros says otherwise," Kelleiden answered, and thought that shaft struck home.

"Your arros has given up that right." A red-haired man rode forward to join the banner-man, armed like his men but helmetless, and with a golden torc glinting at his neck. "I am Reys en Nevenel, Lord Paramount under the Blazing One, and ruler by right of surrender in these Hundred Hills."

Esclin lifted his head at that, as though he would meet Kelleiden's eyes, and Rota said softly, "What is he up to?"

I wish I knew. Kelleiden said, "I see the arros a prisoner. Nothing more."

The banner-man drew his sword, controlling his horse with his knees, and laid the edge of the blade against Esclin's throat. Esclin lifted his chin, gaining a little clearance, but made no other move. Reys lifted his hand. "This is the bargain we struck. Aubrinos will tell you himself. He has given all— land, ruler, and sword—into my hands." Reys drew Arros, the sun gleaming from all-too-familiar steel.

"That is so," Esclin said.

Kelleiden heard the faint equivocal note in the words, and hoped both that Reys did not and that Esclin could make good on it. He looked at Rota, who nodded once, and at Waloner Steward, Maeslin's deputy who had remained behind. He was pale and sweating under his mail but strong enough to nod as well. "So be it."

They opened the great doors of the nenn and let the Riders in, Reys en Nevenel dismounting along with a senior wheelman to lead perhaps a third of his company into the main hall. Kelleiden waited at its end, at the foot of the stairs that led up into the living spaces, and saw the Riders exchanging wary glances at the stone that arched thrice man-height above them. His men were drawn up behind him, the scant garrison that he had left, and he knew that the rest of the household were watching nervously from the upper galleries. There were no more than fifty of them, and he grudged every one.

"My lord," he said, and made himself bow to Reys en Nevenel. At his side, Rota bent her knee. "We give Nen Elin into your hands."

Waloner held out the symbolic bundle of keys and Reys accepted them with a nod, his eyes roving over the company. "I expected a greater company. Where are the rest of your people?"

"Fled." Kelleiden met his eyes squarely, as though he spoke perfect truth. "Word reached us that the battles had gone ill and that the arros was captive. Most of the nenn had no desire to sit out a siege, and feared for their lives and families. These were willing to stay to see this through."

Reys frowned. "You couldn't keep them?"

"I didn't try," Kelleiden said. He thought he saw the ghost of a smile flicker across Esclin's face.

"That was ill-judged," the dark man said. "They should be called back."

Reys lifted a hand. "Angeiles is right, we'll need more than these few to manage the nenn. You'll call them back, Kelleiden."

"I didn't think you'd want our men-at-arms," Kelleiden pointed out.

"They'll lay down their arms and join the other servants," Angeiles said, and Reys lifted his hand again.

"For the moment," he said. "But you will call your people home."

"I will send word of what has happened," Kelleiden said carefully, "and that a new arros has claimed Nen Elin. After that—I can't bring them home like strayed sheep."

"You will tell them that I am their king—their arros," Reys said, a new and dangerous note in his voice, "and that they owe me their service."

"I will tell them so," Kelleiden said.

Reys nodded. "And who are these?"

"Waloner Steward, who gave you the keys, and Rota Speaker, the voice of the Mistress of the Caves, who also acknowledges your mastery." Kelleiden held himself very still. This was the moment most likely to bring trouble: the wheelmen did not honor the Mistress of the Fires, but they hated the Mistress of the Dark.

"I expect no less," Reys said, and Rota bent her knee. Waloner bowed as well, his mouth compressed into a tight, unhappy line. "Lord Reigar will see that the fires are quenched in the caves and in the forge, and will rekindle those that should be relit. You will lead him there, Speaker."

"Hold me excused," Rota said. "I am oath-bound to my Mistress, I may not do this."

"Reigar is chief among the servants of the Blazing One accompanying me," Reys said. "The Blazing One absolves all lesser oaths."

"I do not serve the Blazing One," Rota said. "And my Mistress's will is clear."

"Rota," Kelleiden said, under his breath, but she refused to look at him. He knew suddenly where this was going, how this had to end, and said quickly, "My lord, Sire, anyone here can lead you to the caves. This is not necessary—"

"The Blazing One has made this clear," Reigar said. "You must take me there, in token of your submission."

"I may not, under my oath," Rota said. "And you have no power to absolve it. Only She may release me."

"If you do not," Reys said, almost gently, "I will know you cannot be trusted, and I will have no choice but to order your death."

"As you will, Sire," Rota answered, and Kelleiden could feel how much the honorific had cost her, "but I have no choice."

"Rota," Kelleiden said again, and she glanced at him, a faint smile playing across her lips.

"My Mistress is not yours," she said. "You know that."

He had known it lifelong: the Mistress of the Fires was changeable herself, understood human needs and frailties, dealt in forgiveness; Rota's Mistress was none of those. In spite of himself, he looked toward Esclin as though somehow the arros would have an answer, some clever twist that would save her. Esclin's face was blanched, carved from stone, as though any breath, any flicker of feeling would make things worse—and probably that was true, Kelleiden thought, but he himself was desperate.

"Lord Paramount." He went to his knees without shame. "Sire. I beg you to spare her life."

Reys spread his hands. "The choice isn't mine. She need only do as she is asked."

"I cannot." Rota smiled.

"On your head," Reys began, with a sudden, savage smile of his own. "No, it will be your head, it will cost you your head. Angeiles! Do it now."

Even the dark man seemed momentarily taken aback. "Sire?"

"I want her head off. Now. Here in this hall."

Rota's smile widened. "I won't make it difficult for you, boy. Just grant me my farewells." She patted Kelleiden's shoulder as she spoke, then stepped out quickly to embrace Esclin, whispering something in his ear. Kelleiden saw the arros's eye flicker closed, pain and sorrow and regret, and then two of the soldiers hauled her back from him. She shook herself and they released her instantly, as though their fingers burned. She went to her knees then, her back straight, and reached back to pull the mass of her hair forward off her neck. "There."

"Bring a mounting block," Angeiles said, stiff-lipped. "Something to rest her head on…"

There was a flurry of movement among the soldiers, and one came scrambling forward with what did indeed look like a mounting block. He set it in front of Rota and backed away, scrubbing his hands on his tunic, to hide himself among the other Riders. Rota rested one hand on it, the other hand still holding her hair off her neck, the skin very pale in the relatively dim light of the hall, then bent forward so that her forehead rested on the dirty wood.

"Angeiles!" Reys said.

Angeiles drew his sword—a good heavy blade, Kelleiden saw with sick relief, enough to do the job in a single blow if the man was halfway competent—and braced himself. Reigar raised his hands, calling to the Blazing One in a language Kelleiden couldn't understand, and light sparked from the windows high above the door, falling in an unnatural beam across Rota's kneeling figure. Angeiles swung the blade, and Kelleiden flinched at the sound of the blow. It was clean, her head rolling one way while her body slipped sideways, blood bright in the sun and the air sharp with the slaughter smell of it.

"So be it," Reigar said and the light faded, leaving only the huddled shape, dark robes in a dark pool, one pale hand lax amid the shadow.

Kelleiden dragged himself to his feet, knowing he looked shaken and sick and unable to care who saw. He looked toward Esclin and saw him as motionless as Nen Elin's stone. If Rota was dead, if there was no one to speak for her Mistress— this was what she had meant, this was what she had seen, that the wheelmen entering Nen Elin was its destruction. He imagined he felt her hand on his shoulder—apology, farewell, some attempt at comfort, he couldn't say—and forced himself back to the moment. Already some of the Riders had brought a blanket, were carrying away the body, and as they left the nenn's main gates, he thought he heard a cheer from the men still outside.

"You, Steward," Reys said. "You'll consult with my marshal about feeding and housing my men. Smith, you'll take Reigar to quench the fires."

There was no point in protesting that he was not allowed in Rota's domain. All rule and decency was already gone, but he glanced at Esclin again in spite of himself and saw the slightest tilt of his head. It couldn't be true that Esclin had planned this, or even guessed at it, but a part of him seized it as comfort. "As you will," he said, and beckoned for Reigar to follow.

The master smith obeyed the lord paramount's orders, though he looked sick from the sight of blood, and balked at the top of the stairs that led down to the Mistress's shrine. Angeiles put his hand between the man's shoulderblades to push him on, and Reigar looked over his shoulder.

"And what should we expect down here, Smith?"

"I've no idea," Kelleiden answered. "Ask another."

"There are rooms to either side of a hall, and the sanctum at the end," a woman said. Angeiles glanced sideways, remembered that she was the captain of the archers, a graying broad-shouldered woman who'd named herself Senta. "The master smith has never been there."

"And you have," Reigar said, sounding skeptical.

"I have been to the Dance in my time," Senta answered, "and the Mistress welcomed us home."

"Then you'll lead the way," Reigar said, and shoved her toward the front.

She brought them down the spiral stair, ill-lit by witchlight, and Reigar's attendants were quick to light more lamps from the flame they had brought with them. In the sudden flare of light, the cave seemed no different from the rest of the nenn: a long low hall hollowed from the living stone, with two rooms to either side, and doors at the end carved with a frieze of skeletons and maidens. Two of the wheelmen dragged them open and their lights showed a round space, spare and empty except for a central table and four unlit braziers at the cardinal points. A flame burned feebly on the offering-table, but as Angeiles watched, it flickered and went out.

That must surely be a good omen, he thought, feeling again the shock of the killing blow jolt his shoulder. He had not expected Reys to ask that of him, but it seemed as though it had been the proper choice. Mistress Death was the Blazing One's implacable enemy; her servant's death was the only answer.

There was no threat left in the sanctum or in the inner cave with its crystals. Reigar kindled more lamps, drawing flame from the burning glass. By their light the sanctum looked small and bare, the crystal cave almost tawdry. The master smith stood with his head averted, unwilling even now to see more than he must of the sacred space; and when they were done, he led the procession up through a labyrinth of stairs and passages to the forge near the nenn's top. Reigar doused the fires himself and lit the new coals. There were no apprentices to tend them, and Reigar frowned.

"Where are your people, Master Smith?"

"I sent the apprentices away myself," Kelleiden answered, "and, as I told your lord, the rest fled. If you want someone to tend the fire, I'll send someone from the kitchen."

"Do that," Reigar said, and fixed Angeiles with a stare. "See to it, if you please."

Angeiles bowed, grateful to have work to take his mind off the killing in the hall. He had been a Rider since he went for a squire at sixteen, barely big enough to wield a longsword, but this was the first time he'd been asked to kill in cold blood. It had been necessary; his discomfort paled against that need.

By the end of the day they had the nenn secured, a third of the men billeted in the abandoned chambers to keep an eye on the hill folk who had remained behind and who now toiled in the kitchens to prepare a suitable meal for them all. Messengers had gone out to the neighboring nenns proclaiming the new arros and demanding allegiance, and Angeiles expected they would spend the rest of the summer bringing the stragglers to heel. After that... He couldn't imagine that Reys would want to remain in the Hills for the winter, not when there was still unfinished business to the south. There was no word yet from the army in the Westwood, and that was beginning to be a source of concern. Presumably they would winter at some central spot, where hostages could be collected and some terms made with the rivermaster. With his son gravely wounded, it should be easy to bring him to heel.

They had found the nenn's cells, deep in the mountain's heart, and when the tunnels had been searched and found clear, Reys dispatched him to see Esclin safely secured. "We'll do this thing properly," Reys said, standing in what they were told was the royal meeting hall, "and that means waiting another day or two until we can arrange a proper feast. And with the Blazing One's blessing, lure a few more of the locals to see what we've done. But everyone will see. Nen Elin is mine, and the Hundred Hills with it, and the rest of Manan-Oversea will join me or perish."

That was meant for Nen Brethil, Angeiles thought, seeing the man still standing a little apart and all too aware that he wore no sword in a room full of armed men. He bowed and collected his men and Esclin, still as silent as he had been since Rota's death. Reys seemed to feel that, too, for his voice rang out, stopping them at the door. "Nothing to say on the death of your servant?"

Esclin turned slowly, and for an instant, Angeiles thought he read anger in the movement. "My friend, not my servant. Her death's not mine to avenge."

"Do you threaten me?" Reys demanded, and Esclin lifted his bound hands.

"Like this? Not I, Lord Paramount."

The words had a double edge and Angeiles shoved him forward, so that he stumbled and almost fell. Behind them, he heard Reigar pronounce a propitiatory blessing and the door closed behind them.

Their footsteps echoed in the nenn's empty corridors, and as they wound their way down into the depths the lamps burned low in their brackets, a few guttering almost spent. A woman was passing with a basket, her eyes hastily downcast as though she tried to make herself invisible, but Angeiles caught her sleeve.

"See to filling those." He jerked his head at the nearest bracket.

The woman bobbed a silent curtsey and fled, disappearing into the shadows, leaving Angeiles staring after her narrow-eyed. He would remember her face, and if the lamps were not refilled he would make sure she answered for it.

The corridor sloped slightly downward and the nenn's cells lay at its end, deep in the mountain's stone heart. Angeiles's shoulders tightened, thinking about the weight of rock and earth above him. Out of the corner of his eye, he saw Esclin smile and scowled back at him. Esclin could not have read his thought, that was a gift given only to the most favored of the Blazing One, and not even rumor credited Esclin with that talent. It galled him nonetheless, and he was glad to see that the cells were none too well appointed. They were dark, low-ceilinged hollows in the rock, each with a barred front that made observation easy. The bars were sunk solidly into the stone; the locks would break before the bars pulled free. Each was furnished with a bare wooden cot and a stone pot in the corner, and Angeiles allowed himself a certain narrow pleasure at the thought of Esclin so reduced.

The sergeant found the key and swung the door open. Angeiles gestured for Esclin to enter and he obeyed, but turned back before Angeiles's man could follow him.

"Will you permit me my own light?"

"There'll be torches in the hall," Angeiles answered, and waved him brusquely on. Chain and shackle were ready; Esclin stood quietly enough as they were fastened, like a horse half-broken to harness, but there was a look in his eye that Angeiles did not like. The lock clicked solidly shut and Esclin lifted his hands.

"Will you release me?"

For a moment, Angeiles was tempted to deny him, but common sense prevailed. "Outside and stand back," he said to his man, who scrambled to obey. Once he was out of reach, Angeiles drew his dagger and sawed through the ropes, sheathing it hastily as Esclin worked his fingers, grimacing as the blood returned.

"Tell me," he said, "is this the first time your beloved lord asked you to kill for him?"

The tone was soft, conversational, but the words were like a knife in the gut. Angeiles backhanded him without hesitation, knocking Esclin sideways in a clatter of chain. "I am not in love with him."

"Did I say so?" Esclin protested, and Angeiles struck out again. This time, Esclin caught his wrist, but it was easy to break the grip of numbed fingers, and Angeiles hit him a second time before he mastered himself. There was blood on

Esclin's mouth and a bruise already rising on his cheek: Reys would not be pleased, Angeiles thought, and controlled the urge to blacken both eyes.

"It's no wonder you surrendered," he snapped, and stalked away.

❨

The cot was every bit as uncomfortable as it had looked. Esclin leaned against the stone, knees drawn up and feet braced on the cot's edge, rubbing the last of the pain and tingling out of his hands. His shoulder was aching again, his wrists were raw, and his cheek throbbed where Angeiles had struck him. And Rota was dead. He tipped his head back, feeling again her hands on his shoulder and her lips brushing his cheek. *I know*, she had whispered, *I know, take it all…* Probably she had guessed his plan, her Mistress's gift was foresight, but he hadn't wanted, he didn't want—but he did want what she had given, he could feel still the crash of her death, the power that pooled where her blood had spread. He would have preferred she live, had wanted desperately for her to live, but he would use that power along with his own.

Kelleiden had done as he was told. The sluices were open, the cisterns full and by now over-full, the weight of water massing behind the rock. He could feel it, shifting and heavy, grumbling at being confined, a water horse uneasy in an unlikely stall. He hoped it would be enough. He hoped he could get at least some of his people free—if he could somehow get a moment with Kelleiden, the smith would spread the necessary word. He hoped he could save Kelleiden.

He focused again on the rising water, pressing impatiently against rock and will. He would have to time it perfectly, channel it correctly, but he could do that. Water had made the nenn, and water could as easily unmake it. It was just the cost. Fifty souls, he'd guess, who'd stayed behind with Kelleiden to hold the defenses and staff the kitchens and the stables, just to give him this chance. He could only hope it wouldn't kill them all.

And if it brought down Reys en Nevenel, it would be worth it, though he would prefer to live if he could. If not, Talan was capable of cleaning up the mess, though he would be sorry to leave it for her. And it would end the Rider threat for generations to come.

If only he could get word to Kelleiden. If only Kelleiden were here. He closed his eye again, imagining Kelleiden's arm around his shoulder, the familiar body leaning against him, breath warm against his neck. Kelleiden must have guessed he had a plan, they knew each other too well for the smith to think otherwise.

The guards were playing dice, the rattle of counters and the quiet exclamations unmistakable, their lamps withdrawn to light their game, and he was grateful for the dark to hide in. He could feel the nenn breathing, the exchange of air through thousands of cleverly-hewn passages, keeping the air sweet even in the depths of the mountain. It was cooler than it should be, cooler than night alone would make it: the water was making its presence felt even through the stone. *A little longer,* he told it, *just a little longer, and then you can do everything you've been forbidden. Only wait, and I'll give you everything.*

Brelin knelt beside the low brazier that was the center of the arros's quarters, carefully feeding the gentle fire. He was there, he suspected, because Reigar wanted him watched after so long spent with Esclin's army, and he had no intention of drawing notice if it could be avoided. His answer to all questions had been to point to his calling, priest and healer, and if it was not enough, he would blame Reigar for failing to see true light. Though he would prefer to avoid such a conflict altogether.

The fire had caught, was crackling cheerfully in the metal bowl, and he sat back on his heels. The walls were heavily carved, shaped into the stone shadow of an arbor, a fretted lamp in the shape of a ripe cluster of grapes at the peak of the domed ceiling, empty of the witchlight that should have filled it. Instead, there were half a dozen stands of candles filling the room with as much shadow as light.

The door opened behind him and the lord paramount entered, trailed by a handful of his men. Reigar was among them, to Brelin's regret, as was Nen Salter's nephew, who gave him a nod of greeting. If Nen Salter knew how comfortable he was making himself, Brelin thought, smiling back, he would never have sent the man. Or perhaps that was why he had sent him. Angeiles was missing—but even as that registered, the door opened again and Angeiles joined them, murmuring an apology.

"No harm done," the lord paramount said, and sprawled in Esclin's great chair. "It's been a profitable day."

"Indeed it has, Sire," Reigar said. "The speaker is dead and Nen Elin is ours in truth." Angeiles went to one knee to pull off the lord paramount's boots. The lord paramount rested a hand on his head for just a moment, but Angeiles did not look up. "You'd be wise to avail yourself of his services again," Reigar said. Brelin handed him a cup of wine and passed the next one to the lord paramount, who drank deeply.

"How so?" The lord paramount was not precisely drunk, Brelin thought, but this was far from his first cup.

"Aubrinos has to die."

"Eventually, yes," the lord paramount said. It was clearly not the first time someone had broached the subject. "But it needs to serve my turn."

"If he dies now," one of the Rider lords said, "the daughter will proclaim herself arros."

"Let her," the lord paramount said. "She's a child, they'll be too busy fighting over who's to marry her to put up any kind of fight."

Thedar shifted uneasily, and the lord paramount fixed him with a stare. "You have something to say to that?"

To his credit, the boy didn't flinch. "Only that she's his daughter, she won't be easily led."

The lord paramount waved his hand. "She's a child," he

said again, and looked back at Reigar. "Why now?"

"Because he's the greatest twister living," Reigar said bluntly. "I don't for a moment believe he's tamed, I think he's plotting. Take off his head and that's an end to it."

"I gave my word," Reys said.

"And so did he," Reigar said, "and yet he's breaking it."

"There's no proof of that," Angeiles said. "Is there?"

"The proof is who he is," Reigar said, and the lord paramount nodded.

"There's truth in that. But he needs to be seen to give up his crown—to give it up to me."

"And so he shall," Reigar said. "Tomorrow night, at the banquet—that was your intent, was it not? Bring him in, let him say his piece. And once he has renounced his title, the man may be freely executed."

The lord paramount held out a hand to Angeiles. "I admit, I'd like to see you take his head."

"I'm yours to command," Angeiles answered, and bowed over the outstretched fingers.

The evening ended at last, the pitchers emptied and the candles burning low, and Brelin slipped away, losing himself for a moment in the tangled corridors before he found a familiar landmark. From there, he managed to find his way to the guardhouse, and a man-at-arms pointed him toward the cells. Even Esclin—perhaps especially Esclin—deserved the time to decide how he would face his death.

"You're late abroad, Uncle," the older of the waking guards said.

"I have a message for Aubrinos," Brelin answered, and the man shrugged.

"I can't promise he'll be glad to see you, but that's your business."

The other three cells were empty. Esclin had heard them coming and was already sitting up on the narrow cot. As they came closer he rose to his feet and came closer to the bars, eyebrows lifting.

"I can't let you in to him, of course, not without Angeiles's word, but you can speak with him here."

Brelin was tempted to press the matter, to say he was here as a healer, but the guard was already retreating to his fellows. Esclin rested one hand on the bars. "I didn't expect to see you here."

"As I said, I have a message." Brelin kept his voice low enough that the words would not carry. "I'm sorry. The lord paramount intends your death."

"Hardly a surprise," Esclin said.

"Tomorrow night," Brelin said. "After you confirm that you've ceded your rule to him. He's told Angeiles to take your head."

"I wonder how Angeiles feels about that," Esclin said.

"Don't think he won't do it." Brelin scowled.

"No, I'm sure he will."

"I thought you deserved to know."

"And I am grateful," Esclin said. He looked more worn than Brelin had ever seen him, even the night after his hair was shorn. "Truly."

"Is there anything I can do for you?" Brelin half wished the words unspoken—what could he do, after all?—but recognized the Blazing One's prompting.

"I would like to see Kelleiden one last time," Esclin said. "He and I—we've been lovers since we were boys, I've loved him most of my life. If I could say farewell..."

"I can't," Brelin said. "You know it isn't possible. It would never be permitted."

"Will you take him a message, then?"

Brelin hesitated, but nodded. "Yes."

"Tell him I love him." Esclin's smile was for once without irony. "Tell him to look for the water horse."

"What?"

Esclin looked almost embarrassed. "I'm of Arra's house. If the tales are true, I might be born again..."

"Those are tales," Brelin said gently. His heart ached at the thought of lovers pinning hopes on winter tales. He didn't think the lord paramount planned the smith's death, but he doubted the man would be freed any time soon.

"Will you tell him anyway?"

There was no harm in it, and a kindness to a dying man. Brelin nodded. "I will."

It was late and growing later, the candle dwindling in its socket, but Kelleiden couldn't bring himself to undress, never mind to sleep. He paced uneasily in the fluttering light, poking at possible plans. He and his people were clearly disregarded as a threat; they were certainly outnumbered but that left poison and magic both, though presumably the wheelmen planned some defense against them. Presumably, too, he himself was being watched—Esclin would have arranged it, and he had to assume Reys would do no less. He considered and discarded half a dozen ideas, all increasingly far-fetched, and all foundering on the core of his uncertainty. He was sure Esclin had a plan but had no idea what it was.

There was a scratch at the door, and he opened it to find the wheelman Brelin. He stepped back and Brelin slipped inside. Kelleiden closed the door behind him, aware that the guard at the end of the corridor hadn't moved.

"What do you want?"

"I came up the back stair," Brelin said. "There's no guard on this level, though there is one at the bottom of the stairs."

Kelleiden filed that information for later. "I take it you're not here at the lord paramount's request, then."

"No." In the fading light, Brelin looked exhausted. Kelleiden lit a second candle from the stub of the first.

"So what do you want?"

"I have a message from the—from Esclin." If Brelin blushed for his near-mistake, it was invisible in the dim light. "The lord paramount plans to take his head."

"Yes—" Kelleiden began, but the other rushed on unheeding.

"Tomorrow, at the feast, when Esclin has acknowledged his surrender. Angeiles is to kill him then."

Kelleiden's lips felt stiff as though with cold. "He might have waited a little longer."

"He's in a hurry to claim the throne," Brelin answered.

"And you told the arros?" Kelleiden used the title deliberately, and Brelin did not gainsay it.

"I thought—he should know, not be taken by surprise." Brelin took a breath. "He asked for you. I said I would take his message."

Oh, Esclin. Kelleiden swallowed the words, said instead, "And?"

"He bade me say he loved you." Brelin's voice was steady. "And he said to look for the water horse. After he was gone."

Kelleiden blinked. The first, yes, he knew, and nonetheless he'd cherish the message lifelong, but the second... He couldn't imagine Esclin wasting words on anything but this life. "Thank you," he said, and tried to make his voice choked with sorrow. "You'd best go now."

Brelin paused. "There was nothing more I could do."

Kelleiden eased open the door, peered cautiously out to be sure that the guard's attention was elsewhere. His back was to the corridor, and Kelleiden nodded. "Go."

Brelin slipped into the shadows and Kelleiden realized he hadn't thanked the wheelman. He found he didn't feel much guilt about it and turned back to the room, pausing only to pinch out the second candle. *Look for the water horse*, Esclin had said. What was the real message there? Something to do with the sword, perhaps? With Talan? There was something else, he was sure of it; it nagged at him, but nothing he could think of made any sense. He worried at it for a while longer without result, and finally dragged himself to bed. He would have work enough in the morning if he was to find some way to save Esclin.

Morning came far too soon, and with it a dozen demands

from the lord paramount's people—for food, for the arrangement of the hall, for the entertainment of the troops still camped at the nenn's gates. Kelleiden met them as best he could with Waloner's help but couldn't find a moment alone with the steward to warn him of the lord paramount's plan. A little after noon, as the servers carried the midday meal to the Riders gathered in the hall, Waloner caught his sleeve and drew him aside into one of the half-empty storage rooms.

"The sluices are still open," he said. "The Riders don't know they exist, of course, but—should I send someone to close them?"

"The cisterns are full," Kelleiden said. That was the answer, that was Esclin's water horse, all the water siphoned from the Hidden River loosed at once from the cisterns. That was why he'd ordered the sluices left open, to give himself the chance of bringing down the nenn on the lord paramount's head. And on his own head, on all their heads, but Kelleiden found he didn't mind that so much, at least not for himself. As long as he saw the lord paramount know himself defeated, he could die satisfied.

"To overflowing," Waloner said.

Kelleiden shook himself back to the moment. A little overflow was unpleasant but not dangerous, there were channels to drain the water back to the Hidden River and to the Aurinand. And it would ensure reserves for Esclin. "Leave them open," Kelleiden said. "I have worse news. The lord paramount plans to kill the arros."

"Tonight? There's no place set for him."

Kelleiden nodded. "He has a plan."

Waloner grinned. "Of course he does. What can we do?"

Kelleiden ran a hand through his hair wondering how much to tell. He couldn't risk the Riders hearing anything, but he owed his folk who had remained some warning. "I think he plans to flood them out."

"Thus the cisterns."

Kelleiden nodded again. "We can't warn your people, there's too much chance of a careless word."

"If I tell them to run, they won't hesitate," Waloner said. "Senta told me she and some of her folk managed to hide weapons."

"Bows? Swords?"

"Bows. Some swords, I think, and daggers. She said there were six or seven of them, and her."

"Have her find me," Kelleiden said.

"I'll pass the word."

He didn't ask what was planned, Kelleiden thought, and was grateful for it. Most likely, all they could do was die with the arros—but if they could bring down the lord paramount, it would be well worth the sacrifice. He saw the same decision in Waloner's eyes, and laid a hand on his shoulder. "Esclin has a plan," he said again, and hoped he had guessed right.

۵

For the rest of the day, Kelleiden walked through his duties, making himself visible for Senta while keeping eyes and ears open for any more details of Reys' plan. By mid-afternoon he was wondering if he should have told Waloner to carry a message instead, and he stood in the nenn's strongroom counting silver spoons without being able to remember the numbers.

"Master Smith?" He turned, hiding his relief, and Senta nodded to him from the door. "The steward said you were looking for me."

"I was." Kelleiden could see one of the Rider guards behind her, just in earshot, and waved her toward the table with the spread of silver dishes. "Here, help me count these."

She joined him without hesitation, took the bundle of spoons he passed to her. "Sir?"

Kelleiden passed spoons from hand to hand, lowering this voice as though he was counting under his breath. "Waloner said you have arms."

She nodded. "We do. Bows and swords for eight of us. No mail, but most of us have leather."

"It'll have to do." Kelleiden picked up another bunch of spoons. "Reys plans to kill the arros at the end of the banquet, and I think Esclin plans to flood the nenn. We need to free him first."

"There's not so many men on guard," Senta said, "but what we do after—"

"That's the problem," Kelleiden agreed. Warn the kitcheners, loose the waters, escape themselves—well, the last was probably unlikely, but the rest... Surely Esclin had a plan. "When they serve the last remove, we free the arros. Bring your folk and meet me in the antechamber above the gate to the cells."

"You'll have the keys?"

"I have all the keys," Kelleiden said. He hadn't been about to turn over his own keys to the lord paramount. Esclin would have changed the locks, but Reys had done nothing.

"We'll have to be quick," Senta said, picking up another bundle of spoons. "If they sound the alarm—"

"We'll have to silence them first," Kelleiden answered, and hoped it could be done.

It was hard to keep track of time in the cells. Esclin slept, woke, counted the changes of the watch and received first one grudged meal and then another, hoarding his patience and his strength. If Brelin had carried his message—both parts of it—if Kelleiden understood his meaning, if he himself could shape the water into the needed hammer blow... Best or worst, it all ended in the same place, and he was braced for it. He would have liked longer, would have liked more chance for farewells, regretted the things he hadn't said, to Talan perhaps most of all, but to Alcis and Heldyn and even Kelleiden, everyone whose lives he'd spent to reach this place.

He touched his chin, feeling the bruise beneath the stubble. It was a pity they were unlikely to let him shave—even light-haired as he was, his beard was showing and he felt unkempt.

But that was what Reys wanted, to deprive him of his armor; he might as well wish for silk and jewels and all his finery. He didn't think his jaw was badly swollen, in spite of Angeiles.

But that had been revealing, if painful. Angeiles was a weak point, a man whose blind spots might yet betray him. It was a frail hope, and he tipped his head back against the wall, staring at the dark stone above the cell's bars. He could hear the guards in the distance, the clatter of arms and indifferent voices, and pulled his knees to his chin. There was every chance that he would simply die, and leave Talan—and Alcis, and the rivermaster—to clean up an unholy mess. He could feel the water pressing in on him, the cisterns spilling over, water running on hidden walls, in secret channels, splashing into spreading puddles. If the Riders noticed they raised no alarm, and above them the stone groaned and shuddered under its burden.

❨

Kelleiden dressed carefully for the feast: a good enough outer gown to signal respect, but nothing that would draw too much attention, and a plain dark tunic underneath. The great hall was dressed for a feast, the trappings at once familiar and alien: there were all the tables and the bright banners and the silver plate for the high table, but the wheelmen had kindled a long fire before the high table, reaching nearly from end to end, and there was a haze of smoke high in the hall where the vents were overwhelmed.

The high table was mostly Riders, Reys at the center and Reigar at his right hand, but Nen Brethil and his nephew and Nen Salter's nephew Thedar were conspicuous among them. The hall was well guarded, men-at-arms ready at every door, though cautious investigation showed that the empty gallery at the far end of the hall could still be reached from the servants' stairs. That was, he hoped, a useful option—a few bowmen there could decimate the high table—and halfway through the fourth remove, he touched Waloner's shoulder in warning and slipped away.

He discarded his gown in a niche behind the kitchen and slipped out through the passage that led to the storerooms. He retrieved the sword he had left hidden between two barrels, belted it into place, and let himself out into the more traveled corridors.

The nenn felt empty—everyone was at the feast, Riders and Nen Elin's folk alike, and the lights burned low in their brackets. He caught only a glimpse of a guard here and there as he made his way to the antechamber above the entrance to the cells. The heavy door was closed, but he pushed lightly on it. It swung back, and a gloved hand reached out to drag him in.

"Pardon, Master Smith," Senta said, and let him go. She was fully armed, bow and quiver at her back, drawn sword in her other hand, and her people crowded at her back.

"You're ready?" Kelleiden asked, and she nodded.

"They've got the outer door closed, we'll have to knock to have them let us in."

Kelleiden grimaced. That was hardly ideal—too many chances to alarm the guards, and have the door barred in their faces—but he couldn't see another option. And there wasn't much time before Reys sent his men to fetch the arros.

They made their way down a side stair and out into the main corridor, lit by the guttering lamps. A man in wheelman's robes was making his way toward the cells and Kelleiden lunged for him, driving him back against the wall as he fought to cover his mouth. The man gave way without a fight, and he realized abruptly that it was Brelin.

"You've come for him," the wheelman said softly, and Kelleiden nodded.

"You won't stop us."

He felt Brelin draw a shaky breath. "They'll open for me. They're used to me visiting."

"He'll warn them," Senta said.

Brelin shook his head. "On the Blazing One, I swear it. I'll get you in."

Esclin had won again, Kelleiden thought. Somehow he'd won again. "Very well."

"Master Smith," Senta protested, and Kelleiden shook his head.

"His word is good."

At the far end the door was closed, and Kelleiden waved for the others to hug the corridor walls, out of the guards' line of sight. Brelin shook himself, straightening his robes, and knocked on the door. The peephole opened and Kelleiden heard the scrape of the key in the latch.

"Oh, it's you, Uncle—"

Senta and another of her men leaped for the door, forcing it fully open, and Kelleiden lunged after them, sword drawn. He cut down the first man he saw, and then another, bracing himself for someone to shout the alarm. A man cried out, instantly silenced, and they stood in sudden quiet. Kelleiden scanned the space: four bodies, an overturned table, and the cells beyond, and Senta stooped to retrieve a ring of keys.

"That's all of them."

Kelleiden nodded and found the cell door, unlocked it to find Esclin on his feet, fists clenched. "It's you," he said, and sounded entirely surprised.

Kelleiden choked back laughter that would rapidly have risen out of control, and knelt to unfasten the shackle around the arros's ankle. "Me and eight others. And Brelin."

"To what end?"

Kelleiden paused. "Reys plans to kill you."

"Yes, I know that. I intend to return the favor." Esclin worked his shoulders, wincing, and stepped past him out of the cell. He pointed to the youngest of Senta's men. "You. Run to the kitchens, tell Waloner Steward to get everyone out as soon as I come into the hall."

The man nodded jerkily, and darted away. One of Senta's men pushed the door closed behind him, planted himself to keep watch out the open peephole.

"You can't go to the hall," Kelleiden said. "Esclin, he's going to kill you."

"Yes," Esclin said again. "I intend to kill him first."

"You'll need us for that," Senta said. "And there are a lot of them, Sire."

"If you plan to flood him out," Kelleiden said. "That's what you meant, wasn't it? You don't need to face him for that."

"I need to be sure he's there, and that he stays there," Esclin said. "I'm grateful, but you shouldn't have come."

"We're not all as clever as you," Kelleiden snapped. "Fine. We'll bring you to the hall ourselves."

Esclin paused. "If you do, you'll likely get yourselves killed."

"As will you," Kelleiden said.

"If we're there, Sire, there's a chance," Senta said. "Without us, there's none."

It was true, and Kelleiden saw Esclin recognize it. "All right. And thank you."

"Sire!" That was the man at the door. "The lord paramount's men—they're coming."

Esclin swore under his breath. "How many?"

"Six? With that Angeiles."

"Right. Get the bodies out of sight. We'll have to take them here." Esclin looked around. "Make sure no one gets away."

Three of Senta's men hauled the bodies into the empty cell while three more nocked arrows to their bows and took a stance behind the overturned table. Kelleiden held out his sword but Esclin shook his head, picking up one that the guard had dropped instead.

"Be ready."

◖

Esclin braced himself, listening for the sound of footsteps outside the door. This was not what he had planned, though he supposed he should have guessed Kelleiden would try something; still, it should work well enough, if only they could make sure no one escaped to give the alarm. And he wasn't sorry to have his own chance at Angeiles.

The knock came at last. Senta's man fumbled convincingly with the peephole, then swung back the door. The archers fired instantly, knocking the leaders to the ground, and the others rushed the men behind them. Esclin charged with them, unfamiliar sword in hand.

"Angeiles!"

The younger man turned, parried his blow with a counterstrike that jolted Esclin's healing shoulder. Esclin flinched, and Angeiles saw, struck again on the same side. Esclin parried, shoulder on fire, and flung himself inside the younger man's guard, driving his good shoulder into Angeiles's midriff. Angeiles went down hard, and Esclin grabbed for his dagger before Angeiles could draw it himself, caught his sword hand in the other hand. Angeiles flailed, trying to hit with the pommel of his sword, and Esclin managed to work the dagger free.

"If you'd been worthy, he'd have loved you."

He felt Angeiles flinch at the unfair blow, and drove the dagger into his throat, the body suddenly slack under him. He shoved himself to his feet to see the rest of the escort dead, and Brelin slumped against the wall, a great gout of blood marring the pale robes. He frowned—had Brelin come with Angeiles?—and Kelleiden said, "He's gone. He got us into the cells.

I said I'd be his death. Esclin nodded. "We have to hurry."

"Take their armor," Senta said, and Kelleiden shook his head.

"No time. They'll be expecting them back—"

Esclin took a breath, and then another, feeling the waters roiling at the heart of the nenn. This was the final act, the final choice, and it would take his greatest gift to make it happen. "Kelleiden. Is there any way you can provide cover?"

"In the hall? They've left the gallery empty."

"Can you get to it?"

"Yes, but—"

Esclin put a hand on his shoulder, wishing there were time for more. "Get Senta's people there. But I warn you again, you're not likely to live out the night if you do this."

"We're with you," Senta said, and Kelleiden closed his hand over Esclin's own.

"And you?"

Esclin reached for water and shadow and the flickering lamplight, drew shapes from the sprawled bodies and set them on their feet. One by one, he smoothed death from their features, made them whole-seeming, arranged them around him as an escort. Angeiles's shape lifted sword in mocking salute, and Esclin looked at his people. "These will bring me to the hall."

He had thought himself ready, more or less, but it was hard to keep the illusion and the water both in mind as they hurried through the nenn. Kelleiden left him at the servants' stair and Esclin braced himself as he turned the last corner, the chill of the water pressing down on him. At the hall door he readied himself to have Angeiles's shape answer the challenge, but the bored-looking guardsman swung back the doors without hesitation, releasing a wave of light and sound. The lord paramount sat at the center of the high table, Reigar at his side, and his captains filled the long tables to either side. Arros lay unsheathed on the cloth before Reys, its blade dull in the torchlight.

Esclin stopped halfway down the hall. "I am here."

Reys rose slowly to his feet, a faint frown creasing his brow as he looked at the shapes around Esclin. "Esclin Aubrinos. You have been defeated twice in battle, and you have surrendered your person and the symbols of your reign to me. Do you now acknowledge me as arros in your stead, arros of the Hundred Hills."

"No." Esclin felt the shock of the word, saw Nen Brethil's eyes widen with fear, and reached for the water, directing it to the base of the cistern where a long channel dropped to the bottom of the nenn. *There*, he told it, feeling the water horse turn in its confined space, grown to monstrous size and strength. *When I bid you, strike there.* He felt the floor shiver beneath his feet, the illusion wavering, and saw Thedar and Nen Brethil rise to their feet. "Neither my sword nor Arra's ring make you arros."

"Angeiles!" Reys reached for the royal sword. "Kill him."

Esclin spread his hands, the illusion vanishing, and heard the creak of bowstrings from the gallery. Arrows whistled past, aimed for the high table; he saw Nen Brethil fall, clawing at the shaft in his throat, and another shaft whistled between Reys and Reigar and shattered against stone.

"I gave you nothing," Esclin said, reaching for smoke and shadows, for the sword in Reys' hand. "And I am still Esclin Arros." He released the water, felt it fall, a hammer-blow against the cistern's floor. There was a crack like thunder, stone snapping like rotten wood, and then a grinding rumble that shook the floor beneath his feet. He drew down the smoke to snuff the torches, and in the dark the water horse leaped gleaming and silver from the sword. It rose above Reys' head and shoulders, webbed hooves striking, and in the quaking dark Esclin ran for the gallery stair.

He stumbled up it, hearing shouts behind him as the wheelmen and the Riders fought to raise a light, and someone caught his arm. In the same moment witchlight blossomed, showing him Kelleiden and Senta and her people.

"Well done," he said, and Kelleiden pulled him on, jarring his shoulder painfully.

"This way."

"We'll cover you," Senta said, and Kelleiden dragged him on.

The stairs were shaking, the rumble of stone and water swelling to a roar that drowned even the strongest voice. Esclin took the stairs two at a time, shoving Kelleiden ahead of him as the passage began to twist and crumble. He reached for the stones, trying to hold them together, to keep this narrow space solid and untouched long enough for them to pass through it. He had to use his hands to keep his balance, pulling himself up the steps through clouds of choking dust, and as they reached the first landing he felt the stone fall away behind him, crumbing into emptiness.

Kelleiden caught his hand, dragging him forward so that he fell hard against the smith, and they swayed for an instant before Kelleiden found his balance and turned toward the guards' stair. They struggled upward, this stairway steeper and sharper, but it was carved from living stone, there was more to work with, a greater reluctance to dissolve into the general collapse. He held it to its shape as they moved along it, though the witchlight showed cracks and falling pebble. He saw Kelleiden put a hand over his head to protect himself and ducked sideways as a rock the size of his fist fell past them both.

The air was full of dust, of sound and rock and scything wind; he saw Kelleiden's mouth move as he looked back, but anything he might have said was drowned in the unending rolling roar. The stone's solidity was sliding between his fingers, dissolving as he clutched at it. Esclin choked, his mouth full of grit, dragged himself on hands and knees and finally fell stumbling onto the stones of a watch post. Kelleiden caught his hands, pulling him to his feet, but his eyes were wide, fixed on what lay behind them.

Esclin turned to see the entire side of the mountain vanished into rubble, dust rising like smoke from what had been the plain outside the nenn's gates. Slabs of earth and stone were still falling, sliding off the mountain's peak, and he pushed Kelleiden toward the edge of the platform. Together they scrambled further up the slope, onto grass slippery with early rain, until they could go no further. Behind them, the mountain crumbled, more slowly now, pieces falling into the void that had been the nenn, and Esclin collapsed himself, clinging with one hand to the trembling turf and with the other to Kelleiden. The head of the stairway fell in on itself and vanished; a section of the watch post's paving cracked and slid and fell, the sound lost in the terrible rolling roar that filled the valley. A light rose from the wreckage, a flare of silver, a shape like a water horse rearing from the rubble, nearly as tall as the nenn itself. Esclin stared, dazzled, and it tossed its head and disappeared.

He fell back onto the turf, and Kelleiden collapsed beside him. The roaring had ceased, though his ears still felt stuffed with sound and dirt. Senta and her people were gone, he had felt them fall when he could not hold the full length of the stair, Senta and far too many of the others who'd stayed behind—and the Riders, too, crushed and drowned and broken, though he regretted none of them. The wreck of the nenn would have overwhelmed the camp at the gate; Talan would have heard the destruction, seen the water horse rising into the night, and she would mop up any resistance that remained.

He felt emptied, hollow, every muscle in his body stretched to exhaustion. His shoulder throbbed and he thought of Brelin, dead with the rest. His mouth was still full of dust, too dry to spit; he wiped at it with a shaking hand, but couldn't find the strength to do anything more. He rested his head on Kelleiden's shoulder instead and Kelleiden put his arm around him, saying something that was drowned by the steady drumming in his ears. He closed his eye, intending only to rest for a moment, and fell out of consciousness as though he had fallen with the nenn.

CHAPTER FIFTEEN

Talan found them there the next morning, stranded above the new-made cliff and the great fan of rubble where Nen Elin had been. She dispatched scouts to reach them by a roundabout way, a hunter's track that climbed up the northern slope, and turned her attention to the few shocked survivors lingering on the edge of the wreckage. The Riders among them were in no mood to fight; those of the nenn's folk who had survived were mostly kitcheners and servants, though there was one older man with a badly broken leg who said he had been with the master smith. She listened to the tales and ordered guards for the prisoners and help for the injured, and felt her breath catch in her throat as she saw the scouts making their way back down from the heights. That Kelleiden was alive she had known, she had seen him waving from the edge of the cliff, but Esclin lay unmoving, tied to a litter, and she braced herself for the worst.

"Master Smith."

"He's alive." Kelleiden's voice was choked with dust and stone and sorrow.

"Is he hurt?" Talan peered into her father's face, smeared with dirt and almost unrecognizable under the shorn hair and a half-grown beard. She had only once or twice seen the missing eye uncovered, felt she ought for decency's sake to cover it.

"Not injured," Kelleiden said. "But utterly spent."

That need not be fatal, not if she could help it. "Bring him to Nen Arranme. We'll treat him there."

Despite her best efforts, there was no way to leave the ruin before evening, and she mistrusted the thought of moving the survivors through the night. Her people had brought tents and gear, so instead she left Esclin unconscious in her tent under the watchful eye of the master smith and the troop's healer, and turned her attention to the ruin. Searchers were still combing the rubble, but she doubted anyone else would be found alive.

At midafternoon, she was called to a report of horsemen on the road—*Four of them, coming fast*—and sent scouts to meet them, all too aware that she had brought her people into a vulnerable position. But then the scouts returned, the strangers in tow, and she recognized Nen Salter's son Perrin.

"Thegen," he said, sliding off his horse to bend his knee as though she were her father. "My father sent me ahead with news. The Riders have been defeated in the Westwood, and the kyra's army is in sight from our walls." His eyes strayed to the wreck of Nen Elin, but he was too well-trained to ask outright what had happened.

Talan raised her voice, wanting word to spread. "You've come in good time. As you see, the prophecy was fulfilled— the wheelmen entered Nen Elin, and Nen Elin was destroyed. But Esclin Arros lives, and most of our folk. And we will rebuild." There was a cheer at that, ragged at first and then building, and she waited for it to die down before continuing. "Can I send some of your men back to tell the kyra what's happened? The arros must go on to Nen Arranme, but we can meet the kyra further down the vale."

Alcis met her daughter in the lower meadow, where normally the Aurinand spread wide and shallow, and the nenn's herds and the hill deer came to drink. Alcis remembered the water so clear you could see the schools of tiny fish lurking in the shadows, silver sides catching the sun as they fled from her shadow. Now the stream was choked and clogged, its stones laid bare, and there was something wrong with the shape of the hills above the tree line. Talan had done her best to make herself presentable, but her hair was pulled back ruthlessly and there was dirt on her breastplate and, when they clasped hands, ground into the lines of her fingers.

"What news?" Alcis could no longer bear the formalities, not with the stories they had heard—the nenn fallen, the lord paramount dead, Esclin and all his people dead or wounded—and saw something like relief in Talan's eyes.

"The arros lives."

That was what she had hoped to hear, first and best, and Alcis drew a deep breath. "Unhurt?"

Talan flinched. "Unwounded, anyway. He's—Kelleiden said he's spent himself, all his strength, to get them out. He's unconscious. I've sent him on to Nen Arranme where they can tend him properly, but I believe he will recover."

There was a slight quaver in her voice that betrayed she was not as confident of that as she pretended. "He's strong," Alcis said, as much to herself as to her daughter, and Talan squared her shoulders.

"But. The lord paramount is dead, and Nen Brethil and most of the Rider army. The arros brought the nenn down on their heads, buried them under the stone." She paused. "Will you come see, Kyra?"

"I will," Alcis said.

Even after Talan's description, she was not prepared for the destruction. They came out of the forest into what had been the wide plain outside the nenn's gates, the ground beaten flat before what had been a towering cliff carved with towers and ledges and narrow defensive windows before it rose further to stone and ragged grass. Now there was nothing but a gap in the hill and a jumble of dirt and stone that completely obliterated the Aurinand and spread out to cover most of what had been the open space before the gates. Dust still rose from the pile, carried in the gentle breeze, and the air smelled of rock and death.

She reined in, her people shambling to a stop behind her,

voice rising in the same shock and horror that she felt, and she lifted her hand to quiet them. Heldyn pushed forward to join her, his eyes wide and disbelieving. "How many dead?" she asked, and Talan shrugged one shoulder.

"Of our own folk, thirty-five or forty, plus some injured. Of the Riders... There were some hundred men, or more— perhaps two hundred? We've taken a handful alive. They were camped here on the plain as well as in the nenn."

"It is a victory," Alcis said. "Both their armies are beaten, the Riders won't come back next year. But such a cost!"

"Only Esclin could manage it," Heldyn said, and surprised a smile from Talan.

"Rota—the speaker said, let a wheelman into Nen Elin, and it would destroy the nenn. I doubt this was what was meant to happen."

Clever, twisty old fox, Alcis thought. Of course he'd made it happen, while she saved the Westwood. "You and I must talk," she said. "We must plan how to secure the Hundred Hills and what to do after."

"I have thoughts on that," Talan said. "Nen Salter came with you, did I see? Have your folk camp here tonight, and we'll talk. Then tomorrow, if you wish, I'll take you on to Nen Arranme."

And that was her daughter, the daughter Esclin had made, clever and practical and fit to pick up the reins until Esclin was well again. "It's well done," she said, and did not hide her pride.

Esclin slept and woke and slept again, then woke for longer, enough to know that he was in a nenn, though the scents and presence, water and stone, told him it was not Nen Elin. He slept again before he could feel more than empty sorrow, woke at last to a strange bed and light pouring down from a sun-shaft. The air smelled of herbs and rock and beneath it all the sharp green wind of late spring. He was certainly not in Nen Elin and this time he knew why, a knife-thrust of regret beneath his breastbone, and with an effort he turned his head enough to see beyond the tied-back bed curtains. A gray-haired woman sat in the shaft of sunlight, distaff and spindle in her hands, but she looked up at the movement and wound up the thread to set them aside.

"Sire."

"Where—?" The word was barely a whisper; he swallowed hard, and said, the words easier this time, "Nen Arranme?"

"Yes, Sire." The woman brought a cup, helped lift his head so that he could drink. It was honey-water, cool and sweet and touched with mint, and he drained the cup without stopping.

"More, please?"

"A little," she said, and filled the cup halfway. "You'll make yourself sick, else."

He drank eagerly anyway, and let himself fall back against the pillows. There was no strength in his sinews and he knew he should find that terrifying, but his thoughts were dulled as well. With some effort, he managed to lift one hand, feeling the band of linen laid over his missing eye. He was unshaven still, the sort of beard old men wore when their hands grew too weak to shave them; he wanted to feel his head, to see how much his hair had grown, but could not muster the effort. "How long?"

"It's been two weeks since Nen Elin fell," the woman answered. "The thegen and the kyra will be glad to know you're awake. And the master smith."

But not Rota. And not Arra knows how many others. "Wait. Get me put to rights first."

The woman hesitated—he could almost read her thought, *Do you think they haven't seen you already?*—but said, "Let me fetch my mistress." She bustled from the room.

Even that little effort had exhausted him. He lay limp against the pillows, blinking at the sunlight, and drowsed again before the door opened. He opened his eye again to see Nen Arranme's speaker bending over him, the bones clattering in her gray-streaked hair. Her face was heavily painted, stark white with black around her eyes, and he winced in spite of himself, missing Rota. The speaker lifted a painted eyebrow.

"I know, I'm not who you want, but I'm who there is." Her tone was brisk, but not ungentle. "Lias says you wanted to bathe."

"Wash and shave and preferably a clean shirt, too," Esclin answered, and she laughed softly.

"We'll start with washing, and see how you do." She paused. "Do you remember what happened?"

The brief moment of amusement vanished. "All of it."

She nodded. "I'll fetch my people."

It took them most of the afternoon but he got his way in the end, though his attempts to stand left him weak and shaking, and he slept again after they were done. When he woke the light had faded to evening and a kitchener was busy at the hearth, building up the fire against the coming chill. The speaker examined him, feeling for fever and testing his pulse, and professed herself satisfied. Lias brought extra pillows until he was almost sitting, then disappeared. Talan hovered in the door, Alcis at her back, and the speaker nodded.

"You may enter. He'll tire easily, be aware of it."

"Thank you, Alodie," Talan said, and glanced over her shoulder. "Set the wine on the table and then you can go."

A page—one of Nen Arranme's folk, no one Esclin recognized—busied himself with pitcher and glasses, and hurried out, the kitchener scrambling after him. Alcis frowned at the shadows and lit a second branch of candles. The flare of light showed Kelleiden behind her and Esclin felt one fear fall away. He had known the smith had survived the nenn's fall, but seeing him again made it true.

"Will you take wine, Sire?" Talan asked.

"Please." Esclin let her fill a cup and took a careful sip. It was heavy in his hand, too heavy, and he set it carefully aside, not wanting to show weakness. Kelleiden brought a chair for the kyra and set it at the head of the bed, then retreated to its foot, never taking his eyes from the arros. Esclin waved at the other side of the bed. "Sit."

Kelleiden started to say something, then swallowed hard and settled himself gingerly at Esclin's side. He was close enough to reach, close enough to touch, and Esclin extended a hand he carefully did not allow to waver. Kelleiden caught it, bent his head to bring Esclin's fingers to his lips. Something in Esclin eased then, a knot working loose, and he tightened his hold on Kelleiden's hand.

"I like our daughter," Alcis said. "She's done well."

"I take it you defeated them in the Westwood?" Esclin asked.

Alcis smiled. "We did. I hold their captains close prisoner—or Rihaleth does—and we'll send their men back to Manan as soon as we may."

"I thought you would."

"And you defeated the lord paramount."

Esclin grimaced. "Not in the field."

"It sufficed," Kelleiden said, and Esclin squeezed his hand.

"Who got out?"

"You and I. Most of the kitchen folk. They said there was a fight, some of the Riders tried to stop them leaving, and Waloner and some others held them off."

And died, presumably, along with Senta and her little troop. Esclin nodded. "And the Riders?"

"Fewer than a dozen survived, and those were outside in the camp," Talan said. "We have them under guard, but they're too stunned to think of fighting. Nen Salter has sent his allegiance, and Nen Brethil's widow has said she'll stand regent for her son. She's put Aillard under guard, and I've set Nen Sarn to keep an eye on her. He's her cousin, and they seem in agreement. And we've word from Nen Poul. They've chased the Riders out of the vales, and Kellecost's latest messenger said they'd driven one band back onto their ships." She paused. "We've spread the word widely that the lord paramount is dead, and how."

"Good." Esclin knew he should feel more pleasure, but he could still feel the stone shifting around him, the ghost of the water's weight pressing on his chest. "How badly was the Westwood damaged?" He managed another sip of wine, and felt that was a victory.

Alcis shrugged. "Not badly. They were foolish enough to try to force their way through the wood itself, and Helevys and Rocelyn were able to use its strength against them. We weren't far behind at that point, and that slowed them enough that we could take them." She paused. "That harper of yours, Viven. She harped up a storm for them, too."

"We feared she'd been taken," Kelleiden said.

"She had," Alcis said. "The lord paramount didn't respect harp-law."

Esclin frowned. "Is she alive?"

"She was hurt, but she should mend," Alcis answered. "When she's fit, I'll send her south to Nen Poul. She has a child there. I told her I'd foster it at the Carallad if she'd like."

"Send that scout captain with her," Talan said, with a grin. "Leicinna. That'll help her recovery."

"Or set it back," Alcis answered, and matched her smile.

Esclin felt his eye closing, blinked it open with an effort. Alcis retrieved his cup and set it aside, her fingers brushing his hand. "And you?"

"Alive," Esclin answered. He had meant it for bravado, but the truth spilled out, his thoughts too slow to hold it back. "Unlike so many others."

"The Riders are defeated," Alcis said. "They will not be back next year, nor for a decade after. I say it's worth the cost."

"They died at my hand," Esclin said. "I knew I would kill them, they knew it, and they stayed. I had no right." Kelleiden's fingers tightened on his own.

"I doubt they stayed out of obligation." Alcis's voice was tart.

"No?" Esclin lifted an eyebrow.

"No." To his surprise, it was Talan who answered. "They stayed for love. Because we love you."

That seemed unlikely, but he had no strength left to

protest. Kelleiden's hand was warm in his; he closed his eye and let himself fall back into the welcoming dark.

(Q

Kelleiden woke to shadows and a shaft of moonlight crossing the room, silvering the stone of the fireplace. *Stay with him*, Alcis had said, generous as always, and he had been glad to obey, to stretch out on top of the sheets beside the arros, a blanket drawn awkwardly over his shoulder.

Esclin's hand was tucked beneath his arm, and Kelleiden shifted to take it in his own. Esclin sighed, and Kelleiden couldn't tell if the sound was regret or content. "I didn't mean to wake you."

"It's all right."

Kelleiden edged closer, until they were almost in each other's arms. "Do you need anything?"

"You."

"I'm here."

"Yes."

That sounded more like contentment, or at least relief. Kelleiden said, "I'll always be here."

"I could very easily have killed you," Esclin said. "Along with the rest of them."

"I chose to be there," Kelleiden answered. "We all did, I sent away anyone who doubted. I knew—Talan said you had a plan."

"To lose Nen Elin—" Esclin shook his head, the pillow rustling in the dark. "I thought I might twist free."

"We couldn't beat him in the field," Kelleiden said. "And even if we had, we wouldn't have driven them back. Not like this. This—you've driven them back for a generation. Longer. That is worth Nen Elin, worth all our lives. And only you could have done it. You've saved us all."

"Except those I didn't," Esclin pointed out, but his voice was less grieved.

"Except those," Kelleiden agreed. "But, I told you, we

chose. We knew you—somehow, against all the odds, you'd find a way. And you did. Nen Elin's a small price to pay for the Hundred Hills, and you as arros."

Esclin sighed again and Kelleiden pulled him closer, wishing he had more words or better ones. He had made his choice clear-eyed, long ago, had been willing to die at Esclin's side a hundred times because he knew his life would be spent to a purpose: there was nothing to regret. He felt Esclin relax against him, thought him sliding back into sleep, then felt him stir. "We can't stay here. We'll need to find a new place, build a new nenn."

That brought the tears to Kelleiden's eyes, as nothing else had, the true moment Esclin took the turn for life. He swallowed hard, managed to master his voice. "Yes. We will."

"There are still caves in the hills," Esclin murmured, his voice blurred with sleep. "And along the Hidden River."

"Yes," Kelleiden said again, and closed his eyes, listening to the familiar rhythm of Esclin's breath.

News trickled in from Mag Ausse: Ilgae Marshal was dead of her wounds; Gelern Sword-Hand lived long enough that his people thought he could be moved, but he developed a fever on the road and died within sight of Riverholme. More losses to share with Esclin, and each one keenly felt, no matter how careful Talan was in telling him. It was nearly midsummer before Alcis was ready to leave the Hundred Hills. Talan had been grateful for her presence and her support, and once or twice for the part of the army still camped in Nen Elin's lower meadow: there were always minor lordlings who hoped to use the confusion to enlarge their lands or to pay off old scores. She spent a few harried days forcing the end of a feud in the hills north of Nen Arranme, then held court in the muster field at Nen Salter to resolve a dozen other issues. The local wheelmen came to make their submission then, as well, and she banned them from living within the nenns' walls. The ones who would renounce any allegiance to the next lord paramount and axial were welcome to build their houses outside the walls, and serve the Blazing One there; once their loyalty was proved, she might reconsider the ban.

"I wouldn't have them in my lands," Alcis said, "but I think you've drawn their fangs."

"They have done good here, especially in the south," Talan answered. "And they have a following. But, as you say, this keeps us safe. And of course we'll watch them."

"I'd expect no less." Alcis smiled.

They stood together under the shade of her tent's awning, the camp in motion around them: the last of the army marched for the Westwood in the morning, and there was much to be done. Talan would dine with her and Nen Salter, and see her off in the morning. After that...after that, there were a thousand things to do, from finding some place for Nen Elin's folk to winter over to planting and reaping what late crops could be managed, and she couldn't help a sigh.

"Is there anything you need before I go?" Alcis asked, and Talan shook her head.

"No, we're in good shape—and I thank you for all the help you've given us. Given me! And I know the arros has been glad of your presence."

"It was hard to leave you," Alcis said abruptly. "You weren't even weaned, and you were my first daughter, and I loved you so. But my father was failing, and I could not give up the Westwood."

Would not give it up, Talan thought, any more than she herself would give up the Hundred Hills. She said, "Lysse was a good mother to me, and Cat Meirin better than a sister. And the arros—I could not ask for a better father. I have not suffered, Kyra. And the Westwood needed you."

Alcis nodded. "Yes. But you should know it wasn't easy."

"I never thought it was." Talan paused. "He never even hinted that it was."

"I never thought he would," Alcis said, with a wry smile. "But I worried you might have done."

"I've been the thegen since I could walk. I know what's required." Talan paused again, watching Alcis's shoulders ease a little, and blurted out the question that she hadn't meant to ask. "Do you think he'll mend? Completely, I mean. He's still not himself."

"These things take time." Alcis sighed. "I don't know. I hope so. There's every chance he will. I just wish I could stay to see it."

"I know," Talan said. "I'll send messengers."

"Thank you."

The sun was down behind the hills, the air thickening toward twilight. It would be time for the farewell feast soon enough, and past time for her to change into suitable finery, but instead she held out her hands, and let Alcis pull her into a tight embrace.

It was days before Viven was fully awake, and by then the summer king had brought her into Callamben and placed her with one of the town's physicians. Nestan Timnos was a grave and graying man who allowed that the army's healers had done a passable job and prescribed rest and quiet and the company of a harp. Her shin and ribs were broken and bandaged, and the crutches hurt to use. Her head ached steadily, though over time the pain grew less; when she complained of it, Nestan said she was lucky it wasn't worse. The bones of her skull hadn't been broken, but she had been tumbled like a leaf in the flood and it would take a while for her spirit to settle again within her bones. She had heard of such things, but it was hard to school herself to patience.

Eventually she was allowed visitors, first Aelin, who brought a gift of early berries and the report that the lord paramount was dead and Esclin victorious. Nen Elin was fallen, destroyed in whatever cataclysm Esclin had brought down on his enemy. Viven doubted that—she knew, none better, how tales grew in traveling—but she did not question, all too aware of the joy Aelin took in the story. And who could blame her: Reys en Nevenel had treated her ill indeed.

"Kellecost Sarrasos—Nen Ddaur's nephew-by-marriage—he's granted me Mag Talloc for now, and he'll let me travel there with some of his folk. I wondered if you'd care to come with me."

"I need to reach Nen Poul," Viven said. Gemme was alive and the nenn was back in its proper hands, but she wouldn't feel entirely easy until she held her child again.

"You'd be that much closer," Aelin answered, and for a full day Viven considered it. But she could barely walk the length of the physic-garden without growing dizzy, and had to admit she was in no condition to cross the Dancing Ground.

"You are progressing well, all things considered," Nestan said, and with that she had to be content. She borrowed paper and ink, composed a letter, but there was only a company going on to Nieve. The captain promised to find someone to carry it from there, but she knew how much trust to place in that.

It was midsummer before she could walk without a limp, and then too much exertion brought back the headache, so that she could not work herself back into the shape she needed to reach Nen Poul. The kyra had come home by then, a bright procession through Callamben's streets, trailing painted lanterns and fireworks in her wake. One of the stewards had visited, with a purse for Nestan and another for her, along with the promise of safe housing for Gemme at the Carallad and help when she was ready to travel, but she was still not steady on her feet. Instead, she spent some of the money on a new harp—her old one had been smashed to kindling in the river, not even fragments left—and set herself to play herself into its favor. It was wary, but sweet in tone and touch, and she could feel the beginnings of a bond return.

The moon had waned and waxed again before her next visitor arrived. She heard horses in the courtyard, and then the tramp of boots on the stair, set her harp aside and swallowed the memory of fear as Nestan's maid swung back the door.

"Leicinna Elloras, Harper."

Viven smiled, relaxing into pleasure, and the captain came into the room. She was dressed for ordinary riding, neither armed nor armored, and there was a folded piece of paper in her hand. Viven stared at it, her breath catching, and Leicinna held it out at once.

"From your sister, Harper. I've come from Nen Poul." Viven snatched it from her, broke the blob of candlewax that sealed it, and drank in the familiar hand.

Gemme is safe, we are well, all of us. None of us were harmed. Come to us. We miss you.

She closed her eyes, the tears running down her cheeks, and Leicinna said, worriedly, "But surely—they were well when I saw them—"

"They're fine," Viven said. "She says they're well."

Leicinna nodded. "They looked well. She's a pretty girl, your daughter, and clever."

"Yes." Viven caught her breath. "Thank you. I need to go to her, and then—the kyra said she'd take her as a fosterling—"

"She'd be safe at the Carallad," Leicinna said. "It's a thing to consider." Viven nodded slowly. She trusted the kyra, but she didn't fully trust herself to make any momentous decision just yet. "Also, I'm bound back to Nen Poul," Leicinna said. "Would you care to travel with me?"

"I'm not sure I can ride," Viven admitted, though the thought of traveling with Leicinna was unexpected pleasure.

"We're escort to a merchant caravan," Leicinna said. "There's a wagon you could travel in." She paused. "We don't leave for a week. And I'd be glad of your company."

"And I of yours," Viven admitted. She touched her harp for reassurance, not yet sure what it thought, but she knew it was time.

❦

It was autumn before Esclin was well enough to make the ride from Nen Arranme to the ruin of Nen Elin. They took it in easy stages, stopping for the night in a hunter's hide some four leagues from Nen Elin, where the forest crept closer to what had been the Aurinand's open plain. In the morning, they rode on through the rising light, through groves of quaking aspen where the leaves had already turned to gold.

They emerged from the forest an hour or so before noon, to see the ruin of Nen Elin looming before them. Esclin had thought himself prepared, braced for the destruction, but it was still somehow more than he'd expected. Most of the stone was the familiar bread-crust brown of the walls, but here and there shards of cream-colored stone stood up, and blocks of darker brown and russet and rose. Some of those would still show carvings, and he wasn't sure he could bear to see that even now.

"The Aurinand still runs," Talan said, sounding surprised, and he looked where she pointed. The river was low in its bed, barely ankle deep, and large swaths of the stones were dry, but there was a definite stream two ells wide in the central channel. The water was clouded by silt from the wreckage, but the current was strong enough to whirl leaves down the long straight stretches and pen them against larger stones.

"There won't be much to salvage," Perrin said, from his place at Talan's side, and Estor gave him a jealous look.

"No one expected there would be."

"I'd thought there might be some rooms left within," Talan said, "but it looks as though the mountain's fallen in completely." She glanced at Esclin. "It was well you sent so many of our people away."

With at least some of their goods, Esclin knew she meant. That had made it possible for the refugees to set up summer-houses outside Nen Atha and Nen Arranme, the ones who couldn't be accommodated in the nenn itself, but winter would come and they would need warmer shelter.

As they came further up the river, Esclin found himself looking for caves beyond the wreckage, some sign that there had once been a settlement, but Talan was right, the mountain had collapsed entirely into the void where the nenn had been. They picked their way through the field of scattered stones to dismount at the base of the great heap of debris that spilled out from the mountain. A few of Talan's companions poked idly at its base, as though they might find some token that people had once lived there.

Esclin walked along its edge, to the spot where the Aurinand emerged from the rocks to form a deeper pool. He trailed his fingers in the water, then pulled himself up the steep slope, stopping finally on a slab of pale gray stone that must have come from one of the upper chambers. Even from there, he could see no way back in to the mountain, no way to know how far the destruction had gone. Even if the lowest levels had been spared, there was no way to reach them, not without moving the mountain itself. He hoped no one had been down there when the mountain fell.

"Sire!"

He shaded his eye to look down at Talan. "Yes?"

"We're going to scout south a bit. Will you come?"

Esclin shook his head. "I'll stay here."

He seated himself on a block of stone, watching as Talan detailed a handful of people to mind the horses, and then the rest set off on foot across the broken plain. He wasn't sure what they thought they might find, but there was no reason to gainsay them. Below, the people who had been left went about their business, two kindling a fire while the rest set a picket line and let the horses graze.

He sat in silence for some time, the sun still rising, a hawk wheeling distant across the cloudless sky. He could hear the murmur of voices below and the splash of the Aurinand over the stones, common and plain and ordinary, and heard again the crack and roll of the mountain falling.

Below him, a handful of pebbles rattled down the slope to splash in the pool. Another, larger handful followed, but the people by the fire didn't seem to notice. He frowned, and the ground heaved and split, revealing a horse's nose and forehead and rolling eye, and then a flailing hoof. It hauled itself up and out of the ground, a great blood bay with streaming mane and tail and feathered feet. It shook itself, releasing a cloud of dust, then turned and heaved itself up onto the stone slab. It took one step, its hooves clicking on the stone, then shimmered and shifted and became a naked man, bearded and long-haired and wild.

"Water horse," Esclin said, and the other grinned.

"Well, we've made a mess of things." He was a hand's-breadth taller than Esclin, and broad-bodied, dark hair standing out against his copper skin. "Not that it wasn't entirely necessary."

"I'm glad to hear you say so." Esclin shaded his eye and the water horse came to squat on his heels beside him, looking back down the valley.

"I didn't like them much myself. It was a pleasure to bring them down. That was clever, stopping the cisterns for me."

"I didn't know if it would work," Esclin said.

The water horse grinned, showing square yellow teeth. His black hair fell in tangles over his shoulders, and a line of hair ran down his spine. "It's how the nenns were made. You'll need to find a stone dancer to make you another one."

"If we can find one strong enough," Esclin said. "There aren't so many lithomancers these days."

"They'll come to you," the water horse said. "To make an arros's nenn? They'll come."

They sat in companionable silence, watching the horses graze along the picket line. Several of the escort kicked a rag ball back and forth, their voices sharp as birds'; the others tended the fire, a thin stream of smoke rising into the still air. Esclin could smell that and the warm horse-smell of the creature next to him, familiar and homely amid the rubble.

"I'm sorry about the Aurinand."

"What? No need." The water horse waved his hand. "Give me fifty winters and I'll have the channel clear again." He gave Esclin a sidelong glance and another show of teeth. "Send your mares to summer here, if you want to give me something."

"That's a gift to us," Esclin said. "What can I give you?"

The water horse shook his head. "You've given me what I wanted." The skin of his shoulder twitched, as though he felt a fly. "More. My kind aren't often granted such power. Or such a feast."

Esclin remembered the weight of water, the leashed strength, the wild patience, and then the moment of release. The sound of it still lingered beneath the silence, behind the water horse's calm, like the bones beneath the ruin. "We can't come back here," he said, after a moment, and the water horse nodded in agreement.

"North a bit, there's a cave. The entrance isn't much, but there are more rooms behind it. You might could burrow there."

"How far north?" Esclin turned his head, but the curve of the hills showed no breaks.

"A day's travel? Thereabouts. Look for a white rock like a wolf's tooth halfway up the hill."

"Thank you." Esclin gave him another sidelong look. "If we build a new nenn there, would you come?"

The water horse shook his head. "This is my river, none other. But there are more of us in these hills."

That was fair, and Esclin nodded. Something moved to his left, and he turned his head to see Talan and her company coming back from the Doubtful Scarp. The water horse rose to his feet, seeing them, and took a step away. "Oh." He turned back, holding out his closed fist. "This is yours."

Esclin held out his hand and the water horse handed him a twist of silver, slightly battered, but unmistakably Arra's ring. Words abandoned him, and the water horse bent to kiss his forehead.

"Child of her house," he said affectionately, and ruffled his hand through Esclin's hair as though he were a child indeed. Esclin closed his hand tight over the scrap of silver and the water horse turned away, shifting as he went into a horse and then to mist. Pebbles rattled and splashed in the pool, and then there was a deeper splash, like a fish jumping. The group tending the fire turned to look, and then turned back, shrugging. Esclin took a breath and picked his way down the slope, to meet Talan beside the fire.

"Nothing left there that's of any use to us," she said, and Esclin nodded.

"Let's try north along the hills before we go back to Nen Arranme," he said. "There are caves there we should look at for our home."

❍ ❍ ❍

Acknowledgments

This project has been a long time in the making, even by my usual standards, and followed a meandering path to completion and publication. I'd like to thank the folks who stuck with it from the beginning—the first readers on LiveJournal, the friends and colleagues who listened to my musings and who offered their insight. I'd also like to thank Athena Andreadis for her editorial efforts. As always, it's been a pleasure working with someone who saw what I was aiming for, and offered so many ways to make it better.

About the Author

Melissa Scott is from Little Rock, Arkansas, and studied history at Harvard College and Brandeis University, where she earned her PhD in the Comparative History program. She is the author of more than thirty original science fiction and fantasy novels as well as authorized tie-ins for *Star Trek: DS9*, *Star Trek: Voyager*, *Stargate SG-1*, *Stargate Atlantis*, *Star Wars Rebels*, and the anime series *gen:LOCK*. She has won Lambda Literary Awards for *Trouble and Her Friends*, *Shadow Man*, *Point of Dreams* (written with her late partner, Lisa A. Barnett), and *Death By Silver*, with Amy Griswold. She has also won Spectrum Awards for *Shadow Man*, *Fairs' Point*, *Death By Silver*, and for the short story "The Rocky Side of the Sky" (Periphery, Lethe Press) as well as the John W. Campbell Award for Best New Writer. Her most recent solo novel, *Finders*, was published at the end of 2018 and she is currently at work on the next book in the sequence.

THE ADVENTURE CONTINUES ONLINE

VISIT THE CANDLEMARK & GLEAM WEBSITE TO

Find out about new releases

Read free sample chapters

Catch up on the latest news and author events

Buy books! All purchases on the Candlemark & Gleam site are DRM-free and paperbacks come with a free digital version!

Meet flying monkey-creatures from beyond the stars!*

WWW.CANDLEMARKANDGLEAM.COM

CPSIA information can be obtained
at www.ICGtesting.com
Printed in the USA
LVHW092108210521
688023LV00024B/32